Jackboot

Britain

By Daniel S. Fletcher

Jackboot Britain

© 2011, Daniel Stephen Fletcher

~

Book notes:

This work is fictional, with May 1940 being the point of divergence; the German invasion of France occurs earlier in this narrative. The entire timeline thereafter is fictional. It consists of the following:

a) Real life occurrences, used in this fantasy context with a twist – e.g. Churchill's 'Fight on the Beaches' speech, or the SS Einsatzgruppen, which were in active operation in Nazi-occupied territory.

b) Elements taken from German documentation, such as Hitler and Heydrich's instructions for an occupied Britain, written SS orders, Wehrmacht orders, memos... including stated intentions and beliefs, sourced from Mein Kampf, the Goebbels diary, court testimonies, the findings of Nuremberg, the work of countless historians, Albert Speer's account of his life, Walther Schellenberg's richly detailed autobiography of life in Heydrich's SD, The Protocols of the Learned Elders of Zion, etc...

c) Elements entirely of the author's invention.

Many of the characters were of course real historical figures, but while trying to correlate with reality as closely as possible regarding dialogue, stated views and actions, pre-1940 history and the use of certain anecdotal stories, the depiction of all characters here is fictional.

Author's note:

This novel is based on an original screenplay that was drafted in Ibiza, Spain circa 2011, to which Steve Burdon (1971-2013) made several contributions. JB is dedicated to his memory.

Eternal thanks to my wonderful family in England – Maureen, Stephen & James; Brian & Vera; Elizabeth & Douglas – as well as Andrew, Max and Simon in particular, Anthony, Donny and co. and my positive friends in Asia who have taught me valuable lessons, and whose support gave me the confidence and self-belief to write this and other works.

Heartfelt thanks and gratitude to everyone who gives the book a chance. If you'd like to share any feedback, it would be fantastic to hear from you; please, by all means hit me up via one of the listed websites. Technology, eh?

Cheers, and have a wonderful day.

Peace **L**ove **U**nity **R**espect.

Namaste,
~Fletch

May 10th 2014, Phuket, Thailand.

http://www.amazon.com/author/danielfletcher

https://www.Goodreads.com/DanielSFletcher

https://www.twitter.com/Daniel_Fletcher

https://www.SamuraiLife.net

"Hitler has grasped the falsity of the hedonistic attitude to life... because in his own joyless mind he feels it with exceptional strength, knows that human beings don't only *want* comfort, safety, short working-hours, hygiene, birth-control and, in general, common sense; they also, at least intermittently, want struggle and self-sacrifice, not to mention drums, flag and loyalty-parades... Whereas Socialism, and even capitalism in a grudging way, have said to people "I offer you a good time," Hitler has said to them "I offer you struggle, danger and death," and as a result a whole nation flings itself at his feet."

~George Orwell, 1940

"Political language... is designed to make lies sound truthful and murder respectable, and to give an appearance of solidity to pure wind."

~ Orwell, 1946

"Over the World, rages war.
Earth, sea and sky wince at his roar.
He tramples down
At every tread,
A million men,
A million dead.

We say that we, must crush the Hun,
Or else the World will be undone.
But Huns are we
As much as they.
All men are Huns,
Who fight and slay.

And if we win, and crush the Huns,
In twenty years we must fight their sons,
Who will rise against
Our victory,
Their fathers', their own
Ignominy.

And if their Kaiser we dethrone,
They will his son restore, or some other one.
If we win by war,
War is force,
And others to war
Will have recourse.

And through the World
Will rage new war.
Earth, sea and sky
Will wince at his roar.
He will trample down
At every tread,
Millions of men,
Millions of dead."

~Joseph Leftwich, 'War' (1915) – remarkably apt with the 'twenty years' line.

Prologue

A Priori

The power of language – it can heal and build, or corrupt, poison, destroy, desecrate, annihilate...

Language has a power that can be beautiful, yet it is perverted with far greater ease; twisted sickly to ooze venom, spitefully inciting vicious, destructive thoughts... and rarely in human history has such nihilistic savagery been fostered, skilfully nurtured with unsurpassed malevolence, and ultimately unleashed in such epic magnitude for the greater ill.

While these unnatural, hateful men may use violence in place of debate, the ideals of a peaceful society with some semblance of brotherhood cannot merely be crushed underfoot beneath an army of jackboots. Language will always remain, and retain its illimitable power. They cannot control language – at least in private – nor can they control thought, at least, not of the reasoned mind. Our thoughts are ours; *it is our right to think thoughts, and to communicate them, and only Nietzschean criminals believe otherwise. And so, here are my own, for what they are worth.*

My name is not important. I have a name; I am a person, a human being – despite what they might tell you – and I have a life, family, friends, feelings, emotions. None of that matters in the face of a new order of hatred; of rigidity and compliance, fear and rule by force. Hatred and prejudice does not care about names; not when fired up by the maleficient power of beguiling language, wickedly misapplied to lead a generation of humans astray, and obliterate any prevailing sense of empathy, humanism and brotherhood.

Language has been mobilised and sent into battle; it directs the human carnage of conflict with its enunciation of emotion, stimulating souls to abandon peace.

On one side, monstrous men with bloodstained hands; Hitler, Göring, Goebbels – savage puppetmasters; their calculated language stirring the mindless masses into bestial frenzy. On the other, the humanist scribes; men of the moderate-left, or the socialists and anarchists – for us, the rejection of bloodlust and war, and the supremacy of truth, altruism and advancement. There is no compelling argument against the three working concurrently. Of course, I cannot speak for the men whose talent far outshines my own, but at best I can assert; if language can be used to inspire thought, creativity and love, as opposed to the furtherance of suffering, let its power be harnessed solely for those ends.

At present, Europe's hot blood thirsts for the destructive annihilation of combat. Linguistically; the calculated language of vengeance and fire holds more appeal for the dissatisfied soul than the calming composition of peace.

They of ambition; who stir tribalism and division and set brother against brother man for their own ends; they use language in its most evil, twisted form. Their modus operandi is to appeal to the lowest form of understanding, on a level I hesitate to allow for the term 'human intelligence' to be associated. It is the darkest abyss of psychology; the blackest recess of the soul, the realm of soulless men with machine minds.

Children, fertile minds ripe for molestation. Now they will be taught what *to* think, not how *to think. Language, that twisted poison. It scars purity.*

Extremism stifles true progression in all fields of human advancement; it is a detriment to everything but war, tribalism and the personal power of Nietzschean entities, striving only for the narcissistic vindication of their ego and will. The enlightened mind knows that all is challengeable, ergo questions all and thus, learns and grows; progression. The weak and narrow mind makes its beliefs sacrosanct; fearful of challenge, their creed becomes unalterable, defended with violence. Political extremists, much like religious zealots, are the latter. They destroy what they cannot convert. They annihilate those they cannot control, or force to conform. They have found no peace in life, no love, and so promote war and division, as emotional cripples – inflicting their own pain and misery and malignant stupidity on the world. Their language binds people together, but only by stirring the darkest excesses of the soul; language of hate, and intolerance, fear and conspiracy, and the need for vengeance. In war-scarred Europe, these cripples direct mass-psychology, and would make the world in their own likeness; mutilated by violence and tribalism and hate.

Men speak of God's love for man... but if providence does not come in this hour, where is He then? My conclusion is simple. The Semitic texts from Bronze Age Palestine of which Christianity is comprised still fit uncomfortably well with contemporary life. The Old Testament depicts a God capricious and cruel; blood sacrifice, vengeance, genocide; death and destruction et al. Would He not approve of Herr Hitler and the brutal, tribalistic crusade against Hebrews and non-Christian 'untermensch?'

One thing is inarguable. His church on Earth has produced some of the most vigorous and violent contribution to the European fascist cause.

It is synergy. Man Created God, even if God Created Man; it all exists in the hubris and apotheosis of the narcissistic soul, and alas, all too many of the human herd are willing to follow the beastly trait of leadership. The idea of self-emancipation and advancement, with Europe under the jackboot of fascism, would be Quixotic to the point of mirthless lunacy.

There will be a million and one accounts of what happened here... or perhaps, just one. I expect that the victors of force shall record its history; a forlorn hope, to leave behind a voice that seeks to shed light from the shadows of a vanquished perspective. From a tragically flawed viewpoint; a love of democracy, and the quaint notions of a franchised people, who – even under a plutocratic class – still enjoyed the freedom of civil rights and a Voice. In the new system, the individual human is judged differently, and is essentially worthless. Only the collective matters. *Creativity and individualism, diversity, freedom, independent thought; all abstract notions, consigned to the Dustbin of History that another competing totalitarian system and quasi-religion so recently spoke of.*

The legions are coming, and this time, not even Pindar will be spared. No poets, artists or thinkers shall be allowed to live in the conquered land if they retain their own thoughts.

Even if this is only for my benefit alone, I want to talk about how it felt. How it feels. What their hatred means.

It is a cruel system of control that – much like religion – demands submissive conformity; to do otherwise is to be the nail that sticks out; first to meet the hammer. And that hammer, its arrival imminent, is a black-clad army of death; the SS, and its vicious Gestapo.

These will be our masters; they whose capricious wills shall determine our individual fates. Britain's civilised society will cease to exist, and our ethnicity and opinions will be judged to ascertain those worthy of life, and those unworthy, condemned to die – 'life unworthy of life.'

I am a writer, aged 27 years and four months. I live in London, the capital of England and Great Britain, and the pulsing, hammering heart of a doomed Empire. I have a family; a mother, a brother – serving in Singapore – I have one surviving Grandfather, in Oxfordshire. And soon I, and everyone I have ever met, known and loved, will be ruled by new masters; new leaders with new laws, with a different language; different values, different ideas of what constitutes an ideal society, different perspectives on the way the world should be.

How twisted and frightening our reality has become. Years of vitriolic, violent language; the hearts and minds of men have been sapped of empathy and made machine.

I record this with little hope of future publication; the words form a blur. This diary may well be burned along with its author, but I wish to make peace in it with myself before the time comes. Perhaps one day it shall be read and what we saw will be known and understood; what we felt as the storm approached. Thus, I record; to come to terms with our grim reality; as a poet of yesteryear observed, 'all that we see and seem, is but a dream within a dream.' To live through the surreal is to experience a shattering of one's own notions of reality as a concept; mine, the touch, taste and feel of a broken dream.

The storm approaches and so, I write. In doing so, it will not become less real, but more so, even as collective faith turns to despair.

I've penned enough freely distributed public material – zealously shared – to sentence me to one of their concentration camps for many lifetimes over, if not the gallows outright, or the impartial simplicity of a bullet.

It is their typical reaction; they employ not words and reasoned discourse to resolve problems, but the truncheon, the jackbooted foot, or the gun. Sophistication and reasonable behaviour requires more competence and skill than mere thuggery and brutishness. It is a harder, loftier charge to be civilised than to let the beast in man devour man.

If I am to die, let my final words – as worthy or as worthless as anyone else's – be a condemnation of the new order, and an appeal to reason: never let hatred overcome love. When violence is used in lieu of peace, when cruelty replaces reason, and when hate is stronger than love, humankind is losing; subjugated by unnatural men, with machine minds and machine hearts, its wondrous possibilities flung into a spiritual abyss. Never let peace & love be crushed underfoot by the jackboot, beaten by the truncheon and killed by the bullet.

So, if this were a final written piece – a diary entry, after years of published work both critically acclaimed and derided alike – then let not only myself, but – if you'll permit my presumption – an entire harassed and harangued people be remembered by these words. We did not all conform. We did not all bear the shame. We did not all believe. We did not all surrender our love of humanity, our empathy and our souls to the darkness of their creed.

Quies ante tempestatem

"In the days of Napoleon," Churchill solemnly declared to the silent, hostile House, "... of which I was speaking just now, the same wind which would have carried his transports across the Channel might have driven away the blockading fleet. There was always the *chance*, and it is that chance which has excited and befooled the imaginations of many Continental tyrants. Many are the tales that are told... we are assured that novel methods will be adopted, and when we see the *originality* of malice, the *ingenuity* of aggression which our enemy displays, we may certainly prepare ourselves for every kind of novel stratagem and every kind of *brutal* and *treacherous* manoeuvre. I think that no idea is so outlandish that it should not be considered and viewed with a searching, but *at the same time, I hope*, with a steady eye. We must *never forget* the solid assurances of sea power and those which belong to air power if it can be locally exercised..."

Rumblings of dissent were beginning to form, in the benches behind Clement Attlee. Even at Churchill's back, several of his supporters packed together on the green leather pews exchanged worried, or knowing, glances. But the Prime Minister carried on, bloody-minded, his large face pulsing with truculence; bolstered by whiskey and defiant in the face of an unwelcome atmosphere, doggedly determined to rally the wavering Members of Parliament around to the cause.

"I have, myself, *full* confidence that if *all do their duty*, if nothing is neglected, and if the best arrangements are made, as they are being made, we shall prove ourselves once more able to defend our island home, to ride out the storm of war, and to outlive the menace of tyranny... if necessary for years... if necessary *alone*."

He paused for full effect, sternly peering across the hall to directly meet the icy stares, like an animal. A beast, establishing dominance. It was a challenge, with the highest stakes of all on the line in a moment of inconceivable peril.

"At any rate," he said at last, nodding slightly, "that is what we are going to *try to do*. That is the resolve of His Majesty's Government – *every man of them*. That is the will of Parliament and the nation. The British Empire and the French Republic, linked together in their cause and in their need, will defend to the death their native soil, aiding each other like good comrades to the utmost of their strength."

Once more, the great, bullish leader paused for effect, straightening up proudly, his body language affirming the tenacity of his convictions. Much to his chagrin, the rumblings were only growing in strength and number, and the first rising sensation of a deep fear suddenly pricked him. He ploughed on, a steely edge to his voice.

"*Even though large tracts of Europe* and many *old and famous states* have fallen, or may fall into the grip of the Gestapo, and all the odious apparatus of Nazi rule, *we shall not flag or fail*. We shall go on to the end."

He cleared his throat, and stared around, fixing his steady gaze on the assembled men in front of him, their unsmiling eyes boring into the great orator.

"We shall fight in *France*... we shall fight on the seas and *oceans*... we shall fight with growing *confidence* and growing *strength* in the *air*..."

"With what?"

An incredulous voice cut through the great war leader's speech, chilling him to the bone. Churchill fought hard, and his body did not betray him. But his old, gnarled fists briefly clenched.

"We don't have a bloody fighter force left capable of winning," another, almost despairing voice exclaimed, and the jeers rose. Churchill placed his hands behind his back, and straightened up, sternly casting a wide gaze, staring down the dissenters.

"We *shall* defend our island... *whatever* the cost may be. We shall fight on the *beaches...* we shall fight on the *landing grounds...* we shall fight in the fields, and in the *streets...* we shall fight in the hills... we shall *never surrender...* and if, which I do not for a moment believe, this island or a large part of it were subjugated and starving, then our Empire beyond the seas, armed and guarded by the British Fleet, would carry on the struggle..."

The jeer rose, almost drowning Churchill out and he halted.

"They have quarter of a million hostages, you old drunk," a frantic voice cried.

"Göring beat the RAF!"

"We have no army left!"

"You want to call their bluff? The SS will flay them alive," a quieter, but no less insidiously scaremongering voice remarked, an angry edge to its tone.

"Face it you old *drunk*, it's all *over!*"

Churchill was stunned into silence, and the jeers intensified, pouring down from at least a third of the House of Commons. He turned to Neville Chamberlain, the ousted Prime Minister of only two months previous whom he'd insisted remained on the Cabinet as his trusted adviser and a deputy of sorts, but the man for whom appeasement had been the answer less than two years prior. Neville now knew the folly of such a move, but in the face of political debellation, the man who had bragged that he 'only had to raise a finger and the whole of Europe is changed' could only shake his head helplessly, shrug wordlessly, as the deafening silence of Churchill's advocates and the men who had supported resistance at all costs spoke with even more ruthless eloquence than the jeering, braying mob that demanded an end to the bloodshed.

As the erstwhile chief of appeasement shrugged, gazing around powerlessly, Churchill's head dropped for the first time, and in the midst of loud catcalls, all could sense a silent, haunting moment of defeat.

Allegro

Darkness enveloped the land; England's green and pleasant countryside that so drew the glowing prose of poets through the years was covered in a black cloud, its fertile colour suppressed. It was perfect for the Einsatzgruppen. Already obscured by the fogs of war, their evil intent was further veiled in the grim nocturnal stratagems; cloaked in mist, masked in blackness.

The only light to be seen in the military trucks was the glow of cigarette tips; pinpricks burning bright red in the endless sea of black. Black, too, were the long, sinister trench coats that were wrapped around the men of the SD; drafted from all the many branches of the SS and German police that Himmler and, more pertinently *Heydrich* had gradually monopolised under their control; thousands of uniformed thugs of the state, lumped together as a versatile manpower pool from which to enlist personnel to the murderous tasks of the SD. Heydrich's long, spidery fingers were wrapped around an operational command that the Führer deemed vital, wickedly spinning a continental web of death. Hitler approved; no more would hostile elements attack his Reich. Göring, too, bestowed as much power on Heydrich as was seen fit to allow 'the Hangman' to obliterate all in his path, with a shadow army of merciless killers, built up over the course of seven years of National Socialist power.

Unshackled, unleashed, this was their work. It had the cold quality of a medical experiment, the Germ Theory of Disease applied to society with the scientific finality and totality of death.

Remove the bacteria, save the organism.

The trucks rolled on, up the Selby Road from Leeds and onwards to the outskirts, passing through the quiet, leafy suburbs with silent, evil resolve, stealthily tearing out to the mining village of Garforth, which was slumbering in sleepy tranquillity.

"Are any of these yids," murmured one of the SS men hunched in the truck, whose face looked like it had been carved out of honeycomb granite, chiselled out of a mountain.

"*Bitte*? Yids?"

"*Ja?*"

"Resistance, is all I know," the senior non-commissioned officer replied, himself of an obscenely Aryan posterboy quality; the hard, strong-jawed face of a young Saxon more than willing to embrace the comforting worldview that Adolf Hitler's bible provided, legally enforced by his police. The physical representative of the Party's ideals, the seeds of which had been planted in the malleable minds of a generation of children, taught the glories of Aryan blood, German supremacy and military conquest.

"Resistance..."

A low, growling chortle rumbled elsewhere in the truck. "It will be a fun time, then."

Grunts of affirmation, from men colder than the northern English night.

The biting chill of the trucks was not felt by the vehicle's driver and his brooding passenger, insulated as they were from the outside. The driver cleared his throat quietly, stealing a glance at the officer sat upright beside him, noting obvious signs of tension. The man sensed his attention, and turned cold eyes to face him, two black pinpricks boring into the young man's own... dark brown meeting pale blue in an unequal contest.

"The Wehrmacht used this route, yes?" The question was quiet and rhetorical; his smooth, Viennese tone almost melodic.

"Yes, Herr Untersturmführer," the driver affirmed, using the army-style prefix formality to address his senior.

"How long did it take from the landing to get *here*?"

"Not long at all, Unter–"

"How *fucking* long?" he hissed animatedly. The driver answered in a low voice, cowed, his eyes fixed straight ahead.

"Four weeks, sir."

Newly promoted SS-Untersturmführer Amon Goeth had been assigned to Dr Rudolf Lange's *Einsatzgruppe Leeds* from the notoriously eager Austrian 11th Standarte. As junior officer, he carried himself with zeal, though his mood swung pendulum-like from a restless, nervous energy to quiet menace. The erratic behaviour combined with his cruelty, and Goeth was soon known known and feared. As an *Einsatzkommando* leader he was keen to shine in his new role. Watchful eyes in Berlin, he knew, were fixed on England.

The disconcerted driver sensed Goeth's lingering gaze, and elaborated. "Pockets of resistance pushed from Leeds here to the east, as well as west and south. Mining villages such as these remained stubborn. Many fled for the hills to join the resistance."

Goeth snorted. "To freeze in winter, hiding in rat-holes with dwindling supplies. What do they think this is, the fucking Winter War? It will take more than Molotov cocktails to beat the Wehrmacht. And the SS," he added, as an afterthought.

His brief moment of contempt over, Goeth became inexpressive, and relapsed back into his own unspoken thoughts.

The driver knew as well as Goeth that the organised resistance were equipped with far more than homemade incendiary bombs, having been arranged *in situ* long before the invasion. The Leeds gruppe under Lange had followed in the wake of Army Group Centre's 'Group B' on its journey northwards, smashing through Suffolk, Cambridgeshire, Nottinghamshire and up through Yorkshire into Leeds. And the men of the *Einsatzkommandos* attached to *Gruppe Leeds* all knew that Goeth was a capricious and cruel man; it had been proven in every theatre of operations they had engaged in on the back of a rapidfire advance. Even amongst the hardened killers who had served to destroy Poland's intelligentsia so effectively, Goeth was respected and, when possible, avoided. The lieutenant was one of the new breed of Austrian National Socialists, anxious to prove their worth to the Germans following the *Anschluss* reabsorption of their country with unwavering, unyielding fanaticism.

As such, the driver kept his contradictory thoughts to himself.

"The group we are after tonight, Herr Untersturmführer... they are all resistance members?" he ventured to ask his Austrian passenger, after a lengthening silence began to hang heavy in the air.

"Yes."

The reply was short. Thus, the conversation ended.

Goeth wrinkled his nose in disgust as the smell of manure wafted in, thick in the air, clinging to the insides of their nostrils. Quietly seething, he cursed, fumbling in his tunic to produce a packet of Turkish cigarettes, and with the flash of a match, lit one to overpower the nauseating stench. Immune to the chemical, industrial pollutions of the human habitat, the Austrian could not bear the uninvited intrusion of a natural, if repellent odour. As they rode on grimly through the night, the starry sky helped illuminate a natural vista, but it did not appeal to the sentiment of the Viennese city boy, with his haughty disdain for the provinces deeply ingrained; almost customary for those born and raised in the old Austro-Hungarian capital. The pleasant scenery barely registered in his cold eyes, even as the stars lit its distant horizon across sloping fields and rolling hills from the road's high vantage.

The driver noted Goeth's irritation, as the officer fidgeted in his seat, sucking crossly on the cigarette with each deep inhalation.

"Disgusting, isn't it sir," he remarked agreeably. Goeth gave no sign that he heard him.

The cross-coated convoy banked a sharp left, cutting through the heart of Garforth, a sleepy far-eastern village in Greater Leeds whose remaining inhabitants were sullenly observing the curfew in place, blissfully unaware of the intent of German men now encroaching on their soil. Onwards they rolled, the low sound of their motors the only noise audible in the quiet countryside town, beyond the incessant chirping of crickets.

Hurtling past the train station and eastwards, the trucks finally reached the last turn-off point at the edge of the town's boundary, just before the road re-joined the main motorway for eastward thoroughfare. They turned right into the small estate; silently dozing in the thick of night, in deep, unsuspecting sleep; the low rumble of tyres a deadly lullaby that proved fatal. The Germans maintained pace, until finally, they were there.

Cedar Ridge. The convoy slowly filtered in to the leafy neighbourhood, as the tree-lined lane curved gently right and then left. The road ended three hundred metres further along in a field, but the SS had no call to drive even that far. The first left turn was fifty metres in, and upon reaching its impasse and the cluster of houses, the SS vehicles slowly ground to a halt. Black-clad figures disembarked, marshalled by Goeth. The trucks backed up, in preparation of exiting the estate. The stealthily moving men approached four separate houses in the silent cul-de-sac; scurrying predators, like pack animals preparing an ambush from the shadows at night.

Goeth's hastily scribbled list, memorised, had read *2, 5, 6, 7.*

As quietly as was possible, the *Einsatzkommando* men congregated by the homes of the doomed, and with the awful, sudden noise of threat and violence breaking the silence of the night, four doors were kicked off their hinges, the sacred sanctuary irreversibly violated. The black coats swarmed in like an unstoppable virus, pistols drawn as they raced upstairs in each home, jackboots clobbering on the carpeted stairs.

The surprise of the ambush, perfectly timed to strike at a moment of optimal vulnerability, combined with the instant panic of fear made the ensnarement complete. So unsuspecting were the targets that no weapons for self-defence were found to hand, as the foreign intrusion neared its ugly inevitability. Two terrified married couples were dragged out of bed, their bodies betrayed by shock; frozen from action and still wrapped in bedclothes, the groggy Garforth targets offered only a token, weak resistance to the nocturnal assault. Other adults, resistance members seeking refuge with sympathetic friends or co-conspirators in their continuing struggles against the Germans were hauled from the settees and guest bedrooms of the four detached houses; those capable of attempting to repel their arrest were promptly beaten to a bloody pulp. The cruel blows of the cosh were punctuated by scornful jibes and foul obscenities spat at them in the fearful, harsh tones of a guttural tongue they could not understand, yet feared and loathed with an overwhelming force.

Cries of pain rang out through the sleeping suburb, quickly smothered.

In the fourth house, implacable malice was manifesting in equally odious fashion, as the basest of human instincts surfaced with sinister speed and an indecent urgency. Two stormtroopers roughly held a dazed woman back from her helpless husband as he was hauled away, tearing the nightdress from her back. Utterly impotent, the apoplectic husband was dragged out of sight, his stifled screams receding with every step until being silenced by a final, vicious blow. His wife was stranded; helpless game for the animalistic, predatory men who had shelved a vital part of their humanity. Alone in her own room, helpless in the face of their violent depravity, the shocked young lady made one final, impotent effort to wriggle free. But with her arms pinioned, naked breasts bouncing as she thrashed wildly in a frenzied panic, the unfortunate young woman had her right leg seized with an unbreakable grip. Now held in place by two others, the man facing her grimly clamped her leg as though in a vice, and with horrified certainty, she knew with a terrible shock that their brutal intentions were inescapable. Fear rose up her spine like an electric current; paralysed, she was wracked by overwhelming dread and terror. The two troopers tightly held her spasming body in place as the enlisted Gestapo brute forcibly penetrated her with his swollen flesh.

"Hold her, hold her still!" the senior squad member demanded in their native tongue; lust and excitement adding strain to his eager cry.

Screams died in her throat, as the awful indignity of her attack overwhelmed the unfortunate young quarry of a merciless predator; prey to his pitiless passion. The noise of his animal instincts echoed through the house, with sneering, guttural invectives in German directed at its victim; thrusting mercilessly into a body made compliant by shock and fear. Pain and revulsion throbbed through her as her assailant writhed and grunted, inserted in her, inside her, in violation of the most primitive intimacy of her being. Her jerky, pitiful yelps and pleas were stifled against the hand of another SS man, clasped tight in her savage defilement until the cruel display was halted upon Amon Goeth's entry into the room.

The Austrian lieutenant strode in with fire burning in the dark globes of his eyes. Unhesitant, he struck the enlisted man hard across his angular jaw, flooring him, and the thump shuddered through the silence that had descended on the house as suddenly as the noise of violence had defiled it. The other men partially dropped the woman, who was now shaking in a state of fugue, whimpering pitifully with a wordless noise.

"Unterscharführer Beckenbauer, what the fuck do you think you are doing?" Goeth began, with dangerous calm.

"It's Scharfü..." the trooper began, tenderly checking his injured jaw as he rose unsteadily to his feet.

25

Beckenbaur stopped himself, and stood up straight, withdrawing his still-exposed erection and wiping away the woman's fluid as he did so with sullen contempt, as though her body's unwanted evidence of his crime had been something insulting, disgusting and deliberate. Goeth cut in.

"I don't care what it is. Is this Poland? Are we in Warsaw, or Leeds, England?"

"Leeds, sir."

"Why would you have the men waiting outside, as I'm sure the other arrests have been made, while you commit a crime against Reich policy?" Goeth snarled at him, abandoning the superficial calm of his silky tone and unruffled air.

"Sir?" Beckenbauer asked, confused.

Kriminalassistent in a provincial Gestapo, Beckenbauer had been drafted in to the fold with the *Einsatzgruppen Britain* on the strong recommendations of his chief. Chosen by Heydrich and his Reich Security Office as an enlisted EGB stormtrooper, he had been assigned to the *gruppe* of Dr Rudolf Lange. In his platoon's Austrian *Einsatzkommando* leader Goeth, however, Beckenbauer suddenly saw an imminent return to the province was at hand if he was lucky; perhaps there was even a court martial on the cards. With a predator's instinct, he sensed danger.

Goeth's evil stare continued to bore through the rapist.

"You stupid *swine*."

"Sir?"

"This is house no. 7, is it *not*, Kriminalassistent whatever-your-fucking-SS-rank-is in your shithole province, you Gestapo clown?"

"Yes, sir," Beckenbauer replied, resentfully.

Such a derogatory comment could have been used against an enlisted man and reported, but for Goeth to have been drafted as a chief lieutenant of SD Major Lange meant he was likely protected. The SD, after all, was under the wing of the same man as the Gestapo; complaints from one agency of the other at such a junior level would only serve to aggravate Heydrich the Hangman.

"Well…" Goeth said, jutting his brutal face into the smooth features of the younger man. "The woman of no.7 is a *Mischling*. You just fucked a Hebrew, a full-on *half-breed*, and in *SS uniform*. Bearing the badge of Heydrich's own security *service…*" and he tapped the small 'SD' diamond on the sleeve, with gleeful malice underlying his rage.

Goeth's eyes were terrible; the junior officer could only stand rooted to the spot, mortified, hardly believing his ears. The final words had been hissed with ferocity.

"What would the General say, I wonder," Goeth mused sneeringly, his eyes bulging, "or indeed, Reichsführer Himmler? You fucked a Jew in uniform. I could have you *shot*."

Beckenbauer was horrified. Neither he, nor the others present spoke, and the awkward tension grew, hanging palpably between them in the air.

Then Goeth grinned; a wide mouth full of evil teeth. Beckenbauer imagined them ripping at his throat. Not like a badger from its back, or the darting lunge of an opportunistic snake, but in the style of a big cat, or an angry alpha male of the ape world; a direct attack from the front, like a carnivorous animal. He would overpower by force, every blow and strike thrown with lethal intent. Goeth was more like the vain Achilles than a wily Ulysses. He was a dangerous man. Even the other professional murderers knew it.

"This is not Poland, you foolish pig," an unblinking Goeth softly said. "Do the job you have been assigned..."

Beckenbauer clicked his heel, straightening up. Goeth sneered, framed in the door by hallway light, and he glanced to his right at the SS stormtroopers who were still holding the dazed arrestee in their grip.

"Bergmann, take the Jewess away," the Austrian snapped.

One of the other men, a huge, bear-like figure quickly clicked his heel, and with agility that belied his frame, dragged the still-frozen Leodensian woman out of the room, roughly down the stairs and out to the waiting trucks. Still naked, quivering in the cold night air, she was unceremoniously thrown in to the back of the truck like a discarded inanimate object, of which no further use could be made. Her husband scrambled to the small, sad figure and he held her in comfort, weeping bitterly through the whispered, empty reassurances and soothing words. She was motionless; a shivering, foetal ball of flesh, in fugue, robbed of her spirit.

Back in the house, Goeth continued to stare at Beckenbauer with a half-grin, before turning on his heel and walking out. After a pause to recollect his wits, SS-Scharführer Beckenbauer, NCO of *Einsatzkommando 2* of *Einsatzgruppe Leeds* followed his battalion leader, marching out with purpose, cursorily saluting a still-sneering Goeth before clambering up and back into the truck. None of the other men mentioned what had happened in the cul-de-sac, House 7; sat with eyes facing directly ahead, expressionless and their rifles slung warily in a hair-trigger grip. Beckenbaur's eyes bore into those of the man opposite; neither man averted their gaze. No German spoke. The silence was deafeningly loud.

Thirty seconds later they had left the boundary of the mining town, and drove eastwards and north for ten minutes in the hesitant first light of the northern sky, to a designated field, veering off the main road down a winding mud path to the chosen spot. A crude anti-tank ditch had been dug there, in the shade of a long line of birch trees; the first section of a shallow trench defence built in preparation of the German invasion that they'd all known was imminent after the Fall of France.

Those ditches, dug with defence in mind, were now used for an altogether more macabre purpose. Unspoken amongst Germans, it was one of the many whispered rumours shared across cities and townships, concurrent with similar tales of atrocity that varied from factual to fanciful. But of all the fevered talk of death in the shadows, the purported use of what were now commonplace countryside ditches held the most gruesome fascination.

Under Goeth's baleful gaze and the silent scrutiny of his cold-faced troops, the fourteen adults, and five children aged four, six and ten, were lined against the ditch. Under a cold, grey sky, several of the doomed raised their eyes to the pale morning sun, wincing as though in regret at its underwhelming final appearance to them. Others sobbed, the children cried, but none begged. The fearful confusion of the children made no impression on the *Einsatzkommando*, calloused as they were to such tasks, and the ill-fated women gently turned the small, tear-streaked faces away from the sight of those hard, cold figures, framed against the morning sky with their guns, pressing them instead into their own bodies with a warm, heartbroken love.

They held each other for comfort, as a signal from Goeth summoned submachine gun fire, crackling through the air; a volley of shots that sent the small, sad figures crashing back into the ditch, with brief fountains of blood spraying into the morning mist and then disappearing just as quickly as they had appeared, like a vaporous apparition.

The SD commando doused the bodies in petrol, and left them burning; a small convoy of cross-marked trucks rolling away into the distance, one long smoke plume at their back rising from the blackened ground, twirling and merging into the grey morning clouds.

PART I

The sun rose weakly over northern France.

James looked up through bleary eyes, as he stepped heavily into the pale light, blinking dumbly and yawning. "Fitting," he said dryly, in the laconic Yorkshire style.

"For what?" asked Tommy, similarly dishevelled as he shuffled out of the barrack huts and out to the asphalt parade ground, rubbing sleep from his gummy eyes. Neither cared much for keeping silence. They hardly felt bound by military discipline. The Yorkshireman glanced at him, and with furrowed brows, nodded towards the stony-faced SS officers stood silently watching their approach, clad in their sleek Hugo Boss uniforms.

"For this new start. New dawn, new day," James observed, deadpan. "And this is SS hospitality, which should be interesting."

Tommy followed his gaze, and scowled. The SS, standing out like sore thumbs in the backdrop of the characterless forested area and the ramshackle little camp it enclosed, looked every inch the merciless supermen they'd been propagandised as on both sides of the war; grim, imposing figures. Brian, limping along behind Tommy, noted with interest that while the Death's Head skull and crossbones was visible on peaked caps, their SS jailors had the usual lightning runes on their collar tabs, like the Waffen-SS, and not the skull and bones of the infamous *Totenkopf* camp guards of Himmler's notorious internment system. The uniforms were field grey, double-breasted both above and below the belt and seemed to be cut from the thick *feldgrau* wool of the army. They wore the same jackets as panzer commanders. *Military dress.* Some bore medals.

"Look at them. They're fucking robots," Tommy whispered. Grumbling, James agreed with the sentiment.

"Twats."

"*Look* at this lot. They're a bunch of dustbin lids! Fresh out of school, seven foot tall and carved out of stone. They don't even look human." Tommy shook his head in disgust, and loudly spat a green blob of phlegm into the dust at his feet. "I can't believe I'm 'ere doing bird in a kraut prison camp, stuck with a Yorkshire bastard like you to boot."

James churlishly grinned at that. "What will I do without my whippet and wife to beat?"

"Die, hopefully," he snorted.

Still fixated on the SS guards, James barely blinked. "You Artful Dodgers are all the same. Eighty years since Charles Dickens and cockneys are still a bunch of uncivilised thieves."

"What would you know about civilisation, you northern monkey?"

"Quite a bit, you little chimney sweep. London; *rats, syphilis, Fagin the Jew and the plague epidemic.*"

"That's enough, Private Wilkinson. Silence in the ranks!" Sergeant Stanley called back to him. "Men, move out! Three ranks of eight! Step to, look lively!"

His heart was in it – the Suffolk voice as stern as its refined tones could allow it to be – but the words were jumbled. Lieutenant Smith was dead; bombed in the anarchy following the collapse of the southern front and the BEF's forced retreat along the River Senne to maintain a straight defensive line with the French, and as such, the leaderless platoon fell to the Sergeant. The ranks, though, had been decimated; Stanley's boys numbered a mere twenty-four from the original sixty that had landed in France with the rest of the British Expeditionary Force.

The entire company filed out, and Tommy and James shared a look of cynical apprehension. They'd arrived the prior night in transit trucks, and had been sent straight into their respective barrack huts. Now, lined up for parade, it was apparent that the company only had one hundred men, all in all, less than half its original number. None voiced what they were feeling. Tommy bit his lip.

One of the watching SS men stepped forwards, an officer; good looking, tall and blond. He seemed to be in his mid-20s. *SS prototype*, James thought. *One of Hitler's own supermen.* The grim embodiment of Aryan masculinity in a brave new Europe.

The officer began calling names out; a coarse, rasping tone belying his handsome, boyish visage. Roll call began, as the German ran through his list of names, the first of which were familiar to the group that laughingly called themselves 'Stanley's Boys'.

"Marshall, Brian, Private!" The German barked.

Brian winced. His own name had never before disturbed him, or sounded so unpleasant as it did then; verbally ejaculated in such guttural fashion.

"Here."

"Rawlinson, Thomas, Private!

"Here," Thomas Rawlinson called back.

"Wilkinson, James, Private!"

Expressionless, James remained deadpan for a split second; long enough to make the German look up inquisitively, his brows furrowed, cold blue eyes roving the ranks.

"'ere'," he finally intoned, deadpan, with all the considerable reserves of contempt and pokerfaced scorn that only an unimpressed Yorkshireman could muster. Tommy smirked, glancing round in amusement. The men let out a small titter; quiet laughter rumbling through the ranks as James yawned loudly.

"Watson, Thomas – private!" The German barked louder.

"I'm still here, Jerry," he sneered, drawling his cockney, and this time the laughter rippled loudly throughout the rank and file. Even the Sergeant snorted, before fixing his expression and staring dead ahead, pokerfaced. This time, the German officer definitely scowled.

"Fletcher, James – Private!"

"Here," the other James in the platoon called out.

"Burdon, Michael, Private!"

"Here."

"Clifford, Andrew, Private!"

"Here."

"Hitchman, Stanley, Platoon Sergeant!"

"Here, *present and correct*!"

The British soldiers sniggered, with the men of other platoons mistaking Stanley's public schoolboy properness for mockery. It was not the norm for such an educated man of culture to join the enlisted ranks of the army. Tommy, Brian, both James' and a few of the others smiled indulgently. Stanley would be stiff upper-lipped for the entirety of their internment, they knew. A gentleman. *Show the enemy what civility looks like. Kill them with kindness.*

One by one, the names of each of the hundred or so remaining men from the four platoons were called out, and the new company was deemed all present and correct. The German lieutenant fell back into line with a handful of enlisted SS, but no dismissal was called. An early breeze whipped them, the sun's pale light proving inadequate as a counterbalance and they shivered, listening to the oddly stifled trilling of birds from the trees. Apprehension lapsing into boredom, the soldiers continued to stand to attention on the makeshift parade ground of what were, clearly, either hastily constructed or disused French military barracks.

Finally, just as the men started to get restless, the gates that separated the barrack huts area from the long building on the other side of the fenced camp creaked open, with a loud metallic groan, and through them walked an SS officer.

There could be no doubt that this man was in charge. He exuded a primal gravitas, radiating authority. The black-clad figure wore a long leather trench-coat, under which his uniform looked crisp, sleek and new. Though field grey, its thread was silvery, unlike the woollen military style Waffen-SS jackets worn by the others, and the right collar tab bore the trademark lightning runes. His uniform, from the smooth, creaseless tunic, to the black coat, to the gleaming knee-length jackboots, shining as they clip-clopped across the gravel, was *perfect*.

Striding powerfully towards the massed men, he did not so much as glance at them, marching confidently until he reached a point of equidistance between the British soldiers at either end of the ranks. And then, with supreme assurance the man turned, imperious. Expressionless.

"Good day to you, soldiers of Great Britain and the Empire."

That raised eyebrows. The tone was commanding, yet vaguely friendly, as though stentorian yet tempered with a smile. The proud face, with its pronounced jaw and cheekbones, however, remained cool.

"I am Commandant SS Sturmbannführer Jochen Wolf. The rank is roughly equivalent to major in your armed services. You may call me Major Wolf."

Brian stole a quick glance to his left at Tommy and James. While the Yorkshireman was impassive, listening indifferently to the SS major's peculiarly precise little introduction, the cockney's contempt was visible, etched across his sneering, upturned lips, and the hostile challenge that flashed in his eyes.

"You are my charge," the major continued smoothly. His English was impeccable, even cultured, with a delicate edge to its rhythm and syntax. "If you are wondering why it is that you are... *guests*, shall we say... of the SS and not the Wehrmacht, rest assured that it is no reason to panic. You are not hostages. These were French military reserve barracks. This is not a hostile situation as far as I see it, nor from the perspective of Reichsführer-SS Himmler and the Führer himself. This is a time of great change. There no longer exists, in the practical sense, a state of war between our two Aryan, Germanic, white European nations. *One* Great War was enough, thankfully this time it ended quickly before too many good men were lost in a pointless struggle."

The speech was met with silence, and no small degree of shock. *Where is he going with this*, Stanley wondered. Talk of hostilities being over... and beyond that, just to *talk*? And to address them with such a bizarre, candid entreaty; to view them with something other than enmity? This isn't common practise for prisoners-of-war. And that particular jurisdiction – the custody of captured troops – most definitely falls to the army. Not a paramilitary, regardless of how entrenched it is in the national social structure.

SS-Major Jochen Wolf let his gaze wander across the ranks of proud, defeated and thoroughly confused soldiers. Undaunted, they stared back through narrowed, quizzical eyes at the handsome young SS officer, bedecked as he was in war service medals that were pinned to his impeccable uniform. Momentarily, he cast a lingering gaze around the men in his charge, and then resumed his introduction. "We are in Aincourt, near to Versailles."

"Ironic, eh," James Wilkinson muttered from the second row. But despite the sharp intake of breath from his fellow platoon members, the major merely continued his speech.

"This camp will be known as St George no.5. Your platoons are being reorganised into three groups, and as a company you will remain together. You will enjoy hot water & regular meals. Improvements will be made to the toilet facilities currently in place here. We Germans will assist you in this. And now let me clarify the relationship between our peoples, who share a common blood. I must make mention again – you are *not* hostages of the SS. There will be an opportunity for education here, in history, culture, geography, and language – *German*, of course. All the men here speak the English language to a considerable degree. You have the chance to learn here, to leave this camp as improved versions of yourselves."

At this, Tommy gave an indistinct snort. The major's eyes identified him at once. Smiling pleasantly, he almost murmured, "No noise or interruptions as I speak, please. The penalty for not extending me the same courtesy and respect I show you is severe."

This was met by silence. Major Wolf's smile melted away, replaced by what was known in the SS as 'the cold face'.

"None of this is compulsory; in fact, nothing is, beyond roll call once a week, and the washing system. You can laze around as you will, as shirkers if you so wish. With no privileges, and all the free time you could wish for. Or, you can learn, and grow. As military men, you will continue to wear your uniforms proudly, though spare shirts and trousers will be given to you also. Rest assured, any clothing given to you will be stripped of SS or German insignia before being presented to you, and will not be identifiable as German military field gear.

Lastly..." and though he smiled, the major's voice took on a steely tone. "There are to be absolutely no escape attempts *whatsoever*. Infringements on this rule will result in punishment. I should not have to tell you what that means. Please... bear in mind the advantages of being in our care. Use this camp to your advantage."

There was no response, and he nodded, as if pleased. "Sergeant Hitchman?!"

The Sarge stood to. "Sergeant Stanley Hitchman, Fourth—" he began, but was abruptly cut off.

"Sergeant *major*, as Platoon Leader and *de facto* company head, do you have any questions?

The Suffolk man bristled visibly, his chest fractionally rising.

"As you mention it, I most certainly do, Major Wolf," he began, indignantly. "*I do not personally have any family left, but these men want to speak to their loved ones back home. All the fellows you see before you have families, parents, wives, children... they don't know if they're alive or dead. It would be a most grievous outrage, Sir, not to mention a barbaric desecration of the honourable code of war, if the families of brave soldiers were not allowed to contact their loved ones serving in France!"

There were some murmurings of assent from the assembled. Tommy even gave several open claps of support. Stanley opened his mouth to silence him, but stopped himself. He was deeply touched.

To Stanley's consternation, however, the major merely smiled.

"*I understand your plight. *Trust* me, in time you will be able to send and receive mail and your families will be in regular contact. This internment is simply a temporary measure while the creation of the new form of the British body politic takes place. Our countries will of course have to diplomatically square away the unfortunate differences brought on by German reclamation of stolen territories to reintegrate our people back into the Fatherland, which were unlawfully signed away to Poland quite nearby in these forests, and of course, the criminal conduct of your government in not only declaring war on the Reich, but commissioning war crimes on German troops, breaching the Geneva Convention in several deeply disturbing ways..."

He trailed off, the blue eyes sliding downwards in an affectation of disquiet. Stanley rankled at the impertinence of the German officer, in leaving the issue vague – a matter of honour! Some of the more knowing of the assembled rolled their eyes; others scowled. It was no secret that SS and, it was said, even

Wehrmacht conduct in Poland had been abysmal. The legitimate persecutions of Germans living in the lost lands of the 'Polish Corridor' that separated East Prussia from the rest of Germany after the Great War, was used to justify embarking on an orgy of unadulterated violence and terror, news of which slowly seeped west. Fire, bullets, bombs and rope; the four weapons freely wielded by the SS in the excessive brutality of their campaign. However, some of the more naïve British soldiers looked uncomfortable or even ashamed; embarrassed by the ungentlemanly conduct with which they were being accused of waging war.

"Furthermore," Stanley blustered, indignant. "I should like your word of honour as an officer and a gentleman, that the rumours we heard of an SS massacre of British POWs as the Pas-de-Calais front collapsed, is categorically not true, Sir!"

"It is categorically *not* true, Sergeant Hitchman," Major Wolf instantly replied, unwavering and firm.

James noticed shrewdly that the younger officer who had read roll call had looked down at his feet, as though embarrassed. The major added, "Waffen SS participation on the battlefield initially caused elements in the Wehrmacht command to register their resentment, to effectively have the panzer formations folded into the army and the divisions absorbed. False complaints of SS military capabilities and conduct were a natural by-product, but ultimately fruitless as the Führer was most delighted with the performance of the Waffen SS, the military bearers of his *political will*, if you like, and as such, the regular army dissidents in question have been brought to heel."

This was met by silence.

"Are there any other questions?" The major asked, affecting an air of innocence. At least, that's how it looked to Tommy, who piped up.

"When are you krauts going to let us go home?"

Again, with uncanny sensory awareness and speed, Major Wolf's icy blue eyes found Tommy, fixing on the young man with unwaveringly intensity. "I'm sorry, Private?" he asked softly. Shouting was unnecessary; the only sound heard was faint birdsong from the thin, sickly trees around the camp, their gnarled branches twisting grotesquely in living death.

Tommy was unrepentant, to say nothing of unfazed. Being under fire in the terrible German onslaught had changed the men; all were hardened, calloused by combat. Stung by defeat, but unbroken. The German sized him up impassively, calmly holding the cockney's stare with an unwavering cool. Tommy did not drop his gaze. Major Wolf approached him, unhurriedly, the dull thud of the jackboots echoing slightly in the total silence.

Before the major physically reached Tommy, the British soldier preempted the threats he suspected would surely follow. *In for a penny, in for a pound*, he thought darkly.

"I said *when* are we going to be let home, Jerry? The war is over… *unfortunately.*"

The clip-clop of jackboots continued at the same maddening pace, until Major Wolf reached Private Tommy Watson of the BEF. Despite himself, at close proximity, Tommy began to feel uncomfortable. Wolf was roughly the same height – six feet – but with the jackboots, cap and the impeccably sleek uniform, medals on his chest visible through the open black trench coat, Major Wolf was an undeniably commanding figure. The icy blue eyes weighed him up and down, neutrally. *Calmly. That terrible calm.*

"Is it not customary in the British military to address a superior officer by his rank title?" he asked.

Tommy suspected that punishment would follow. *In for a penny...*

"As long as he's in the military too," he blurted.

At that, Wolf smiled; a small, toothy gesture. Perfectly neat, white teeth in a straight row. There was not an element of his personage that wasn't kept immaculate.

In the shocked silence, he stepped forwards until he was unnervingly close. When he spoke, it was with the same awful calm.

"I hold the rank of *Sturmbannführer*, or 'Major', young *Private*. It applies throughout the SS. I served on active duty in the Waffen-SS; Czecho-Slovakia, and then Poland, where I commanded a panzer battalion, and then once again when we conquered Holland, Luxembourg, Belgium, France and *Great Britain* in the space of twelve weeks. Now, I have a new role. You will address me as Major, Private, and I will not ask again."

Tommy willed himself to hold the major's gaze, but wilted under their resolute will of steely blue.

"Private?" Wolf asked.

"When do we go home, Major Wolf," Tommy mumbled, looking at the floor.

"As soon as the Führer deems it appropriate," the SS officer said with a pleasant smile that did not quite reach his eyes. "In the meantime, any problems you gentlemen have settling in to life at St George no.5, please do not hesitate to bring to my attention any problems that you have, through Obersturmführer, or

Lieutenant Hoffman, my immediate subordinate here at St George no.5 and the designated liaison officer between you enlisted men of the British Expeditionary Forces here, and the *Schutzstaffel* officer class."

And as he began to briskly stroll back to the gates, he turned, briefly, to address the ranks of men, saluting as he did so. "Good day, gentlemen."

Major Wolf turned back, and marched briskly through the gates leading back to the long brick building, which he entered, disappearing from sight. Lieutenant Hoffman, the officer whom had barked out the roll call, resumed the position left by the camp Commandant.

"Sergeant Hitchman, this company is yours to organise. Lunch-time in the mess."

If Hitchman was taken aback, he recovered quickly.

"All right men. Dis…MISSED! Fall out!"

The men filed out in orderly fashion. Stanley surmised they were glad of the continuation of military discipline. In tough times, the military order was a comfort in and of itself. It was their salvation after catastrophe.

Tommy, Brian and James Wilkinson hung back. James Fletcher winked, muttering "fill me in later. I'm hungry." They filed in just before Stanley, marching off to lunch like some strange training drill, under the still watchful eyes of the SS, and then they sat straight down at a table with Stanley.

"That's not wise, Tommy old boy," Stanley began. With 'his boys', he didn't bother with military rank; he'd enlisted too, after all, and he enjoyed the affection they bestowed on him as the older man. Their collective bond was strong; *had to be* strong, after the Meuse, retreat, Dunkirk… capitulation.

"The last thing we need is to start antagonising Jerry while we're fenced off here in the damned forest."

"I was only saying what everyone was thinking, Sarge," Tommy scowled.

James raised an eyebrow. "*Aye...* maybe there's a reason no one else said it though? Oh, and uh... nice touch in disrespecting him."

"Well someone had to stick up for us, and I didn't hear your contribution you gormless nancy."

"Ah, interesting choice of insult from a London boy."

"What?"

"You *soft* southern *bastard*; London is nothing but plague, perverts and chimney sweeps. I'm not gonna be called a coward by the retarded uncle of Oliver Twist."

"Yes you bleeding well are, you sheep-shagging scallywag."

"*Original* Twist, the sequel."

The flat, deadpan Yorkshire attitude and dry northern humour was his primary tool against the more headstrong cockney. Naturally sardonic, the northerner is often more than equipped for the verbal spats with their southern counterparts, whose lazy reliance on 'caveman' stereotypes often results in a verbal unravelling. Sarcasm is a weapon, and James was the brand of Yorkshireman that had difficulty answering the first question of the day in a serious manner. Tommy, too, came from a close-knit urban community, and carried its traits of easy argument and masculine chest-beating. Something about the debate just appealed to the tribalist nature of an island people with imperialist goals; *in lieu of external enemies, fight and hate each other.*

James and Tommy – neither man harbouring any real ill will – both privately enjoyed their silly squabbles, and with the stress of war, had come to rely on the routine for its assuring familiarity. It gave them a semblance of home life, however slight. Being interned had, thus far, done little to change either man or the dynamics of the wider group.

"Shut up, you northern ponce," Tommy snapped back.

"Shandy."

"It's *grim* up north…"

James nodded, supremely pokerfaced. "*Shandy.*"

"Pigeons, whippets and coalmines," Tommy sneered, before reciting, "Yorkshire born, Yorkshire bred, strong in t' arm an' thick in t' head!"

"*Compelling*! Leeds United. Parks. Trees. Country pubs. Cheap beer. No shandy."

"You're not even *from* Leeds, you Yorkshire twat!"

Tommy's voice betrayed angst. James was calm. The others suspected that he would have worn the same pokerfaced expression had he been part of the *B Company 2nd Battalion* that faced the Zulus at Rorke's Drift.

"Shandy."

Stanley sighed at the familiar argument. "All right, all right," he interjected wearily; clipped Norfolk tones cutting through the distinctively accented north and south spat. James tipped his typically Yorkshire flat cap to the cockney, and looked to Stanley, who resumed: "We're in a bad spot right now, chaps. A *bad* spot. The jolly *good* news is that we're apparently a damn sight more worthwhile than the Poles, and the SS are being uncharacteristically nice. I say until we work out what the devil is going on around here; we do our best to keep it that way."

"So what do we do?" Brian asked. It was the Yorkshireman that answered.

"Go to class and learn how to be a perfect Nazi. Learn some German while we're at it." James scowled. "Then we'll be able t'order sauerkraut in Hamburg, and one of those giant mugs of ale without using a translator. Family 'olidays..."

"Hilarious guv'nor," said Tommy sourly.

"No, it's very much not," the Sergeant said, and shrugged. "But given the circumstances... in all probability, he's right. Let's just see what our new SS friends like Major Wolf have in mind."

James, unusually talkative but warming to his role as a sardonic commentator, looked over to the SS guard on duty in the dining hall. "I'm not looking forward to t' next full moon."

"The Land That Time Forgot," the man intoned to himself, under his breath. The words were lost to the winds. As the gusts subsided at intervals, the sound of his footsteps echoing in almost total silence was unnerving; it felt like the main street of some remote Texan ghost town; a desolate chunk of humanity in the desert. Certainly not a central district of the capital of western civilisation; London, the city and beating heart of the world's largest empire.

"For *now*," he muttered again, verbalising his thoughts. All senses tingled; he was conscious of the rustle of leaves, shrill whoosh of the wind He crept on, through the eerily silent streets of Bloomsbury.

The windswept street on which proudly sat the Royal Oak public house was a cobbled, stony testament to hundreds of years of London history; the loves, lives, blood sweat and tears of the capital's melting pot of people had bled themselves over the stones until they were etched into the very fabric of the city itself, becoming part of its eternal energy, ethereal and tangible alike. The road seemed indistinguishable from the multitude of identical streets around that part of Bloomsbury, reassuringly in the interregnum between fashionable and unintimidating to the common man, and was a welcoming enough place for the Londoner in need of a drink.

"Perfect," old Arthur Speakman the landlord would say. "From the writers to these *petit bourgeois* the commies always chelp about, workers, students, graduates, locals to passing trade from the centre, we 'ave it all. We're the hub."

Famed for its group of resident writers and intellectuals that took the area's name as their own, and with a hotpotch that covered all bases of the lower-middle and middle classes, Bloomsbury was, much like Camden, a mixed bag. It was not uncommon to hear a medley of dialects from around the capital spoken there;

indeed, several regular voices in the Royal Oak had more than a hint of Bow Bells, as opposed to the more local twang of vowels and consonants that is fostered within the sound of the church bells of St Pancras and St George. The trademark garden squares that punctuated the dense mass of duplicate streets and the Royal Oak attracted clientele that often stretched from as wide as Camden to Covent Garden, right across the capital's central districts. On summer's days, with birdsong and sunlight brightening the appeal of the Bloomsbury garden squares, the Royal Oak pub was a heaving mass of booze-soaked Londoners whose city experience was only brightened by its energy.

But in these dark days, the once welcoming street had an eerie gloom to it, as though a cold shadow had crept in with the early autumnal winds and taken its people unaware. Its icy grip was wrapped around the hearts of every living thing in sight; even animals no longer lingered, their scurried patter through the shadows encapsulated the mood among the human populace, whose bowed heads and hesitant gait betrayed latent unease. Verbalised thoughts were shared cheerily enough; foreign invasion and occupation was not enough to quell black humour in England. Even death cannot crush the spirit in which it exists.

However, it would take more than banter to genuinely lift the mood. People were thankful that alcohol had not yet been rationed in the way that fruit was, yet the sight and sound of uninhibited laughter was long gone.

"Ten at bleedin' night, would you credit it?"

It was the grumble of an old man; taking advantage of a lull in the wind, he retrieved a thin wooden pipe from the multifarious interior of his great coat, and emptied a tiny clump Dunhill tobacco from a crinkled pouch into its small opening. "Bloody curfew. Makes you feel like a bleedin' child."

The swarthy man, sat beside him on the garden square bench, murmured his agreement.

"Be indoors at *closing time*; anyone caught out after a pint liable to be denaa'nced... makes your heart bleed, don't it?"

The weather-beaten Londoner took a thoughtful toke on his cheap cigarette; some low end brand from the black market, which variously did and did *not* taste of tobacco, depending on the week. Its red tip and the two silvery smoke plumes were the only lights in the square.

~

Leaves noisily fluttered over his feet as the dark figure clad in thick woollen fox-fur-collared overcoat crept over the cold, dry cobbles, stepping smartly past the public square which he watched warily; too many times had he wandered unwittingly past some assailant hid in undergrowth, or from the shade of a tree. The two old men ceased their grumbling instantly, on hearing his footsteps, and raising themselves up as quickly and quietly as possible, they silently crept away. The silent figure paused behind the square's foliage that grew over that section of fence, waiting until satisfied that he was alone. Crossing the empty road, with the Royal Oak in sight, he kept to the shadows, quiet steps echoing horribly loudly to his ears in the silence of an eerie London night.

The wind all but flung Jack Harrison into the public bar of the Royal Oak as he shuffled in; recovering his poise, impassive, wary. The 1930's had taught him that he lived in times in which walking through the wrong door with the wrong look was a potentially fatal mistake, and on this occasion, as ever, caution prevailed. The young man surreptitiously glanced left and right in a quick appraisal of the scene, but his poise visibly relaxed as he strolled loosely towards the bar, leaning on it with a practised casual air.

Strange memories of Spain loomed up in his mind. In Catalonia; ears pricked for the dialectical or behavioural idiosyncrasies of an outside spy. *Here and now*; familiar but occupied ground; informants replacing a 'fifth column'; the four columns in power, holding the country to ransom in an iron grip. The odious and malignant unspoken presence of the secret police lingered in the air like a foul smell of death. Jack had lived through similar times – the bitter, cannibalistic internecine intrigues of Republican Spain, and following fascist victory, the police round-up squads that later became Franco's *Brigada Político-Social.* They, however, had nothing on the Gestapo with regards to combining competence with murderous intent.

"All right?" Jack intoned to no one in particular.

There was a non-committal grunt from the two older men. The old barman polishing his glass smiled; a wide split in the middle of a ruddy face.

"No worries," Jack muttered. "Don't all get up."

The Royal Oak's public bar was all wood; known as one of the finest looking pubs for miles around, its owner took great pride in its appearance. What had been a well-stocked bar ran along a wide public bar, around the corner of which stood a grand piano, to Arthur's back. There was nothing in the old pub landlord's manner to suggest he was aware of Jack's presence, lounging casually at his bar with a nonchalant air. Instead, he turned to serve the bleary eyed regular who lurched to the bar behind him, adjacent to where Jack stood.

"Pint of stout, Arthur," he mumbled, three days of stubble evident on his strong chin. Arthur served him with a smile.

"There you go, Super," he said kindly. "This one's on me."

The unshaven man nodded, seeming to barely hear him. He was former Superintendent John Thomas of the London Metropolitan Police, and had been relieved of his job when the SD background checks of police officers in southern England unveiled him as a former card-carrying communist party member. The SD was the intelligence service of the SS, set up by Reinhard Heydrich and a sister organisation to his Gestapo in the 'Reich Security Main Office', which was now the responsible body for UK police policy and direction, as well as Germany's own secret, political and criminal police forces.

They'd not arrived in force yet, but their jurisdiction held; Heydrich's position as INTERPOL President transcended national boundaries, with the help of German military conquest. John Thomas had been rapidly flagged, with a speed that dismayed him. Told to go home, the veteran policeman was advised in strong terms by a stern, tall young blond man in SS uniform to not attempt to leave the capital "pending further investigations."

With no wife, married to the job and devoted to the Met, Superintendent Thomas had slunk home to be haunted by his empty house, spending most of the subsequent weeks in the Royal Oak, stewing in a stagnant pit of his own loathing and listlessness, solidly drinking through the palpable fear.

Now, Arthur turned to Jack Harrison.

"Good evening, Sir, what will it be?" He smiled expectantly. Jack returned it, amused by the formality.

"Pint of stout please, old boy. How goes it?"

"Could be worse, son. Could be a lot *better*, mind."

"You're not wrong, mate." Jack gestured towards the two glum, familiar figures sat on tables in the public bar with a tilt of his head. "Three sheets to the wind?"

"Blotto," Arthur replied, quietly. "Both absolutely bollocksed. Both been in since I reopened. Don't have the 'eart to refuse them, truth be told…"

Much like before the occupation, public houses continued to close for several hours in the afternoon, before reopening later for the evening crowd, men and occasionally their wives whom had just finished work and were in need of a pint.

Jack looked to the piano, nestled around the corner of the bar to his right, past where the morose figure of Thomas was sat unresponsively, close to a slouched man who had the disorientating aura of a powerful prize-fighter gone to seed. His name was Bill Wilson, and he had been a regular at the Royal Oak for nigh on twenty years. Few paid him attention; the man was as taciturn as the table he sat at, and less conversational than a mute lunatic; just another mental casualty from a doomed war generation of young corpses, haunted cripples and orphans. Countless parents who'd outlived their children. A lost generation.

Arthur's head was balding, cheeks rosy, nose red and streaked with tiny burst blood vessels, giving him the air of an ageing drunk whose body was in the midst of betraying him after years of substance abuse. But his eyes remained alert and wary. They followed Jack's gaze again, with a knowing look. "Brushing up on Wolfgang," he said, with just a hint of sardonicism.

"Any complaints?"

"From this lot?" was the murmured rebuke.

Jack briefly closed his eyes to the music. "I always loved Mozart," he smiled. The pianist was quietly playing *Requiem* – Jack recognised '*Dies Irae*' and surmised that he was around ten minutes in to the epic composition.

"Yes," Arthur intoned, smile fixed. "Wonderful music. Fitting, I thought."

Jack marvelled. The unctuous manner and classical German composition was the perfect foil to con a Gestapo informant or operative, while few drinkers would make the connection between the hated occupiers and the piano's discreet lull. Plus, Mozart was magnificent, Jack thought. *Absolutely magnificent, heavenly music.*

He leaned in to Arthur.

"Mozart is fantastic."

Jack's impetuous nature had long ago been quelled by necessity in the intrigues of Spain, but caution still frustrated him. Arthur finally relented, recognising a somewhat teasing determination in Jack's eyes, and he dropped the act.

"Aye. But..." and the old publican's voice dropped to a barely audible, croaked whisper, "this is not the Germany we know."

Arthur turned his face ruefully, and began to pour Jack a pint, his hands slightly tremulous.

"No. And these aren't Mozart Germans."

Only as he said it did the full realisation dawn on Jack that he was profoundly disturbed, and saddened by the thought. The nation of Mozart, Beethoven,

Goethe, Nietzsche and all the other names whose work William had introduced him to, and whose *magnum opera* he'd greedily absorbed… that nation no longer existed, to him; replaced by automatons, repeating slogans and racial ideals screamed at them by a crippled dwarf, a fat Renaissance emperor-complex opiate-addicted narcissist and a syphilitic moustachioed psychopath; three maniacs. That nation, a sophisticated country of culture, music, literature and psychology had been supplanted by a nation of strong-armed Aryan supermen; ideal soldiers, machine men, with obedient, unthinking minds and pitiless logic replacing human kindness. The conformists praised, and exalted; the ruthless rewarded; the dissidents, rebels, dreamers, thinkers and heroes tortured, interned, brutalised, killed. Vanished from history.

And now, that will happen to us, Jack realised. These robotic sauerkrauts will inflict that soulless system on us; good blood isn't enough, conformity is of equal necessity. The neurological ability to critically analyse and process information forever switched off, *Ja mein Führer* in its place. Nothing less than a reshaping of human thought.

The thick beer frothed over the top of his glass, and Jack noticed the small wince that crept across Arthur's thin lips. Beer had not yet been rationed, but with the prosperity of the average man fading under Berlin's rule, and the wealth of England already reportedly being bled out of her flanks, even the pubs were being hit. The German mark had been fixed at 9.6 to the pound sterling, but the existing British currency was still being widely used; pennies, shillings and the like. This was still a good rate for the Germans, and their legal purchases were of a notably good value, to say nothing of the illicit siphoning away of art, gold and iron ore that had been quietly reported. Göring, it was said, had obtained some priceless arts for his collection at Karinhall.

Arthur set his beer down in front of Jack. "Thank you, Sir, that will be six and three pence please."

"Cheers."

Jack laid the money down in front of him, a full shilling; three pennies more than had been asked for. Arthur took it gratefully, nodding towards the door leading into the saloon bar where the rooms were partitioned.

Jack turned on his heel and headed through into that section of the pub, its floor thickly carpeted in red and booths replacing tables and chairs. He slid into the furthest booth, occupied by a young man and woman of similar age – mid-twenties – both dressed similarly. No words passed between them, but almost as though by instinct, their hands slid across the smooth table surface and meet, grasping each other firmly.

"Any joy, old boy?" William asked quietly.

He was slightly taller than Jack, with near-shoulder-length dirty blond hair from which he had long since deflected any suggestion of cutting for anonymity's sake. A quiet and more scholarly nature than the others in their collective merely disguised the same burning desire they all shared. His convictions had been expressed in no less violent a manner, at times, though he was free of the almost compulsive impulsivity of the others.

Jack shook his head slowly. "No joy at all."

He sipped his beer thoughtfully, and looked at Mary, sat directly facing him, her dark, Latin eyes scrutinising his. He added quickly, "the rendezvous didn't happen." Theirs was a bond that neither required nor allowed for melodrama or one-upmanship.

"Why," she asked simply, the 'y' lingering a little with the Latin lilt on her tongue. She tilted her head curiously.

"I don't know."

She pursed her lips. Jack loved her unique movements, the way she physically presented each spoken sentence, though he was careful to keep that view private from William, her lover and fiancé. Jack had long since resigned himself to never acting on any impulse with her, nor expressing his deep lust and affection; quite deliberately spending little time over the past four years with her without William, Alan or another comrade being present.

"I've no idea," he admitted.

Beats of dejected, contemplative silence, before Jack realised the impact of his words, and he hurriedly elaborated. "No word at all from recon. No message to, or from, anyone. Forget the War Office, there's no word even at recon level if there's any kind of organised..." before William could hiss at him to be quiet, Jack nodded quickly, recognising his friend's expression. He whispered "... *I know...* no intel, no radio operators broadcasting, no word if there's even an organised resistance movement left, what happened or what's going on now. There's silence in every direction."

No one spoke for a moment. They all knew the gravity of being cut off, acting independently. It wasn't in their nature to just turn their backs on the responsibilities they'd been entrusted with. But with no discernible support network, for supplies, information, instruction; they were adrift. The three of them all knew that their life expectancy could be measured in weeks, if not days, if they went ahead with any mission whatsoever.

Jack leaned across the well-polished table to William. "I take it you didn't get a note with your change?"

William shook his head.

"No such luck. Old Arthur hasn't heard anything but radio static since the Germans took London."

"He was supposed to be our bloody focal point of information," Jack hissed. William shrugged at him, pointing out the flawed logic.

"We were *supposed* to kick Jerry's arse in France. Hitler was *supposed* to be happy with reintegrating the poor Sudeten krauts back into kraut-land with the other sauerkrauts, one big happy kraut family of non-aggressive sauerkrauts," William complained, his lilting Scottish accent more pronounced as he warmed to the sardonic commentary. "Munich was *supposed* to be 'Peace in Our Time'. *Baldo*lini and the Iti's were *supposed* to keep Hitler out of Austria. Someone, somewhere, surely, were supposed to help the Republic when the fascists revolted – never underestimate the Catholic Church, of course. Versailles was *supposed* to keep Germany docile. The League of Nations was *supposed* to *prevent* war. The word 'supposed', all things considered, is evil bollocks."

"You have a point," Jack conceded dryly.

Mary scowled. "All the preparation, weapons dumps, radio operators sharing information from cell to cell, and then *los fascistas* come here nada, no word at all."

She tossed her head impatiently, clearing a thick strand of dark hair out of her eye and awarding Jack a view of her profile. Despite himself, he felt the unmistakeable first flush of arousal. The spark of her eyes, the smooth Latin flesh. To a London-raised English boy, hers was a ravishing beauty made terrible by the impossibility of consummation.

Jack turned to his friend. "Look, I didn't want to ask this but does he... y'know, have any other contacts?"

"You know the score there, old bean. *Total* deniability and compartmentalisation. Arthur doesn't know anything other than who commissioned him, us, and what he gets told on the radio. And that," he said bitterly, sipping his pint, "... is bugger all."

He leaned back, and scratched his chin, as though deep in thought. But as Mary turned to him, William shrugged, as though to avoid raising her hopes. He was as lost as they were.

"How are you two holding up?" Jack asked. He saw little point in further ruminating on their situation. William shook his head sombrely.

"We could be better, my friend. Came down to make a difference, not sit drinking stout quietly in a German city, rubbing shoulders with Jerries." He scowled. "I still can't get used to the swastika flag flying over British soil."

Jack nodded sympathetically. William was the intellectual of the group, but his hatred of fascism was even more deep-rooted and bitter than was his own, and Alan's. Never much minded to fight for as long as Jack had known him – he'd moved down from Edinburgh to Bloomsbury, London in 1934 as an eighteen-year old, compelled by the area's literary reputation and proximity to the hub of central London. Jack had taken an instant liking to the studious Scot. William was prone to quick bursts of intensity, as though social norms only repressed his natural state of being – it was as though in taking up arms in 1936 he had renounced his pacifism in some existential war, reluctantly losing some nobler part of himself to pragmatics and the need to fight fire with fire; only to return back to Britain defeated and, in the cruellest of ironies, find himself living under Nazi rule anyway.

"I never thought we'd see the swastika fly over this country," William continued sadly.

It was a bitter pill for them all to swallow – even having being recruited in the Auxiliary Units. Alan had threatened suicide twice the day the first German troops landed at Dover, and had to be pacified and even sedated.

Mary looked down, and Jack leaned forwards and gave her hands a squeeze. They locked eyes, briefly; no words were needed.

"We're fine," she told him softly.

"How's your Mum?" Jack asked William.

"She's not too great. Still in hospital, her last letter said, and she's got the Jerries' to worry about an' all. She sends her best, anyway."

Mary poked him playfully, and then turned to the recent arrival. "How's your sister, Jack?"

"She's fine," he replied. "She's getting on with it, like everyone else."

He pulled out a small notebook, ripping a piece of blank white paper from it on which he wrote "no recon." He took out a shilling and some pennies, giving them to William, along with the note.

"Here you go old boy, get the next round in."

At that, William seemed to raise himself a little bit. But before he could squeeze out of the booth, prodding Mary back several times in kind, a very distinctive voice came sharply through the bar from the public room. The tone was argumentative, and rose higher.

"That's bloody Alan," Jack snapped redundantly. "For Christ's *sake*. I told him the saloon bar. Thick as *bloody* mince..."

Muttering irritably, the Londoner rose smartly and strode through to the public bar, noting Arthur turn at his arrival to shrug helplessly. The man to whom the Geordie accent belonged was clad in a typically buccaneering black leather jacket with fur lining, his hair cut short into a businessman's neat side parting, as though in conscious irony; the dichotomy of a man stood strained with unreleased tension, green eyes lit by the fire of fury as his voice rose to a scream:

"You're fuckin' pathetic, man! Sitting here drinking yourself into oblivion while there's a *war* and *killin'* out there – you do *realise* there's a war aye?"

But his red-faced admonitions were for nought. Bill Wilson remained as impassive as ever.

"I am quite well aware of the hostilities, thank you." Bill said quietly.

The tone was a sort of softened cockney; the vague hint of underlying Bow Bells remained, but had been smoothened into the kind of generic delivery that could have come out of any north London suburb. Somehow, the clear and reasoned elocution didn't seem synergic with his appearance; bloodshot eyes, a heavy overcoat as weathered as Alan's own jacket, and several days' worth of stubble on a haggard, drawn face, not to mention the lingering pungency of the strong tobacco odour that relentlessly followed him. Bill was a tired man, whose age was almost impossible to determine, with the vestiges of a rugged, yet still youthful handsomeness visible, but overwhelmed by the wild facial hair and weather-beaten skin. Yet for a man suspected of all manner of things, from idiocy to outright lunacy, he rarely betrayed emotion, much less emotional immaturity. Faced with an irate Alan, the fatigued, battered-looking Bill betrayed nothing; no fear, resentment, anger, sadness, bemusement... nothing. The calm response only served to further rile Alan up. Bill's composure was unsettling. Worse, the man's slovenly state made his reasoned tone seem exaggerated, which his Geordie tormentor seemed to sense as he visibly bristled, railing even louder than before:

"Then get off your arse and do something constructive you drunken *shite*! You didn't even put your name down for the reserves or the Local Defence volunteers or the fire service or *anything*, you draft dodging *bastard*!"

In the ensuing silence of the pub, Bill sipped his pint again, thoughtfully. In no obvious hurry to answer, nor concerned at all for his own wellbeing, he scratched the stubble on his chin with one overgrown, blackened fingernail, before raising his eyes to Alan, calmly inquisitive.

"What exactly are *you* doing?"

Jack had seen enough. The reply was maddening for Alan, who recognised and quickly bit down on his dangerous anger as it threatened to boil over into violence. He began sneering "if only you bleedin' well kn..." just as Jack grabbed him from behind, and jostled him away to the threshold. "Alan! That's enough!"

Steering the incensed Geordie towards the door, Jack looked around at Bill. "Sorry about that," and to his friend, "let's go outside and cool off."

Alan gently removed Jack's hand that was still clasped on his shoulder, and they walked out together, the anger instantly quelled. With no sun in the darkening sky, the frosty wind bit as they stepped out into the chilly air, both silently noting that such conditions were ideal to speak in. On this uncommonly windy evening, few informants would be inclined to face the chill, with fewer still potential or tangible enemies in proximity capable of hearing much of what was being said in the silent streets.

Despite this, Jack suddenly grabbed the Geordie, and dragged him over to the alleyway next to the pub. He didn't let go until they were several metres into the shadow, finally allowing himself to let loose with a flurry of recriminations.

"What the hell do you think you're *playing* at? Were you really about to *tell one of the locals* that you're doing something to be proud of, *for the war*? When the war is officially over – making scenes in public when we've got to *stay anonymous or die*?"

Jack's face was aghast, but he left it at that, letting the words take effect. Alan knew the risks involved. It was a stressful time for all of them, and his judgement had lapsed.

But no mistakes could be made. Their lives depended on it.

Alan shrugged, unsmiling. "Stupid man, aye, I just got wound up by that old drunk. He gave me a right look up and down when I walked in the place, it fired my blood–"

"–But we can't afford that, Alan. And I know; only Arthur, John, Bill and a few of the old boys were in there but you know better, mate. Even if things look safe, we can't afford to take those risks."

Alan looked at him, silently holding his gaze; rather pointedly, Jack thought, and bit down on his temper.

"Who else was in there, apart from the old fellas, Super and Bill?"

For the first time, Alan looked discomfited. "The pianist."

"Yes, the pianist, the one I've never seen before, sat playing fucking Mozart. How about Wagner? *Ride of the Valkyries*? I hear he's doing the *Horst Wessel Lied* as a closer."

Alan scowled. "All *right*, all right. You've made your point."

"That geezer could have played at Göring's fucking wedding for all you know–"

"I've got it man! Howay..." Alan chuntered, still slightly riled up.

Jack continued. "It doesn't matter how bad things get, or who says what. What matters is what we've got to do. Anything out of the ordinary, we get tortured, and hung, or shot. They'll hang our fucking cobblers from the Tower, mate. This lot will rip our bollocks off and tear us to shreds. That comes with the territory. But to get caught due to mouthing off in the pub? No, mate. I'm not dying for nothing."

The Geordie held his hand out. It was rather pointed; the familiar mark, where a bullet fired from a fascist's WWI era pistol had tagged him in a village battle near Aragon, was still evident. He'd saved Jack's life that day. That man now took it, briefly, but grinned at the gentlemanly gesture, and hugged him.

"Howay man," Alan snapped loudly, as they separated and walked back towards the pub entrance. He punched Jack's shoulder without looking at him. "Buy us a pint, you tight southern bastard."

They strolled back in, towards the counter but Arthur diverted them back into the saloon bar with a nod and a wink. Alan quickly stepped in front of Jack and swaggered in to the saloon, where he was met by a bear hug from William and a few good natured punches from Mary. William sat back down, and pointedly slid a pint across for Alan, who gratefully lowered himself into the booth, for the first time showing a sign of weariness. Jack wondered when he'd last sat down to relax.

"Howay, son. Best greetin' you could've given me!"

They all clinked glasses. Alan caught Mary's eye. It was a pleasing eye to catch. She beat him to the punch, though, and clasped her hands in entreaty.

"Speak English. *Please...*"

It was a familiar riposte, but they laughed anyway. Such is comradeship and the solidarity of shared struggles in dark times. Alan swigged mightily from his glass, tipping it to Mary and winking at the *Barceloniña*.

"Anything for you, lass. Even if you want me to take you away from this one." He nodded at William.

The pair raced to answer him; Mary won.

"I tell you so many times now; I love you but *no comprende nada*. You do not speak in a way my brain understands."

"I tell him that too," Jack interjected.

Alan affected a grudging acceptance as they chuckled. "Guess I'm out of luck. William, you've got them both. To the victor, the spoils." He raised his glass in salute.

William winked. "You've got lovely hair though, pal. Assuming you make it through the next year, you could always get a job in a bank somewhere. Just pretend you're mute. And Jewish."

Mary prodded him again, in tolerant disapproval. Alan winked at her.

"*Shalom*, sister."

"Beso mi culo, mariquita," she replied, smiling sweetly as the others snickered.

At that, Alan's jollity gave way. He cleared his throat.

"The next year..."

"So what have you heard?" William urged him, leaning in.

The good mood rapidly evaporated, and a sense of purpose was restored. Alan sighed, emptying his glass with huge gulps, pouring the dark frothy ale down his throat with indecent gusto. Jack slid his own, barely touched pint over to him – anything to hasten the process of news on which they'd all keenly waited.

Alan was a well-connected radical figure; it had been he who'd arranged the Spain travel, he who encouraged the defection from the International Brigade of Communist Party members to the POUM militia, upon meeting Mary in Barcelona; he, or so he claimed, was responsible for their being recruited as Auxiliaries. On the latter point, William knew otherwise but he had no intention of revealing it. Loyal, clever – despite an infuriating lack of tact and diplomacy – and a passionate fighter for the cause; in intrigue and action alike, Alan was worth his weight in gold.

He cleared his throat.

"Not good. German Army all over London –"

"–are they?" William interjected. "Excellent work. I knew you'd know."

He smirked, flicking his hair out of his eyes, and tipped his glass to Alan before swigging from it. Mary sarcastically applauded, and they silently toasted him, feigning admiration and reverence. The Geordie returned a baleful stare, his bright eyes narrowed crossly.

Jack's objection died in his throat, and he chuckled. Good spirits were essential in dark times. Morale in all forms was to be cherished.

Alan continued, pokerfaced; "Anyway, with the agreement of William Wallace over here, Wehrmacht is crawling all over London... obviously occupied Whitehall and... everywhere that matters, really."

"And their operational base?" Jack enquired. "We've all heard conflicting reports, most of it pure rumour, and they're a bloody bureaucratic lot these Jerries. Wehrmacht, SS. SD and Gestapo."

Alan nodded. "SD were..." but before he finished the sentence, he hesitated, and glanced at Jack, who guessed what he might be about to say. Hurriedly continuing, Alan explained, "... Wehrmacht have jurisdiction, and Hitler named a General von *Brauchitsch* as commander. Nice name, eh? Just some lapdog, but he's in command of the ongoing battles in the northern zone."

This really piqued their interest.

"So what *exactly* is going on outside this city?" Jack asked.

"It was as we expected. What passed for a home defence army; stragglers, Great War vets and odds and sods from all over were forced north as the front line spread. Government capitulated with the army *proper* captured en masse in France, but there were still plenty of fighters on the home front. They were forced north with the German advance, and have banded together with the resistance in the northern zone and who came down from Scotland."

"So what's going on in Scotland? Where are the front lines, and where are they occupying?" William asked, his voice betraying concern.

Mary glanced at the worried face of her lover. His family still lived in Edinburgh. His mother's letter from weeks ago had just gotten to him; she was in hospital but assured him it was nothing. She'd wanted to pass on her best wishes to Jack and Mary. She had mentioned neither Germans nor Scotland.

Alan considered. "Well, *that's* where the line becomes blurry. The government imploded, and capitulated with no army – only auxiliaries, as we well know – and then radio operators went down…" He looked at Jack again. "I'm sorry, but I have to say it. I think Fifth Columnists are the reason the radio stuff didn't work."

"Preposterous," William immediately interjected, quite indignantly. But Alan and, to the Scot's surprise, Jack, both shook their heads.

"Not treachery. Spies and saboteurs in this country. SD. Agentur. Not the people risking their lives for Britain. That's the only thing to explain the collapse of our networks."

William nodded, reluctantly. "Perhaps. Scallywagging includes intel, yet we've heard nothing. Arthur's not heard from a village priest on a church radio, a countryside bunker, northern Special Duties officer, Ops Patrol – nothing. The whole country's bedlam."

Alan quickly continued. "Point being; the government imploded, but people formed resistance armies *anyway* to fight back. So here's the crazy part. The Germans sent over representatives and task forces of the army to help facilitate a BUF takeover of Edinburgh and Glasgow, right? And the London government are kaput. Oswald Moseley's waiting in the wings, ready to be installed as a Hitler puppet."

"Prime Minister Moseley, Christ."

Alan shook his head. "No. Just a lackey."

"Thank God for that."

"Anyway, the people wanted to resist, and with the front lines in England stretching up to the Liverpool-Manchester-Leeds west-to-east line, thousands of Scottish blokes went south to join up with the partisans, and thousands more are dotted around your homeland trying to sabotage German plans. It was all set in place like us, with shelters, weapons dumps. Now, they don't know where the front lines are, if the border is fully held by German troops, if the three northern English cities south of it are fully occupied or what. It's all a bit chaotic."

William's eyes were open wide, fully grasping the dire consequences of this information:

"What you're saying is; the north of this country and the south of mine – the entire middle chunk of this island – is a volatile, bloody warzone filled with Jerries and partisans?"

"From what I gather, that is the case, mucker. Partly, at least."

"My God," Jack breathed. "No wonder they're keeping a tight lid on the whole thing."

William snorted. "We're all *Saxon brothers,* and all that. A PR campaign until things settle."

Alan shook his head ruefully. "There's little chance it will last into winter though. For a start if they converge on towns and villages for shelter and food, the Jerries would just raze them to the ground. There's too many resisting to just creep home at night and live normal lives in their towns and cities. Too many jobs left empty, posts deserted. Too many German patrols in the cities and big towns. So, our boys will eventually run out of food, hiding places or bullets. Unfortunately there's a possibility that thousands of British lads could just freeze to death, or run out of time and territory. We're talking about an army that conquered Europe against the leftovers of ours who didn't go to France, and the older lot who fought their fathers. Even with the weapons dumps, incendiaries and all that, they've got no chance long-term against the Wehrmacht."

This was grim news. Jack hurried him on.

"Where is the army command? I take it the civil administration is the same HQ? We're obviously not under SS rule."

Alan gave another snort, this one mirthless. "They took over Churchill's Blenheim Palace."

William snorted too, in derision. "How *poetic*. Winston's in exile, the war's fini–" now it was his turn to catch himself "–... invasion's over and Hitler still wants to piss on Churchill's shoes."

"A message to all of us," Alan pointed out. "Downing Street is nominally left for whatever puppet government they decide to elect. I think they wanted Chamberlain but he refused."

"Poor bastard. Between Munich and the Phoney War *sitzkrieg*, he'll get all the blame." William mused.

"Forget blame! History? Any future under fascism is worthless, it doesn't matter what history records. I'd rather die than see it."

The sudden eruption from Mary silenced them all. There was no trace of mirth now.

After examining his glass for what felt like minutes, Alan cleared his throat again and looked up.

"The Royals got out safe, obviously, so did Churchill. They had to drag him to the plane. Canada. The rest of his cabinet stuck around, obviously not knowing they'd be grabbed and held. Chamberlain and Halifax are being left alone, there's talk Hitler wanted to set up a puppet government under them instead of Mosley for now, just to keep everything in place and running smoothly. But from what I hear Chamberlain's ill, and not expected to see Christmas."

"Probably a blessing," Jack opined gloomily. They all murmured assent.

"So Hitler remembered the Munich conference," William noted. "Interesting."

"Aye, probably why they scratched Neville's name off the arrest lists. Viscount Halifax has been spared, but I don't know anything else about arrests."

He looked confused for a moment, as well he might. It was the most curious thing about the occupation thus far – relatively peaceful in London. This *den of Jews and subversives,* as Hitler and Goebbels had ranted, and everything Lord Haw Haw had silkily purred on Radio Berlin; *the British warmongers*; the communists, the socialists, the 'decadent' writers; why had the city been spared the customary bloodbath? Why hadn't the SS-Gestapo and security police arrived in force to turn London into a thick-walled torture chamber?

"Alan," Jack queried, "Why aren't the round-up squads operational yet?"

He hoped if he verbalised the thought, that at least one of them may be able to offer some insight. But there was silence, and the Geordie shrugged.

"How do we know they're not? I've not heard about the big guns landing or anything, but for all we know they're attached to the army rear-lines. Or focusing on the continent. France and Holland. Or still busy slaughtering Poles. I don't know..." and his lack of knowledge on a vital issue seemed to almost pain him. He didn't have a source in the know. It was a mystery.

There was another silence, as each of them collected their thoughts. Finally, it was broken by the least impetuous of the group in William.

"Well... whether we know about it or not, it's safe to assume there'll be the usual cleansing. Let's just see how things pan out..."

"In the meantime," Jack added solemnly, "we hang tight. No foul play – yet."

With that, each of them drifted into their own thoughts, as a sudden flash of lightning signalled an imminent lashing rain, which pelted against the pub windows like a possessed spirit bringing threatening auguries for the serious young people inside, lives dedicated to a grim cause from which there could be no escape now, no compromise, no surrender. They, or it, would fall. It was the irrevocable nature of the fight, on either side of the dividing line.

Simon lit a cigarette, deeply thankful that he'd stocked up on his preferred American Lucky Strikes prior to tighter rationing. *Lord help those on the black market cigarettes*, he thought. *Just smelling them is bad enough. Having to actually smoke one would be like volunteering as a chimney sweep in some Charles Dickens novel.*

It had been a good day, in the circumstances. The writer reclined at ease, in the large, studded leather chair he'd bought for the desk, and running his hands gently through the thick clump of knotted hair on the crown of his head, breathed easily for the first time in what felt like days. Only as he did so did the realisation set in that his chest had been contracting, and his trapezius muscles were tensed. Sucking gratefully at the Lucky Strike cigarette, he began to pen a diary – his own private act of defiance.

Printing subversive materials extolling the people to resist German propaganda was his outward contribution, though how long he'd last, the young journalist was blissfully, worryingly unaware. But this, his diary, was the private resistance that he himself used, in the forlorn hope that perhaps the leather notebook and his thoughts could possibly survive the mayhem to be read one day, in a free world, by a free people; an insight into occupation and life under the jackboot.

It had taken him several days to relax. A member of the dissident writer's movement named Walter had been captured in London, and punished mercilessly. Simon did not personally know the man –an acquaintance of Eric, and other familiar faces of the '30s who had been at home on the political left – but regardless, the ghastly nature of the news still shook him to the core. It was not so much the failure and resulting arrest that disturbed him, but the baffling, brutal barbarity of German vengeance. Evidently, Walter's Hebrew heritage swung the balance. The freelance journalist had gotten careless at the printers;

snatched by the Gestapo or SD, he'd been hauled in for interrogation. Days later, the poor writer's family received his severed tongue in a box. A note written in blood explained in vicious, vivid detail that by the time the poor, doomed writer had died, Walter was not only missing several other limbs – diabolically heinous – but even worse; that he had been castrated and blinded prior to death.

"Sic Semper Reichsfeinde."

A sinister Nazi paraphrasal of the old Roman reproach in Latin; thus always to tyrants. How sinister the world now; *Thus Always to Enemies of the Reich.*

Presumably, blood loss had spelled Walther's demise, given the protracted torture and the nature of his many grievous injuries. Simon found himself fervently hoping that the mercy of unconsciousness had descended on him as early as possible, acutely sensing his empathy surge, before realising with a cold sensation in the pit of his stomach that it was inconceivable that Walter had not suffered tremendously and at length, given the horrific nature of his tortured ordeal.

Such horror was unfathomable, and it hit hard with those guilty of the same crimes as the condemned man. Reverting to cannabis was misjudged; it merely led Simon to protracted bouts of intense introspection, after which it took several sober days and a considerable mental readjustment for him to recover his flagging spirits and resume writing, encouraged as he was by the others.

Today had been a revival. Musing over the materials he'd typed, the young writer even dared to consider the possibility that his day's literary yield was equal to Eric's standards. Restless, he rose and approached the mirror, peering into the flecked brown of his own eyes. He was not Orwell. Shaking his head slightly, the writer resolved to return to the hemp; ego-checks were essential, in order to keep progressing. Packing his huge wooden calabash with the cannabis, he puffed happily, allowing the tempo-switch to come into effect, sensing his thought processes changing along with his vision. *Slow down,* he told himself, setting the tone. *Never get ahead of yourself. Keep going. You are not Eric yet, but you could be.*

He returned to the great desk and with fountain pen in hand, he opened the leather notebook, dipped his quill's nib into ink and he inhaled deeply, preparing to write.

Possibility is limitless.

Smiling, the scribe repeated his simple mantra thrice until satisfied, and then reached for the calabash, his good humour returning.

Simon used none of the four comfortable rooms downstairs as an office, preferring to dedicate the space to bookshelves and homeliness; tables, rugs, ornaments. He liked writing in the quiet solitude and security of his own bedroom, with its wide desk and ample drawers, reclining couch, four poster bed and comfortable chair. Each room of the house was adequate to host a number of guests in, tended lovingly by his mother, whom he'd insisted move in after the death of his father. At any rate, her house had been in no less peril during the Blitz than had his own.

"But I couldn't possibly get under your feet, my darling boy," she'd tried to protest, voice crackling. "You don't want your old Ma around."

"Why?" He'd inquired, with genuine curiosity.

"You're a young man," she warbled, "a bachelor. You don't want *me* cramping your style..."

Chortling to himself, he'd responded by promptly packing her valuables into a suitcase, deflecting her protestations as he forcibly moved her possessions. It took a considerable time; Simon's family were well-to-do, and both the houses were filled with trinkets and assorted items of taste and style, nothing chintzy or kitsch; a large assortment of material wealth that had been discerningly collected over time.

Looking around his large, spacious bedroom almost compulsively, with its thick carpets, ornate rugs and furnishings and gleaming mahogany, the writer tried to settle; dipping the nib of his quill into a small vat of ink, and he set to recording his thoughts; praying, even as he did so, that one day the words *could*, and *would*, be read by others. Deciding that having not made a diary entry in weeks, it was best to explain what *had* happened first and foremost, before chronicling what *was* happening.

Perhaps it would survive, perhaps not. How many Samuel Pepys' had been lost to history? How many chronicles of human drama; from love to fear, suffering and triumph alike, had been swept into the dustbin of time; lost in the annals and archives of humankind's bloody advancements..

Cigarette-holder clenched in the corner of his mouth, tasting its smoke on his breath, a pale sun setting through the glass panes to his back and even with something approaching hope; Simon began to write:

London attracted, with horrible suddenness, an array of leeches, parasites and social scavengers congregating in the symbolic site of national terminal erosion; sucking the spiritual lifeblood out of their injured host in the dying days of The World's Great Empire. These vultures, skulking; buying knockoff goods sold in desperation; selling weapons and 'essentials' to a terrified middle class at extortionate prices; offering safe passage across the Atlantic to Canada or guaranteed escape to Gibraltar, fake American passports, cut-rate stimulant drugs which were so impure and diluted with everything from sodium bicarbonate to the as-yet unrationed salt that there was never enough to have much effect... slinking villains, who were viewed with a mixture of contempt, gratitude and indifference, depending on the constitution of those that observed their trench-coated, solicitous scurryings.

A tiny minority, no longer fearing the criminal charge of 'defeatism' in the wake of Dunkirk, had even sold pocket sized German language handbooks; utterly taboo, though even with a discerning approach to choosing potential buyers, most would still fall victim to particularly vindictive assaults from enraged patriots, and those with family and friends in France. Two died in Liverpool, with an astonishing thirty-seven stab wounds *reported on a middle aged male found slashed to pieces in a market. Stabbed and slashed THIRTY-SEVEN times... evidently, Scousers hate Germany. To everyone's shock; the practice soon migrated from working class areas...*

Everything is in short supply for the average man; vegetables, meat and tempers. Queuing up for goods when the lads fought in France, and especially when the night raids happened, that was fine. All anger was directed outwards, frustration turned to humour.

'Fat Göring should spend a month or two in England', they'd say. 'No wonder he wants us so badly. To be able to live in a country whose bread tastes like cardboard, milk like puddle-water with cheese curds or rat turds, and who only get a combined 480g per week of cheese and butter – it will do him the world of good... he'll look normal again in no time!'

Or talking about some obvious sign of bomb damage on a building, asking how big the mice must have been to chew an 'ole that size! Or any number of other brilliant examples of the British sensibility in times of suffering. Had we been Latin, Mediterranean types, there would have been panic everywhere, every time a Jerry plane flew overhead. Here, people made jokes in the queue about how the pilot was off to find the sausage factory, to crash land, as the Berlin rationing was killing him. Truly astonishing humour, in the circumstances.

The British spirit warmed your heart. Now, all I hear is grumbling.

They've lost the incentive to stay cheery. Positivity has no meaning, only food and the continued survival of their families matter; all else is quixotic, abstract, antiquated. To some, astonishingly enough; creativity, positivity and even love seem to belong to some long lost time already. Shouldn't times of suffering necessitate such contribution even more? Alas, countless husbands and sons in the army, dead or captured, or conscripted to factories – the warm women I knew are hard-faced, locked in private grief which they do not show, and have essentially become entirely self-serving survivalists. Atavistic urges reign. Collaborators are brazen. London is an isolated entity in its own right; most assume the north is lost, even those who disbelieve Haw Haw on the radio and the Goebbels Ministry broadcasts. Many of the unwashed, unfed people no longer care. I fear that many would indeed heed the call to 'hail Hitler' if he fed them better. The jokes have stopped, or they meet only with painful silence.

War has dehumanised even those who did not fight in it.

Simon paused, sitting back in thought, and absentmindedly flicking ash onto his smoking jacket. How to capture the madness adequately, with the written word?

Those horrendous days, with opinion so massively divided, when all seemed lost but the refusal of surrender remained?

Churchill wanted to fight on. No army, 300,000 men captured in northern France and God knows how many more. Now we know he wanted to sink the French fleet, use mustard gas on the Jerries. They stopped him; everyone knew all was lost. He tried rallying the people with epic speeches of defiance, and ended up being deposed in a coup. Halifax enquired about an armistice, but by then the Germans had already set off. They seized their opportunity. Italy and Spain sent ships, and a six-figure number of men. Vichy-France contributed a volunteer infantry battalion, along with its navy. A fleet of landing barges assembled. Landed in three spots. The Kriegsmarine Wolfpacks, causing terror at sea and a quadri-national naval force to tie up the Royal Navy. The Luftwaffe, clinically depleting the Spitfire's of Fighter Command with awful relentlessness...

He hesitated briefly, before adding, *it was all so fast.*

The radio broadcast had been perhaps the most shocking moment of his life. Remembering it was like recalling a horrific, disorientating nightmare. He'd been at the office, in a crowded room of industrious journalists and drunken hacks alike. One of the older men had swigged from a whiskey flask, tears rolling down his face as the unspeakable words were uttered to the nation. He'd seen too many dead friends in the mud of Ypres and Flanders Field to fully comprehend what the broadcast said:

"To the people of Britain, I have the odious assignment of informing you that the government of the United Kingdom of Great Britain and Northern Ireland is engaged in peace talks with the German High Command. I must express to the

British public the dire military circumstances at present, with complete frankness. The capture of the British Expeditionary Force and allied French troops numbering almost 400,000 men, the loss of valuable equipment, heavy armour and artillery, tanks and supplies; the hostility of a French state and its willingness to ally their navy with the Kriegsmarine against ours, the Italians and the Spanish poised to join them in the assault upon our land, our men in captivity – most with the paramilitary SS – the loss of fighter planes over France, and regrettably, the continued German superiority in the air, creates what is *all in all* a hopelessly defenceless position from which to continue to wage war against Germany.

I have received assurances from the government of Herr Hitler that peace with Britain was most acceptable to him, and that he saw no merit in subjugating a great European nation and, as he put it, a racial brother. Herr Hitler stated the following; 'England's willingness to compromise is the best option available for all, and to end the lamentable state of war that was forced upon the Reich by the Chamberlain government ten months prior. The Reich's only goal against England was driven by the necessity of eliminating Great Britain as a base from which a war against the German Reich could be, and was being, fought.' Now, as ever, said Herr Hitler, with no malice towards the western nations of a shared Christian civilisation, his eyes turn only to the reclamation of land taken from Germany, and the German people lost in the reshaping of Europe from a criminal treaty and again, as he put it, the bastard children of Versailles."

Simon had stood dumbfounded, the cigarette clenched between his teeth burning out in the holder, ash falling down his front. Several of the men present began yelling at the radio, as if that would help, and all were silenced again as Halifax's tired voice resumed its cracked delivery:

"The German government wishes to extend the same message of friendship to England as it did two years ago. They reiterate that, regardless of pacts, and treaties signed by paper, that the English and German people are bound by blood, and that the two Christian nations and Aryan peoples of Saxon blood have a duty to their shared civilisation to look elsewhere, and see that while large tracts of land may come under the rule of an international conspiracy of... parasites and... *Jewish* leeches – *excuse me, I am reading verbatim* – that the Aryan peoples of Europe must *unite* to preserve the long continuity of our institutions, our Empires and our civilisation. We must brace ourselves to our duties, and bear ourselves so that history will record we behaved with *honour*, and in the defence of our people, our empire and western civilisation itself."

In his bedroom now, back in the present, the contemplative Simon again took his pen to the notepad. Ruminating briefly, he tore up the terse notes he'd written, deciding to start over. Regardless of the 'brotherhood' shared with Germans, he thought bitterly, with any luck this notepad condemning their bestiality will survive all of us as a testament to the true spirit of democracy-loving people.

After Dunkirk, the Luftwaffe had turned its sights onto England. We'd seen the destructive force of German military might playing to universal horror across cinema screens up and down the country, and with our army gone, Hitler and Göring's eyes turned west to the white cliffs of Dover. Warsaw, Rotterdam... was London next? Leeds, Manchester, Liverpool, Edinburgh? They bombed us relentlessly for a fortnight, even before France signed her official surrender. Night-time bombing raids on London, now called "The Blitz". Fires in the night sky, women and children screaming, the shriek of the bombers, the deathly silence that briefly, fatefully follows. And then dust, blood, sirens. Noise and smells and screeching yells, panic and terror. The rising panic of a people under fire, who knew they had no army left to defend them when the enemy came.

Hitler called off his air strikes on the cities, obviously fearing that continued indiscriminate slaughter would result in vastly increased resistance to even a partial occupation of Britain. He was right.

Focusing solely on the battered RAF, Whitehall was apparently – so I hear, anyway – threatened with the mass-execution of tens of thousands of the captured troops. Hard to tell if it's truthful or one of the other ludicrous yarns being spun on the rumour mill; perhaps even an expedient Parliament lie to excuse the cataclysmic collapse. But, as it goes, apparently the SS have custody of large numbers of enlisted men, not the Wehrmacht. The pressure was too much.

The entreaties to America to send quarter of a million troops 'for training purposes' to England was rejected. Did they see it as an ill-disguised attempt to unofficially bring the US into an armed defence of Great Britain? Did Lindbergh and that awful Kennedy chap sway opinion in the States? Either way, we were done. No army, Parliament in uproar, numerical disadvantage in the air, thousands of soldier hostages with SS guns pointed at their heads... the worst start to summer in recorded British history.

Simon thought to himself. How could we have defended, he wondered? Who's to say the RAF couldn't have beaten Göring's boys? We have the best navy in the world? What if we'd called Hitler's bluff with the POWs?

The grim reality was that with French, Spanish and Italian ships joining Germany's, even that naval invulnerability *would* have, and was in the process *of,* been broken. And we could not risk the lives of our men abroad. Sentimentality; the Achilles heel of our democracy.

The French Navy stood firm against British threats to scuttle their fleet entire – weeks before, our allies, and now pledging their ships to the Hun. Spain promised naval and air support against us, in return for Gibraltar. And after Dunkirk, there was not a single shred of hope left for a ground resistance. The families of the captured soldiers begged for peace. Whitehall turned against the war faction. Churchill was finished. The tide had turned.

Simon realised his cigarette had burned out. He opened a great carved wooden box on the felt desktop, selected one of the loose fags within – a Chesterfield, it looked like – and inserted it into his silver holder, lighting it with a quick snap of the tin. Satisfied by several deep intakes of smoke, he resumed writing.

The air of capitulation hung heavy. Halifax headed up the new cabinet, with Winston and Neville out of the picture, but confusion still reigned. Many still wanted to fight on. Half the civilians said they'd fight regardless of any pact with Hitler. By the time they decided to reach out it was too late; they'd already launched the attack, barely five weeks after French surrender. Thereafter, on-land resistance came down to the fury of civilians, not official policy.

The horrors of the Blitz had enveloped Victoria Embankment, Bloomsbury and the East End of London in its misery. Simon had set off for the East End the morning after a particularly vicious blasting, after spending an interesting night before in the Savoy hotel where a gang of hysterical East Enders led by a Stepney councillor had commandeered the hotel's shelter.

"If this shelter is good enough for the bloody Savoy parasites, it's good enough for the decent people of Stepney under German bombs!" the man had screamed.

Simon had felt fortunate indeed to have been dining in the hotel restaurant that night, with a well-to-do businessman he'd interviewed several weeks prior. As darkness fell, the tired journalist had considered booking a room upstairs, until hearing the scream of a Stuka bomber. With the screeching sirens and sinister sound of the bomber planes combining to eerie effect, Simon decided he was better off staying in the shelter with the group of victorious cockneys, whose 'invasion' of sorts had met with token opposition from a management staff who knew that to deny shelter would be a public relations disaster; unsurprisingly, in the face of bad press, the Savoy had quickly relented.

Elated, the cockneys sang most of the night. *I'm Forever Blowing Bubbles* and Vera Lynn. It was really quite fun, come to think.

"Pretty bubbles in the air!" Sat perched together on the makeshift bench, a thick woollen jumper-clad cockney happily yelled into Simon's ear, while reaching to wrap his short arm around the significantly more suave, svelte scribe. From the initial conversations, Simon had gleaned that the group was of a distinctly socialist persuasion, but the heated talk of class war had soon morphed peaceably into song. As he leaned across, draping his arm over the journalist's shoulder, the cockney simultaneously offered Simon a flask with his free hand. Gratified, he unhesitantly accepted the small metal decanter, drinking without so much as an inquisitive sniff, wary of the tinge of guilt from the slight surprise he felt, as was sometimes experienced by the upper class upon encountering proletarian generosity. He soon regretted it, as the flask was filled with gin; taken by surprise, the journalist coughed and spluttered as his cockney companion cheerily continued the singalong:

"They fly so 'igh, they reach the sky, and like my dreams they fade and die! Fortune's always 'iding! I've looked everywhere! I'm forever blowin' bubbles, pre'y *babbools*, in the *air*!"

Laughing uproariously, the man beseeched a grimacing Simon to sup more of the gin, and with a brief parody of reluctance that he genuinely felt, the bemused writer tipped the rest of the foul-tasting alcohol down his throat, as the watching East Enders cheered him. Minutes of unpleasant stomach rumblings followed, until the class-conscious Savoy staff, to whom Simon was known, realised that he was fighting the urge to be sick, and despite his protests, they hurried to fetch him water, whiskey and ice – German bombs be damned.

Before resentment could fall on their haven, Simon extended some notes and bought a full bottle of Scotch, which he insisted be passed around the bunker. With a quick one-sip-pass procedure, morale soared. The Savoy waiters, less sullen than management over the earlier confrontation, followed up with silver trays carrying ornate pots of delicious, real tea for the East Enders who had commandeered the hotel bunker, drawing deep sighs of pleasure from those for whom only ersatz was available. Soon after, more platters arrived, this time laden with thickly buttered bread for the children. Brandishing money delicately, to ensure compliance from the staff but while avoiding ostentation in a somewhat more Marxist-friendly environ than he was accustomed, Simon replenished the whiskey supply and observed the happy interactions in the room. *Unity, sans division*, the writer thought. *These people are genuine, warm, and real. My brothers in this human family, no more or less than a chap at the Oxford & Cambridge Club, or any of the clubs on Pall Mall. This is humanity at its realest, not the kids upstairs flying planes to bomb people for the agendas of their political masters.*

No religion or even politics down here, in this basement. What would it take for whole communities, countries and creeds to feel this solidarity?

Cannabis, the sensation that had reignited in America and helped bring hemp's recreational usage back to prominence in a quiet, steady British counter-culture, had helped dispel much of the prejudice, entitlement and arrogance that had eluded the careful eye of Simon's mother, undermining her care during the once-restlessly energetic yet gentle soul's dedicated mothering of the studious boy. It took root in his thoughts and expectations. Bravado and projection replaced genuine yet understated confidence; much of that which had been endearing in him ceased to be seen, to his mother's despondency. A bachelor of the arts, the blissfully apathetic raconteur left university, having renounced his faith and openly claiming to feel *no connection, either socially or intellectually* with the student life and further study. Personal failures and parental despair combined to sober the-21yr old frustrated essayist and tentative poet. Cannabis, ironically sought following the conclusion of his stimulant-filled student years, had finally levelled him out, and provided the introspection needed to dispel the lesser demons of his nature. *Reefer Madness*, such insanity – freely distributed for the mass-consumer audience of the west! Curiosity pushed the wealthy young man's interest in the plant to an isolated purchase, and thence to regular use. Wracked by introspection, the young man struggled through several months of instability and self-doubt before readjusting his focus to chase goals. Once humorous, *Reefer Madness* no longer amused him, and he dedicated an entire afternoon to writing an ultimately unpublished critique of the film, that descended into an impassioned defence of the plant. He began to watch with keen interest, as the critically-panned debacle of sheer slapstick silliness successfully struck terror into the hearts of a large section of non-marijuana smoking people in the west. The dichotomy of his own understanding and perception only increased the profound sense of gratitude Simon felt for the directional change his life was going in. It had helped him escape from earlier attachments to the advantage of his upbringing, and destroyed the arrogance that, he realised with shock, had served to cloud years of his judgement. Thus, positive energy led to forward momentum; the mental readjustment silenced doubts, which in turn brought peace, and hope.

In the basement shelter of the Savoy, sat drinking whiskey with a ragtag mob of cheery cockneys, singing songs in the dingy cell of their enforced troglodytism – *hope* in humanity is exactly what the writer felt.

"Pretty bubbles in the air," he burst out loudly into the general buzz of conversation, having refrained from prior participation. "They fly *so high*, they reach *the sky*..." and then warping the clear elocution of his cultured tone into a self-parodying East End London accent, "and like those *krauts* they'll fade, and *die*, the *Führer's* always 'iding... RAF looked everywhere... *We're Forever Blowin' Bubbles*, pretty bubbles, in the air!"

With delight, the laughing group took up the chorus from their basement mate, who mused that perhaps without the transcendental perspective changes that cannabis had brought him, he would not have experienced the connection of that moment with people that in all likelihood, he would not have deigned to converse with.

German bombs strafed the bricks and concrete of England's primary proud, sprawling settlement, with terrible fire and light and noise burning demonically in the London night. Safe in the Savoy shelter, cocooned from the world's malice, it was with a warm glow that the writer took his rest that night, moved as he was by goodwill and his sense of amity, shared in solidarity by circumstance with a group of people whom he had never met, and quite possibly, would never lay eyes on again.

The next day, upon leaving the Savoy and heading east, his naked eyes witnessed true carnage for the first time. Hope seemed obscene, and was dashed in his heart as the spiteful carnage that others had inflicted on the world as they lay insulated beneath the ground revealed itself to him with as bleak a visage as was imaginable.

It was that nightmare image of Guernica; the new face of war and indiscriminate suffering. England jolted out of its peace by the screaming 'Jericho siren' of bombs. Human warfare no longer required the personal application of violence; passionless murder meted out from afar, from the skies, undiscerning in its application of thoughtless evil. Whole streets turned to rubble; houses demolished, corpses stricken and inanimate with the pulsing life force extinguished... a shell of human habitat, and a shadow of life.

Dusty, grime-covered cockneys stared at Simon through hollow eyes, and at the hordes of curious West Enders who'd travelled to see Göring's destruction of the capital.

Is this is what things have come to? Is this western civilisation?

"You seen this?" A Jewish East Ender shouted at him, covered in brick dust. Simon had been quietly asking the locals to share their feelings with him, as they all silently gazed upon the debris.

Dumbstruck, he nodded. The journalist felt any consolation offered would sound hollow to this man, whose grief was more palpable than those around him, his bloodshot eyes already carrying the haunted look of a survivor. The acrid stench of a chemical smoke and the hot dust of the ruined street hung heavy in the air; poisonous toxicity merged with destructive inferno, blackened and burned. Simon could taste its noxious bitterness in his dry mouth. The visual consequences equalled the olfactory assault; a settlement razed, yet ruined scientifically, with chemical malice. It assaulted every sense possessed by the body and mind with more awful power than he could have ever imagined.

The angry Jewish cockney lumbered over, his eyes red and wild.

"Well, you tell the world this," the middle aged East Ender had snarled at him, his shaking finger pointed at Simon's face. "That Mr 'itler can drop as many bombs as 'e bleedin' well *likes*, the people of Britain won't submit to a bunch of German *ponces*. Tell that fat bastard Göring what a *Jew* in London says to 'im. German *cunt*. Even if you come here yourselves, we aint done *by a long chalk*."

Simon heard similar defiance from others that day. It had been heart-warming.

But the awful power of bombing raids was seared into his memory.

"My friend George fought in Spain," he would later tell his mother, "… and he wrote in a *Time & Tide* piece; "the horror we feel of these things has led to this conclusion: if someone drops a bomb on your mother, go and drop two bombs on *his* mother. The only apparent alternatives are to smash dwelling houses to powder, blow out human entrails and burn holes in children with lumps of thermite, or to be enslaved by people who are more ready to do these things than you are yourself; as yet no-one has suggested a practicable way out…" and now I know what he meant." Shaking his head helplessly, the journalist struggled to add anything further, and as his mother tried to embrace him, the agitated writer turned and quickly left the room.

Remembering the awful day, Simon quickly recorded a cliffnotes version of the tale, and continued with his narrative.

Hitler correctly predicted though, by dropping the civilian raids and not causing further damage, the anger simmering elsewhere under the occupation was manageable. They focused on knocking Fighter Command out; it worked. Goebbels dropped his hysterics for once, to magnanimously conclude that the diplomatic moves towards peace following Germany's incredible triumphs in all fields, and the refusal to follow orders of 'the criminal government' to sink the French fleet and use mustard gas on the landing German troops, showed England's 'civilised Aryan spirit.'

Göring, on the other hand, bragged nastily that even if the British army had been able to withdraw back to England, and the focus not shifted to the aerial dogfights, his Luftwaffe could have bombed Britain's capital flat.

Recording that statement, Simon fervently hoped that he would live to see Göring fall. Even if Hitler lived to a ripe old age, dying as President-Chancellor, the writer had a sudden hunger to see Fat Hermann torn down from his pedestal and put face first into the dust. *Perhaps an opportunity will present itself to Heydrich*, he mused.

Clearing his head of anger, the scribe resumed his journal:

The people were divided. With the north of England still, so the rumours had it, embroiled in savage guerrilla fighting and the random chaos of sabotage, the southern section of Britain and London itself in German control was comparatively closeted from the madness of occupation which had prior been a purely continental concern. Rationing on certain foods had been upheld and enforced, but fruit had been scarce from the onset of the war anyway, and with the Reich's carrot and stick policies, much of the male populace had sunk into a sort of resigned slump. Those veterans of the Great War and the filth of Flanders Field and the Somme, the men of Passchendaele and Ypres, could not comprehend the apparent quiet with which the rest of the men left in the cities apparently accepted their fate. These can always be spotted, still; the ones who thus far have avoided the surprisingly well-informed forced recruitment policies of the Germans to send able-bodied workers to the factories and Organisation Todt – well-recompensed, they assured the public –they're conspicuous at a glance. To a man they carry the unmistakeable, haunted look of inconsolable misery and heavy-hearted widespread dejection felt since the first Germans in feldgrau *landed on British soil.*

Simon stopped. That was enough for today. He knew that the spirit remained, even *here*, deep in occupied territory; peace pacts and nominal sovereignty be damned. Even those not actively resisting, out with the rebels and hiding in shelters, made do with mocking remarks about 'Jerry' – actual pleasure of the foreign victory was rare; even a conflicted Oswald Moseley's fascist interests had supposedly waned. British pride still lived. But with forced factory conscription, prisoners-of-war overseas and the awful uncertainty of the future, the jokes rang hollow; less the bleak cynicism of Britain, and closer in essence to the *gallows humour* of the condemned. No matter how reassuring the radio broadcasts were, fear remained. Even those with sons, husbands and brothers in factories, captivity or shallow graves soon came to be shaken from their apathy with a real and pronounced trepidation of what might happen to them too, and to Britain entire.

About to finish, the word 'apathy' triggered him, and he penned a conclusion in the hope that he could properly capture the zeitgeist of the moment, wryly noting even as he did so the German origin of '*der geist seiner zeit.*' The pen scribbled assuredly; words flowing with rediscovered confidence.

All men, women and children can fall prey to war's capricious, indiscriminate evil. The inimitable George Orwell – dear Eric, of course – penned a marvellous account of the war in Spain (non-fictional, unlike the American Hemingway), a tragic prelude to Europe's wider suffering, and victory for the fascist forces of Franco. Sadly, I believe that to date, it has sold only several hundred copies, overshadowed as the Spanish conflict was by the growing menace of Franco's foreign allies. But had this country bothered to pay attention to that epic clash, and read this book, the warning at its conclusion might have resonated; "... all sleeping the deep, deep sleep of England, from which I sometimes fear that we shall never wake till we are jerked out of it by the roar of bombs..."

London, much like Leeds, Bristol, Birmingham, Wolverhampton, Liverpool, Manchester, and just about every other city and town within four hours' drive of the capital have certainly been jerked out of that slumber; explosions, gunfire, artillery; the ominous stuttering of distant guns drawing closer, all the nasty apparatus of war and destruction, and the panicked anguish of the dying as war's hell finally reached them and shattered their gentle peace.

Fearful, darting eyes could be seen blinking behind curtained windows; despite the weather, there was a repressed tension in the air that was brutally palpable, almost electric. Everyone knew – soldiers and civilians alike – that someone, anyone, could strike sparks anywhere. In Leeds, Wehrmacht soldiers who were billeted in the centre and at Armley Palace to the west patrolled cautiously through the central districts that still bore the marks of what had first been defence, and then frenzied, desperate rebellion. It had collapsed in impotent fury and defiance, much like the rival ideologies and social paradigms that had proven weak in the face of the insurmountable jackbooted beast that was international fascism; Mussolini's lovechild had grown to an irrepressible, unruly and violent shyster; far outstripping the limits of power, murder and empire than even he could have foreseen in his halcyon days of the *March on Rome.*

Could Mussolini have possibly *dreamed* that his movement would snowball into a continental revolution; aided and abetted by the world's oldest, largest and most powerful religious institution? Ten years later; Hitler's Germany and Franco's Spain rising up at his heels, the re-emergent German titan; teeth bared at the world that opposed them.

Everywhere Victorious. Gods on Earth.

Bloodstains remained as grim scars on the pavestones of wide Leeds streets; the city centre tram shuttled its silent passengers east down the dual-carriage York Road throughway, all eyes averted from the quiet scenes of recent hellish, thunderous shouts, booming explosions and screams. The meeker members of the northern populace began to feel – even hope, to themselves – that their husbands, sons, brothers, neighbours of whomever the men in the movement may be would perhaps, in retreating, have ensured that present and future violence be kept away from the city. Some were glad, though none dared voice that selfish, survivalist hope. A *Trojan* hope, ultimately; the forlorn pipedream of a spectator that a victorious Hector's duel on some distant plain would keep the bloodshed away from Ilium's sacred walls, and the families sheltered within.

Public sacrifice had been made; a notable scapegoat horribly executed in warning.

The Lord Mayor had voiced public support for the continued armed struggle and defiance of London's armistice that had been widespread across the north, following the capital's June designation as an 'open city'. After encountering fierce resistance along the Liverpool-Manchester-Leeds-Hull northern belt line, the Wehrmacht chose to exemplify the futility of opposing German arms. Leeds' Lord Mayor Wythie's fate was sealed. Under the express orders of Commander von Brauchitsch himself, the Wehrmacht had publicly hung the Lord Mayor with piano wire from the Leeds Town Hall, watched by silent, saddened crowds.

Almost comically inadequate, the most perfunctory of public announcements had informed the city's inhabitants of the impending death of Willie Wythie, and the next day, hundreds of mostly soundless observers saw the spectacle of the old man jerking pitifully as he choked to death. Most claimed that a sense of decency and decorum prevented them from witnessing such a horrid event, while those few that did pointed out dryly that Hitler aside, the death penalty was still occasionally applied in Britain by the British themselves. Most, though, suffering losses of their own and in the immediate aftermath of recent conflict, declined to comment. Distress was widespread; at least one third of all families had lost one or more relatives, and many more still had sons, brothers, husbands and fathers with serious injuries, or who had been captured in battle, or conscripted to forced labour. Others fled for the hills, a disorganised rabble of resisters; well-armed, as each surprised rumour-monger had it, but *up against it* in every conceivable sense.

Lord Mayor Wythie, now thankfully still, was left hanging from the Town Hall turrets for the first month of occupation in its entirety, serving as a macabre reminder of the days of fighting, and a nasty warning against future dissent.

After initial hostility and a widespread attitude of what Wehrmacht chiefs deemed to be disrespectful, the watchful Germans were presented with another opportunity to instil fear through a single act of calculated callousness. Wythie's target of the support that proved fatal was a known left-wing activist, who had been instrumental in drumming up support for the 'people's defence of Great Britain' against its invaders, organising some structure to those in Yorkshire with arms, who were willing and capable. His name was Andrew Knaggs.

Quite by chance, the firebrand was snared during a clandestine meeting with members of a major trade union, whom he'd been passionately petitioning to rally round to the cause; an attempt to attract more men to the growing resistance. German troops were highly trained; the ambush had been performed clinically, with all potential belligerents eliminated with ease, save the target. The small, wiry figure, bearded and youthful, had tried to commit suicide upon capture, realising that escape was impossible, but was failed by the cyanide capsule he had bitten to no avail, its expired poison utterly useless. He was made an example of.

Spouting nothing but obscene curses and profane condemnations of the Germans, Knaggs refused to be cowed in the face of his tormentors as the Wehrmacht staged the most cursory of trials, quickly sentencing Knaggs to join Wythie on the gallows. It was with some regret that the soldiers assigned to the task sent the brave man to an excruciating, choking end, impressed as they were by his courage and the mesmerising vitality of his snarling defiance. However, every German who witnessed his fury was glad that such an enemy, one of revolutionary charisma and élan, had been eliminated from the fight.

"Andrew Knaggs, for crimes against the German Reich and serious contraventions of the Geneva Convention's stipulated legal code of waging war; you are sentenced to death. Do you have anything to say?"

"Yes," he sneered quietly, before raising his voice to the massing crowds at City Square. "Germany is a nation of fools! Fight, England, *fight*, and *fight*, and never quit, so that one day our children can live in peace–"

The executioner abruptly interrupted his exhortations, and the partisan leader slowly choked to death on the wire, blood bursting from his eyes and orifi.

To diminish the rebel's continued legacy, Andrew Knaggs' body was immediately taken down, and transported out of Leeds for discreet disposal. It was strongly rumoured the Gestapo tradition was to incinerate bodies and scatter the ashes in sewage. If this fate befell the rebel Knaggs, it is not known. The body of Leeds' unfortunate Lord Mayor, by contrast, continued to dangle from the city's symbolic administrative building, dangling eerily on the wire that killed him. Even in the weeks following his eventual removal, no children were to be seen for at least one mile in all directions from the great Hall.

To the north of that city centre past the park, St Mary's school stood as a grand red-brick testament to Victorian England, its ornate architecture rising past high window arches to gothic spires and ridges in a formidable mound, like some kind of grim municipal building of a bygone medieval power-centre or 19th century French lunatic asylum. To the more imaginative eye, one could envision some kind of sinister ritualistic neo-pagan festival taking place in its cavernous depths, or row after row of padded cells in a labyrinthine hell; the insane screaming and babbling their disjointed outpourings in a giant, man-made testament to the darker realities of human life, shut away to spare the sane from the discomfort of acknowledging them. In contrast, the parish church nestled into a space three times smaller on the other side of the leafy lane looked a poorer representation of God's omnipresence. Older members of the parish maintained a haughty silence on the matter, while the younger, less religiously inclined joked that only in 'God's Own Country', as Yorkshire was known, could such a thing be allowed.

In reality, the great building was host to a school of great warmth, and the invariably tentative, fearful first steps taken by five year old boys and girls into its high-ceilinged interior were for nought. Teachers here were young; so many of a lost generation had bled out their fledgling lives on the fields of Flanders, Ypres and Passchendaele that the following batch of teens nationwide were thrust into the adult world at a tender, school-leaving age. For St. Mary's, youth had brought vigour, enthusiasm and fun. The corridors along the south side of the building were unfettered by additional storeys above them, and as such both they and the Cathedral-like Great Hall curved high overhead, supported by cast-iron arches and great beams.

"Back at the old castle," the receptionist smiled from behind the glass of her partition. "Good to see you, Miss Rosenberg."

"Good to be back," Naomi replied fervently.

It really *was*. But already, there was a change, something almost imperceptible. Oversensitised by the implications of German victory, the young teacher was sure she detected something in the way Agnes had said her surname. *Rosenberg.* Perhaps she had merely imagined it.

"So…" Naomi continued, slightly nonplussed by her own suspicion. "Same as before, from the little I've heard? We continue as though nothing ever happened…"

"So no more tackling fires?" Agnes asked brightly, neither confirming nor denying the implied request, as though unaware that it was a probe for information.

"No," Naomi answered with regret, abandoning her planned enquiries. "Back to usual."

Usual. As though there could ever be such a thing again. Perhaps there never was, she mused, just a series of drastic changes that generations grow accustomed to and which get taken for granted by their young. *Perhaps in fifty years England will be full of dedicated Nazis*, she thought, and shuddered. It was hard to picture it, but she knew that after years of occupation, what seemed so quaintly 'normal' to her now would appear to be impossible fantasy. Perhaps even *misguided*.

"Well," Agnes chirped, "I suppose it's best."

"Best?" Naomi replied, a little loudly. "Agnes, who really knows what's *best* anymore? All we can hope for is peace, for which we have to sacrifice our pride, or otherwise it will be repression, and then more of us sacrifice our lives."

Peering through squinted eyes, Agnes gazed at Naomi curiously, her amused poise briefly broken, and the young teacher instantly regretted losing her own composure.

Just stay normal, and neutral.

"Anyway," she resumed, more cheerily, "I guess you're right. All we can do is carry on. It's great to be back at the school."

She smiled as sweetly as she could, baring her teeth for maximal effect, and then extricated herself from the unnerving chat, strolling out and into the great corridor. Agnes' eyes followed her until she disappeared from sight, before turning and sharing a *well-what-have-you-now* look with her fellow receptionist, whose nose was so high in the air that her mouth resembled the *Arc du Triomphe* entryway in miniature. The shared look was full of an unspoken meaning.

Naomi Rosenberg had once been a pupil at the school herself. The tall, slender long-legged young teacher turned the heads of older pupils as she strolled confidently through the corridors; emitting bonhomie, smiles and warm greetings were her currency, which she spent freely. That same long-legged lady had once been a slightly gangly, early-developed little girl with neither physical beauty nor mental focus, blundering through academic and social life alike with a graceless charm, showing little sign of the adult she would ultimately blossom into.

The school had closed upon the start of the war, remaining as such throughout 'sitzkrieg', and despite not being particularly patriotic in the standard sense – to King, Empire and flag – Naomi possessed a great love for the democratic ideals instilled in, and espoused by, the people of Great Britain; not to mention a profound dislike of the dictatorial fascist craze which had swept through the continent like a particularly unpleasant domino effect, with its totalitarianism and anti-Semitic persecution.

Furthermore, she loved Leeds. The city was perfect to Naomi; its place at the heart of the industrial revolution of the prior centuries in northern England was a transformation of grand development that nevertheless left room for large inner city parks, tree-lined roads and leafy suburbs aplenty. She loved the Leodensians, or 'loiners', the people of Leeds who, while being part of a modern city, often shared the particular Yorkshire idiosyncrasies of laconic humour, as fearlessly honest as they were broad in tone and dialect, and a prevailing dry understatement that she found endearing.

Spending time in nearby Roundhay Park by the lake, the public squares near her home, the city centre and its smaller park to the north, or even her own mostly terraced inner-city urban estate with a book, or in the company of friends, were the simple pleasures that city life in Leeds allowed Naomi to enjoy. She'd long since inwardly acknowledged her thankfulness that of all the places in the world her grandparents could have settled in the diaspora, they chose Leeds, Yorkshire, in the north of England.

Furthermore, Naomi possessed a fiercely independent streak, and on telling her father that she intended to join the Women's Auxiliary Air Force – and being firmly rebuffed, on the grounds that *his* daughter 'would *not* put *herself* in danger for another stupid war' – Naomi rebelled. With the quiet pretence of acquiescence, the energised lass signed up for the Auxiliary Fire Service the very next day, slightly nervous, and then thrilled when acceptance came. Her response to the predictable outburst of anger from her father was to move out, and she found a nearby flat of her own. In the context of the time, it had seemed like nothing of import given the dramatic magnitude of the island's predicament as a whole.

Sat on the roof, trying to seek out a blaze; underlying the collective fear and misery, Naomi was unashamedly thrilled with her role.

Months of fire service; the sense of duty and belonging intoxicated her. Then, initially with a savage anti-climax, the Germans came to British shores. Calamity ensued; before long, violent conflict scarred the streets of Leeds and the feeling of anti-climax soon dissipated in the awful midst of war. Thankfully, guerrilla action in the urban settlement was as quick as it was bloody. Calm descended. The smoke began to clear.

After a while, St. Mary's reopened, now incorporating the 11-16 class along with the smaller children. And Naomi, ruefully, returned to her vocation. The new, older pupils stared with the transparency of youth, their instincts for tact not yet honed. Some mumbled embarrassed replies at their own feet, as she beamed in greeting.

Only when she'd turned a corner did she lean against the wall, burying her face in her hands. After what felt like hours but was likely a legitimate twelve seconds, she heard a familiar little cough, which was usually attached to the shadow of a smile and slightly raised eyebrows, an affected air of near-permanent amusement. It was a friend. Naomi looked up with dry, if tired eyes into the boyish face of Paul Heggerty.

"Paul!"

"Hey," he replied, so quietly she sensed rather than heard him.

"Can we talk?"

"Not here," he said quickly.

She followed him through the great doors to the stairwell, where they ascended one floor to the library, footsteps echoing on the polished, gleaming wood. When they got there, Paul opened the door but seemed to think better of it, in case old Betty the librarian was lurking in some quiet corner amidst the dusty tomes. They stayed in the corridor outside. Naomi leaned against the wall tiredly, worry lines bitten into her pale skin.

They didn't exchange a word, and he embraced her. They clung tightly to each other, and he felt a shift in her body's tension as she relaxed into him. The two friends had touched before – a nudge here, a playful poke in the ribs there, a cheeky pinch or, as at Christmas the year prior, a prim peck on his soft cheek, while flushed with wine – but never like this. Despite being her junior by two years, he held her as a father would; fingers running through her hair, surreptitiously stretching on his tiptoes as the tall Naomi laid her head heavily into his shoulder. He quietly breathed in her scent, nostrils grazing her curly, jet black locks. For all his jokes and jibes at her expense, which were repaid fully in kind, underneath the good-natured teasing Paul was slightly in awe of his friend's staggering physical gravitas – a combination of beauty and a perceptible goodness of spirit – and even more so of her total ignorance of it. She seemed entirely unaware of her own physical splendour. This embrace, however, was one of concern.

Eventually he broke it, suppressing his self-congratulation in doing so. He often second-guessed his actions even as he performed them, and at the worldly age of 23 Paul Heggerty was trying to simultaneously eliminate as much of the self-regard and the introspective recrimination as possible.

Naomi's head remained bowed after he released her.

"How are you?" He started tentatively.

One wide-eyed look in return was enough to tell him all he needed to know. But she too was surprised; gone was her jovial, sharp-witted, cocksure, mocking friend and in his place stood an uncertain and worried man.

"I know this must be hard for you," he tried again. She forced herself to perk up. It was good just to hear that broad Leeds accent, which somehow didn't suit his baby-faced appearance and cheeky, jesting nature.

"It's hard for everyone, Paul. We're all in the same boat."

He contradicted her, partly out of habit.

"Perhaps, but your boat is a little less safe than the one I'm floating along in. For a start, there's a big Star of David-sized hole in it, and a bloodthirsty shark with a moustache swimming underneath."

She glared at him. Even now, he could still bring himself to wind her up. She did concede, though, that the familiarity of his jesting tone helped normalise the situation.

"I can swim."

"I know that," Paul replied, more evenly. "There are a lot of people in the same situation who can swim. Sometimes it's best to be on dry land, with the ground under your feet."

"Well, we're all under the same thumb, anyway."

"It's a nasty thumb to be under."

"Don't worry."

"I *do* worry," he told her, voice noticeably softening, and he seemed so obviously sincere that she couldn't help but smile, even snigger a little bit. But not a trace of amusement showed in his green, hazel-flecked eyes, or the slightly open pout of his thick-lipped mouth. He held her eyes, briefly, and then looked away without smiling. A small tilt of her head drew no reaction, and she whistled.

"Good heavens, you really do care don't you?"

"Yes."

The grin faded, and as he calmly turned she held his eyes, compelling him to elaborate. He sighed, without melodrama, with only the small involuntary movements of his hands accompanying the entreaty he made.

"I'm worried for you, Naomi. I *am* worried. I've seen Berlin under this lot. Visited for t' Games in '36, and it were' bloody ugly I tell you. If the Nuremberg Laws were owt to go by, you'll be out' a job at the very least, perhaps an 'ome too, and if t' rumours are true about German-Jewish relations in Poland as we speak then employment's the *last* thing you should worry-"

"Paul! I get it! I understand!"

She'd tried to interject breezily, just to cut short such disturbing ruminations, but stress forced its delivery out in a sharper tone than she'd intended. She sounded scared, and knew it. *With reason*, she conceded.

Silence was compressed in the great hall, made more intense by the immensity of its surrounding space. When Paul answered, after twenty undemonstrative seconds, he spoke soothingly. "I know. I just want you to be very careful, me lass. *Very* careful. Head up, ears pricked. Even with the racist rags taken off the newspaper stands and the whole thing toned down, we still saw some very ugly scenes in Berlin. Over here they might not get to every man, woman and child for whatever mad scheme they've got going, but teachers, doctors and lawyers–"

"I know–"

"–which is why you should consider dropping out quietly, and perhaps even going underground," he finished without missing a beat, his voice louder. "Cos eventually your lot over there 'ad to register. They'll be watching certain professions 'ere. And teaching kids? The next generation, the future?" Paul shook his head bitterly, partly in sadness, but tinged by scorn and contempt. "You know what's going on."

And she did. While the south remained under an uncertain occupation, by all accounts, the bile and fury of Germany's enmity of England raged *here*, and against the Scottish rebels to the north. Leeds, and Manchester and Liverpool to the west had been securely occupied by now, after bitterness and revolts. Then word had gotten out; SS-Gestapo were quietly operating behind the Wehrmacht's back, acting in secrecy, their quiet suppressions obscured by the fogs of war.

Even as life continued as before, ugly reprisals had been taking root.

"We don't know for sure that the Gestapo raids are happening," she said quietly.

Paul shook his head sadly, but firmly. "SS raids. Whatever their label, they're not even bothering with the plain clothes schtick, I'm afraid."

Naomi smiled wanly. "I doubt they'll care about a twenty-four year old Jewish girl up north who teaches kids English."

Paul hesitated, briefly. "Education, medicine and law were the first professions to be hit in Germany after the Nuremberg Laws. Naomi, please don't underestimate the news that SS raids are transpiring on British soil. These are *death raids*," he hissed, instantly regretting his lack of tact as her bloodless face fell.

Those great enemies of the National Socialists, whose implacable enmity was eternal and assured, were attacked openly and with righteous indignation. It was in the style of a crusade; liberation by violence, the bacteria of society removed from the organism to save it – that being, the ideal human society as held dear by the Nazis. The freemasons' lodges had been smashed, as had various other institutions deemed conspiratorial and working for the destruction of western civilisation. Synchronising the concentration of public demonstrations of a worldview that was *everywhere victorious,* the British Union of Fascist Blackshirts burst triumphantly back out into the open, and in greater numbers than ever. Preening with naked arrogance, those who did not renounce the foreign occupation as an affront to their British identity were happy to assist German and Italian efforts to enshrine fascist ideology on newly claimed soil. Outside the pre-existing British fascist party, local chapters of the Anglo-German Friendship Bund were springing up, although here and there, it was commonly known, solitary arrests were being made in the dead of night. Some, it was said, were for reasons that seemed entirely preposterous and impossible to reconcile with the victimised people in question.

One rumour persisted, strongest of all; some kind of book existed that identified *Enemies Of National Socialism.* 'The Black Book', people whispered; peculiarly, Naomi thought, as though its colour mattered or made it more sinister. Death lists could be scribbled on newspaper scraps from *The Yorkshire Post*. It was the actions that were fearful.

Fear of books and lists. It seemed ludicrous. People with guns, without empathy and given immunity from illegality were the death plague.

Naomi smiled, her poise recovered. "Doubt my name's in their book, Paul."

"Well that's one thing I'm not gonna joke about."

"You don't like book jokes?"

At that, he winced.

"Come on Paul," she winked, tone breezy. "Books? Is *that* what we're worried about?"

He stared resolutely at her, determination bleeding green in his eyes and Naomi looked away, discomfited by the vehemence of his concern.

No one was quite sure, but most of the arrests reported were being attributed to this 'black book'. Men of fighting age were by and large either with the resistance, were working quietly in their 'necessary' jobs ('collaborators', it was said, with not inconsiderable guilt, that the resisting men and women were calling these mostly city-based workers who continued to maintain and produce under the Germans) or had been conscripted en masse with tens of thousands of others to the continent. Meanwhile, there was some tittle tattle regarding the book – it was now widely claimed that some of the names on it were dead, or had emigrated years prior. The running joke was that Sigmund Freud was to be arrested posthumously, and that California resident Aldous Huxley was sentenced to death in absentia - *A Brave New World*, indeed.

But for all the gallows humour, the SS Security Police and SD were no joke. *SiPo und SD*, as they were called, comprised of the Gestapo secret police, the German criminal police, and the SS-secret intelligence service – each branch under Reinhard Heydrich's tender care, and apparently entrusted to some sinister

Colonel named Six in England; another doctor, one of the intellectual gangsters Heydrich had staffed his SD with.

"You know full well they run the camps in Germany," Paul pointed out.

"Yeah," she replied nonchalantly, trying to deflect his blunt observation.

"And they've taken over army and RAF barracks here…" he pressed on, hesitant to drum the point home. She sighed.

"Yes. I have thought about it."

The SS, so rumour had it, arrived soon after the Wehrmacht's inexorable advance and apparently acquisitioned the main Yorkshire army barracks at Catterick Camp, which could hold 40,000 people. The visions of barbed wire camps filled with emaciated internees in typhus-filled long-huts were at the forefront of everyone's mind.

"*Laying low*, let's call it… is better than potentially ending up in there. *Potentially.*"

She contemplated it quietly. Paul did not move a muscle.

"Underground… like a rat?" she said flatly. "Like the vermin they say we are?"

Paul's reply was firm. "No. Like a wonderful, flawed human being the same as me or anyone else, but one who's in danger and needs to be safe."

The words felt awkward and clumsy on his lips, but he neither blushed nor stammered. She changed the subject; not out of embarrassment, flustered though she was – and had been for weeks – but to explain herself.

"I can't, Paul. Besides, losing my employment might not even come as a result of ethnicity."

He looked at her blankly, and she sighed.

"Have you ever noticed I'm a woman?"

"Yes, but I don't think your parents would approve of me," he quipped.

She mused inwardly that in times of stress, he seemed to revert to little wisecracks as a safety mechanism. In all fairness, it was an admirable attitude.

"With good reason. Anyway, I am. A *woman*. And Nazis don't like women, not outside in the world doing man things… like working. They don't want us doing anything ending in 'ing' – I'm sure they'd ban us from eating and fornicating if it weren't for childbirth."

"You can…" he began, but the joke died on his lips. As radically liberated as her humour and tastes were for a modern woman, even post-Pankhurst, the implications of her ethnicity were too serious to act the fool, as ludicrous as the Nazi definition of a 'Jew' was. Paul realised how naïve he would appear should he continue to make flippant jests, and he stifled his instincts. Taking advantage of his uncertainty, Naomi pressed home her point.

"Paul, you should know my job's at risk anyway. Forget race. The woman's place is at home, producing good Aryan children. Not so Aryan in my case, obviously…"

"That doesn't matter. Fu… bugger the job – you'll always teach. You're born for it. But –"

She interjected, resuming her point: "–Have you seen what they want us to teach?"

He looked discomfited, but nodded.

"They want the Protocols taught as *fact* to the children of this country. They've been debunked by more journalists as a fraud than the Dreadnought Hoax, let alone scholars. Have you read them?"

He nodded again, a little hesitantly.

"Skim read, yeah."

She laughed bleakly. "Illuminating, aren't they?"

"Bollocks, is what they are."

That was met by a small, sad shake of the head. "Who will say that in two years? Or five? Or ten?"

"Or never."

Naomi's head continued to gently shake. "If only that were true, Paul."

The Protocols of the Elders of Zion detailed a plot of hegemony from Jewish financiers and shadowy power-players to seize global economic domination, supposedly leaked from a secret Zionist organisation at the turn of the century, and serving up such juicy apéritifs as the plans to poison the populace with pornography, destroy their religions and control the world's press to perpetuate these aims. The texts 'proved' that the total global enslavement of gentiles was the aim of the mysterious, as-yet unnamed Jewish elders. Henry Ford published them far and wide across America, to undermine national opposition to the Nazi cause. In Germany, Hitler and Göring had decreed that the Protocols were a mandatory staple of school education since 1933. Julius Streicher's *Der Stürmer* adopted a different approach – referencing the sacrifice of children in 'ritual murder', and calling on other historical allegations made against the Jews – but Goebbels and the party 'intellectuals' more often than not took the Protocols and world hegemony theories as their licence to persecute; their warrant to wage war on the *evil agentur* forces of world Jewry and its scattered wanderers of the diaspora.

Naomi had referenced them impersonally, but now couldn't restrain herself. Suddenly, the pent up aggression that was her natural response to the slanderous provocation of these documents came rushing out.

"They want *me* to teach our kids that my own blood is poisoning them and their lives."

"I know, I know."

"'The *Jew* controls *all* media and economy, owns politics and creates all *war, enslaves the Goyim with debt; the Jew poisons Christian civilisation and Aryan blood*' – how can I do this, Paul?"

"You can't. Listen to me…"

He gripped her shoulders, keeping eye contact determinedly until she gave relented, with a short jerk of the head in acceptance.

"You need to *lay low*. We both know that eventually the Gestapo will tire of its arrest lists, or will run out of subversives to deal with. There's only so many J.B Priestleys' and Noel Cowards' out there…" he searched her eyes for acquiescence, and saw a small semblance of acceptance. "And then, if they haven't already, they'll one day come to remove *all the Jews,* and the gays and communists and everyone else that caused Germany to lose the Great War and go bankrupt twice and rejected Hitler from the Viennese art gallery, and all t' rest of it. Aye?"

She nodded, frowning slightly.

"Good," he resumed. "Those Germans we see patrolling the city centre? Nothing. Wait for the Nazi police ruling openly. They'll take away your jobs. And if they've taken your *jobs*, they'll take your *citizenship*. And later, they'll take *you*. And… assuming that all this is an aberration, that some good will eventually come out o' this and the old world's values don't completely perish, there's a future that still needs you."

She was genuinely stunned into silence. Paul had always been good company and a fun friend, but to hear him now was like listening to a different person. But, she was her own woman. She couldn't fold so quickly.

"You're a good man, Paul."

"Naomi–"

"But I've a feeling if you were the Jew you'd think differently."

Usually, the younger man would have interjected with a joke about how the yarmulkes wouldn't suit him, or that he could never abandon pork, but even he knew this certainly wasn't the time or place. He opened and closed his mouth, like a goldfish. A lot of people were doing that, these days. Naomi continued.

"Every time they say the Jew is *vermin*, the Jew is a *rat*, and make things harder for us here the way it is over there, they'll expect us to crawl. They'll expect us to scurry and hide like rats. And if I do, it will become a self-fulfilling prophecy. The kind that Hitler and the fat one and Goebbels love to make."

"But Naomi –"

"I love you."

She stopped in her tracks, alarmed. Where *had* that come from? Perhaps just to shut him up. But, she conceded, she was deeply touched by his concern, by the obvious and open fear for her wellbeing and the advice that only he – no other friends, or colleagues – had been able to actually say. There was something in the others' eyes; a kind of fear, something indiscernible, or wariness. She couldn't tell if some of the other teachers were afraid for her sake, or worried about being denounced for cosying up to the school's own subversive pet parasite. But not Paul.

"That got your tongue," she teased him, her tone deliberately breezy. "Seriously Paul, you're a good man and I know you mean well. But I love my family, teaching, Leeds, you... even the kids! You think I should *react* to their hatred? They want me in a *sewer*. I can't do anything other than continue on as a *human being*."

He just stood, dumbfounded. Naomi realised she'd gone too far with the casual term of affection. Where had *that* come from? Where *had* that come from? The intent had been casual, its delivery less so; regardless, there was no use backpedalling and demeaning them both with a silly explanation. Still, though... there had never been so much of a hint of romance between them, she mused, attractive though he was. In the two years both had been at the school, after determining they were of similar age and both unmarried, they'd somehow adhered to an unspoken rule of never raising such topics beyond an occasional unobtrusive jest. Paul had never intruded on her privacy, insofar as probing for the otherwise negligible details of her life that she kept from him, in a refreshingly transparent and well-intentioned bond. For whatever reason, Naomi – Paul or no Paul – had simply never been highly sexed. She was remarkably undersexed for a humorous, vivacious young woman, particularly one so relentlessly eye-catching.

"I'm scared," she admitted with some reluctance.

He found his voice. "I know."

"I'm scared of what they'll do to my old parents. I'm scared of what they'll do to me…" she paused, ears pricking up at a slight noise in the stairwell, but it was only some far-flung vibration resonating from elsewhere in the great building. She resumed, "I'm scared they'll set up some kind of city ghetto in Leeds like in Poland. I'm scared they'll set camps up like in Germany. Yes, I'm scared."

Paul tried his usual smirk, defying the gravity of the current situation in which the whole country was trapped. Hoping he could cheer her up; knowing, even as he spoke that it was a foolish misstep. "Relax. This is Leeds, the biggest city in Yorkshire and a northern hub. In *York*shire, *Jorvik*. This is Viking land. We're Leodensians, our lot are gonna be fine."

Briefly, the ghost of a smirk flitted across her pouted lips and he hesitated, gauging her state of mind before plunging forwards:

"Anyway lass," he boomed, "… *cheer up*. You'll look more Saxon with some peroxide – even real Aryans in Germany use it. Bit o' *Schwarzkopf*, even if schwarze *is* black – I reckon it's a Jerry joke. Stick a picture of Göring on your desk; you can say you always loved pilots, even fat morphine addicted ones with a God-complex. Goose-step into class. Change your accent to sound less Heeb. Salute every copper. In the meantime let's get you sorted with some false ID and rename you Helga. Throw your skull cap away. No circumcision to betray you – I assume, eh? Use some Barnsley dialect, *tha knows, cocker...* and buy a Bible. Ditch the Talmud. There's tons of tricks, aye? They'll *never* know..."

Paul's babbling finally ground to a halt; his jaw bunched, cursing at his own verbally incontinent drivel as he gyrated slightly on the spot, his hands gesturing as he cheerily spewed a stream of nonsense quips at the poor, frightened girl, his friend who was at risk. Had the war done *this* to him? Made a fool of him, completely incapable of communicating properly with the person he felt most comfortable around, in her hour of need?

To his intense relief she chuckled, though it was noticeably with neither enthusiasm nor humour.

"They'll know when I sacrifice an Aryan child after class. It's been a while since I drank your pure Teutonic blood. What will the Elders say? I'm letting the tribe down."

A deep wave of affection washed over him, recognising the valiance of her flimsy attempt to dignify, and even play up to his weak buffoonery.

Deciding to operate on instinct after the prior foolishness, Paul placed his hands back on her shoulders, resting a steady gaze on her again to confer earnestness, while fighting his body's natural reflex to break away. Her eyes, even scared, were mesmerising. "Jokes aside, lass; I can *protect* you. Even if they stop your pay, I can... I could sustain us until the whole thing settles... we'll work it out. It will be fine..."

It had been his turn to blurt something impulsively. He'd shown his youth before and had wanted to make amends with the serious solution, which he'd ad-libbed on the spot. It was the kind of decision that had been made – or not made –

across Europe for seven years, with life-changing consequences for the people involved. But, while touched, Naomi was set on her path. Her decision had been reached.

"I'm scared, Paul, and I appreciate it. But –"

"–You think if they see the name 'Rosenberg' on a teachers list they won't pay you a call? Think, lass." Paul interjected in vain, attempting to dissuade her, yet even as he resorted to observing the painfully obvious, the young man could already sense her rejection. She was bloody-minded, which he found quite endearing, but in this context it worried him sick.

"Fear or not, lists or not, Paul," Naomi replied gently, "I'm not a rat, and I'm not vermin. I *won't* hide; under a bridge, in a wood, not even in your basement. I'm *English*, this is *my* country. The values we believe in protect the citizens of this country. If we hide, they really *have* won."

Naomi squeezed her friend's hand, briefly, before turning and strolling back down the steps with an affected confidence. There was no more she could say. Paul watched her legs, back, and then finally her head disappear from view, and buried his hot face in his hands, letting it boil against the skin of his palms for a while. For every one of the nineteen seconds it took her to reach the bottom floor and exit into the back foyer, she expected to hear his voice call out to her, or hear footsteps thumping on the floor behind her. There was only silence.

~

Violence lingered in the cold, thin air.

The deathly silence continued through Naomi's lonesome journey home; first down past Hyde Park into the city centre as she breezed through the Headrow, where the cobbled roads rubbed smooth by the countless shoes, hooves and tyres of centuries sloped down to the Corn Exchange and the open markets. Millgarth Police Station, a hulking, ugly dark monstrosity was still operational, but everyone knew it was under German supervision and the few that had to use the city centre regularly gave the dark bricked building a wide berth, as though it was haunted. Naomi was sure that years from now, children would say it was.

The main Leeds market lay directly in its shadow, with a cavernous warehouse room and stalls that spilled out into the open square. The young teacher strolled through, as ever, but there was no fruit available, and no laughter. A lethargy hung in the air, as stall workers completely bereft of their spirit barely put forth an effort to attract the attentions of the few stragglers wandering aimlessly through the rows of quiet counters filled with second hand garments and tins of thick, cloying milk; a sustenance so viscous in its gelatinous dairy form that parents would layer it over bread with a spoon for their children to eat, wincing at its sickly sweetness.

Naomi, seeing the 'bread milk', wistfully remembered her mother, stingy with jam even prior to rationing. "Watch it with that jam," she had always snapped. "Remember there's other people in this 'ouse!"

She walked on, viewing the sparse food available with her rather limited collection of coupons.

Further on, trouble was brewing.

Two German soldiers were harassing a leathery faced little stall owner, who had the misfortune of being burdened with an inescapably large nose stuck in the middle of his rather tired, haggard face, weather-beaten by the potent combination of time, stress and alcohol. It was the kind of Talmudic nose that would escape attention only in the context of a Bar Mitzvah or a synagogue, and even then, Naomi suspected that few others would match him for length, girth and the pointedness of its wickedly hooked curve. Clean-shaven, pockmarked and small, the man had not been blessed with aesthetically pleasing looks, yet one attractive attribute that he did seem possessed of was courage. Despite his gaunt and wearied appearance, and the disadvantage he faced in every aspect of his confrontation, the little market man was determinedly defending himself.

"I don't bloody 'ave 'em wi' me, a'right?" He chuntered crossly.

Utterly impassive, the two Germans shared a look, before returning their hostile stares to the stall man. The larger of the two, whose boulder-sized head sported cropped blond hair and pink skin, began cracking his knuckles menacingly. He looked like a gigantic wild pig, preparing to charge at some hapless creature in its way. A vicious, stupid creature that only moves forwards, and always attacks.

Naomi doubted he could fit through an average doorframe.

"Papers," his smaller comrade purred; the soft, silky demeanour equally threatening.

"I'm tellin' you," the local snapped, "ah've left me papers at home! That's t' long and short of it. All right?"

The larger Wehrmacht patrol man laughed, falsely. "*Ja*, with *that* nose. OK, Moses. Prove it. Papers."

His body language resembled a rabid dog straining at the leash. Visible tremors shook his body as the huge pig fought to stay calm. Incredibly, the bloody-minded little Yorkshireman did not seem to recognise the imminent threat he faced.

"I'm *tellin'* you, they're at 'ome! And you know what, so what if I *were'* bloody Jewish anyway! I'm a market boy, what do you bleedin' care? Fucking *idiots...*"

Naomi winced. He'd gone too far. The German who had demanded his papers flinched visibly, as though the retort had affected him physically, though with predictable spite, he recovered quickly, reacting to the verbal scorn with physical aggression. The market boy had barely lowered his outstretched finger when the soldier ducked low and struck him hard in the stomach with a great fist; the piston-like attack from the big brute doubling the little man over, and he tottered dizzily for a brief moment before sinking to one knee, desperately gasping for air. It was a cruel blow from such a powerful specimen, delivered to a tiny stall boy who was barely five feet tall. Outraged by the ugly spectacle, several of the nearby stall sellers piped up.

"Oi! What are you doing that for, you bloody Boche twat!"

"No call for that *at all*, young man, no call for it."

"What you goin' off on one for, you great big *pillock*?"

"Hey 'ey 'ey, pack it in, will you?"

"*Fuck* off Jerry!"

Faced with open dissent from the disgruntled and irate Yorkshiremen, many of whom had approached to voice their anger, the oversized young German hesitated. His comrade, a shorter, squat man with dark hair, felt his own surprise dissipate quicker; raising his palms outwardly in a peaceful gesture, he offered some token placatory words. Smooth as his performance was, the appeasing words of conciliation seemed at odds with the menacing scowl of his fellow soldier, who glowered around him at the furious faces, looking as though he wanted to brutalise them all for the verbal dissent. His squat comrade let tensions wane, and then warned everybody in earshot that while *they* did not want any trouble, rules *must* be obeyed, and regrettably, that even mild resistance to basic laws could only lead to conflict. Everyone, he said, has to choose correctly, and play by the rules. Breaching that would only lead to self-inflicted trouble.

Having said his piece and diffused the tensions somewhat, skilfully employing a combination of veiled threats and ingratiation, the soldier swiftly moved on, followed by his taller *kameraden*. He, though, left with one last lingering glower at the little stall man, who had been violently sick in the meantime, wriggling in discomfort as he emptied his stomach, and then rolling onto his back, sucking in pained lungfuls of air as he gasped through the pain. Several rushed forwards to check on him. The man was helped to his feet, and taken away to clean himself up in the market toilets. The noise of excitement quickly faded. In less than half a minute, it was as though nothing had happened at all.

They weren't used to being stood up to, Naomi realised, still stood in the market centre reflecting. And obviously to them, Leeds is not Warsaw... or Jerusalem. But blood or not, they are conquerors. How long will they respond with reason and appeasement?

Slightly shaken, the young Jewess bought some fresh bread and two ounces of cheese, her full week's allowance. "Not cricket eh? Jerry bastards. Takin' bloody liberties, they are," the stall seller said to her as she paid for the food, referring to the German soldier's conduct with the little fellow who had the unfortunate nose.

"No," she agreed. "It's out of order. Hopefully that's the worst of it."

But in her heart of hearts, she doubted it. The fear was manageable, but it still remained, beneath the surface, intruding her thoughts in moments of peace.

Boarding the tram, she nibbled tentatively, willing herself not to finish the luxury before even reaching home. The stares of other passengers helped in this; sensing their open hostility, Naomi wondered if it was due to their hunger, rather than some breach of etiquette she had made in ignorance. Food *had* become a sensitive issue; astonishingly for the people at the heart of a global empire. The hated rationing was still in effect. Well-to-do types had aroused anger by continuing to eat at the designated restaurants that were exempt from rationing, and the privilege of immunity was soon withdrawn; ironically, in a move meant to placate the people, the Germans reintroduced the exemption system only weeks later, in an early decree.

Self-conscious under scrutiny due to a prevailing shyness, the young lady quickly stashed the food down by her feet and out of sight, watching the tenements and terraced streets of East Leeds flash by in a blur of grey and green until they reached Harehills. Her parents were not in. Naomi set off on the long walk home towards Chapeltown, where the largest Jewish community in not only Leeds, but Yorkshire entire could be found, ever-flourishing right up until the day lightning runes flew on flagpoles above British police stations. SS de jure spelled more than the end of that, as the liberal spectrum entire was ruthlessly eradicated from British society, but there was nowhere in England that the *Schwarze Korps* were feared and loathed with more bitterness than in the persecuted ranks of the Jewish community.

Enjoying the stroll past red brick terraces and eventually the park; Naomi took her time, feeling the wind whip her hair as it blew with a gentle coolness, and then gushed faster at intervals, wafting strongly as she walked through its trajectory. Inside her flat, she settled down with some bread and half the cheese ration, and began to read her copy of *The Protocols*.

It sickened her.

Twenty-four protocols...

"Three: *Methods of Conquest,*" she murmured to herself in disbelief. "Four: *Materialism Replaces Religion... Despotism and Modern Progress... Takeover technique... World Wide Wars... The Totalitarian State... Control Of All Press... Ruthless Suppression... Attacks on Religion... Brainwashing... Financial Programme... Loans and Credit...* unbel*ievable...*"

Prior to the Nazis, she'd been faintly amused by the concept of the Protocols. With a regime that wholly sponsored nationwide anti-Semitic persecution within its own borders now holding sway in Britain, Naomi felt her blood run cold as she read through the chilling warrant for that said-same persecution; the forged imprint of the global conspiracy of her people. The justification for all violence committed against them as 'self-defence' – the implied protection of a saintly world from the menace of their corrupting perversions.

The end of her world.

~

She suddenly missed her parents.

When Naomi's father, apoplectic with anger, threw a predictably *ad hominem* tantrum at her for joining the Auxiliary Fire Service, Naomi had moved out with as much dignity as she could muster, and found a small flat further north above a shop; still close enough to be part of the family, and ironically enough, closer to the main body of the Jewish community than her parents. Her father quickly made the peace, which she warmly and magnanimously accepted, but she chose not to move back. A young woman in the flush of early adulthood, Naomi was enthused, and with a combination of excitement and fear, succumbed to the national fervour of unity and resistance; doing her part for, if not the *war*, which she disagreed with as she did all wars, then the people at least, and finding a fantastic solidarity with her fellow AFS members. To feel such a bond can be a powerful thing. Naomi shared their pain as the men in their ranks were labelled 'War-dodgers', with such little action domestically for the first nine months of hostilities, and then their grief at the culmination of what amounted to the only bloody but brief action in its entirety, which ended with the complete collapse of the BEF in France.

Despite her induction into the AFS, Naomi had been deeply disappointed to find herself in no position to actually put out a fire. She did, however, surprise a few of her male colleagues with her driving which, by consensus, saw her reach the scenes of the fires just as quickly as would they. Doubling up as a fire watcher whenever a shift ran spare was seen as less glamorous, too, waiting with binoculars on the long, cold nights, but she found it inexplicably thrilling.

Such thrills seemed like a lifetime ago. Now, Naomi found herself wanting her mother.

Pulling herself back into the present, the young teacher finished the last of her cheese and lit a cigarette, finally steeling herself to properly acquaint herself with the hated text. Even in being prepared for its prejudice, opening the text still made Naomi's flesh creep.

Methods of Conquest, Doctrine III: "There remains a small space to cross and the whole long path we have trodden is ready now to close its cycle of the Symbolic Snake, by which we symbolise our people. When this ring closes, all the States of Europe will be locked in its coil as in a powerful vice..."

Naomi spoke the paragraph aloud. She shook her head, wearily, before reading on, underlining the more pertinent, pernicious parts.

In order to incite seekers after power to a misuse of power we have set all forces in opposition one to another, breaking up their liberal tendencies towards independence. To this end we have stirred up every form of enterprise, we have armed all parties, we have set up authority as a target for every ambition. Of States we have made gladiatorial arenas where a lot of confused issues contend ... A little more, and disorders and bankruptcy will be universal... Babblers, inexhaustible, have turned into oratorical contests the sittings of Parliament and Administrative Boards. Bold journalists and unscrupulous pamphleteers daily fall upon executive officials. Abuses of power will put the final touch in preparing all institutions for their overthrow and everything will fly skyward under the blows of the maddened mob... The GOYIM have lost the habit of thinking unless prompted by the suggestions of our specialists...

Naomi blanched at the capitalisation of 'Goyim'. Pausing to hydrate with some water, she composed herself and read on:

... The word "freedom" brings out the communities of men to fight against every kind of force, against every kind of authority even against God and the laws of nature. For this reason we, when we come into our kingdom, shall have to erase this word from the lexicon of life as implying a principle of brute force which turns mobs into bloodthirsty beasts...

Naomi shook her head again, slowly. The dark locks cascaded down over her eyes, and she shook her head a third time, like an impetuous horse, before continuing to underline key parts. She had only thus far read through Protocol III, out of twenty-four.

Glancing through the financial protocols on loans, credit and gold, she was merely bemused. Hatred of the financial elites was easily understood; were Jews not under the thumb of the same economic system of slavery as were gentiles? Did Jews alone hold the keys to the financial palace? Were the majority of the world's Jews privy to the machinations of the richest Israelites, whomever and wherever they may be? Was she responsible for the Court Jews of prior centuries, or the bankers of this one? Were not the right-wing governments and Churches fully cooperative with the financial institutions?

Naomi snorted. These protocols were an irritant. But a dangerous, pernicious irritant.

Protocol VII, though, thoroughly disturbed her, and shook her to the core. Even more so than XI and XI, *Totalitarian State* and *Control of All Press*, the seventh, *Worldwide Wars* was the warrant for persecution.

Most malicious of all; beyond economic and political conspiracy, the seventh Protocol blamed all gentile wars specifically on the machinations of her people.

Throughout all Europe... we must create ferments, discords and hostility. By our intrigues we shall tangle up all the threads which we have stretched into the cabinets of all States by means of the political, by economic treaties, or loan obligations. In order to succeed in this we must use great cunning and penetration during negotiations and agreements, but, as regards what is called the 'official language,' we shall keep to the opposite tactics and assume the mask of honesty and complacency. In this way the peoples and governments of the GOYIM, whom we have taught to look only at the outside whatever we present to their notice, will still continue to accept us as the benefactors and saviours of the human race.

"Life *unworthy of life*," she noted, sombrely.

The Protocols in effect bolstered the current German theories of scientific racism and lent justification –superficial and contrived as it was – to the gradual process of enacting the continental exclusion of her people from the chain of heredity. Acceptance of these texts as truth was tantamount to conspiring to de-humanise a race.

Jews conspired to enslave the world; ergo, Jewish life was *life unworthy of life*.

Naomi remembered an incident from her childhood.

"Get out of here you Jew," the eleven-year-old boy had screamed at her, his mouth contorting nastily with the words as he pushed her away from the children's park.

"What have I done?" the eight-year-old asked, bewildered.

"You're a fucking *Jew*! *Fuck* off or I'll *smack* you!"

She tottered away, thoroughly puzzled, and strolled off towards the distant swings at the other, nearby playground. Before she got there, halfway across the adjoining grass, a fist slammed hard into the back of her head, its thudding impact momentarily blurring her vision while sending her undeveloped, childlike body flying forward into the grass. She blocked the fall on instinct, but the blow itself had depleted her senses, and she lay confused and stricken for several seconds.

Trying to collecting her wits, Naomi prepared to stand back up, silently waiting for the dizziness to subside. Before she could manage it, the boy leaned down to spit in her face. The huge gobbet of mucus ran down her nose and mouth; she spluttered and coughed as some entered her oral cavity, momentarily shocked. Seconds later, her senses returned and tears started flowing freely; hot on her wet face as she cried in painful shame and degradation.

Snarling, her attacker showed no pity.

"Get out of here, Jew scum. This park isn't for you."

The boy was eleven; as Naomi realised later, he didn't know *why* he hated her, or even what a Jew *was*. He just *knew*, with a surefire certainty in his cocksure confidence of his arrogant, eleven-year-old mind, that a *Jew* was *bad*, and she was a *Jew*, ergo she was scum and he *hated* her.

As a young adult, Naomi became a teacher to help inspire children; to aid the creativity and channelled passions of their fertile minds. Now, the kids would read these Protocols; that 11yr old boy would be joined by an army of thousands, countless thousands, even millions. How long until the twisted poison of language could scar purity, and forever pervert the children of Britain into a hateful, vengeful, violent clique of racists?

Jewish life was life unworthy of life.

How could she have ever ignored and belittled this work? So maleficient was its content, to perniciously penetrate the conscious fears of all European nations – and presumably the rest of the world – to transcend cultural differences, and encompass all facets of cultural decay and parasitic operation to insidiously affect the thinking of – and thence bind together – *all* peoples of Britain, America and Europe to the modern form of anti-Semitism and scientific racial loathing. From the medieval beliefs of sacrifice and well-poisoning to this modern resurrection of ancient fears, with its sinister new ambition and devilish upgrade in scale; Naomi realised with trepidation that once more, her people truly *had* been chosen.

Maisie had the cheerful disposition of a girl who'd been blessed with an intelligent sibling, a loving mother and enough combined personality and looks to never be short of friends or popularity. That disposition had been sorely tested just ten minutes prior, with the visit to her shop on Tottenham Court Road from a gang of swaggering Blackshirts; BUF party members, old guard, enjoying their newfound hero status with its legal license to be loutish.

"Here we go," she murmured to herself as the doorbell tinkled.

The fascists strolled in, glancing contemptuously at the modestly dressed young lady tending the shop. The youngest lad amongst them had a swarthy face, what looked like severe vitamin D deficiency and the kind of greasy, hook-nosed gargoyle visage that could have leapt off the pages of *Der Stürmer* to rape an Aryan child. He looked every inch the Jewish Demon that Hitler's government wished to implant in the nightmares of every Aryan child in the Reich. The man's face alone, sat perched on top of a skinny frame with its long torso and contrastingly short limbs, made her wonder exactly what *master race* it was that the Germans spoke of.

"Heil Hitler," the runt in lead sneered at her. She responded by scowling.

Maisie had quickly found that it was these types who were more liable to be the loud, zealous defenders of Reich racial policy; slithering little imbeciles with slack jaws and Slavic features. The tall Wehrmacht soldiers on patrol merely looked wary, or bored; even resentful that after having their hatreds directed against 'world Jewry' for seven years that they instead had to fight, and then stand guard over, fellow Saxons; stuck in the ugly, grey-skied chilly environ of England when they could all be slaughtering Russian Jews in the east, or drinking champagne in the sunlit summer of Paris. As for the BUF muscle – including the three big ones that sauntered into the shop with the young man – they were now Britain's SA.

"Heil Hitler," the second of the two shaven-headed mountain-sized lumps grunted at her, without saluting.

"My name's not Hitler," she replied flatly, with a wan smile.

The strategically-shaved silverback gorilla was about to retort, the loose skin of his huge face bunching up angrily, when his friend who resembled the runt of the litter quickly interjected to complete the self-glorifying tale that he'd been in the process of droning through as they entered the shop.

"... *wha' a lit'wl fackin' kike*. Where he belongs, the *fackin' floor like a snake*. Next time I'll make him lick the road, clean the street with his tongue the *cunt*. He was trembling in his fackin' boots wasn'e? *Eh*, 'e was *fackin'* shiverin'..."

The dark-haired man spoke with an exaggerated cockney; the overeager drawl and self-conscious bite into each pronunciation betrayed him as a *mockney* of the highest order. His act was transparent; posturing with the pathetically eager air of a schoolboy whom had attached himself to the biggest bullies on the playground, just being in proximity to him made Maisie nauseous. His desperation to please, or to flaunt, gave rise to a slight shrillness and rising intonation in his voice, which was universally viewed as an incredibly unappealing trait on the English side of the Atlantic. Like most forms of mockney, it would have been a slow, sneering drawl but for his obviously ingratiating intent; eagerness lending haste to his foul stream of verbal incontinence.

"Good to see the filth show us the proper respect, these days..." he declared, drawling his leer, "not lookin' d'aan their noses at us. You could be anything in the old days, as long as you had a bit of bees an' 'oney... queer, rent boy, Jew, commie... not now, o' course!"

"Not now," one of his goons intoned dumbly.

"Thanks be to God, for Adolf Hitler," the runt smirked with relish, playing with a coin between his fingers. Maisie had only ever seen one person do this before as habit, and the man had been a thief from Bermondsey, openly proud of his sleight of hand.

Surreptitiously ogling the shopgirl, the undersized runt of the fascists drew nearer, until Maisie was awarded a close-up view, to her regret. The man's unappealing visage was only heightened at close range. His pockmarked cheeks were slightly flushed with red, like a child left outside for too long in winter, or a drunk whose blood vessels had mutinied in the face of excessive alcohol consumption and committed mass-hari kiri. Sporting a lined forehead, heavy bags under his watery eyes and a crooked nose, she realised with surprise that the man whom she'd thought was an arrogant, slimy teenage boy must be well into his forties. His oily skin was weather-beaten, flecked with scar tissue and dotted with small, almost imperceptible spots. Maisie mused that she could have played braille with the blackheads on the crooked spire of his bent, off-centre nose. All in all, the man was a gargoyle.

"Hello," she said with the unmistakeable air of sardonic cordiality. It was wasted on the fascist.

"*Awroight*," he drawled, barely glancing at her as she moved around the shop, gazing disinterestedly at the various items the owner had added to what was essentially a tobacconists, in an attempt to make good during rationing. The fascist bit down on the 't' at the end of the word, a letter usually omitted in the quick, natural pronunciation of real East Ender cockneys; as a result, it seemed he was almost self-parodying the mockney-cockney routine.

"All right," she replied scornfully, mocking him.

"'ow's it ga'an then, *lav*?" he asked disingenuously, without looking round.

"It's going."

He chuckled. "Yeah, it's ga'an quite well, all things considered."

"That's an intriguing opinion. Not a valid one, but it's interesting."

A small double-take of surprise, and then the fascist chuckled again. "Well, you and everyone else will come to see sense soon enough, love. Don't you worry your pretty little 'ead about that…"

"Who or whatever 'sense' is, coming from you I can only hope I don't see it."

The swarthy man opened his mouth to retort, and then decided against it, scrutinising the girl with a grin. She realised he had probably been a confrontational mental midget for much of his life, and only now was he realising that he actually wielded some real, tangible power. Seeing him in this light, she shuddered slightly to see his volte-face, hoping he wasn't planning a methodical attack, be it verbal or otherwise.

Maisie cast a disdainful glance at his friends; big, thickly set, close cropped hair, boulders for heads, and all clad in ominous black. They looked like bear wrestlers. The greasy braggart, on the other hand, looked like a Jewish troglodyte. If ever an ugly caricature of Slavic 'untermenschen' came to life from the pornographic pages of *Der Stürmer*, it was this fascist. Maisie couldn't understand the dynamic of the scene playing out before her eyes. How were *they* waiting around for *him*, listening to and tolerating his inane, nasty fluff? And all a member of the exclusive blood family, Mussolini's baby of 1922 that had grown to monstrous proportions. It should have died in Rome, stillborn and unmourned, buried in an unmarked grave.

"I've read about you somewhere," she blurted out suddenly, impulse once more getting the best of her.

The monster nearest her uncrossed the massive arms that were straining at his shirt sleeves, and looked over at the shopgirl with dull eyes. "What?"

"You were..." Her eyes flashed, as though having a brainwave. "Aha! You... were under a bridge, waiting for the Billy Goats Gruff."

If Maisie expected an explosion of rage, at least after the period of silence required for the big man to register the joke, she was left sorely disappointed. The bear wrestler, scratching the cleft under his ear where a bushy sideburn grew, merely grunted incoherently, and then asked her to explain the remark. She shook her head, and he dropped the issue, scowling suspiciously as he lapsed into a brooding silence. The young man, however, took umbrage to her humour, and decided to cow her into the proper deference that he felt was only right and due.

"Well, you're pretty funny aren't you?" He leered at her with yellow, if evenly sized teeth.

That was *something*, Maisie thought. *If there's one thing that's right with him, his yellow teeth are perfectly even. Not jagged, or crooked. The colour of bananas, perhaps, but at least they're even.*

She smiled, maddeningly pleasant.

"I don't know… my brother used to tell me my jokes were rubbish, and he wouldn't make me an honorary boy."

She shrugged, regretfully, flicking a strand of curly fair hair out of her eyes. "He laughed, but said it was because they were so bad. Jokes *so bad* they were funny, y'know? Then we'd play-fight."

"So you're a fighter," he sneered, looking to his pals and awarding her a profile of his misshapen head and teeth. "Shame you weren't in France."

She pretended to consider. "That *did* occur to me… though at the time I must admit I was glad. Too many *fascists* there. The risk of coming across some violent, racist idiot was *far* too great. It's a real shame how things turned out."

Ratlike eyes bulging; the slimy runt could not answer at first, absorbing the impertinent retort with barely concealed anger. Yet the eruption of rage never came; controlling his breathing, the runt simply stared at Maisie for twelve seconds, before his eyes lost their fury and began insolently roving over her body at leisure. This was a more effective insult than verbal barbs, and one that she couldn't simply toss back at him with scorn. Fascists, of varying nationalities, *de facto* ruled Britain. He was a party member. That's how it worked. He was in power. For all her bluff, she was just a shop girl.

Mortified, she sat back behind the counter, so that only her head was visible to the odious fascist. Deliberating, the runt flexed his jaw, and then performed some further theatrics to simulate rumination, in the pretence that he was in the process of considering her situation with some significance, wielding some as-yet unspecified power over Maisie.

"Well…" he finally said, "… you're obviously not a *Jew* at any rate. Which is a shame, cos I'd *lav* to paint a big star on your window, perhaps come in and trash the place every naa'an' again". He glanced at her little pile of books behind the counter. "Perhaps take a piss. Or see if your little book piles are harbouring any *subversive material…* that would be fun." That leer again, the two curled slabs of raw meat that were his lips twisting grotesquely. She wondered if he was born with them. He added, "Best to be sure that things are properly above board, after all."

She nodded slowly, as though in sympathy with his burden as a defender of All Things Fascist.

"Well, future plans aside, if you're not here to buy anything, I'd 'lav' it if you and your friends here…" she stopped herself, before using a profanity. They wouldn't make her lose her dignity. Not this idiot. Not this bullying, sneering little nobody; a child in a man's body, albeit a malnourished, misshapen one. Not this cretin.

"… Would pack it in. And leave. Thanks!"

She smiled sweetly, noting to her satisfaction that his eyebrows rose in surprise at her coolness. Much to her own amazement, the fascist duly turned and walked out, his friends following, rewarding her bravery with one last, lingering sneer.

Her mood though, had dipped as they left, emitting menacing vibrations even in exit. She knew it wouldn't be long before the hundreds, or even thousands of idiots like the young weasel of a fascist who had bothered her would grow accustomed to their roles as legally accepted bullies. That was the nature of brutal regimes and dehumanisation. How many *Sturmabteilung* brownshirts had been good sons and brothers, nephews and friends, in Munich, Nuremberg, Hamburg, Berlin? How many nice boys in Madrid and Barcelona, Rome and Paris – capitals of European culture – had taken to the worldview of scientific racial superiority and right-wing political extremism? And how many in the nightmare Germany had become warped and transmuted into powerful men of ugly actions; how many good sons grew to beat communists with coshes, fire bullets in street skirmishes, throw glass and chairs in beer hall brawls, and force Jews to lick pavements, sweep up the broken glass of their own shops and houses, parade them through the streets with bloody noses and humiliating placards, burn their properties on *Kristallnacht*, support the legal privations inflicted and contribute to the persecutions and misery; all done with the sole intent of unifying one tribe by robbing their fellow man of dignity?

And – unthinkable as it was – how many had turned against their own friends and family?

The idiot would be back, Maisie realised. And he'd return meaner, more cocksure and a more dangerous enemy.

She returned to the counter, choosing a familiar book without so much as a browse through her pile of potentially subversive materials, to while away the remaining hour of a quiet day reading Arthur Conan Doyle's *The Hound of the Baskervilles*. Even though she'd left cigarettes behind in her teen years – an old, furtive rebellion of yesteryear – Maisie was strongly considering opening a packet of Dunhill's or Chesterfields and lighting up a fag, just for a leisurely, calming smoke, to mortify any Nazis or British fascists who might walk in and see her poisoning *the life-giving vessel of Aryan blood...* when a tinkle of the doorbell signalled the glass-panelled door swinging open, and two German soldiers stepped in.

They looked earnest, she thought. Still, don't discount some capricious act of arrogance or cruelty. Not from this lot.

The taller of the two approached, glancing left and right as though to ensure they were alone. This was odd. Germans who wanted behind-the-counter goods didn't pay attention to whoever else was in the shop – not those in uniform, anyway. They paid no heed to queues. In any event, with so many of the British fighting men or those of age absent for various reasons, there was little perceived threat anyway in the more established occupational zones.

"Hallo," he said. His voice was slightly singsong; distinctive, though she did not know what accent it was. No doubt they'd all come to be versed in the intricacies of German nuances soon enough, she thought tartly. She smiled pleasantly in response, with a level of cool sardonicism that an outsider to the British Isles would likely miss.

The young soldier smiled a little wryly, as though he correctly surmised her coolness to him.

"May I have some Chester... *nein*, ah... perhaps, I should like to have some Dunhill cigarettes please?"

The tone was over-exaggerated, a level of careful precision in his elocution that no average Londoner would ever employ. Nor most of the country, come to that.

She turned, eyes sliding to the shelf behind her and she retrieved them for the young soldier. His friend stepped outside to wait for him, a small tinkle announcing his exit. Maisie serenely tossed a packet of Dunhill on the counter, which seemed to amuse him.

"I have never tried British cigarettes before," he said pleasantly.

"It's a filthy habit, it will kill you," she returned coolly.

"I suppose you are right. At least this death would be my choice, however…"

"Choose wisely then."

He laughed at that; neat white teeth in a wide, smiling mouth, the corners of which were slightly upturned in his dimpled cheeks.

He was, she noted with annoyance, a handsome lad. Perhaps three-to-five years younger than she, possibly still a teenager. Blond hair cropped at the sides, the longer strands of his fringe swept across an unwrinkled forehead and strong, angular face with pronounced cheekbones and jaw. His eyes were the pale grey-blue of Hitler himself; one of Nazi Germany's supermen, the new breed of master race.

"Ja, I will try. Perhaps some Lucky Strikes if you have any, or…" his slightly sing-song voice trailed off. They both knew that with shortages of American cigarettes and roughly two thirds of the available pre-war imported goods, that one must consult the black market to satisfy their needs. Even with the post-Churchill usurping government's capitulation, and the black day of Wehrmacht troops marching through London, many of the parasitic scavengers and opportunists had remained in the shadows. Even previously respectful citizens had turned to the black market for income to help support their families.

"Afraid not today, Hermann."

He laughed again, widely, utterly unfazed by her cheek. "'Fritz' would be the German way, fraulein. Like your 'John Smith'. As soldiers, you are Tommy and I am Jerry."

"Well, enjoy your Dunhills, Fritz. Say hello to the other Jerries."

"I shall," he smiled, stifling laughter. "I am billeted nearby here, now. When it's time to make my next choice of death, I shall see you again. Auf wiedersehen, fraulein."

One last smile, which split into a toothy grin as the young soldier tipped his cap, turning away to the door. Maisie didn't utter a goodbye, but instead looked down with an effort of will that was not inconsiderable, and somewhat flustered, the London lass reopened her book. To her chagrin, it took her a minute or two to properly refocus on the prose of Conan Doyle.

I shall. So proper in his English. Such *quaint* language, the berk. It was *laughable*, really... what did he hope to achieve what that ridiculous attempt to be polite? With his sing-song voice, eyes paler than a ghost the colour of Caribbean sea and his stupid dimples...

Maisie slammed her book down, crossly. She grabbed a packet of cigarettes herself and lit one, billowing smoke as her eyes filmed with thought.

Outside, the young soldier inspected the reddish, regal looking packet and its 'Dunhill Superior Cigarettes inscription' with interest, before tearing the seal open in haste and producing a fag each for himself and for his fellow *obersoldat* Johan. Even now, he mused, with wars and invasions and privations, rationing, curfews and whatever else, the international corporations continued to make their profits. Cigarettes and whiskey would always sell. The fat cats' profits would still flow like a river. Goebbels at his most hysterically socialist was right about that much, at least, even if he no longer said it, with his master Hitler and superior Göring embracing investment in the Reich from foreign big business, and relying on oil and iron ore agreements. And with the industrial conglomerate of the *Hermann Göring Werke*, and numerous corporate power plays and mergers, the Reichsmarschall himself was a major player in the business world now in addition to dual roles of almost unsurpassed authority in both the political and military realms.

"British?" Johan queried in their native tongue. There was doubt in his voice.

"Don't be a German snob, you nationalist swine," he chided. Snorting, Johan lit them both. There was little danger in such remarks; the two men knew each other well, and there were large sections of the Wehrmacht that held no love for the Nazis, even those who supported the expansionist policy. Both had shared many conversations regarding the transparency of post-Versailles military glorification that had permeated everyday German life for two decades.

The young, blond soldier looked around with interest, surveying a hesitant blue sky specked with clouds and grey streaks of water droplets and vapour. "It's not too bad, today."

"We're not supposed to smoke until we're off duty, anyway," Johan reminded him, accentuating his East Prussian manner in mock-haughtiness. "Duty to the Fatherland comes first. The Führer is a teetotal non-smoker, don't you know."

"We can't smoke because Fat Hermann orders it?" he asked coyly, puffing away at his Dunhill and grinning. "He breaks every law Hitler ever made."

"The Reichsmarschall–"

"Fat Hermann's Luftwaffe adjutant is a Jew. That's a breach of the race laws."

"*Reichsmarschall* Fat Hermann to you, obersoldat. Don't you forget it."

"How could I forget Prime Minister, Reichstag President, Master of German Forestry, Nazi police founder & Marshal *Kummerspeck* of the Greater Reich?"

Johan chuckled; smoke billowing out through his mouth. "How you avoided Dachau I have no idea."

A typical East Prussian soldier, though enlisted, Johan shared the consensus opinion of the officers about the 'Bohemian Corporal' and his paladins. He was twenty-four, but had already developed the Prussian military manner, cloaked though it was in knowing humour.

"Just in case you ever do get sent down," Johan added, "you might as well tell me about those old friends of yours who disappeared. God, it's not like you are the only one in that regard."

"Another time," came the sober reply.

Johan recognised something in his tone, and did not press the matter.

The strolled on southwards to the end of Tottenham Court Road, and rounded the corner on to New Oxford Street, which was a busier hub of life. Two women aged around ten years older than they approached on the pavement, and both soldiers gave them a cheery greeting.

"Don't you leer at me, you Jerry bastard!" one of them snarled.

They marched past, scowls etched into their faces. Both soldiers halted, caught by surprise, and turned to watch incredulously as the women stomped away.

The two women put a safe distance between themselves and the Germans before speaking again.

"Can't stand the bloody sight of the bastards," Nancy spat with feeling.

"Same, Nance. Just glad they're not crawling all over the East End."

Which Goebbels had promised they would. Which had scared, and then confused them. Which they left unspoken.

"Every time I see the filth I start thinking 'you could have killed Tommy'."

Her friend tutted sympathetically. "Don't be daft, Nancy. Tommy aint dead."

"I must say," Sergeant Stanley finally relented under Tommy's insistent pressure, "we have indeed fallen on our feet here, chaps."

"Yes!" Tommy cried. He slammed his card deck on the round little table in front of him. "I knew you'd come round. It's all right."

James, sat on the barracks steps behind them, snorted loudly; a derisive explosion of phlegm and scorn.

"Bloody fan*tastic*. Tables, chairs, get to play cards, smoke cigarettes freely, drink beers and learn German. You'll be bloody Seig Heil'ing next you twat."

Tommy reddened. Had that particular assessment come from anyone other than one of the handful of men present, he would have leapt to action and torn chunks out of them. Even so, he struggled to maintain his composure. The cockney and James had a shared bond of mockery and humorous northern-southern antipathy, at any rate. But the Yorkshireman had touched a nerve. Brian stood between them, just in case. Tommy's face bunched, running through a gamut of emotions. James stared at him blandly.

"Watch what you're saying," Tommy blurted finally. "You're from fackin' Leeds anyway, what do you hairy, incestuous slags know about anything?"

"Bradford. Borders' to the west."

"Oh my days," the cockney mirthlessly chuckled, his jaw clenched. "You are without doubt the biggest berk I 'ave ever 'ad the misfortune to do bird with in my life."

"So you've done porridge before? Typical of an Artful Dodger, chimney sweeping, pie-and-mash bubonic plague-carrying cockney criminal–"

"*Fuck* off!"

Stanley intervened, amidst general amusement. Brian informed James that he was 'a belligerent northern bastard,' and he agreed happily, lighting a cigarette and finally lapsing into a congenial silence.

"I'm just saying," Tommy pressed on, "it's *all right*. They're not what we thought they were. No beatings, starvation, threats. The guards are all right. This *camp* is all right."

James didn't answer, lighting a Woodbine instead and looking up to the sky. It was a dull day, more akin to England than France; the sun a small orange disc in a sea of grey and white wisps, ominous swirls of an ugly atmosphere. He sucked in the smoke with gusto, exhaled, and then snorted again without looking at his friends.

Tommy scowled at him. It *had* been all right.

Weeks had passed now, and after a fairly stiff first day, the following days were a succession of surprises.

~

The first had perhaps been most significant, given how quickly into their internment it had happened. They group had been sat in the very same place – five in chairs around one of the small tables that had been plonked down by chuckling Germans outside their platoon's huts – Tommy, Brian, the Sarge, James Fletcher and another fellow from the 'Stanley's Boys' platoon, big Dave. James Wilkinson sat smoking and brooding on the top step, then as now; it soon become his natural state. Wincing periodically as it stung, Brian was sat discomfited, hunched forwards with his injured leg stretched out straight before him on a wooden crate.

"You're definitely a raspberry ripple, mate," Tommy had told him. "Chances are you'll never walk properly again."

"Good," grunted James, without looking. "You southerners walk like you're carrying carpets. It's like you spent too long watching apes at the Regent's Park zoo. Makes me beat my chest just *watching* you."

Sighs from the men, anticipating the inevitable; Tommy turned, leaning towards the stocky northerner with his hands outstretched. "Oi – flat cap. Listen, son. Seriously now... *please*... think about it... one of your main *stereotypes* is a man removing his shirt to fight, *while chanting the name of your county...*" the men broke into loud sniggers; one began parodying the territorially proud, shirtless northern man, and the laughter increased threefold. Brian slapped his knees, hooting as James let out a reluctant grin. Tommy couldn't contain his smirk as he resumed. "Cavemen, us? What about, '*you can always tell a Yorkshireman... but you can't tell him much*'..."

Laughter pealed out amidst scattered claps and slapped thighs; James himself grudgingly smiled, even as his counterpart tried to embark on a roll of momentum.

"Yorkshire's most exotic attraction was a shop that sold *foreign food...*" the laughter got hysterical, "... and it shut down after a week because a Leeds local *didn't like that foreign muck*, so he took his shirt off, chanted *Yorkshire, Yorkshire* for ten minutes, told everyone he's *not eating that fucking crap I tell thee*, and then torched the place. That northern geezer had a punch-up that night... in an empty room, by himself. Cockneys carrying carpets? *We* play Billy

Big Bollocks? Coming from you! Don't you talk about giving it the big 'un, you daft melt…"

"Yeah that's interesting and funny," he muttered quickly and quietly, before booming: "For a twat. Aye, I *will*. *Cockneys*," he declared unhurriedly, loudly, in the typical Yorkshire style, "… are the *only* people who practice swearing at the mirror. And you talk in rhyming slang…" James shook his head in genuine disbelief. "How much in love with the sound of your own voice can you buggers get? And it stemmed from a covert criminal code, which you accept with pride. Cockneys are nutters."

"You aren't fully evolved."

The reaction was instant. "*Whoah*…" he cried, turning round in a sudden burst of animation. "You can *speak* to people in Yorkshire you've never met, pal, and engage in *conversation*. Try that in London; only rapists and street-crawlers do it, and the odd fruity pervert like Jack the Ripper and your uncles…" they locked eyes, and Tommy laughed, unable to hold it in. The pokerfaced chain-smoker continued, exaggerating his accent for effect:

"The Great Fire was Biblical; a modern Gomorrah. Sodomites flock there. You have rapists, rent boys, murderers and plague-infested rats running around London, and they're the only ones who enjoy it. You pay too much for beer that you can't even drink. Yorkshire is *green*. Fresh. Beautiful. Your lot *hang, draw and quarter* people and hang their *dismembered body parts on the Tower*. We swim in clean country lakes; you have a river of poisonous pisswater running through your shitty concrete nightmare, build a bunch of crap buildings around it and expect me to be impressed. Unevolved? All right, Dodger. You lot are fruity."

"And you are the only person who's sarcastic in his sleep. You sleep talk at night, and I hear you arguing with yourself. Yorkshiremen have the largest county, and the smallest gene pool. You sound like a slow Glaswegian with mongolism that's been hit with a brick..." and he mock-bowed at the cheers. "Your people are like the Scots, but more aggressive, uglier and with the generosity squeezed out of 'em. You're a bunch of inbred ginger beers who bother sheep. Button it, will you?"

Beats of silence passed, before James concluded the argument in his chuntering, methodical style, as they all knew he would. "Oh *aye*? Is that right, lad? Let's get down to brass tacks, here. You sound like a gay Australian who can't surf, can't swim and swapped the beach for a rat-infested concrete hellhole full of plague and rapists. You're a cockney named Jack; named after a rapist cannibal who ate prostitutes and dead cats. Your people... cockneys actually have a *phrase* for unemployment and petty crime, *ducking and diving, bobbin' and weavin'*, and you *all do it and admit it*. And I'm unevolved? Well... there were no Great Fires of Bastard *Yorkshire*, was there, eh? Even God hates cockneys. Now shut it, *gloyt*."

Sharing an amused glance with Brian, Tommy of the East End let his friend's mocking finale pass unanswered, silently thanking some unspecified person or deity or energy – he wasn't sure – for James' survival in May. The stubborn, bloody-minded, chuntering monkey could end up saving his sanity in the camp. That made him worth his weight in gold.

As they'd reclined at ease, enjoying what they later came to realise was the rare sound of birdsong, the camp medic had approached. Accompanying him was Lieutenant Hoffman, and another German trooper of the SS.

Every man save for Stanley mumbled "Heil!" in unison, and then a medley of German sounding noises followed by 'Führer', to mock the SS rank.

'Oberlebbenhoffer... BadenBadenjerryführer', from James Fletcher, the longest and most obvious wind-up. They waited on baited breath for a response. Hoffman, though, merely raised his eyebrows and even seemed to smirk. *He doesn't look angry*, Tommy thought. *There's a turn up.*

"Private Marshall, Brian?" Hoffman had asked. His voice was far less harsh than it had been during roll call. Nevertheless, the question was met with silence.

"Private Marshall, I am led to believe you have a leg injury from battle?" he asked, glancing thrice at the obviously-injured Brian as he looked around at the English men.

Tommy piped up. "Don't say anything; let him guess who it is."

The men chuckled, their initial recalcitrance gone. Hoffman looked at him, and his own face split into a grin.

"My guess is you," he smiled, pointing at the stricken-looking Brian. "How is the leg?"

Brian pretended to examine it. "Still there!"

This time Hoffman laughed; the chuckles of the English died in their own throats.

"Do you mind if the medic has a look?"

"Not at all," Brian replied in surprise. "Help yourself mate."

The medic, sporting a walrus-like moustache and a freckled face, did not resemble the typical SS man. Nevertheless, he sported the Hugo Boss *feldgrau*. After a minute's worth of examination, he spoke, in a voice that seemed altogether too high pitched for his large frame and half-crazed appearance.

"Well it seems to be healing very well. I have brought you some new bandage and gauze. I also have a little bit of surgical spirit for cleaning the wound, and not drinking!"

"Drinking?" Tommy piped up again. "Drink surgical spirit! What do you think we are, Scottish?"

Everyone laughed at this; the SS lieutenant loudest of all. The medic briskly walked away, both sides of his walrus moustache visibly bobbing up and down as he heartily cackled all the way to the creaking gate.

Hoffman had stayed chatting for ten minutes longer. He offered them German cigarettes, which were surprisingly good, and assured them that as the British Expeditionary Force-SS liaison officer, he would ensure he found a football, and even explicitly promised goals to be built on the flat, grassy area inside the fence, directly situated behind their barracks.

When he'd left, Tommy stood up and turned to the others, astonishment etched across his features.

"Did you bloody *see* that?!"

They looked at him in alarm. Had they missed something?

"That Jerry laughed at my jokes!"

James turned to him sourly from the step. "And?"

"I didn't think they had a sense of humour!"

"You miss the point," the Yorkshireman replied dryly, his eyes narrowed.

150

But Brian commented, "Lads, we might have fallen on our feet with this camp. Things are looking all right."

James spat on the ground in response, drawing snorts of laughter from his boyish namesake James Fletcher. Tommy ignored them both. Their name alone was starting to grind his gears. *James, Jackboot, Jerry.*

Though, he conceded, the latter one had proved to be a turn-up for the books. Idle conversations with Jerry... and regarding the krauts in this camp, they were an undeniably friendly bunch. Hell, they're bloody soft!

"Let's just see how things settle..." he decided aloud.

Predictably, it was James that replied. Scratching the prickly four-day stubble growth on his chin, the northerner queried his hopeful friend.

"But what will we see, Tommy lad? In what way will it 'settle'... they'll continue to treat us with courtesy, on this weird 'We Are All Blood Brothers' kick that Hitler's on–"

"Hitler said that long before they beat us, old chap," Stanley observed, pitching up after a long silence. "In his book, in tens of speeches, in public appeals. Not that the wider public were told."

"What?" James retorted, incredulous. Stanley held his hands aloft.

"Avoid the easy temptation of *judgement*, old bean. Forget *me*; it was purely observation. *Fact.* Beyond the semantics, though, the point being is that their attitude and the spiel that the Hoffman kid and that commandant are coming out with is *nothing* new... said with all respect, old chap," the gentlemanly Sergeant added.

Opening his mouth to speak, James caught himself and considered, finally nodding. "OK. Fair point. We fit their racist views. But either way, there's something amiss."

The higher voice of James Fletcher piped up in agreement, voicing his own concern with German intent. The men discussed the issue for some minutes, and Tommy and Brian were almost certain they detected a note of nervous tension in James voice, underlying the gruff, deadpan Yorkshire tones. The prospect appalled them. As they scrutinised him, after sharing a knowing glance of acknowledgement, James was impeded by the huge gust of wind, nixing his valiant efforts as he tried in vain to light his cigarette. His hand raised slightly, ready to launch the packet of matches into the air. Stopping himself, the steady northerner let frustration overcome him, and he openly cursed. Releasing a string of humourless obscenities, the young Yorkshire lad stuck the unlit cigarette in his mouth and snarled:

"Well, I don't trust them."

But the others were placated by the medic's visit, and Hoffman's seemingly genuine, genial nature. Tommy frowned. He had never been cerebral, tending to live by his emotions; James, on the contrary, his sarcastic foil from the north was reserved and cynical, and generally never betrayed a lack of equilibrium. The man's emotional control up to now had been extraordinary, holding up in extreme conditions. Even under fire, James had been ice cool, thinking clearly under pressure and helping keep others grounded in the most hellacious moments of sensory assault. Here in the camp, it was somewhat off-putting to see his poise slip now.

"Cheer up mate," he called over. "Let's make the best of it."

There was no response. Tommy rose to his feet and approached, patting his comrade's strong shoulder and lingering by the steps. James looked up to meet his gaze and nodded, winking. The cockney reached down to take his abandoned cigarette, lighting it for him with his own body shielding the match from the wind, and he knelt to place it in James' mouth, with a friendly tousle of his increasingly bushy hair.

James seemed cheered somewhat, shaking hands with the cockney before turning to smoke with relish. Tommy watched him for a moment, until James muttered "ginger beer," the cockney slang for homosexual. Smiling, Tommy turned to the group with hands held high.

"I tell you what though, lads... God *bless* her, I feel rotten for sayin' it but the food in here's a better than my Nancy can knock up!"

At that, they'd all been forced to agree with Tommy, the rather well-to-do Stanley excepted. This was better food than they had either expected in captivity, and for some, the quality German cooking tasted considerably better than the cuisine they were accustomed to at home.

~

Later that week, Hoffman had turned up in their platoon barracks with whiskey, claiming his superiors thought it was merited due to fifty-two men, or roughly half the surviving company entire, attending that week's camp lectures – nineteen of whom had come from Stanley's Boys! Hi-fives were exchanged, and the alcohol was gratefully accepted.

The lessons had been thirty minutes of basic German and thirty minutes of recent European history, daily. Three nights later, Hoffman upped the ante – heavenly delight, both James' had almost cried – the SS man brought *beers* to the barracks.

"German beers, Bavarian beers..." he said, with a mock-conciliatory tone. "That should be no hardship; even you Tommies have to admit that Germans do beer very well."

Meeting the scattered jeers and bantering English with open humour, Hoffman stayed with them for twenty minutes, and around half the men felt comfortable enough to lower their inhibitions to drink with an SS officer. Hell, beer was beer.

Tommy approached Hoffman. "How, and why?" He asked curiously, having had James' suspicions playing on his mind.

The German shrugged. "They made me liaison because of my English, and said I could use beer as a means to cheer you all up and make you happy. I love beer! This means I get to drink on duty, with permission!"

Justifying it as an inherently selfish act was an endearing statement to British ears. Often a cynical people by nature, had Hoffman launched into some spiel or other they would have shut down on him, smilingly drinking his beer while letting him spout unappreciated gibberish. But a man who perverts the course of his professional duties in order to drink? British 'Tommies' had to respect it.

With genuine magnanimity, a decently-sized chunk of the group actively welcomed Hoffman into their midst to get drunk. Questions comparing the two countries soon flowed, and common ground was quite easily reached.

James Wilkinson, on the other hand, drank three full flagons' worth of ale in quick fashion and then, thoroughly contented, he retreated back to his bunk bed at the far end of the room. The Yorkshireman refused Tommy's entreaties to join him in a toast; instead, lighting a cigarette on his bunk with his face disfigured into a leering scowl, and he began to read his battered old copy of Joyce's *Ulysses*, refusing to pay heed to the catcalls for some time before belching loudly. After the beer, James struggled to focus on the strangely worded text of the novel, but he persisted, ignoring the continued merriment only twenty-five metres away. He spoke not a word to Hoffman.

~

The beginning of the fourth week, after several more surprise beer drops and other assorted amenities, Tommy had been sat in the furthest corner of the camp, near the fence and at the edge of the grass. An upturned barrel was the makeshift table, and two logs on either side made it perfect for card games, checkers or chess, all of which the Germans had provided. Tommy though, had been writing, when he heard footsteps approach.

"Hello, Private Watson."

Lieutenant Hoffman doffed his cap. The thick military wool jacket was gone; Hoffman wore the sleek grey SS tunic as had Major Wolf. An Iron Cross dangled from his left breast. Tommy made no move to stand, but touched his forehead.

"Hello Lieutenant."

Gone was the gibberish noise for his SS-Obersturmführer rank, Tommy's own being 'unterschlieffenkrautführer". No one felt any inclination to mock Hoffman anymore, after the first days, or indeed, most of the other guards, most of whom had a good grasp of English; even more surprisingly, the German attempts at humour. The aloof, menacing types, on the other hand, all seemed to guard the outer perimeter and the long building adjacent to their barracks where the dining room was located, situated in the other section separated by the inner chain-link fence that split the camp grounds.

"Writing to a loved one?" The German had asked.

"Yes, my Nancy..." he hesitated, hating to ask. "Look, Lieutenant, when are these going to be sent? And when can we receive mail?"

"It will be taken care of. The same rules will apply to you boys when you get to send mail as we SS, though; they will be censored. Just as I cannot say certain things, nor can you."

Tommy was shocked by his frankness, and more than a little grateful.

After a moment's silence, Hoffman asked "may I sit down?"

Apologising instantly, Tommy gestured him to sit down. The Lieutenant did so.

"My girl is called Claudia," he said. "Do you want to see? I have pictures."

Pursing his lips slightly, the lieutenant took out a small leather wallet and handed it to Tommy with a relaxed smile.

"Yeah, she's very pretty," Tommy said, impressed. Blonde, wavy hair, full bosomed and smiling, the picture showed Claudia sat on Hoffman's knee in the garden, two huge jugs of beer on the slab of wood in front of him. He was wearing civilian clothes; a white buttoned shirt, with a thick brown tie loosely hanging from a neck slightly exposed by his open top button. The strong jaw and unavoidably Nazi-stereotype features of Hoffman were as pronounced as ever, but with his girl and stripped of what James Wilkinson called 'the skull and crossbones clobber', the stern-faced SS man looked utterly peaceful, and free of inhibition. Claudia seemed to be caught mid-speech, and his young face was captured on camera, splitting into a wide grin as he watched and listened. They both looked happy. Drunk and happy, even. *Normal.*

"And you?" Hoffman had pressed. "Do you have a photograph of Nancy?"

Tommy slowly nodded, and retrieved it. Their personal items had not been confiscated. Many of the men kissed the photographs of loved ones at night, and said prayers. Tommy did so.

"She looks nice," Hoffman said approvingly. "Are you happy?"

"Very," he'd replied defensively.

"It's very difficult to be so far away from home, isn't it?" the Lieutenant remarked, sadly. "I miss them very much."

"Them?"

"We have a daughter. Helga."

Tommy smirked. "I guess she's blonde?"

"I would be worried if she was not," the Lieutenant smiled back.

He looked across at the camp's yard and parade ground area.

"I'm glad to do this duty. Not just to improve my English, which is already very strong, but because it confirmed everything I thought about this bullshit war."

Now Tommy was intrigued. He snorted, in the derisive style of Yorkshire James.

"Bullshit is right."

"We're not so different, Tommy. We're the same." Brooding, his pensive blue eyes swung back around to face Tommy. "Politics created a war when there need not have been one. My duty *here* means I mingle with English, and perhaps Scottish, Welsh and Irish – northern Irish? – soldiers. Normal men like me. We're not so different," he repeated thoughtfully.

Tommy was taken aback. "Well... I suppose not, Jerry."

The SS-Obersturmführer glanced at him, and the British private winked. Hoffman grinned.

"Not at all, Tommy. Ha, of course, that *is* your real name."

They chuckled.

"But seriously, ja? Just a group of normal men caught up in this struggle, both wanting to protect our fatherlands, our civilisation, and to go home to our women as soon as possible..."

Tommy smiled ruefully at that. Hoffman continued. "Surely we can both agree we prefer our women to war! Cigarette?"

"Yeah lovely, ta."

They smoked in silence for a while, enjoying the quality.

"You have any other kids?" Tommy asked as he exhaled a thin cloud of smoke.

"Nine."

"Bloody hell, nine kids?"

Hoffman chuckled again. "No. Not 'nine'," he said, holding up fingers. "*Nein, mein England soldat,* I have *no* other kids."

"Can you imagine nine kids? *Strewth,*" Tommy pondered, exhaling the last drag of his cigarette. Chortling, Hoffman gave him another, which he lit it for him.

"Do you have *kinder*?"

Tommy's eyes grew wistful, filmed by smoke. "Yeah, just the one. Vera. That's my princess."

Hoffman looked at the picture the Londoner passed him.

"She's an angel. What a beautiful girl."

He suddenly offered his hand across the table. No hesitation, no glance to check it was unseen; Hoffman took Tommy by surprise with the naked frankness of his gesture.

"I'm Walther."

"Tommy."

They shook, firmly, and the German grinned at him; a little conspiratorially, Tommy thought. His liking for the officer was growing.

"Why do you really bring us beer, and stuff?" he heard himself blurt.

The German betrayed no surprise at the question. Hoffman looked across the camp, puffing thoughtfully at his cigarette as he considered.

"Well, orders for one. But it makes sense to me, anyway. I don't know what your politicians and media were saying before all this, but in Germany, nobody wanted a war with England. Just France and Poland, to reclaim our land and pride. The English are brothers. The Führer himself has always said so."

"Fair enough," Tommy shrugged, once more impressed by the lieutenant's candour.

The SS officer stole a glance at the Englishman, and chuckled. "Do you mean that?" And before Tommy could protest, he interjected smoothly, "I know it all seems quite a bit crazy, as you say. Some of our boys were confused. Those of lesser brains and wit. Our beloved Dr Goebbels took England's enmity quite personally, Tommy, and for a year he tried his best to stir up eighty million people to hate you..."

Inquisitive, his eyes again sought those of the cockney; the two men held each other's gaze for the final exchange.

"What about *you*? Are you ok?"

"I'm ok, Jerry."

He nodded, recognising truth in the words. "Good. No need for any of us to worry, 'mate.'" He winked at Tommy, amiably. "Things will work out for the Saxons of Europe the way things are meant to." And at that, the British soldier looked away so as not to betray his confusion.

Hoffman stubbed his cigarette out on the side of the barrel, and crushed it underfoot.

"OK, I must go. A German soldier is never off-duty, or so they tell us!"

He rose to his feet, and shrugged. "Speak to you soon, Tommy."

"Yeah, see you soon pal…"

Obersturmführer Hoffman placed another cigarette down on the table for him, and then walked back across the grass to speak to Sergeant Stanley Hitchman, who'd just emerged from the barracks clutching a paper the Germans had given him. They spoke for a minute or so, with both men visibly and audibly chuckling several times, and then Hoffman strolled on to a different barrack. Smoking the neatly rolled German cigarettes that the lieutenant had left him, Tommy had watched him all the way.

It had been around the time when the scale of the Dunkirk disaster was becoming widely known that William had been summoned to meet with the Colonel.

They'd never met before, nor had he heard of him. Nothing in his, Mary or Jack's personal lives had suggested that such a meet could, would or was going to take place. Alan was busy trying to reconnoitre with non-party members of old who'd helped lead workers strikes, trade unionists and other Spain vets who'd become disillusioned with the party. But this was a colonel of the British Expeditionary Force. This was no haphazard plan to gang up to sabotage dock work or factories, concocted by ideological opponents or simply English workers stirred to rebellion of the coming invasion by some form of base patriotism; an islander's tribalistic reaction to foreign threat. This man had a colonel's epaulettes adoring his shoulders. It was contact from The Establishment. No, this was something else.

"No pasaran," Jack had told him solemnly, teasing. William laughed.

"Yeah *yeah*, no pasarán, old boy. Eyes up. Look after the lass."

Whistling to himself in the sun, William went on alone, striding away with purpose to the meeting while Jack and Mary went to wait in a nearby tavern, *The Sherlock Holmes*, nestled away from the main streets around Trafalgar Square. It was a convenient drinking hole for whenever they needed to meet around Westminster and anywhere in the central section, west of the Embankment and river; most importantly, unlike many pubs around Soho, Covent Garden and the government quarter from Trafalgar Square to the Victoria Tower Gardens, it was quiet, and most definitely free of spies and informants.

As they reached the square, Jack and Mary had peeled off wordlessly, and the young Scot was left in the windblown national landmark, in a sea of pigeons, heavy gusts throwing his entangled hair up across his face. Having separated from his best friend and lover, William strolled through the square, taking a prolonged look at Nelson's Column; symbolic, a monument, free for soon-to-be the last time? Will it be hauled away to Berlin or Nuremberg soon, piece by piece? William considered it, glancing around at the quiet, almost sombre square; a grim foreboding was keeping many indoors, or fleeing north. The difference Dunkirk had made; if only evacuation had been possible. William watched the pigeons pattering about the base of the monument, in their comical drunken goosestep. The thought of Hugo Boss-clad *Schutzstaffel* men of the Waffen-SS clip-clopping their way through the square, goose-stepping the symphony of a thunderous roar of thousands of jackbooted feet was almost too much to bear.

From Beethoven's Ninth Symphony to the *Horst Wessel Lied*; from Wagner to the banal beer hall brawler marching songs, and the current favoured patriotic symphony of martial music and marching feet. No matter how many countries Hitler brings down, William thought, none will fall as far as Germany already had.

Lost in thought, he strolled on sedately through the square and around the deserted roundabout, breathing in an uncommonly fresh lungful of central London air as he gazed down Northumberland Ave to the Embankment, passed the War Office and Charing Cross Station and, almost warily, to Whitehall no.7, the altogether more anonymous, nondescript address that he'd be cordially invited to by a "Colonel C.G." Unlike the great War Office that separated the two main roads leading west from the Thames to Trafalgar Square, the entrance to the no.7 offices was next to an unprepossessing restaurant, closed, its lettering faded on the black paint of its frame. Inside the modest doorway, a short, smiling brunette of around 30 took his coat in the undecorated threshold, and showed him to a surprisingly cramped corridor upstairs, and thence, a small office, occupied by the man to whom he'd been summoned.

The Colonel was short. The first though that entered William's mind, as the man rose from behind a desk to shake his hand, was that he rather resembled a neat little spy and secret policeman from Franco's Spain that they'd encountered, which was an unpleasant instinctual first impression to have, though the decided friendliness of the Colonel's greeting dispelled his intuitive dislike just as quickly as it had appeared. But even as he heard himself agreeing to the two fingers of whiskey that the Colonel was pouring into a glass for him, sliding it across the desk, William's mind drifted back eighteen months to times best forgotten.

The Fifth Columnist in question to whom the Colonel bore resemblance had worn a tatty, short leather jacket improvised with a fur lining, thickly collared with some kind of heavy material, which was probably expropriated. With his neat, narrow moustache and slicked back hair, he was a younger, sharper featured General Franco in miniature. Seen on leave at the Hotel Falcón – a go-to for POUM militiamen on leave in Barcelona – and up and down the Ramblas at all the favourite cafés of the Socialist Workers Party and the anarchists, CNT and FAI alike – he'd resembled many of the fierce little Italian militiamen in Catalonia, who were by and large, an illiterate mob of worker peasants yet ferocious and loyal to a man – perhaps made moreso with Fascist Italy and their countrymen occupying nearby Mallorca, in their support for Franco's uprising. This man, though, had been unmistakeably Spanish. He was a familiar, engaging face, and then the neat little man had vanished in the uneasy aftermath of the May Days fighting, and the insanity that followed. Treachery, good men incarcerated, quiet murders. No disappearance was thought much of; it was taken for granted that any missing face was languishing in what amounted to overcrowded dungeon cells; so many young men, flung into squalid imprisonment to rot away like an animal by the same side that in most cases they'd travelled hundreds of miles to Spain to fight for.

But after escaping northwards from Catalonia and out of the fascist nightmare that Spain had become; they'd seen the neat little man in Banyuls. It was an uncomfortably pro-Franco southern French town, full of the suspicious and hostile glares from a populace foreign to the war but with seemingly instinctive and natural predisposition towards the victors against whom the now-ragged English visitors had fought. But Mary was in a terrible state; she had survived the retribution of her capture, but the horrific conclusion to her struggle left her a hollow shell of the fiery woman of passion they'd known, and they too were emotionally fragile. They needed rest, sanctuary.

And so, the languorous group, as though trapped in some nightmarish dreamlike state, sought refuge in the nearest drinking establishment they could find. It was a quiet bar with sun-faded wooden café chairs and tables, filled with Frenchman playing card games, for the most part clean and wearing good quality clothes; there he was. He'd spotted them too, of course – they were a conspicuous addition to the clientele in their weathered jackets, bearing the obvious burden of the war that had raged south of the border for three years and whose slaughter was not yet at an end. They stared in disbelief back across the bar, to where he was sat engaged in what looked like a hearty, wine-soaked debate with a group of rotund Frenchman, putting the world to rights with an unmistakeably high familiarity with all present. Evidently he was some kind of intelligence gatherer for the Falange; the quintessential Fifth Columnist, though whether his loyalties were as such due to fascism, Franco or the Catholic Church they would never know. He'd winked at William, and waved over to the group, oily, hair still slicked but altogether more distinguished in appearance. Even *suave*. William felt the sensation of being physically winded, just seeing him in the flush of his personal victory. As they stared in astonishment, the little man gave an anti-fascist signal from across the room, which proved so uproariously funny to the Frenchmen that the whole bar collapsed into paralysing shouts of raucous laughter, in what seemed to the recent war-escapees like a sick parody of helpless hilarity in humourless days, as though the ugly townsfolk of Banyuls were permanently under-humoured, resulting in deeply inappropriate moments of release, such as this disturbing mockery of all the merciless slaughter wrought by cruel usurpers, at their expense. The group quickly stepped out, restraining a livid Alan and making straight for the train station to flee, to put the nightmare behind them, to lose themselves in the comparative anonymity of Paris and thence, home.

It was the final ignominy of a strange and surreal war.

William's mind had wandered, with such a stark and unwanted resemblance to a forgotten face of a bygone nightmare, and he forced himself to concentrate.

"So I trust that you were discreet about this impromptu little rendezvous," the Colonel was saying. His hair was thinning slightly, but the brow was strongly pronounced, the moustache neat. His uniform was immaculate, and curiously, had a red carnation through the buttonhole. William detected the Highlander in his Scot accent, though distinctly public school elocution was tempering it. The man seemed charming enough, his features open, eyes bright and searching. He had the air of a great energy being contained.

"Yes, Colonel."

"By that, I assume that your friends know about it?" The reply was fast, but not sharp. William decided to meet him head on with honesty. Lies didn't appeal to his honed sense of morality, and it was too early to jeopardise whatever it was that this strange Colonel in no. 7 Whitehall had in mind with him.

"Yes they do, Colonel. They're my comrades. We've fought in the trenches together, in war."

"And by that, you mean Spain?"

"Yes."

"You have experience fighting fascism..."

"Yes." William resolved to give no further one-word answers; though relatively sweet tempered, he shared the egalitarian zeal of the previous decade and all the untold millions who subscribed to socialism in its various forms, or anarchism. Alan would have bristled at the thought of him being interrogated by some public school toff; Scottish or not.

The Colonel smiled. "But I dare say, my dear chap, you don't quite believe in the social system of this country? In the Empire, capitalism and the King?"

William hesitated, wary of blowing some as-yet unspecified opportunity to do more than be an auxiliary fireman when the Germans came, and with anything from a quarter of a million to 400,000 men captive after the Dunkirk debacle, there was nothing more cruelly inevitable.

"I believe in a more egalitarian system that represents us as brothers," William began cautiously. "Although I'm certainly not a communist." He saw the Colonel's eyes narrow almost imperceptibly at that, and realised that he'd underestimated him. Thinking fast, he continued, "... of course I joined the party, but it was to secure a means to entering Spain. Myself, some friends and a handful of other members of the party all shipped out together. Once we reached Barcelona, three of us joined a Marxist militia instead. A year later the Communist Party outlawed them as 'Fascist Trotskyites', and the aftermath of that lunacy is when I stopped believing in the naïve idealism of the dream. Nothing wakes you up quite like betrayal."

The Colonel nodded. "I see."

William decided to reinforce his position. "Point being is we were there to stop the rising tide of fascism. No pasarán; *They Shall Not Pass*. That was the idea, anyway. But that ideal, that dream, hasn't died. It's not even so much fascism, per se, although that word has come to symbolise evil. It's German fascism. Hitler's fascism. National Socialism, a doctrine of hate and suppression, racial Darwinism. That's what I fight for. Not Comrade Stalin, death to the rich, collectivised produce and concrete tower blocks for all."

The Colonel had nodded again, satisfied. "Good. Because personally, my lad, I don't care what your politics are. I care about your passion to defend Britain against the enemy. Because this country, make no bones about it, is under the biggest threat to its survival it has ever encountered. Even the little French weasel Napoleon Bonaparte was child's play, compared to this..."

He gestured in a vaguely south-westerly direction, towards where they both knew the Germans were massing. No mercy in their grey eyes – the average Jerry, the commanders, and the four greyest and coolly bluest eyes of all, those of Hitler and Göring. No respite. They had France, and Britain's army was taken. The U-boats were slaughtering at sea, targeting shipping and cleaving through Royal Navy patrol boats. Even if they didn't get the French Navy – *could we scuttle our Allies' ships, kill their men* – that still left the Italian Navy, and with Franco eyeing Gibraltar, Spain would soon join the *Great Struggle Against The Jew Puppetmasters of London*. Only the Royal Air Force held out, and with a massive Luftwaffe concentration expected to supplement an invasion force that had already captured the bulk of the army supposed to defend Britain's shores, the situation looked doomed.

"I'm a believer in unconventional warfare. The extent of that is, perhaps, unclear; but do you think for a moment that Germany is neglecting offensive bacteriological and chemical warfare? Do you think they will adhere to Geneva?"

Scorn was etched into the colonel's face; William could see his naked ambition to fight Germany using any and all means.

"You may just be the fellow I'm looking for. You won't know this, and in truth, even among the chaps like yourself I'm going to recruit we'll be sparing with the details, in case they're captured of course. But you, I know are dedicated to fighting these scum. And I served with your father, Lieutenant *Lawler*. It is 'Lawler' with an 'e', aye?"

William was astonished, but recovered quickly.

"Aye... uh, still Celtic but aye."

He tried to elaborate, but his lips mouthed wordlessly and he gave up, waiting for the Colonel to explain. The old veteran nodded slowly, gauging his young charge.

"He was a *good* man. Fought at the Battle of Quentin, died 1st April 1918, as the Expeditionary Force halted the Germans. I myself was evacuated from the trench soon after." He did not elaborate further, nor did he need to. His guest was dumbfounded, and this time made no effort to disguise it.

The Colonel smiled. "You seem surprised?"

"I daresay I am a little bit, aye," he admitted, inclining his head. His host picked up the silver cigarette case that lay on the neatly ordered desk in front of him, by his left hand, and offered it to William. The younger man accepted a smoke gratefully, which the military officer lit for him with the lift-arm lighter that had been next to his right. He took one for himself and lit it, all in one smooth movement with the grace of a man who'd performed that manoeuvre several thousand times.

Both sucked in their first drags of the cigarettes with gusto, nursing the smoke in their lungs before releasing it contentedly. Then, business-like once again; now the Colonel had his full attention, and he leaned in. This, they knew, was the crux of it.

"You're from good stock, and while you may not want to defend this country for the *King*, I'm certain that you and your mob – your *comrades* – will do it out of some different kind of patriotism; a kinship with democratic values, if you like, or at least with fairness, and a good old fashioned hatred of racist, tyrant scum. And regarding central London, you may just be the man I'm looking for."

William absorbed it all, nodding slowly. The invoking of democracy was amusing, given their ideals on the outset of war in Spain, but he wasn't going to argue now. Left-wing extremism, they now knew, held as much malevolence for those who did not fit within its parameters as did fascism. But the colonel was a persuasive man. William was beginning to see where this was going, after being initially confused by the Whitehall office, and the mixed signals that this whole rather bizarre summons had sent out.

The Colonel continued. "Against an enemy such as the Germans, less-than-conventional means of warfare and resistance have been considered. Are you aware of any such plans?"

The young man shook his head.

"Nor will others recruited in similar vein to you. You and your mob; I have the feeling somehow that you won't be captured, and if so, that you won't talk. So, for your benefit, I *will* tell you that a certain major – now colonel, back on active duty – explored such possibilities in a national security service section and in doing so, happened to set wheels in motion for what I am being commissioned to implement. Let's call them 'D'. And the justification was clear, let me read you an excerpt from 'Colonel D's' closing report..."

The Colonel cleared his throat, and turned the page of the notebook in front of him – neat and immaculately kept, much like the rest of his appearance – and found the correct page on the first attempt.

"... ok here we are..." he cleared his throat, "'The section was motivated to total war tactics by Adolf Hitler, who harnessed to his war chariot the four horses of treacherous diplomacy, lying propaganda, racial persecution and economic blackmail'. Furthermore... 'With the sudden drastic misfortunes suffered on the military front, the menace of enemy occupation in part of the British isles has increased exponentially. This section conceived and began implementing plans for a closely coordinated sabotage and intelligence network among the civilian population who would be left behind in any territories which the German armies might temporarily be able to occupy...'"

William smiled at that, despite himself. *Temporary*. The British spirit wouldn't allow for permanence.

"... as such, Section D completed several thousands of secret dumps throughout the country of incendiary materials. Our own additions are the D-Phone – a telephone capable of encoding and decoding the human voice, and the Duplex Transceiver; a wireless telephone with a wavelength too short to be picked up by any other known receiver..."

The Colonel looked up briefly at William. "And this is where it gets interesting for you and I."

He continued reading. "In light of the present dangers faced and the need for coordinated action through a network of Operational Patrols and Special Duties officers, in sabotage, intelligence and all means of subversive activity, Section D's Home Defence Organisation network of agents and the means and materials with which to conduct guerrilla war, sabotage and subversion in German occupied territory now passes to the unified single command of the GHQ Auxiliary Units'."

He looked up again. "That means us, my lad."

William was momentarily speechless. Neither the Czechs, nor the Scandinavians, Poles, Dutch, Belgians or French had had the foresight for this. It was a resistance organisation in the making before the krauts even landed! Jack, Alan and Mary would be ecstatic. So much for Auxiliary Firemen, perhaps picking up some Great War era pistol at the end to make some desperate and quite pointless last stand against an enemy of overwhelming power. This was more like it.

He found his voice. "I understand fully and we are ready to do our part."

The shadow of a smile played at the corners of the Colonel's mouth at that, noting the young Scot had not said 'duty'. But the fervour for German resistance was no less because of it; in fact, he was glad that his new recruits were driven by ideological hatred of National Socialism. That, or the visceral fear and loathing felt by older men who'd fought 'Jerry' knee-deep in mud and blood in the Great War, were far more reliable motivational factors in fanatical resistance than loose, crude patriotism and some vague sense of duty to the King.

"You readily accept that the life expectancy for this kind of work is not high." It was rhetorical, not even qualifying as a question. They both knew it to be so.

"Yes."

"Good. For now at least, I will not ask of you anything regarding weapons that are outlawed by the current conventions of war. But unconventional methods are needed. Sabotage, assassination, perhaps even direct combat."

William nodded, and the colonel's eyes bore into his.

"Elsewhere," he continued with a low urgency, "you need not concern yourself; you are perfectly situated in Bloomsbury – your base, as it were, is central London. You will receive intelligence regarding German troop movements from other parts of the occupied zone. Radio operators are located all over. You will have access to one, and there is a weapons cache located in the following place; memorise this now…"

As William listened rapt, his forehead bunched in concentration, the old Scot described directions to the hidden storage dump, outside the city limits in a field bunker.

"And as for Bloomsbury… do you, perchance frequent *The Royal Oak* at all?"

Another surprise, William thought wryly. Old Arthur.

"Sometimes. We mostly drink in The Portland Arms…"

The trademark smile once more split the Colonel's face, stretching his skin and alleviating some of the lines. "Try the Royal Oak. Arthur will keep you informed."

He stood up, a proud stance with chest stuck out, and William joined him. It was as though some unbreakable bond of kinship had been fostered between them; two Scots, more than two decades apart in age and who'd not laid eyes on each other more than twenty minutes before.

"The Germans are coming, William, and they're a bloody ruthless lot I tell you. And with their army will come the SS, and with the SS will come secret police. I'm sure you're as aware as I am of what 'police work' entails to these people."

William nodded. They'd helped set up Franco's own round-up gangs, and they'd been active enough in their own country for long enough. Concentration camps, emaciated internees in dirty pyjamas, dying of typhus and maltreatment in squalid pits of their own stinking waste. Floating corpses turning up in the canals, rivers and foetid becks of the cities; autopsies bypassed when the penis attached to the dead body in question was found to be circumcised; the criminal police, which had been seized in a Heydrich-Himmler coup to consolidate all Reich police forces, ordered by Heydrich to look the other way when their sister forces created fresh crime scenes whose victims were undesirables in the Reich. SD sabotage and intrigues on foreign soil. *Protective custody,* and other such sinister euphemisms. Ghettos being set up in Polish cities, Jews displaced from their homes in Germany itself, persecution having almost become ad hoc law.

Yes, William knew what *police work* entailed. They all had their reasons to fight the Nazis. And in his case, and his friends', they had more reason than he hoped most ever would.

He shook hands with the colonel, who, as the door swung shut behind William, was already leafing intently through the sheaf of papers on his desk, head filled with schemes and machinations, working in quiet intensity as though William had never been there at all.

~

Jack's eyes had widened with the exciting news. He suddenly seemed to enliven; re-energised, galvanised, not a trace of any fear or concern for the personal danger that would be an all-engulfing feature of their chosen life. William had been surprised; his own stomach had churned knots since his slightly dizzy exit back into the windy gales of London, which thankfully had slowed to a manageable breeze as he passed the great square once more, Nelson's Column overhead, the great admiral standing proud above Whitehall.

The flickering fire-light that lit the pub played shadows across their faces, three quiet figures hunched in the corner table. Great patriotic symbols were hung variously around the dark walls; other marks of the great detective of Arthur Conan Doyle were visible, in homage to an institution of the land. Such ostentation was apparent everywhere, driven by the fear of change and the inevitability of further war, and likely defeat.

William spoke quickly and calmly, in a low, urgent tone not unlike the colonel's own as he laid out the grim task to his friends.

"This goes beyond anything we did, including village attacks," Jack noted.

Mary nodded, glumly. "I prefer to meet the enemy."

"This *is* meeting the enemy," William hissed, suddenly animated. "But it's intelligent. We can't just charge a whole army of fascists. Krauts, Iti's, Franco cunts, probably frogs..." his voice trailed off wearily, numbed by the enormity of their duty.

"Alan would," Mary smiled.

Jack and William both caught her eye, in disgruntled surprise, but then let the ghost of a chuckle play over their lips, realising the intent.

They'd all faced danger before. Fighting in uncertain trench warfare, the blood-curdling terror of village battles, the uneasy treachery of the Barcelona May Days and its palpable ceasefires that none dared to trust; the three young men had learned to grow accustomed to the strains and fear of conflict situations, and with the maleficence of civil war, Mary had accepted the modus vivendi of a life in combat, conflicting as it did with her humanist upbringing. But as partisans? They were civilians engaged in acts of war.

And with a racial subversive in their midst, and the notorious barbarity of the Gestapo, William's fears were completely justified.

But Jack's eyes lit up wide.

"This is it," he hissed suddenly, lightly tapping the wooden tabletop they sat at in his great excitement. The enormity of it sank in; Jack had been contemplating a somewhat redundant resistance, as they all had – this task, sanctioned from the shadows of the system, gave them the platform and the means to make a difference before any end.

It was almost indecent, William thought, happily anticipating a coming enemy with the martial zeal of a Viking. Saxon blood, he thought wryly. Hitler would approve.

"It's not a cause for bloody champagne, now is it?" the Scot snapped, berating his friend. "Pack it in man."

Jack shrugged, grinning and unrepentant. "We can make a difference. We're not lying down for the scum."

William made no response, and instead turned to glance at Mary. His dark-haired lover did not meet his eyes. Strange, he mused, the excitement of his dear friend in the face of almost certain death, compared to perhaps the most dedicated anti-fascist in their midst; his beautiful, vivacious, feisty girl, whose wooden expression betrayed nothing. It unnerved him; his creature of passion, silent and portentous.

Simon lit up a Woodbine, his eighth of the evening, and set himself down at the desk in agitation. Fidgeting compulsively, he tried to write as quickly as he could, putting little thought to the torrent of simple words. To *flow*.

"Dear Diary.

I've been invited to cover a soiree of the well-to-do types at the Savoy. They made me sign an official secrets act of sorts to be involved, but only thirty journalists or so are to be involved. By all accounts, indeed judging from their behaviour alone, this is a big one.

He paused. How could he properly convey the dread and apprehension? No words could do justice to the low sensation at the pit of his stomach. So, then, he decided for honest description. If anyone ever reads this, Simon thought, *and they think I'm too expository and bland, to hell with them.* He dipped his quill in the vat of ink, attached the Woodbine to his little gold cigarette holder, and continued writing.

I cannot capably describe the awful sensation of waiting in dull dread for some bizarre or ugly occurrence, the next drastic change that further advances the fascist system and makes democracy, its idiosyncrasies and silly failings and charming ideals, seem yet more distant.

They're hush-hush about all this caper. Cannot really say any more, nor dramatise this entry as yet. No doubt it will be some self-gratifying little SS thug promoting victory in some internecine power struggle; an SS viceroy in England for Hitler, the Wehrmacht side-lined, Brauchitsch an insignificant desk jockey. Won't that be quite wonderful? The only way I can look them in the eye and smile is in knowing that there will be an alternate version of this news printed outside the conventional press soon enough. I have my pride. I'm no gunman or soldier, but I'm helping to build the resistance in my own way.

He paused. Too self-glorifying. Simon rose, and stared himself in the great mirror self-critically. Lethargy had put weight on his belly and face before the war, but while he knew he could avoid the constraints of rationing with the best of them, his conscience didn't allow it, and as a result he had slimmed back down. His cheeks though, looked pale and gaunt. His eyes were lined, and small purple bags puffed under them. At 22, the young journalist had been baby-faced, leapfrogging older and wiser heads through a mixture of family connections and his own considerable talents of the quill, quietly resented by his peers. But at 27, he looked like man well into his thirties. Flecks of grey streaked his sleek hair.

He dressed, wearily donning his best, and only, three piece suit; an ostentatious combination of formal black morning coat, matching waistcoat fitted in the tighter, snug style that the Americans still favoured, and some cashmere striped trousers of charcoal grey; bought in a fit of youthful exuberance, with money from his first three wages when finally earning serious, adult pay at the paper, aged 23. Completing the ensemble was a grey tie and white dress shirt, black felt top hat, and a wrist watch that had been his father's. His mother appeared at the open bedroom door, rapping it lightly.

"Simon dear? There's a man here for you. It's time you went to your thing."

Her son, viewing his new appearance sombrely, turned to her. "It is," he agreed sombrely. "*Tempus fugit.*"

~

No equipment was necessary, the invite – or was it a summons – had said. Only his presence was required. Transport had been provided for; Simon surmised – correctly – that the German agency responsible for this (*whoever it is*, he wondered) had allocated the petrol and the cars. He rode in a large, sleek Bentley.

"Hello," Simon said loudly, projecting false confidence.

The man that drove him had ushered him into the back of the car silently, and ignored the subsequent greeting. His face was taut. Strong-jawed, sporting stubble, and large; the forbidding figure wore a Fedora and a long, double-breasted, belt-tied beige trench coat over a suit and tie, and had responded to neither "hello," nor "so, tonight should be fun..." and then finally "are you a sauerkraut, or real person?"

Eventually, Simon gave up trying to bait him. The man was as distant as the North Pole, and twice as cold. The man could probably freeze molten lava with his tongue.

On reaching the Savoy, he saw that both the perimeter around the hotel and a stretch along the riverside gardens path of the Strand down towards the Embankment were lined with all black figures holding sub-machine guns slung across their chests. *Awful*, he thought. *With Big Ben and Parliament a stone's throw down the river, in* sight. *Just down the Strand there at the Embankment Gardens is where Charles Dickens worked in a glue factory, as a boy. What would* he *think about the SS flanking the Thames?*

With quiet horror, Simon realised that his driver must be a Gestapo agent; at the very least, some kind of shadowy figure in the Himmler-Heydrich police system. The thought appalled him.

They pulled up at the river entrance next to the Embankment, and the silent agent purred away. As Simon peered out to the river, taking in his surroundings in the surreal atmosphere, a slow procession of Rolls Royces and Bentleys stopped in the same spot by the riverside entrance to disgorge passengers, all well-dressed in the extreme. They all filed in to the great hotel, where none other than Simon seemed to blanch at the sight of SS sentries lining corridors, motionless, standing sentinel outside the great suites. They all filed in twos and threes up to the River room. Simon took a spot by the windows, and stood gazing out to the black water, lit by Embankment street lamps. Minutes later, he was startled out of his reverie:

"I say, aren't you that young journalist fellow? You covered the races in '38?"

An old man with a particularly enormous moustache clad in a flamboyant three piece suit came up on him suddenly. There was no escape. Simon was forced to converse, that is, to share awkward small talk with the old gentleman and several of his acquaintances that joined them. One was a lord, one a business tycoon of some sort – he left it unsaid – another was a banker ("of some renown, wouldn't you know") and lastly, a man he didn't recognise that appeared to represent the BUF, with a similarly aristocratic air. *Oswald couldn't make it, or wasn't invited*, Simon thought darkly. He held his tongue with patience, which was made harder when the talk came around to the Germans.

"Well, I always said the Parliament would have its day. Democracy turned out to be a damp squib, what with all the problems facing Europe today. Look at Spain – by Jove, what a *dreadful* business. Thank heavens the little general crushed those communist swine. Burning churches, shooting priests; good heavens, would you *credit it*!"

"Unbelievable!"

"Quite."

"Well, fascism creates a stable and *strong* country, wouldn't you know, and of *course*, led by the people of its *blood*... none of the subversive *decadence* or *unstable* elements, strikes, crim*inality* and what have you. As long as people obey, the world works rather perfectly wouldn't you say?"

"Oh a new order in the world, for sure. Once the whole nasty business is tied up and hostilities are officially over..."

"I must say, *your lot* do seem to have the right i*dea*, those who took point in Italy and Germany... fascist countries *are* rather ideal to work with. They're a *damned* sound investment, wouldn't you know? Stable, *strong* economies..."

"I say, chaps," the journalist broke in, his body tensed. "Do tell me what your thoughts are when it comes to *life unworthy of life*?"

Silence, first in surprise and then tinged with disdain, and the pervasive negative energy of contempt.

"Yeah," the writer resumed, coldly. "Well, I've got to go *what thing there like yeah*..." and muttering incoherently, Simon continued to mumble gibberish as he extricated himself from the men who now stared daggers through him. He snorted, uncaring, and walked away before he felt inclined to attack one of them. Perhaps all of them.

Lighting a cigarette without asking permission – having noted that no one else smoked in the banqueting rooms – the journalist resumed his scenic spot by the window, sucking in cigarette smoke as would a prisoner on death row. Eyes tracing the London skyline, he hoped that tonight would not continue in such an excruciatingly painful manner. Several minutes later, a neat, unctuous little man with oily slicked-back hair called the waiting group into the Lancaster Ballroom. They filed in, in the same dribs and drabs to a table and chair arrangement facing the stage, behind which stood eight SS guards, framed by a huge banner lined with ornate swirls and somewhat obscenely decorated with the swastika and the Union Jack. It was a startling image; stark, a brutal visage. The seated men sat directly beneath it, adding an element of choreography to the grim charade. And as Simon was ushered towards one of the tables closest to the stage, the reason for the evening and everything surrounding it became apparent. Suddenly, the reason for all the security surrounding the Savoy was crystal clear. Sat in front of him was Reichsmarschall Hermann Göring.

A hot summer sun beat down on the Berghof, its light glinting off the polished exterior of the house that sat proudly overlooking Berchtesgaden on the Obersalzburg peaks of Bavaria. An orange ball lit up the surrounding green mountain slopes with brilliance, contrasting sharply against the clear blue of the endless sky, a medley of colours accompanied by a serenading by birdsong. Air so fresh it hurt the lungs swirled in a light breeze, and the smell of the summer grass was fresh and clean. It was a place of apotheosis; a high castle of fairytales from which all-powerful man could be an Olympian God.

The black Mercedes purred past the ranks of saluting *Reichsicherheitdienst* men, clad in SS grey, and rolled up the curving drive to the base of the stairs. There an honour guard met them. The organisation of police and internment across a cowed Europe was known as 'The Black Angels', and present on the mountaintop of Gods were the two blackest angels of them all.

Heinrich Himmler and Reinhard Heydrich strode up the steps, past two saluting guards at its base.

"Back at the Eagle's Nest, Reichsführer," Heydrich purred quietly, as they marched up the steps. He was looking out to the great ravine past the Berghof plot. "Do you think the Führer loves the beautiful nature, or is more fascinated with the great abysses?"

Himmler glanced at his nominal subordinate, unsure of his intent. His suspicions were confirmed by the slightly mocking smile playing at Heydrich's pinched lips. He could never tell when the SS-General, Security Police and SD chief was being sardonic – even about the Führer. He brushed the thoughts aside. They were at the Führer's *own residence*.

"I'd imagine the Führer is fascinated by the whole landscape, my dear Heydrich."

The security chief suppressed a snort. He knew from detailed reports, and a chance remark from Reichsmarschall Göring that the Führer didn't give a damn for dreamily contemplating the beauty of the snow-capped peaks. He stared only into the future, and gazed fatalistically up at the mountaintops or down the abysses; symbolic of the earthly struggle by which he saw life, and shaped his own worldviews and thus, that of the German people whole. *A great Darwinian struggle for survival.* Heydrich had watched him on their Obersalzburg visit the previous year, before the outbreak of war with Poland. He had engaged in discussions of suppressing the Polish intelligentsia, and poring over maps and death lists on the terrace. But the old man, who pored over the plans for Speer's architectural monstrosities with such rapture, had not so much as glanced at the view.

They reached the top of the steps, greeted by more saluting guards on the terrace, and along with Himmler's adjutant Joachim Peiper, the SS and police leaders were ushered in through the threshold and arched gallery beyond it, over marbled floor lined with expensive rugs, and into the Great Room.

There, framed against the huge glass window and the mountain scenery of the Obersalzburg stood Adolf Hitler, the Führer of the Greater German Reich. Conqueror of Poland, Czechoslovakia, Scandinavia, and all of Western Europe, basking in triumph over France. He wore a field grey jacket, with his Iron Cross 2nd class dangling from the left breast pocket. Hands clasped in front of him, flanked by his Deputy-Führer on one side and their ever-present subordinate on the other, he looked for all the world like the godhead he strove to be.

Himmler and Heydrich stood to attention, and clicked their heels. Their right arms shot out.

185

"*Heil!*"

Hitler raised his own right arm, straight up at the shoulder. The stern features softened, and allowed for a small grin.

"Heil, Reichsführer, my dear Himmler, and Gruppenführer Heydrich, the man of iron."

The two SS men approached their leader, flanked by the dark-browed figure of his Deputy-Führer, Hess, and the leader of the Party Chancellery under Hess, Martin Bormann, a fleshier figure with an unprepossessing face. Both were brown Party jackets, marked with the swastika armband. Hitler shook hands with the visitors, each in turn, before they saluted the two high Party officials. Heydrich gave Bormann a knowing, wry smile, curling across his cruel lips in naked amusement, which the Reichsleiter observed coolly without deigning to pass comment.

Hitler acknowledged Himmler's adjutant, a soldier familiar to him, who was stood to attention further back.

"Hauptstürmführer Peiper, greetings to you. I trust you are well?" The celebrated Waffen-SS officer clicked his heels again, saluted for the second time and gave a short bow.

"Mein Führer, I did my part for the Fatherland, and am on top of the world," Peiper solemnly declared. Himmler and Hess nodded approvingly. Bormann glanced at Heydrich's own newly decorated tunic, bedecked with honours.

Heydrich imagined the Führer sat here in this room for hours, or stood framed by the great marble fireplace and great paintings; a bust of early party ideologue Dietrich Eckhart present; Frederick the Great gazing down on the Führer as he delivered lengthy monologues to an eager Hess and Bormann under the crystal chandelier. Or perhaps stood gazing out of the window, in contemplation of history and destiny. How *greatly* Himmler must *wish* he could spend more time up here, he mused. How badly Goebbels must miss his permanent place by the fireside; still publicly the third or fourth highest ranking Party official and Reich Minister, yet within the inner sanctum, still languishing in semi-disgrace with the Führer after the Baarova affair and his handling of Kristallnacht. Such *envy*, mused Heydrich. How the ever-present Bormann was part of the furniture while his nominal chief Hess was now irrelevant to the man he deputised; legally third in command! And countless others, all vying for their spot with the Führer. *Little Führer's* of their personal realms, the kings of their own inner circles of fawning sycophants, but while longing to be honoured with a seat at the table, to listen to the Führer's monologues and gain favour.

The thought amused Heydrich.

After exchanging pleasantries, Hitler suggested his visitors join him on the terrace outside, to take advantage of a fine day. Himmler eagerly agreed. Heydrich wondered what it was that Hitler wanted to say to them in private, presumably away from the ears of Hess. It was a surprise to see the Deputy-Führer there; Bormann, his Chief of Staff and de facto deputy-head of the Party, had suggested that Hess spent comparatively little time at the Führer's side now, unlike he, who owned one of the few residences on the Obersalzburg complex – under the 'Eagle's Nest' proper and overlooking the Berghof itself – in addition to becoming the Führer's personal secretary.

During his declaration of war, September 1ˢᵗ of the prior year, Hess had been named the successor and leader of the Reich in the event that both Hitler and Göring fell. The third man, above even Goebbels, whose political redemption was not yet secure on the outbreak of war. Yet Heydrich knew that not only had Bormann replaced Hess in importance, the Deputy-Führer was no longer even welcome to dine with the Führer at the Reich Chancellery in Berlin, having irritated him with several new bizarre eccentricities.

One by one, would the dominos fall, Heydrich knew. Just as the former paladins had, the current crop would fall, with the inevitability afforded by stratagem. *Strasser, Röhm... Goebbels, Hess. And later, Bormann, Himmler, Göring. Even the old man, when the time is right.*

The Führer led them outdoors, blinking in the sunlight, and the three men strolled to the terrace and its parapet on the edge. Birds shrieking only quietly intruded on their moment. The Führer looked out to the mountains; downwards, Heydrich noted wryly. He gazed into the abyss. In the distance, over the tops of great pine trees, Hitler's native Austria could be seen, as a green triangle framed by snow-capped mountain peaks under the clear blue of a glorious day.

"I trust you travelled well, my dear Himmler?" Hitler asked.

Himmler's usual prim disposition had collapsed into eager ingratiation.

"Yes, mein Führer. Isn't all travel free and light in these glorious times?"

Oh God, Heydrich thought, fixing a warm smile on his wan face to mask the contempt that threatened to overcome him.

"Your view is as beautiful as ever, mein Führer," he intoned smoothly. "I remarked to the Reichsführer that it was fitting to imagine the Führer of the Greater Reich gazing out to the great mountaintops, planning the reawakening and conquest of a Great Germany. It's very majestic... very German."

Hitler surveyed him, sternly.

"You have performed well yourself, Herr Gruppenführer. I see beyond your role in the Security of the Fatherland, you have earned an Iron Cross for active service."

He pointed at the Iron Cross that adorned Heydrich's own field grey SS tunic, with a handful of other assorted decorations including medals for service in Danzig, the Sudetenland and during *Anschluss*. The Iron Cross, though, held pride of place. It was attained by the display of heroism and clear bravery in active military service. Heydrich's was an Iron Cross, Second Class. It matched Hitler's own.

"I merely did what I felt was my duty, mein Führer," Heydrich replied smoothly. "As a General of the SS, chief of the SD, leader of the criminal and political police forces, I have to lead by example. To represent the ideals of the Schutzstaffel elite and all that the Reich and National Socialism stand for."

The Führer nodded intensely, and clapped him on the shoulder, just once. "You are an exemplary officer of the Fatherland. A fearsome opponent of our enemies..."

His voice trailed off, and he stood and once more gazed outwards to the Obersalzburg vista. Heydrich noted that his narrowed eyes were filmed with thought; he looked out unseeingly, not in appreciation, but in his own mind. He lived in the imagination.

"As beautiful as ever, mein Führer," Himmler said, standing beside Hitler at the parapet and gazing out. Heydrich sensed he felt threatened. Usually, *Uncle Heini stands as a barrier between myself and the old man*, he thought. But now things will change.

"It is indeed beautiful, my dear Heinrich. Indeed it is. It is a great shame your noble work for the Fatherland prevents you from joining the others in residence here, somewhere nearby. I could speak to Reichsleiter Bormann? Perhaps, when our war is truly won you can retire out here with the children. Bavaria is in your heart."

Bavarian sentimentality now, Heydrich thought darkly.

Himmler beamed, almost clicking his heels. "That would be wonderful! Of course, when the time is right, and the Order is ready to be passed on to the next generation. Speaking of which, how is the Reichsmarschall? Is Herr Göring here in Obersalzburg yet?"

"No, the Reichsmarschall is still on his diplomatic mission to England, after which he will return to Karinhall for a short but well-deserved break from political and military matters," Hitler answered.

"Indeed, I have seen first-hand the results of his Air Force," Himmler smiled, a little falsely. As he did so, Heydrich met his eyes with his own proud smile, and Himmler's faded. Heydrich had been part of that very air force.

But Hitler had plaudits, too, for his high priest.

"You were well received in the Low Countries, is that not so, Herr Reichsführer?"

"Yes," Himmler answered readily. "Holland in particular, as we expected, the racial quality is remarkably high. I joined with the Waffen-SS *Germania* as we advanced through the Low Countries. I personally took the surrender of a

Flemish town near Antwerp called Rumst, with Herr Peiper and Gruppenführer Wolff. No resistance to be spoken of, and in the Netherlands in particular we were treated graciously, and met many ardent believers in National Socialism. They are a fine addition to Germany."

Himmler switched his reverent gaze from his Führer to the mountain vista once more, and as an afterthought, added: "I was surprised by the lack of resistance. We simply rolled through. Attacks were extremely limited."

That's because it was an empty rigmarole, Heydrich thought, greatly irritated by the blatant pandering. *You weren't in France, near the frontlines. It was a shoring up exercise to bolster rear-lines and your non-existent credentials, with the real battles elsewhere and the war already won.*

The Führer, however, seemed satisfied.

"Good, good... knowing you as I do, Reichsführer, I imagine in the weeks and months that have passed since, the wheels were long set in motion for an SS-Netherlands legion in the event of our great showdown in the East?"

"Yes, mein Führer. And the French, for whom fascism represents national liberation. An embryonic SS-Charlemagne division promises much."

"Good, good. Excellent work."

"Mein Führer, what are we to do with England?"

At this, Hitler turned, and beckoned they follow him. Leading back into the now deserted Great Room, the SS leaders took seats by the marble fireplace, while the Führer remained standing.

"Ah, yes... England. A disappointing affair, it must be said. With a hopeless, quite hopeless military position, I'd hoped the inevitable removal of Churchill would lead to a quick and proper armistice. The Aryan bankers and industrialists wanted it. The ruling classes wanted it. King Edward wanted it. Aristocrats wanted it. *No one but Jews* wants war between Saxon peoples! No one but the Jews! Even with the remarkable work of Herr Heydrich here... utterly ruthless, a great example of the true use of power as an instrument of national strength!" Hitler cried, losing his train of thought as his deep-rooted approval of pitiless initiative politically applied overwhelmed him.

Heydrich smiled at the praise. Himmler waited, impassively. Hitler collected his thoughts, and continued. "As it was, the British, *absurd* people, *still* hesitated to see sense and come to terms, that criminal clique in Whitehall. We had to launch the invasion while we could, as soon as we could, with them in disarray, only for them to offer peace after all, depose the lunatic fringe and stand down the ludicrous, criminal orders Churchill gave for the island's defence. And the result? Neither full blown *war* nor a truly honourable *peace*. Neither a stable occupation, nor a protectorate-state, operable without German military presence. We are trapped in the uncertainty between war and peace; a compliant government and an unruly populace. It needs to end. We need *stability*."

Heydrich sensed he was stirring himself up to rage; a ranting diatribe against the Jewish infestation of Downing Street and Whitehall. But then the Führer unclenched his irritable hands, relaxed his posture, and then lowered himself gently into one of the armchairs.

Himmler leaned forwards in anticipation. Heydrich couldn't help but anticipate the Reichsführer's disquiet, which was surely coming any moment now.

"I discussed this at length with the party. Herr Bormann was very clear and forthright with his views."

I'll bet he was, thought Heydrich.

"The Reichsmarschall agreed wholeheartedly with the idea."

Undoubtedly so, agreed Heydrich, silently.

"I need you, Heydrich."

Himmler's pale, hamster-like face dropped, his jowls bunching momentarily though the Reichsführer-SS quickly recovered. The cool Heydrich held the Führer's gaze, masking the intense thrill of the moment. Hitler, holding the gaze of his 'Hangman' was nodding to himself, his pale blue eyes fixed intensely on those equally icy globes of blue set closely together on the equally pallid, hard, severe face of his most feared paladin.

"Peace with the British Empire is vital," he continued. "Capturing their army en masse led to political confusion and the overthrow of the warmongering criminals, which allowed for Operation Sealion's success. Even so, dealing with their Navy alone almost cost us, let alone the disaster had the troops we did been stranded with no reinforcements or supplies! Four countries against one – an island in disarray less – and we still got lucky. It's clear that aircraft production would have continued in defiance of any armistice – weeks later and even the Luftwaffe may have struggled. We are not infallible, my Reichsführer, and Reichsicherheitsleiter. Armed resistance in England, even if it is partisan, ragged and doomed to fail, will be costly, economically and politically. We need stability, and peace, to establish the New Order."

Himmler was silent. His usual attentiveness was heightened, if possible, by the as-yet unspecified news that his SS subordinate was integral to the Führer's plans. Heydrich for his part noted the catch-all title the Führer had used for him as he glanced from Himmler, "Reich Security Leader." Had the old man slipped that in to bait Himmler, perhaps to stoke rivalry? Musing on the odd handle, Heydrich briefly considered its use with his lengthier ranks and positions. It was fair game now, of course. *Führerprinzip*.

"Herr Heydrich, as the Reichsführer reported to me in detail, you already implemented a Security Police system in place operating behind the Wehrmacht's frontlines of resistance pockets, for clandestine special actions in the cities and townships."

Heydrich's answer was readily available and detailed, as was customary.

"Yes my Führer. Einsatzgruppen were set in place under SD-Brigadeführer Dr Six of the Reich Security Main Office, for unleashing at the moment of choosing. SD overseers were appointed, and Gruppenführer Nebe was drafted there due to his enormous policing experience, in a senior role. Meanwhile Dr Six took control of the major police forces in the occupied zones on behalf of the Reich Security Police and SD, and the transitional period was quite smooth."

Heydrich enjoyed declaring Six an 'SD Brigadier-General', of 'his' security office. He could sense Himmler's discomfort growing with the irrepressible confidence of his powerful junior in the presence of the old man himself. And Nebe? He was the Kriminalpolizei chief, appointed by Himmler. Heydrich had attached him to *Einsatzgruppen Britain* as a Gruppe commander, subordinate to a doctor of lesser rank, a Brigadier of the SD.

The Blond Beast felt his infallibility increase, swelling powerfully in the presence of Hitler and Himmler and fighting hard to prevent his body betraying the force of his pride.

"Some of the Special Arrests List have been completed, quietly," Heydrich reported. "Others identified as being known subversive elements have gone underground; others still, such as Lord Halifax were seen as vital in the capitulation and integration process, and as such were allowed to remain in an operational capacity, under close observation. But all in all, the focus remained on smashing the resistance movement across towns, villages and rural areas stretching all the way north to the Scottish cities. In the towns and cities themselves, the majority of the people are resigned to the new order. The army continues to hunt the remaining pockets of bandits and their special hideaways. Cleared from settlements and aid, they will not survive into winter."

"They should not have survived this far!" Hitler screamed.

The piercing shriek echoed slightly through the great, high-ceilinged halls of the house. Then the leader calmed himself, and his fists unclenched.

"Of course, you have done as excellent a job as ever, Heydrich. But I need you there in person. I have lost what little faith I had with the military commander. They are not the bearers of the National Socialist political will. Bormann and Reichsmarschall Göring agree, that Reinhard Heydrich as *Reichsprotektor of Great Britain* is the best means to achieve the complete pacification of our enemies while maintaining the profitability of our coming arrangements and total efficiency, with no untoward disruptions to that isle."

Heydrich had expected it – even putting the term 'Protector' in Bormann's mouth, although Britain was not a Protectorate, nor an Axis partner, an occupied

Commissariat or Gau – post-armistice, it simply remained a prickly thorn in Germany's side; huge swathes of land occupied, including the main southern chunk, while sections of the populace continued to refuse the new order. But even in knowing what would come from the Berghof meeting, Heydrich still revelled in hearing the Führer bestow more power on him, delighting in his spoken word. Basking in the hated language of bureaucracy, and political jargon of the Reich.

Himmler again had to recover; after all, his chief SS deputy had just officially been granted administrative jurisdiction over a nation; a great nation, no less. "That is a most brilliant idea, Führer. General Heydrich is best placed to perform this vital task for the Fatherland. But the disruption to –"

"Oh, nonsense," Hitler cried, waving him away with a dismissive, impulsive jerk. "The Security Main Office has nominal chiefs of each department. Herr Heydrich's bureaucratic excellence means that the proper delegations will ensure minimal disruption. And you are still present in Berlin as Chief of SS and Police."

That mollified him somewhat. Heydrich had consolidated the criminal and political police forces, Kripo and Gestapo, and married them to his SD intelligence service, seizing the position of INTERPOL President just some weeks prior and merging it all into the Reich Security Main Office. But Himmler remained SS chief and overlord. The unified German police as a whole came under the office of the Reichsführer-SS.

Hitler eyed them keenly, trying to ascertain if there was a change in their dynamic. He loved to stir rivalry between his lieutenants. It was the irrefutable law of Darwinism; the strong shall survive. It was the perfect metaphor for the new Germany.

But, he needed Himmler. The man was too capable an administrator, too loyal to leave by the wayside to be cannibalised by his iron-hearted subordinate. However brilliant he was. However cunning; the most dangerous enemy of the Reich's enemies.

"Herr Reichsführer," Hitler began, smoothly, "I know your plans to establish a *Britisches Freikorps* with Heydrich's hostage army were underway as soon as the SS were granted custody, yes?"

"Yes, my Führer. There were considerable difficulties with the Wehrmacht, until Field Marshal Keitel stepped in to acquiesce to Waffen-SS jurisdiction on this matter."

The Führer nodded, and the glint returned to his manic eyes. Even Heydrich found it difficult to not stare into the depths of his mania, and the suppressed rage of his hypnotic power.

"Now Himmler, let me outline the importance of this," Hitler leaned in, his voice taking on a steely edge, as it always did as he lived in the future. "SS actions in Britain will help determine the face of the New Order in the World. Upon it could rest the very fate of our world struggle, with Russia and the Americans to consider. *There are only two possibilities*; the triumph of the German Reich, or the complete subjugation and annihilation of its people! The SS *must become* the *driving force* of this vision, as we shape the world to our ends and become masters of our time, to ensure the *mastery of our future race*. You must ensure Britain is culturally cleansed, and set to establishing the correct system of integration and cultural harmony between our peoples. To achieve it...," and the Führer's intense monologue resumed its conversational tone, "... you will go to England yourself with Heydrich. You can direct the *Ahnernerbe* personally, ensuring that this historic task is completed on behalf of our cultural integrity. Go with Heydrich. You are commanders of the most valuable mission of the Greater Reich. The two tasks are one and the same. They are intertwined. For cultural purity we must have security, and we need security to ensure cultural purity."

Himmler and Heydrich both nodded. Evidently, Heydrich realised, he wasn't entirely free of the Reichsführer's protective arm around his shoulders. The usual idiocy that would ensue; no doubt the Reichsführer would commission some archaeological digs and make vapid noise about cultural matters; SS authority would be alluded to in political language, and the office of Reichsprotektor would require a boost. Himmler would not stop there. More digs, with an obedient press nearby. There would be some tedious public spouting about the discovery of ancient links between the Teutonic peoples and the pre-and-post Roman English; a bunch of old Saxon and Viking history dredged up. Even *Hitler* mocked such Teutonic lunacy, he knew from Göring, whom Speer had told. Thus, the Reichsführer would *ensure the mastery of our race* in England.

Meanwhile he, Heydrich, Reichsprotektor, would suppress all subversive elements and simultaneously keep the population sweet. The real work would fall to him, as ever; *The Dustbin and Handmaid of the Third Reich*. At least, finally, he was now being granted the power by official decree. His value was acknowledged. Heydrich was now a Minister.

"What of my work here in Germany?" Himmler asked the Führer, whose back was turned to them, gazing out of the window. Once more, Hitler waved his hand impatiently.

"The Großbritannien question must be solved. You have delegated considerable work to capable administrators. The Reich is stable."

Hitler returned to his two paladins, and began pacing in front of the marble fireplace. Himmler sprang to his feet, but the Führer waved him back down. Heydrich was reclined, at ease. Hitler continued his speech. "Popular opinion for the government has never been higher. All we ever had to do was take France and reattach East Prussia. Even the workers' districts have renounced the Kozis. Taking Paris avenged the memory of Versailles. Our position is secured, *forever*. In the here and now, working towards the racial and political reliability of a National Socialist Britain is of paramount importance, and this is my unalterable will. You are the Reichsführer-SS. No Wehrmacht general has any power over you, to impede you in your great and historic task for the Reich."

The SS leader bowed his head. "It is a great honour, mein Führer."

Hitler gazed beyond them, again, his eyes misty and unseeing. "We need England, my *Reichsicherheitsführers*. Controlling Europe with a British Empire amenable to German goals gives us a foothold in every corner of the globe. Frederick the Great could only have dreamed of this triumph. We have succeeded where the Spanish Empire failed... where Napoleon and the French failed! We took on the English, and won; our troops patrol British soil. But," the Führer lowered his tone, and began pacing:

"... It is unnecessarily bleeding the Reich; intolerable to waste time and blood on Saxon brothers with the real ideological and racial enemy to our east. Why fight the British when need an *alliance* with this strong empire, by pacifying their volatile island? We need the resources and support of this white European power in our noble struggle against the freemasonry of Jewish-Bolshevik world tyranny! There are *only two possibilities*; we succeed, or we fail, and if we fail in this task then the Fatherland and Reich face complete and total annihilation by the Bolshevik menace..."

There was a brief silence following the Führer's pronouncements that the SS men felt was appropriate to the profundity of his statements, and the seriousness of the Reich's predicament.

Heydrich waited until Himmler shifted in his seat, showing signs of preparing to speak, before he found his own voice. "My Führer, just to clarify with regards to operational policy; is the decision to attack the Bolsheviks unchanged, and set in stone?"

With the Blond Beast's interjection, Himmler's own question died on his lips, and Heydrich sensed his punitive master's irritation rising. There was a tension in his poise and movements. Hitler, on the other hand, was shaken from his reverie, and fixed unwavering eyes once more on the tall, pale 'Hangman' that commanded his police.

"It is our sacred duty for Germany and the thousand-year Reich. The Judeo-Slavic untermenschen and their poisonous freemasonry, the insidious weakening of culture, the seizing of institutions, the subversion of economy – the WARS they cause, the violations of our German blood – the *untermenschen* are our mortal enemy, and nowhere is this more apparent than England!"

He was almost frothing at the mouth, his calm tones having risen to the trademark yell of a Nuremberg rally speech. Himmler was mesmerised. Heydrich, utterly immune, wondered why the Führer bothered when there were only he and the Reichsführer-SS present. But Hitler continued ad nauseum, nonetheless.

"England has been slower than the French to embrace the Reich's work in its struggle against world Jewry, but they will come to join forces with us, in time. Before democracy softened them, they were revolutionaries in the field – England expelled the tribe in 1290! Look at their greatest writers; from Shakespeare, with *Shylock the Jew*, and Dickens, with *Fagin the Jew*; Marlowe – if indeed an entirely different playwright to the former – with *Barabas The Jew*, and Chaucer's Jewish rabble; England's greatest artists and literary minds have always known what Germany's Wagner's and Luther's and Hohenzollern's have known and warned; the Jew is a vile corrupter of the nation!"

The Führer took a deep breath, which Heydrich suspected was theatrical. Nevertheless, he drank in the Führer's every word, as ever. It was useful to do so. Himmler, for his part, sat rapt.

"England's creative minds are a model..." Hitler said, thoughtfully. "These men; Shakespeare, Marlowe, Dickens... they are Saxon men of sentiment and creativity, like Goethe. They understood that the Jew is a microbe of decomposition... capable only of analytical thought, incapable of true creativity..." he paced, slightly, while Himmler gazed at him, as completely spellbound as ever.

Heydrich, however was deeply amused, and listened in high good humour. The old man was a failed artist, a bum living rough in Vienna before the Great War. No doubt some *analytical* Jews had rejected the Führer's *creative* artwork at some point.

Hitler shook his head sadly. "England is a great model – THE great model – and as such, was targeted and poisoned by the Jews. Nowhere else in the great nations is the Jewish menace more profoundly seen and felt as in Whitehall. Parliament – what a system! The dignity with which the Lower House fulfilled its task for the people... could a people have a more exalted form of government than this classical democracy? It showed the Austrian parliament as the unGermanic embarrassment that it was! Polluted by Slavs, a bastard mongrel of languages and peoples; a *total* failure that was utterly unworthy of the great example of England."

Hitler paused again for effect. It *was* a speech, Heydrich thought. *The old man's table talk, government meetings, party rallies, probably his bedtime chat with the little laughing blonde bitch – all just a big fucking monologue.*

Yet contained within was the direction of Europe's future, Heydrich knew, and much like his dissection of Werner Best's intellectual ideas and leanings during Best's time deputising for Heydrich in the SD, he knew it was practical to absorb the Führer's words.

"This model must continue," Hitler pronounced, "... But first, with people whose synergies to the new order reflect ours, as opposed to an embarrassing rabble led by the anti-fascist, Anglo-American Zionist clique of Churchillian warmongers. Moseley and his fascists are less agreeable than you might think. Sir Samuel Hoare, Lord Halifax and the old king are much more promising with regards to a strong junta of Heads of Government and State."

"Halifax was identified on the *Sonderfahndungsliste G.B*," Heydrich interjected quietly.

That was the Special Arrests List he'd commissioned SD-Major Schellenberg to compile for Great Britain. Most of those listed were prominent politicians, writers, intellectuals, homosexuals and Jews. Heydrich had personally added Aldous Huxley and George Orwell to the list, though he suspected the former was in California. He included Putzi Hanfstaengl; purely as a sop to the Führer, who no doubt would love to be reunited with his old friend who had defected in 1937 after falling victim to a Goebbels practical joke.

Hitler nodded, calculating. "I understand, Heydrich. Halifax beat the drum of war. A time of reckoning will come for this paladin of the Chamberlain-Churchill regimes. For now, it is expedient to use the man who offered armistice. We must *adapt*, to *advance*. The world is changing, and we must impose our new order before fate turns its hand against the Reich," Hitler declared, stepping out toward the great window and the mountains beyond. "Japan is reconquering Asia, an *honorary Aryan* people, though completely without any creativity of their own. Yes, Japan..."

The Führer faced down Himmler and Heydrich, in stern solemnity.

"There are two possibilities. When their war escalates, and they suffer from sanctions, faced with economic hardships, they will be forced to take on the Slavs, or America in the Pacific. This is unavoidable. It is in the Reich's favour that when they attack, that it is to the north and west. If Stalin has to fight Japan's armies in Siberia, it leaves fewer men to defend European Russia and the heart of the Jewish-Bolshevik beast."

The SS men murmured assent.

"I have arranged for you, my dear Himmler and Gruppenführer... *Reichsprotektor* Heydrich, to be flown to one of our bases there. You will enter London as conquerors."

Heydrich was delighted. This was more than he could have asked for. To enter in triumph like a warrior Viceroy of Alexander the Great, the perfect way to cap his personal power coup.

The Führer concluded his invective; hands clenching, pointing and gesticulating as was customary in his speeches to thousands. "With regards to Russia, Japan and America, we need to be in a position of overwhelming power, backed by an ally of overwhelming reach. England's air force, navy and the strategic positions of its empire will ensure that none, not even the Jews in Washington will stand before the Reich. Only then can we ensure that the Aryan civilisation remains the dominant power in the world. You must find the political and racial undesirables, my chiefs, and remove them as combatants in the war against our civilisation. Do that, and a Greater German Reich and the Aryan World Empire will last for a thousand, *thousand* years!"

Heydrich leapt to his feet, seizing the chance, followed closely by the Reichsführer-SS, anxious not to be outdone by the man he'd first brought into the SS only nine years ago. Together, they now de facto ruled a police empire from the Soviet border to the south of Spain, and back up to the northern tip of Scandinavia spanning northwest to Glasgow. Under the Führer, they ruled a European empire without parallel, with absolute power of life and death over its peoples. Heydrich smiled. *Godlike.*

"To the thousand year Reich!" three giant men of fate cried in unison.

London was yet to stir from its gloomy occupied slump, as the missing men of the resistance, prisoners of war and the conscripted factory workers – soon dubbed 'The Pyramid Builders' by the British public – cast a huge shadow over the post-war recovery.

Morale was flagging. Everybody knew somebody, or knew someone who knew a person that had broken down. The two variants of this were a sort of hysterical, shrieking grief through loss or the enforced separation from a loved one abroad, often resulting in total emotional breakdown, or equally bad; outright attacks made on Germans in a fit of full-blown diminished capacity, all thought of consequence and self-preservation flung to the wind. This one was ugly; there was no salvation for such fated men. In several Suffolk villages along the east coast, such incidents led to a mass-execution one bitterly cold day early into the occupation; assorted men, alternately wild-eyed with anguish or quietly defiant, were lined up in village greens, to coincide with the shooting of forty saboteurs in Ipswich, at Alexandra Park. At precisely eleven o'clock, watched by silent, still crowds, sombre Wehrmacht troops opened fire, and a combined ninety-four British civilians fell dead in 'Suffolk's Black Day'.

~

In the Far East, Japan was doing some significant sabre-rattling, and the eyes of the world had turned to the Land of the Rising Sun. Even with most of China still unconquered and vast armies opposing them, Japan's trade agreements with the west were disintegrating, and the noises coming from Tokyo were of aggression and war. The political spectrum of the Rome-Berlin-Tokyo Axis had immediately changed, even as the pact was finalised; the seizure of London, with its key areas in Africa, the Middle East and most crucially of all, in East Asia, meant that what constituted Japan's 'sphere of influence' was now in question. The British Empire abroad continued to function. Some even claimed that the forces there – regardless of what Berlin demanded – would continue to hold out, brush off 'the little yellow men' and 'push them back into the sea'. If Japan had reacted to this provocation, if indeed it were true, then none in Britain had yet heard of it. Outwardly, Germany made positive noises about the three-way pact that Japan had signed to formally join the Rome-Berlin axis. But it mattered little. The Far East was a powder keg, waiting to explode.

"Tokyo is feeling threatened," Arthur Speakman murmured to Jack as he collected pints for himself and the Scot. His caution, as Jack saw it, was quite pointless; the Royal Oak was entirely empty, save for old Bill Wilson in the public room, sat hunched in his usual state of torpor, reeking, and rendered senseless from hours of ale.

"What do you reckon, old boy?" Jack asked him.

The old publican shrugged.

"I don't know. They attack Malaya for the port of Singapore, risk losing to our lot and having the Americans jump in, on top of pissing Hitler off. If they go for the Philippines, which they'd need to if they took any more of the mainland, the yanks would be forced to have to with 'em. Or... they ally for an attack on Russia which leaves Hitler with Moscow and an empire stretching from west Wales to the Urals, and Japan with the world's largest snowfield... and direct control of the largest collection of forced labour camps on the planet."

Jack grinned. "Decisions, decisions. Mainland Asia held by demoralised Brits and looking juicy, or Siberia. All those slaves with frostbite."

He chuckled lowly, but the joke rang hollow for a man who had once believed in socialism, and pledged his loyalty to the CPGB. The thought of old POUM comrades toiling in a godforsaken Siberian death trap in the wilderness, frozen, hauling logs of wood under the whip of some vodka-soaked Russian tyrant in minus-thirty conditions was almost too much to bear.

"What do you think, young fellow?" Arthur asked him.

"... I think... Japan doesn't care much what anyone thinks."

"And?"

Jack considered. "Well... depends what old Adolf offers. If in return for invading East Russia, they get some army or SS help heading down into Chiang Kai-Shek's western stronghold in China, then Tokyo already intends to join Jerry. Japan is as good as there already. If not, the US Pacific fleet had better watch out, and so had our lot in the territories..."

Arthur nodded, to which Jack threw up his hands in exasperation.

"But who knows what all these godlike maniacs are up to, behind closed doors?"

He picked the brace of beers up, and started off towards the far booth, where William waited for him.

"At least we live in interesting times, Jack," Arthur called to his retreating back.

"Yeah. We live in interesting times."

~

London, outwardly disconsolate, was filled with the buzz of murmured conversations; behind closed doors; those with dampened spirits were awakened by the possibility of real developments in an outer world that they suddenly remembered with interest. Covent Garden's pubs were awash with Gestapo spies and informants, it was now widely known – the area's location in the heart of central London in close proximity to Soho, Trafalgar Square and the very heart of government in Whitehall made it inevitable. Many knew, and older hands adopted a policy of avoiding pubs from which the Embankment and Westminster Bridge could be reached on foot in ten minutes. But, the network of Heydrich's pet spider Dr Six was proving most adept at spinning its webs; ensuring the news Berlin could or would not officially endorse would be cast far and wide, if it served their interests. From Covent Garden, across Soho, up north to Bloomsbury and Camden and beyond; in lieu of acknowledging the grim realities of what had happened – what *was happening* – in Britain, interest in the wider sphere of political tension suddenly exploded, and gossip spread like wildfire. Cartoonists got back to work – their fear of retribution having passed – and the satirical serials and newspaper cartoon strips were back in circulation.

With the swirling rumour mill, fires stoked by spies, they certainly had ample material.

The Soviet seizure of Lithuania as France fell, despite the Baltic state's acceptance of the harsh terms dictated by Moscow had sent Hitler and Göring into apoplectic rage. Still, they restrained Goebbels, and quietly, smilingly accepted the pokerfaced Molotov's rebuttals of the official complaints. Now with the heart of the British Empire in Hitler's hands, and an increasingly belligerent Japan to their eastern border, Berlin knew that Moscow would be deeply regretting their 'cynical Bolshevik imperialist aggressions.' Stalin's pact with Hitler was beginning to look like a piece of paper as worthless as Chamberlain's Munich Agreement had been.

Fascism was the ascendant force, having swept across five of Europe's great nations; four of which were aggressive. A continental 'Rome-Berlin-Madrid-Paris' axis was the latest pun from the cynics. All were hostile, even the late convert who only months before had fought *against* Germany. Vichy France, smarting over Britain's intention to scuttle their fleet and all-too-quick to embrace any prevailing anti-Semitic sentiment, gladly bade au revoir to a 'decadent, Jew-run decade of decline', and promptly built up a huge force of Nazi auxiliaries, the 'French Legion of Volunteers' whose stated goal was to oppose Bolshevism; colloquially they were immediately christened the *SS-Charlemagne* division. Franco was growling about the return of Spain's gold, half a billion dollars' worth of which the 'godless Judeo-masonic dogs and hypocrites' at the helm of the Republic had sent to Moscow for safekeeping three years prior. Italy and Romania, too, had their hackles raised and fangs bared at Stalin. Goebbels deviated from official policy, sneeringly calling the dictator "a rabbit mesmerised by the fascist snakes". Göring, it was said, playing on his famous 'I decide who is a Jew!' pronouncement, supposedly proclaimed to a packed Carinhall that Stalin was to be held as a Jew when Moscow crumbled. Soviet Russia was beginning to look vulnerable.

William Joyce a.k.a Lord Haw Haw's Radio Berlin broadcast, which had eclipsed the BBC's in popularity, had taken to casually listing various Soviet incidents in the Baltics and referring in glowing terms to the Japanese struggles in China where the densely populated east coast and thus, most of China's major cities were completely subdued and under the tender care of the Imperial Japanese Army. Reichsmarschall Göring, it was relayed, praised the 'tenacious' Japanese;

his usual jollity deserting him and Hitler's 'Iron Man' of old resurfacing in his naked brutality. He even quoted *Mein Kampf* in his speech, shared with relish for English ears by Joyce, directed at the American condemnation of, and sanctions against Hirohito's Empire:

'The world Jewish press and insubordinate saboteurs that infest global politics are conspiring to turn their host nations against the great yellow Asiatic Empire, whose civilisation combined with that of the Aryans to become the undisputed *herrenvolk* of the Far East!"

By now, with the majority of British eyebrows shooting upwards with as much cynicism as can possibly be expressed by the human face, Göring's vitriolic paraphrasing of the only man in Europe who outranked him either politically or militarily reached its antagonistic conclusion: "... in thousands of years of adaptation, the Jew has tried to turn the great nations of Europe into raceless bastards, but knows he cannot in the East with no bridge to the Asiatic... and now, the Jewish world menace seeks a war of annihilation with Japan in the East, as it tried and failed to with the Reich in the West!"

Goebbels, too, pitched in – never one to miss the opportunity to take centre stage and agitate – with a series of truly hysterical articles in the *Völkischer Beobachter,* a televised rant in the Reich, and a radio broadcast that invoked everything from Horst Wessel – a dead Nazi pimp-turned-martyr, it was said – The November Criminals and Walther Rathenau to Downing Street, American politics, the Rothschild banking family and references to 'millions of Christians brutally butchered in the east.' He railed over the airwaves for twenty minutes, and it was later translated into English in full by 'Haw Haw' Joyce – the *Mahatma Propagandhi* fully upstaging Göring in the process. The little doctor promised a swift and brutal vengeance on the Jewish warmongers, and that

Germany and Japan stood allied together against international Jewry, ready to defend their spheres of influence and each willing to assist their great ally in doing so.

Plots thicken on the rumour mill; public remonstrations aside, the frenzy of unofficial rumours on the grapevine suggested things weren't quite so simple. Germany continued to offer support for Japan; but with the rumours of an Anglo-German alliance with the British Empire, as opposed to outright enforced debellation from a vengeful Hitler, the Japanese were being subtly held in check from the perceived threat to Britain's eastern colonies. Singapore in particular was a vital port. The British no longer supplied Chinese resistance to the Imperial Japanese Army, and in return, it was said, their assets must be left untouched. Japan's seizure of East Russia would be perfect for the Axis, for Berlin. Singapore and British Asia was key to trade. Should British Malaya fall, too, along with neighbouring Thailand and the already occupied Indochina, then British-held Burma would surely follow, and a direct route into India would be available for the Japanese. This, it was said, Hitler could not abide. The British territories in the Far East were no longer Japan's sphere of influence; they were Aryan. London was de facto his; therefore, India belonged to his vassal. Perhaps, some suggested, he intended to march troops in there himself one day, through Russia and the Caucasus and right into Asia. Hitler a modern Alexander; Germany and its allied empires of Britain, Italy and Japan globally triumphant; the massive power of America and Russia cowed into acquiescence or subdued accordingly. The daydreams of *Mein Kampf* made reality; an alliance of 'Aryan' empires, a Global Reich, the Führer *Godded*, Hitler; King of the World.

Others argued; these rumours made no sense. Hitler's next target would be *Russia*; no one was fooled by the Non-Aggression Pact. Sabre-rattling with Japan at the isolated Americans was a ploy. He needed Japan to attack from the east, to keep Soviet armies in Siberia fighting a hopeless two-front war; the dreaded double invasion. Why would he care about saving Singapore and the rest, it was asked? All he needed was America to leave Japan alone. British colonies didn't matter compared to the two-front war in Russia, and control of continental Europe in whole. What could it mean?

The same argument raged across pubs and living rooms all over the capital, which was by far the biggest source of information and gossip:

"Adolf will let Japan do what they like – draw the Americans west, to the Far East! Let them fight it out and weaken each other while the Jerries watch."

"No, he wants a double-pronged attack on Stalin! Make Japan invade Russia, away from the Empire and just leave the Americans out of it."

"He doesn't want the Empire, they'll have all of Europe and Russia; what does Hitler want with Malaya? Jerry just wants European civilisation in power."

"Bollocks! They're allies – *real* allies, not bloody conquered enemies who have to smile at them. When push comes to shove, Hitler won't say a word, or Japan will tell him to get lost. Our lot are doomed out there."

"Rubbish! Didn't you hear what Churchill said? Fortress Singapore is impregnable!"

"He bloody said Fortress *Britain* was impregnable!"

"We got stabbed in the back!"

"Anyway, if China ever officially surrenders, Hitler doesn't want Japan spreading and overthrowing the white man. No, as long as they all turn against Russia, the Empire will be intact."

Still, the people of Britain referred to 'The Empire'. Then would come a sad lull, as those speculating realised that at the heart of that imperial swathe of British conquest in every sphere of the globe, German soldiers patrolled the streets, and German officials dictated police policy. The Friendship Bunds might be springing up, here and there, but Parliament no longer had final say over the Empire and its subjects. Ultimately, the last word came from Hitler.

~

It had not been a good day for Maisie. She looked out at the famous street on which she worked; unusually quiet, for what had been a thronging hub of humanity.

Tottenham Court Road in London connected southwest Bloomsbury and the southeast of Regent's Park down to the northern stretches of Soho and Covent Garden, its base connecting with the great New Oxford Street. The narrower road stretching north had its own fair share of shops and eateries, a great hub of life in the thronging heart of life in the capital. Theatre goers would use its public houses, resulting in a bizarre medley of cross-class mixing in certain establishments that would be unthinkable elsewhere; petite bourgeois engaging 'toffs' from Mayfair and further west in discussions on Wagnerian opera and which adaptation of *The Merchant of Venice* was best. Now, though, conversations with the upper classes were best avoided. *Shylock, see; even Shakespeare himself knew what these Jews were all about, let alone the great Spanish Catholic dynasty. Mosley and these fellows had the right idea all along. From Martin Luther to Shakespeare; Marlowe, Wagner, Bakunin, left wing, right wing, and every monarchy going; there is no place for the Jew*!

In the higher reaches of society, such views were being met with cheers and the clinking of glasses. Former Jewish business partners, merchants and traders became pariahs overnight. Those of mixed race who were in prominence became vocal defenders of western culture and blood, often having had no strong views in the years before 1940.

And those Jews rich enough merely smiled at all the subjective idiocy of the little people.

The middle classes and petit bourgeois were not immune to the grief-stricken torpor of the proletariat; the upper classes, most of whom had supported Franco in his authoritarian fascist/Catholic defence of the 'old Spain', were much more adaptable to the changing spectrum – being mostly above and untouched by its consequences – and ideologically more aligned to the centralism and stability that the extreme right imposed. Nationalising much of the industry and attacking unemployment was one thing; ensuring big business flourished and 'old money' prevailed was another. The toffs, all in all, seemed quite grudgingly accepting of the new order.

~

The tobacconists' bell tinkled, and Maisie looked up from her copy of *The Hound of the Baskervilles* to see the young German soldier smiling at her that had bought a packet of cigarettes three days prior.

His friendly expression faltered in the face of her cool indifference; like a wave breaking against a cliff, before rolling back. The young man paused, discomfited, before quickly doffing his cap to the impassive girl and her steady gaze. He was certain that his failure to have done so *immediately* upon entering was obviously a cultural breach in the land of English gentlemen – hence her disapproval – and his face betrayed disappointment when she snorted quite openly at his attempt to win favour. Finally deigning to put the book down she approached the counter, her face an impenetrable mask.

The young German's mouth opened and closed, briefly, and she reacted to his noiseless greeting with a firm, thin-lipped smile, tinged with a tiny trace of contempt.

"Hello again," he smiled pleasantly, pulling himself together, having mentally abandoned the idea of flirtation and deciding to just replenish his smokes.

"Oh hello… still alive then?" she asked without interest.

He grinned, unused to such front from a woman. Particularly one so young, and vital. Girls close to his age had grown up under the Nazi yoke; the only real confidence and zeal any of them seemed to show was during suitable 'Germanic' activities or statements. Fear and caution stifled spirited girls elsewhere. Just like the boys. And their parents, and grandparents. Fear was insidious.

"Yes, still alive…" he smiled, "and I have decided to take a chance on *one* more packet."

"It's your funeral," she deadpanned.

By now his awkwardness had disappeared, and the soldier was more than a little amused by the spunky English shopgirl, and his own previous inability to communicate.

"May I have a packet of Woodbines, please?"

She turned and collected them, at a leisurely pace. The light struck her hair and sent a blonde glow out, reflecting against the brown of polished wood. Maisie's poise was loose; she almost sauntered back to the soldier with his cigarettes, before dropping them carelessly onto his outstretched hand. The packet bounced off his fingers and hit the floor; he quickly ducked to retrieve them, straightening back up to see an utterly unapologetic Maisie lighting a smoke of her own.

"Are you sure it is the right job for you, working at a Tobacconists?" he asked her, some incredulity breaking through his amusement.

"You have to take whatever is available in these times," she replied, brushing a tuft of hair out of her eyes. "Are you sure being a soldier is the right job for you?"

He stopped his in tracks, letting out a half-laugh.

"Sadly, no." She held his gaze, and he decided to trust her. "But I had no choice."

To his surprise, she smiled at him in what looked like genuine sympathy.

"Never mind, eh."

The tone was much softer than before, and the corners of her mouth twisted wistfully. She was sympathetic. Not so tough after all. Not such a cold fish.

Maisie passed the young soldier his packet of cigarettes.

"Danke," the German said, gently.

She looked at him curiously. "Perhaps I shouldn't tease you for cigarettes. There are more dangerous things happening out there, after all."

He nodded, slowly, scrambling to find the right response in English.

"That is true. Anyway, who wants to live forever? I am sure that old people who cannot fight or make new children are probably considered unGerman in some way. There are laws against them."

Maisie could not bring herself to reply.

"Do not worry," he smiled again, the expression slowly splitting his boyish face. "English, German, it is the same to them. As long as we are young and it is possible to fight or produce children... we are in no trouble..."

He blushed, furious at himself for the clumsy attempt to backtrack, but determinedly maintaining eye contact. Blue on blue, his steady and strong; hers equally blue, but flecked with the slight gold of hazel specks. Freckles dotted either side of her perfect, narrow nose.

"Well," Maisie replied quietly, clearing her throat. "That is a good one. I'll have a smoke myself, today."

"Danke," he repeated quietly, tilting the paper packet slightly.

Beats of silence, then he plunged: "You don't seem like the kind of girl I knew in Germany?"

"Oh?" she replied, eyebrows raised. But he could sense her interest.

Leaning in to the counter, he gave her the full beam of his smile. "Yes," he purred, softly. "You are different. German girls my age grew up under Hitler. They are all the same; scared of being different, Aryan, talk about the same boring Germanic things, they all hate Jews…"

She stared at him, her eyes flickering fast from side-to-side in small movements, weighing him up. For his part, he did not blink; there was a twinkle in his eye.

"*You* are different. Anyway… I am needed. Auf Wiedersehen, fraulein…"

He held her gaze, searching for a semblance of warmth or compassion, or humour or dread in her eyes. He saw none; just curiosity, as she considered him keenly, judging his demeanour after the unexpected remarks. Despite himself, he could not help staring, maintaining the eye contact for several seconds after his goodbye. But she did not buckle under the pressure, with her composure regained, and when her right eyebrow lifted almost imperceptibly in bemusement, he knew he had pressed it as far as he should, if not, indeed, a little further.

Replacing his enlisted soldier's field cap, he dropped his gaze, only briefly discomposed, before doffing the grey wool to the English girl. Turning on his heel, the young soldier quickly exited out into the rare sunlight, moving away from the shopfront before sliding a cigarette into the waiting crevice of his lips.

For the first time in three days, Simon was calm.

Sat at his desk; attaching the Woodbine to his little gold holder, flicking open the heavy lighter and sucking down the smoke. Blowing swirls around him, letting it absorb into his flesh. Breathing deeply. It was his routine, the routine that calmed him. The routine that soothed him in the darkest hours of his life. His time alone, at the desk, expunging.

Placing the holder between his teeth where it pointed outwards, away from his eyes, Simon picked up his pen to write.

Diary,

I feel like I'm trapped in a dream from which it is impossible to awaken.

Walking through my own streets, the busy roads, the garden squares and riverside embankment and Fleet Street and Whitehall and every other monument and sacred place of London there is... and seeing the German soldier.

But no horror can equate to the spectacle seen at the Savoy.

Göring.

That corpulent beast, swollen, having eaten Europe whole. His air force bombs barbecuing cities in their entirety, in preparation for his monstrous appetite to come along and gobble them up, like the fairytale villain of a Brothers Grimm story.

The man himself, in framed pictures, television broadcasts to his adoring German public, those left alive, who see him as a happy, fat figure of fun.

The WEASEL next to him, grinning ear to ear. Shyster! Montagu Norman, the Governor of the Bank of England!

"This man," cried Göring, "more than any other fought to protect the Aryan peoples from economic enslavement from world Jewry and the odious financiers spawned from Europe's Court Jews."

The rest of his speech beggars belief. Turns out old 'Monty' signed away the wealth of Czecho-Slovakia, and literally transferred their gold to the Reichsbank after Hitler's armies absorbed the rest of their country – so much for his sole aim to rescue the Sudeten Germans, mind you!

Simon paused, his hand shaking. Göring, fluent in English, a monster apparition in the room. A handful of well-to-do friends and acquaintances having flocked to him – ambassadors, diplomats, lords, men who had visited Carinhall and hunted with Göring in the days before war. He basked in the limelight; a fat, perfumed, strutting Nero, a deputy-Caesar.

Simon could see why he'd been advised to 'dress formally' – nothing but a sea of morning coats, top hats, sleek American businessmen with neatly parted hair and older, aristocratic and upper class British toffs clad in their dapper best. Most were laughing. Every table, including Simon's, had been laden with wines, champagne, cheese and meats, and assorted cakes, pastries and delicacies. Rationing was still in effect. Simon wrote about what he'd realised at that very moment, gazing across a sea of smiling, flushed faces.

This class of people will never go without. They'll never be affected by war. They'll always prosper, regardless of what happens at the political and social levels. They are above everything and everyone. The world is run on money, and money runs the world.

After thirty minutes of singing plaudits and platitudes to the assembled, the Reichsmarschall called, "and now, dear friends, leaders in our western world – this shall not be a usual night of German speeches and bombast! Let us enjoy a night in the company of friends and associates!"

"Hear hear!" cried dozens of British and American gentlemen in response.

The journalists' pool was summoned to him back in the River Suite, in between the conference and the buffet. The lights of cameras flashed; all taken by Germans in some kind of uniform or other. Journalists crowded around with pens and notepads.

Reichsmarschall, what have you... what do you... does Herr Hitler... economic partnerships between... who instigated... the questions reigned in, and Göring, his large belly stretching at the sleek fabric of an all-white uniform obscenely bedecked with medals, roared his answers back jovially, the huge, glowing moon of a face beaming, the very epitome of conviviality. He *radiated* power, like a great, benevolent authority.

"The reorganisation of a world freed from economic and cultural slavery is a matter for the governments of the Rome-Berlin-Tokyo Axis, the British Empire and the leaders in each field," he'd declared, with gusto. "With such men as Montagu Norman, and a new system of cooperation, the great Aryan nations will continue to grow from strength-to-strength! And perhaps even our American friends across the sea will come to see the advantage of a great union of the world's leading nations and cultures."

The cunning instinct of a fox, the body of a pig, and the empathy of a pure sociopath. Not to mention, the understanding of human judgement and emotion. He watched us all drink in his words and his jovial nature and attitude and smile, yet no one seemed to identify the small light of triumph that shone in his eyes through the good-natured posturing.

Unbelievably, the banker had been worse. Simon had longed to ask Göring about the violent SA purge – an organisation he set up – the concentration camps, and the Kristallnacht pogrom. Of course, he couldn't. But Simon, let alone ask questions, found himself unable to so much as look at Montagu Norman without feeling queasy. His vicious, rat-like smirk. The glint of triumph in his eyes when Göring sang his plaudits. His almost knowing amusement when the titanic figure in world politics draped his arm lazily around the little man's shoulders.

They told us to expect pictures, that we only had to provide written copy and yes, the assured of us the importance of the occasion. The news would only be released two days from then, with the Reichsmarschall safe and sound back in Germany. In the meantime, it's time you gentlemen enjoyed the buffet! Eat and drink your fill, esteemed guests!

Simon stopped. There was little need to go on.

In the event, he'd not touched the sumptuous buffet laid on for them, nor had he sought the company of any of the guests. One journalist he knew tried to engage him in discussion, affecting an air of secrecy as he pontificated in low mutterings as to where this could lead. Simon, though, had detected the underlying excitement of the man, and had rudely turned away, making an abrupt exit to the Savoy's American bar; unusually quiet, for nine in the evening, with plenty of free tables. The glitzy bar gleamed white and yellow, its brightness reflected and magnified by the mirrors, sleek and flashy. There, several cocktails at the bar and then smoke in a far corner of the seated area calmed him, as he absorbed what he'd witnessed elsewhere in the grand settings of the hotel. Neither the tuxedoed pianist playing Wagner's *Tristan und Isolde*, nor the other guests in the bar interrupted his rumination.

The sound of classic German artistry was an almost unbearable assault on the senses. But this was not the night to complain.

Eventually, when enough time had passed, Simon rose to his feet, slowly made his way down through the high domed ground floor back to the main foyer, footsteps echoing horribly in his imagination. He briskly stepped through the great halls, down to the river entrance, and faced with the frosty night air, the journalist grudgingly accepted his ride home.

It had been an uneasy decision, but with the horrible feeling of isolation and gloom setting in around them – even in the comparatively nice surroundings of Bloomsbury, with its quiet garden squares and leafy, tree-lined lanes – the comrades-in-arms had settled on trying to enlist the help of old fighters and with it, all being well, the concurrent support network that had proven so reliable.

The trip was not taken lightly.

It was a dangerous risk to take, travelling across the occupied city together and as such, they insisted that Mary stay in Bloomsbury, taking care to reassure her it was common practise leave a soldier behind should the excursion lead to disaster. Either way, the Barceloniña had not been happy; unleashing the first Latin rage and tantrum at her William in two years; eyes burning as she babbled a relentless stream of perfect English interlaced with Catalan curses, vehement, spat at speed.

They understood her frustration; the old war had been equal rights combat, and before communist cannibalism, many female fighters had signed up to the anarchists and Marxist militias. Mary, caution abandoned, released a torrent of furious passion at her friends. But, the context was extreme, and they all loved the girl with a fervour they were once hesitant to admit. It was quite impossible to retain any anger towards her, and even enraged, she found it difficult to maintain her rage for long. Mary embraced them all before they left, squeezing each of them tightly and blessing their journey.

"Go time," Alan muttered quietly as at long last, they stepped out into the cool, dark London evening.

William snorted. "We're not going to face anything scarier than *that*, anyway... perfect motivation."

Jack and Alan guffawed at the resentful, sulky tone of the chastised lover, and the Scot soon joined in the group laughter.

Stealthily, the group rolled through the city with exaggerated care. They circumvented the very centre of the city, where they knew that German patrols were likely to accost them, to check identification as standard procedure, if nothing else. Their papers would be of no help to the discerning eye, they knew; three men in their early and mid-twenties, of military age, travelling after dusk across a watchful London ruled by wary conquerors. A straight easterly route for several miles before heading south would take them through the East End and on to where they suspected they'd find their old comrade.

An old fighter... Alter Kampfer, the fascists would call him. But he was a veteran of the left, and had vanished from their radars; consumed as they were by the irresistible Germans, *victorious everywhere.*

They knew Duncan McGrath of old; he had been an older head who greatly helped ease the teenage Jack's transition into the communist party and thence, along with William, into Spain. Both had torn up their CPGB Party membership cards as soon as was safe in the aftermath of betrayal in Barcelona, when thousands of Marxist militia members of the POUM returned on leave from fighting fascism at the front to find themselves labelled 'Trotskyite Fascists' and criminal traitors. Their own status as communists and the helpful usage of a veritable thesaurus of Lenin jargon likely saved their lives, but the affair destroyed their belief in the international communist cause. When Franco's tanks rolled into Barcelona, the group barely escaped north and into France, after which they vowed to never support that ideological extreme again. To their shock and bewilderment, even as they returned to fight the last eighteen months of a doomed war as part of the organised communist army – the PSUC proper, suspecting that their preferred ideological comrades the Catalan Anarchists would be next in line to be outlawed and cannibalised – they realised then and later that General Franco's secret police squadrons were merely *continuing* the ignoble work of the Russian security police services and their seemingly subordinate Spanish Communist Party allies. Night arrests, imprisonments and executions were not a consequence of fascist rule; only the persecutors changed.

Indeed, unlike the chillingly efficient NKVD of Russia, Franco's civil guard militias – now referred to as the *Brigada Político-Social* – shared the Gestapo's zeal, but wholly lacked their ruthless competence and the savagery of their clinical slaughter.

"Where do you think the big bastard was?" Alan wondered.

"Who cares," Jack intoned bitterly. "Doesn't matter. The war was lost, and we got out. Don't ever get sucked in to caring about the communist collective again–"

"D'ye think that's fuckin' likely, man?" Alan demanded, bristling.

"No. But remember those days, mate. Don't bother worrying who did what."

Duncan had not been in the POUM, and after escaping back to England in '39, none had yet found it in themselves to seek out their former comrades and allies. Some of their light and optimism had died in the dust of Spain, along with their friends and comrades who subscribed to slightly different socialist beliefs, fought fascism under a different banner and as a result, many of whom were killed by their own side.

But England was occupied now, and the swastika flew over London. That was all that mattered now, regardless of whose slogans a solider spouted.

Duncan was a mountain-sized man, with an equally large-sized heart. He looked like a circus strongman; built like Primo Carnera, the Spanish had named him 'Basajuan', and he became an unofficial mascot to the few Basques they encountered fighting in Catalonia, outside their own embattled land in the north. He had been – and still was, they assumed – a dock worker, inhabiting one of the narrow terraced streets that edged the quays; the dockland factories and machinations of heavy industry casting an inescapable shadow across their private lives. It was hardly a surprise that the communist party had flourished here. The U-bend of the River Thames that housed the Docklands was cockney workers' territory, and flashing the party cards they'd left in tens of torn pieces on the floor of what was an unnaturally pleasant little hotel room in Perpignan – Mary had torn hers up in Barcelona, thoroughly unconcerned – would have been sure to get them instant solidarity. Half the docks had claimed pre-war to have took part in the demonstrations against Oswald Mosley's British fascists, a feat which they were careful to keep quiet now. Nor did the Jewish population of East London greatly help the anti-fascists' cause; the smaller groups of SS Security Police in the city were focused primarily on perceived Jewish and communist strongholds; the East End and the Thames U-bend Docklands were areas that were sure to be patrolled.

"All quiet on the Western Front," Jack stated bitterly, as they worked their way through the old, familiar East End streets of Whitechapel. They knew what he meant.

"Too bloody quiet," Alan mused. "No patrols as yet, but hardly any bloody people for miles. It's only eight o'clock?"

"Thought the krauts would be all over the East End," Jack mused.

"Threatened it enough," William snorted. "All the Jews will suffer, and all that."

Alan turned to glance at him, concern etched into his features. "They're goin' about all this in a pretty daft way, like?"

"Is it?" Jack considered, as the Scot nodded in bemused agreement. "They're keeping us guessing, and it seems to be working."

"Yeah well, we'll keep them guessing with a few sticks up dynamite up the arse," Alan chuntered, sick of second-guessing German tactics and intent. "I've got one Jewish friend, just one, and it's your bird you lucky bastard," he said quickly, gesturing at William, who grinned. "But I tell you what," Alan continued. "I'm painting the Star of David on any bastard bomb I throw at these fuckers."

Jack encouraged the Geordie to grumble for several minutes longer. Much of it was hot air and bluster, but their clever, rough northern friend certainly knew how to cheer them up.

They rolled on through the stillness, imaginations running wild. As the car edged through the last grim, quiet lanes of lower Whitechapel, William piped up from the backseat.

"I loosely translated a Goethe poem that applies to our predicament."

"Let's hear it then, old boy," was Jack's instant reply. He could sense that his friend was nervous, and felt a small rush of gratitude that Alan hadn't objected to German poetry. Indeed, there was even the ghost of a smile playing at the corners of his mouth as William began to recite. They'd just finished praising the prose when the car slipped south past the Commercial Road and on to the turn southeast to the docks.

Fortunately, they passed through to the Docklands outskirts completely without incident – seeing neither German patrols nor London police, whom they feared would be compelled to check papers for anyone heading to the vitally important industrial nerve-centre of the docks. Alan drove slowly to maximise the precious petrol that they had been given. They were stored in one of the munitions dumps, and only Alan and Jack knew their location, for the sake of plausible deniability in the event of enemy capture. Of course, the combined civil and military administration – as yet not publicly declared by Germany – had issued their own coupon currency for essentials, and had fixed the German Reichsmark at 9.6 to the British pound, but Alan's coupons that the Colonel had provided had already been traded in for a significant amount of petroleum gasoline; certainly enough given the average life expectancy of an Auxiliary fighter.

"Forgot how grim all this shite was," William observed.

Jack knew that Duncan lived near Millwall to the west of the Isle of Dogs, in one of the terraced streets wedged in near the Phoenix Heights that was filled with the classic London two-up two-down homes in neat, squat rows. The big docker used to drink in a pub on Cuba Street, an old tavern called the Dock House, in which all the three of them had shared a boozy night together with several of the other communists on the eve of setting off for Spain. William's status as intellectual of the group hadn't stopped him from competing with Alan in a drinking contest, with the bravado and melodramatic pre-war uninhibited zeal that suggested this was their last night of celebration on Earth; the end result had been a sort of bleary truce at nine o'clock in the morning, a full three hours after both had vomited outside into the street, yet shown no subsequent inclination to quit, staggering back inside to where fresh pints of ale were waiting for them, and the mocking applause of their friends. Ice water had been needed to get them in shape to travel down to catch the Calais ferry. Even big Duncan had nursed a hangover that lasted long after the boat began to drift along the coast of France.

But to their dismay, in the present, the three partisans arrived to find the Dock House tavern closed down. It seemed somehow indecent to mourn the loss of a pub with so many human lives extinguished in war, so they cruised on without comment, a silent pact of sorts, on through the eerie dockland terraces and past factories and warehouses that had been blasted by the Germans, and were still being rebuilt; the black scars of incendiary flame and inferno from the skies defacing the mutilated area that had been the hub of London's supply and production, one of the beating hearts of a vast and great empire.

They came upon *The Islander* pub, and found nothing but begrimed rubble; an eyesore of man-made ruin. Broken brick in a mound of dust and ruined, jagged blocks were all that remained of a former hub of life. No attempt had been made to remedy what was clearly a direct hit sustained by the building, and obviously, a kind of grim torpor must have set in for the locals on the visual evidence that Jack, William and Alan silently observed. The lack of reconstruction – even on a popular pub – showed just how apathetic the British defeat must have been for the proletarian communities – sons, husbands, brothers in France, or in continental factories, in hiding or resisting up north. All those who remained had internalised the torment and grief.

In the third pub, they got lucky. Nestled in the far corner of the public bar, in one of the three booths along the northeast corner was the unmistakeable wide-domed, pronounced forehead and colossal frame of Duncan McGrath. The man was gigantic.

There was another half full pint glass in front of him, but the high back of the booth obscured him from view and from the threshold, none of them could see who it was. Sharing a glance, William and Alan strolled over. Jack stepped briskly to the bar; "all right!" he chirped to the barman, in an accent dripping with as much Bow Bells as he could muster, drawling his cockney. It would only have served as an impediment to be viewed with suspicion; three unknowns strolling into a docklands pub to confront a worker during foreign occupation. Who knows what would happen if they were suspected of being informants. Stories were in circulation of awful retribution meted out to collaborators; obscured, of course, by the typical routine of urban legends, exaggerations and Chinese whispers.

But in the Docklands pub, neither Jack, William nor Alan could afford to wrongly expose themselves to suspicion.

Duncan saw them long before they reached him, but gave no indication until they were at the table. They approached him with faint smiles. Alan did not waste time with formalities.

"So you are still alive, you stubborn *bastard*?"

Duncan put his pint glass down, carefully, as though his great size necessitated exaggerated care with the frail glass. "Just about, Alan. Sometimes I wish I weren't though, truth be told…"

He stood up, and any misgivings they'd had seemed in vain. The three men embraced like old comrades, and Duncan introduced them to his drinking buddy; much younger than he, but older than the three young veterans who'd once shared party allegiance with the bear-sized man now squeezed into a corner of the booth. This companion of McGrath looked like a boxer, with the stern eyes, big squashed nose and confident air of a prize-fighter.

Meanwhile, Jack brought five pints over, and the introductions were restarted. A jovial Duncan drew attention to his friend.

"Geordie, Billy, Jack the lad; this is another Jack," he smiled, pointing out each man in turn.

They all shook hands with the stranger, who said "Jack Dash, good to meet you, brothers."

William surmised him to be thirty-five or thereabouts. He had a white face, high hairline and a wide, rounded nose; unfortunate, William thought to himself. A big nose was the last thing you could afford in a German colony.

The man had the air of a worker with serious ideological views; you could tell the sort from a mile away. In the infectious spirit of the 1930s and the solutions offered by political extremes, to channel one's dissatisfaction and drive into some kind of revolutionary movement was the crowning act of self-vindication. It made William's head hurt, now; looking at this slightly older man with his weathered leather jacket – much like Alan's, though his bore dust of the trenches – and small flat cap in the worker's style, he remembered his own days in the early '30s, *devouring every word that Marx, Bakunin, Godwin, Volin, Lenin, Trotsky and Stalin had ever committed to print. Heads swirling with slogans and theories, debating the best hybrid of all the facts and the avenue down which to pursue the People's Movement...* all hot air and bluster. He'd seen what happened in reality; just a power grab from the opposing end of the social and political spectrums. Communists labelling fellow anti-fascists, *fascists*. Torture, murder. The anarchists later banned; that anti-authoritarian system the natural state of being to the Catalan peasants. In William's disillusionment, he considered communists and any kind of political thinking worker a naïve, idealistic fool if they hadn't been to Spain or Russia and witnessed first-hand what Stalin's vision truly was. They justified Franco's claims that he'd purged Spain of the godless infidel savages, and *this* with the camaraderie of the first anarchist uprising and outpouring of popular sentiment, the glowing workers' solidarity of Barcelona in 1936, and the essential decency of the Spaniard! Political extremism and centralism on their own 'side' had condemned them and their vision just as much as the combined fascist and Catholic extremists on the other.

It made William uneasy, now, looking as the fiercely garbed proletarian in his jacket. He imagined the slogans and the communist spiel that would come outpouring in a cascade of worker's pride if he set him off. Another pathetically eager, pro-Soviet zealot. If he revealed that their old militia had been labelled Trotskyite-fascists, the tough-looking little man would probably smash his pint glass over Jack or Alan's head. Yet, William mused scornfully, *still* be unable to articulate why Trotsky, Lenin's chief lieutenant and proponent of permanent socialist revolution, was a 'fascist' – unless that term now jointly included all people exiled or murdered by Stalin's regime.

Duncan was speaking.

"So... what brings my old comrades back around here? Makes for miserable bloody sightseeing." He gestured round at the unprepossessing pub, its stone and sawdust surfaces and naked electric lights resulting in an ugly yellow ambience. The pub's patrons looked tired, and were for the most part stationary and inexpressive.

Jack, perched next to his namesake Dash, leaned across the table pointedly. There seemed little point prolonging the inevitable entreaty, and besides, none of them felt particularly nostalgic for the days when they pledged their loyalty to Comintern.

"We need to speak to you about something important. We know we can trust you. What we don't know is whether we can trust *him*." He turned to the older man beside him. "With no offence intended, Jack."

"None taken, brother," the oddly fierce little Jack Dash replied. "And rest assured if this matter concerns a topic not quite... how shall I say, to be in the best interests of this city's masters – new or old, mind – of either German or capitalist persuasion... you have nothing to worry about, mate."

He raised his own glass, and took a mighty swig out of it. Jack glanced at Duncan, who nodded his assurance.

"We wondered if you were interested in–" Jack began, before William interjected with a hiss to speak quietly, and he leaned in. "... interested in resuming your role in fighting the forces of tyranny, and the like."

Duncan McGrath's face betrayed nothing. William wondered what had happened to the big man who'd been so enthused about travelling for the noble cause. There was once not a prouder proletarian in the docks, nor one so versed in the slogans and theories.

Seeing a vital force broken in a person, an internal light extinguished, was commonplace in wartime. But not in people as proud and as fierce as Big Duncan. Not in people who'd fought tooth and nail for their beliefs, bitterness only growing as they saw the collective effort come to naught, thirst for blood rising with time. But William recognised it in his face. There was no sign of the old Duncan McGrath.

If Jack saw it, much like Duncan, he too gave nothing away.

"We have the means and the information that could potentially make a difference. But it's not without danger."

As Alan waited expectantly, Duncan McGrath sipped his pint unhurriedly, as though lost in thought. Finally, he swivelled round and addressed Alan.

"Make a *difference*. Really? Overthrow the German Army? Kill Hitler? What?"

Alan was astonished, but scrambled to find his voice. "Well, bloody right man! If we can't kill a quarter of a million men, we can kill a quarter of a thousand, or quarter of a hundred, and if everyone did their bit then yes I reckon we would overthrow the German *bloody* army!"

Duncan was calm. "But they won't."

Even his friend Jack was staring hard at Duncan now, emotions warring on his face. Alan looked across the table to him.

"You, Dash – is what I'm saying right or what?"

He nodded slowly. "It's right, brother."

"Well tell this big *lump* would you man? You'd never think he'd already fought these bastards in Spain, the way he sounds!"

Even as he entreated, he could see in Duncan's eyes that it was useless. The big man was almost lethargic; everything in his posture and speech was withdrawn and laboured, a shell of the vital man he'd been.

He raised one palm. "Let's be honest, lads. You're not going to recruit Jack here without me, because that's not how it works. You can't be sure of him without your old comrade joining up too, so let's forget using a brother worker here as some kind of bait to lure me in..."

He took a mighty swig of his pint again, with the eyes of all at the table settled on him, and sighed regretfully. Whether it was to do with the empty glass, or the situation at large, none could tell. He resumed, consigned to the fact that an explanation was needed in his incredulous company.

"Look. Nothing changes, nothing ever will. This isn't Russia —"

"Fuck Russia" Alan snapped, and the pub went quiet. Workers in flat caps turned, and cast surreptitious glance over, ears straining to overhear more. Alan noticed, and belched sneeringly with a scorn that William quietly marvelled at. Jack laid a hand on his friend's arm, and McGrath continued in the same slow, quiet tone.

"Perhaps, perhaps not. Whatever; the point being is that Marxism in any guise or form will never triumph in Western Europe now. We fought in Spain, and lost. Some of us went to fight under Britain's flag in France, and lost. And now fascism is everywhere; worse, it's this bloody Nazi nonsense about pure blood and racial superiority and all that bloody cobblers. Regular people, workers and petit bourgeois alike are just getting on with it. Carrying on, feeding their families. That's just the sad truth. The fighting's over for most people, and you won't radicalise them to think otherwise. You're trying to turn back the tide, like some bloody Ancient Greek hero trying to fight Poseidon. You might as well fight gravity. These buggers are in charge now, and forget flags; the international working class lost."

"Fuck – *international...* and flags, you *berk. This* here is *our* country, and it's occupied by bloody Germans. *Fascists*, you twat." Alan hissed at him across William.

But still, the same dismissive, slow nod and indistinct mumble from Duncan. The words had no effect whatsoever. There was a rumble of noise across the pub, however; Jack realised that their noise had been carrying in the silence. He glanced around; quiet, unchallenging eyes met his briefly, and looked away. He snorted, and turned back to face Duncan, who was calmly answering Alan's incensed entreaty.

"We chose to believe in a class struggle; the *salt of the earth*, the people who make the system work. Us. And we lost. But, it turns out that all is not entirely lost."

That shut Alan up. His mouth opened and closed, like a goldfish, blinking dumbly. *Not entirely lost.* William himself was mortified, and forced himself to look across the table at the two Jack's, sitting side by side. He winced as Duncan continued, verbalising that which was unspeakable, unutterable.

"Because, it turns out that this Nazi piffle is actually a kind of warped socialism after all. Now, don't get me wrong; look at it closely enough, and they're in bed with plutocrats and corporations," Duncan suddenly came alive, revitalised like his former self. The most politically passionate worker they had ever chewed the fat with over beers, with a formidable mind. "Big business funded these reactionary shysters. The same plutocracy they blame on Jewry, they're happy to accept funding from to maintain control. Capitalist monsters have nothing to worry about investing in fascist foreign countries; they're *stable*. They invest, and rely on a murderous police force to keep things on an even keel as the investment starts to bear fruit. Look at the war! You don't see the bankers in top hats shuffling through London, do you? They're not affected by this, are they? Not for all the tea in China. They're still laughing every morning. Fascism is just as good as democracy to them, if not better."

"*Not entirely lost,*" Alan repeated pointedly.

"Yeah," Duncan sighed, realising that such a taboo statement had to be defended. "OK... the Nazis are swollen, fat and greedy with German big business, American dollars and, let's be honest, British pounds. There's still a ruling class that sits above law and borders. But look *beyond* the racist bollocks. They've tried to eradicate unemployment in Germany. They want to do the same *here*. Every home-grown industry goes under the state, totally nationalised, and programs are set up to help assimilate people into the system of work. Public projects, a permanent need for labour."

He stopped, taking a small sip of his beer, knowing that no interjections were likely. Sated, Duncan continued quietly into the accusatory silence. "Beyond the factory conscription, there's plenty of workers who have it just fine staying and working *here*. Families are being fed. Why d'you think that after London was secure there's not been bombs all over the place? And once they've secured Leeds and Manchester and Glasgow, strewth, who knows where else – why would it be any different for the northern monkeys as here? People don't fight when they can eat. The majority just want to be led, earn money and live as easy a life as possible."

Duncan shook his head slowly, retreating back into himself. "Like it or lump it, lads, we can't overthrow them anymore, they're not even breaking the British Empire up and bleedin' hell, as workers we may even come to accept this regime as it rebuilds and builds a new, strong system for a new decade."

In the astonished silence, Jack Dash found his voice. "That's bloody hard for me to hear, brother. But I do concede; Jerry does want to reward the worker, build strong nations on the foundation of the working man, and they're keeping things good... and until then, I'm not sure I could advocate more of our boys throwing their lives away on –"

"*Hold* on," William interjected, cutting the monologue short. "What you're saying is; National *Socialism* is better than no socialism at all? The worker still wins? That's a justification for not fighting?" The young Scot shook his head in disbelief; Alan, meanwhile, looked like he was ready to attack the two Dockers; lips fixed in an ugly sneer, fists clenched. His whole body betrayed fury and tension.

William inhaled the slightly sour air of the pub, collecting his thoughts. How had this happened?

When he spoke, his voice was full of suppressed anger, and he found himself unable to look to his left at the big man. "So the Stalinist, communist, pro-Soviet Duncan McGrath follows the word of Comrade Joe to the letter – I assume the POUM are Trotskyite-fascists in your book, aye? We never did clear that up, us being former POUM of course. We're fascists. But *National Socialism* is an *accepted* form of socialism. Well, *viva libertad*, you fucking *bastard*."

The charged atmosphere was unspeakably foul, its vile tension insidiously spreading through the dank and spacious pub. The vile smell grew in strength, and with it, the nervous pressure of the moment only intensified. Jack realised it was a lost cause, but still spoke into the deathly silence:

"So with the dead in France, the prisoners of war and the practically forced recruitment of tens of thousands of able-bodied workers to German factories, as long as the workers get paid on time and not hassled, and a few more slackers get bunged into jobs building roads and tanks, it's ok to do nothing... even *accept* the way things are?

Jack Dash shook his head. "Not quite. I can't abide this. And as soon as things take a turn for the worse – and at some stage, they will – I'll lead a group myself."

"Will you now," Alan sneered, oozing contempt. But Dash held his gaze.

"Yes."

"So why not now?" But even as he said it, he knew that they wouldn't take him. They came for an old comrade of the old war, who'd fought the common enemy. They couldn't take in some new blood in occupied London that they didn't know, hadn't met and had never heard of, whether he was willing to fight or not.

And Dash knew it too. "That can't happen. But one day, when the wounds have healed, when our lads are allowed home and when we're ready to strike, we will. Wrongs will be righted. There will be liberation, brothers."

They believed him, but it was useless waiting with him. When you'd tackled the enemy, been hurt by the enemy, assailed by the enemy's malice, and felt the breath of the enemy on the back of your neck, there could be no biding of time, no waiting for stability, no licking of wounds. They were irrevocably set on their path.

But Duncan? He'd fought, too. There was a moment's silence, as they looked at him, compelling him to speak in his shame, and then he did. Duncan began to unload as he hadn't before, as he *never* had before. It was as though each word pained him, a savage burden that grew heavier with each reluctant syllable.

"You speak of overthrowing the enemy. You can't know how it felt, when the fascists won. I was still there as the northeast fell. I saw the tanks roll over the bodies of our comrades. I saw the executions. I saw the rapes."

Alan's hand slid under the table to grab the wrist of William, who'd gone instantly white. The roles had reversed; now William was in danger of doing God knows what to the big dock worker he'd once called a friend. Spain was still raw for all of them, but for him, some wounds would never heal. The muscles in his jaw bunched as he bit down. William was desperate to break his glass over the docker's face, and slash his huge face until it pulsed and flopped; dangling, torn flesh, leaking life-blood. The Scot was infuriated, barely able to maintain his calm.

Duncan continued, completely oblivious to the change in his former friend.

"... And I saw all our blood and sweat and tears, our beliefs come to naught. Do you know what I did? Came home, spitting thunder, about how I was going to murder every fascist and Nazi and Falangist I saw for the rest of my life. Cried myself to sleep at night. I wasn't a father, any longer; my little girl barely recognised me. Agnes tried to reach me and couldn't. How can you reach out to them, to explain what it's like?"

He shook his head. "And then Poland. I tried to sign up the next day, September 4th. Wouldn't let me; too old. Well, bloody hell..." a bitter laugh escaped him, hanging harsh in the quiet. "You'd think they needed every man they could get. And then, defeat, and I knew they were coming here. All the ideals and dreams, a brotherhood of workers stretching from Moscow to Warsaw to Madrid to London... gone. And you know what?"

"What?" Alan asked, sourly. His hand still gripped William's wrist.

Duncan shook his head yet again, this time in disbelief. "When the Nazis touched down here I couldn't even care. Trying to remember my *anger* and *hatred* of them, and what I believed in and fought for, and fought against... it's like looking at an old photo album of school days, or reading my childhood ambitions. 'I want to be the heavyweight champion of the world.' 'I want to be Viceroy in India.' I can't even bloody remember what that anger felt like. It's a different person. I'm *dead* inside."

He looked at each of them in turn, dumbly wondering if they understood. Jack and William weren't sure what to think; it shocked them to see what had become of Duncan McGrath. But it was easy to hide behind depression and pain. Jack was sick at heart, and he stopped himself retorting to Duncan's apathy. Instead, the Londoner caught William's eye.

"Do you remember what you said to me, when we first reached Barcelona?"

"What?" William asked blithely. He just wanted to leave this miserable tavern now, no longer caring about what McGrath had to say. He felt suffocated, and wanted to get as far away as possible from the baleful influence of a defeated comrade consumed by misery, who'd given up on everything – including himself.

But Jack reminded him of his old words.

"'A strong man doesn't let fate overwhelm him, he fights for his cause, and he isn't afraid of the future, he creates his own'." Jack quoted. Alan remembered with sudden vividness the moment those words were spoken, as they waited to disembark from the crowded train, cramped and jostled but exhilarated, finally heading out to find people thronging joyously through the Barcelona streets.

William laughed hollowly.

"How very poignant I was."

He drained the dregs of his ale, and stood up. Alan sprang to his feet and stepped aside to let him out, and Jack, too, slid out of the booth wordlessly, without looking at the veteran communist or his friend. He headed towards the door, as Alan and William cast a last contemptuous glance at the shell of Duncan McGrath.

"No pasarán, Basajuan…" sneered Alan, and he turned disgustedly on his heel and stalked out. William raised a mock fascist salute before following. With the haunted eyes of the pub boring into their backs, Alan hawked up a wad of bile, and spat a great blob of green phlegm onto the dirty wooden floor on which their boots smartly clip-clopped, echoing as they exited the threshold, leaving broken men in their wake.

~

Later that night, Mary lay with her neck nestled into the crook of her lover's armpit, a thick cascade of hair flowing down past the ribcage and tight muscle under it; a small figure nestled against his larger frame, breathing in his scent. Neither had bathed that day, and the addition of alcohol to their chemical balance had contributed its own almost-indistinguishable odour trace, but Mary breathed in deeply, nostrils flared, filling her lungs with the smell. It was a scent only identifiable with good things, for her, in a world becoming crueller and starker by the day.

Through the window she could see stars in the black sky. For minutes she'd gazed sightlessly at them, her thoughts invariably wandering back to the march of jackboots and sight of uniforms that filled her dreams, until their pinprick lights came into focus. *If there is a force out there, let it be one that deals in kindness and peace. Let it shine on those that wish peace and forgiveness to the world.* She had no time for thoughts of the God worshipped in the west, or any religious institution or following, cult or creed. And after her desecration of churches on the Aragon front, joyful retribution dished out in the vengeful spilling of priests' blood, she was certain that if there truly was a Christian God, he most definitely would have little time for her.

If there was, though; let it not be said that Franco, and now Hitler and Mussolini's purges were righteous retribution. Seven years, her people had been persecuted, and at various times for one thousand years before that. Hitler's Thousand Year Reich had only seen its seventh savage summer; if the Führer had his way, his Reich would ensure that her people suffer for a thousand years more.

Mary believed in life's beauty and solidarity, but the era she lived in had betrayed her innocent ideals and dreams. Europe in the 1930s had turned her from a pretty, wide-eyed child into a fiery, bitter young woman with vengeful thoughts.

"Are you ok?" William said softly. She knew what he meant.

"Don't worry. We pretended to be Catholics for centuries in Spain. History is full of Hitlers for the tribe."

"I mean you. My girl."

She chuckled, lowly. "Sí, guapo. Siempre."

William gently ran his fingers through the threads of her hair, an almost fatherly tenderness to his caress. Life had been hard and tough for his girl, since the dread nightmare of the uprising and the unspeakable torment she'd endured in The Fall of Catalonia. Her physical allure was obvious; after four years he had still not become accustomed to it, nor had familiarity diminished his awareness of her fierce Mediterranean beauty, with its high cheekbones, pouting lips, dark eyes flecked as they were with colour and passion; an expression that could range from intense focus to anger to happiness and back again, in the space of seconds. Yet the abhorrent realities of her experience tempered his passions for her with a gentleness, something paternal or avuncular as well as love and attraction in the sexual sense. The fierce little girl had grown up in a cruel world, and no loved ones could protect her from it. She had been disillusioned from parental and social protection in her teenage years, with the outbreak of a savage war between her own people. Mary had learned first-hand the basest cruelties of a cold world, and that no one could protect her. William had sworn when they left the Spain that whatever happened, from that point onwards, *he* would.

"*Te quiero mucho, me querida...*" he breathed softly into her ear. He felt her smile play across the skin of his torso. His attempts at *Castellano* Spanish – having given up on Catalan after only a day or two – always amused her, whether he tried in vain to adopt the fast lilt and rolled 'r's of the *Española* tongue, or delivered the Castilian words in his own distinctive Edinburgh lilt, 'tay kee YAIR OH moochoh?'

"I know, darling."

They lay in silence, comforted by the other's warmth. Despite it, William felt a coldness that had not yet gripped him with such raw fear, as tonight; seeing Big Duncan such a lacklustre specimen, broken by circumstance – when *Mary* still had spirit – had shaken him to the core. Not in any way that would jeopardise their mission, as-yet undefined though it was, but indiscernibly. Almost imperceptibly but in some real, definite way, like a sprained wrist the night before a football match; not enough to directly hamper the player, but a niggling setback and drain of focus and will nonetheless. It was tangible. Nothing Duncan could have said would deter any of them, but his pervasive hopelessness had made William consider the hopelessness of their own situation for the first time, and the ugly, barbaric reality of Britain for the coming 1941.

But still, he had to be strong, for her. He'd vowed – they all did – that no matter what, they'd look after each other, and they'd protect Mary from harm. She could never again experience the evil of men, unless she had a gun in her hand in even combat and only by her own volition. But then, the fascists came to England, they seized Britain, and he had been totally unable to protect her.

Like so many other proud men with families and loved ones.

"Mary... I translated a poem from Goethe earlier. Read it to the boys... thought it was fitting in our current predicament, with the Germans and all... and being written in warning by a great German himself..."

She winced a little at the 'great German' line, in the split second that it took her brain to correctly process and translate the sentence, but she gave no mention to it. Instead, she planted her luscious lips on the tight skin of his chest, staring up into his eyes with all the considerable warmth of her nature and visage.

He smiled down at her, before raising his eyes to the ceiling. The effort to maintain eye contact with Mary while reciting his own take on Goethe was too much for his competing senses; cognitive and visual alike. *Here goes*, he thought:

"With iron will; to our dismay,
By brazen fate, endowed with fame,
He'll conquer worlds, and yet one day,
Be flung to hell from whence he came.
In that great anguish, he just may

Resist in vain, yet he will fail,
And they will perish in the fray,
All those who followed in his trail…"

He looked down to see that her beaming expression had turned wistful.

"I hope so, my darling," she smiled. But there was a sadness in her that suggested her hopes were minimal. Her warmth was superficial; its reality was love and fear, affection and, William realised sadly, a concurrent deficit of hope. They had been dashed by life, and the menace of an unwritten future.

As well they might be, William thought, his heart breaking. This veteran of the *Mujeres Libres*, and then Female Secretariat in the POUM, and trench fighter until the ban – serving as a cook and a medic, just to be close, defying the ban whenever possible. Ideologically, the communists – he, Jack and Alan at any rate – had found they identified more with Anarchism than communism per se, having been swept up by the incredible buzz of arrival in Barcelona, 1936. And then they met Mary, of the *Partido Obrero de Unificación Marxista* as the Castilian name had it… and her passion… her beauty, spirit and beliefs had bowled over Jack and William, after all the long hours and nights and weeks and months and years up in Jack's bedroom of his family home, debating ideology and dissecting slogans and meanings, exasperating Jack's mother and sister with their endless earnestness and obsessive recitals. In Catalonia, she won them over; William mused that all three of them fell in love with her that first week. This girl with fire in her brown eyes, flecked with green. Dazzling, radiant, *brilliant*.

"She's amazing," Alan had proclaimed loudly in a packed café bar on the Ramblas, drinking his fourth cupful of the sweet Andalusian spirit that was not yet banned. It was morning. Duncan had left to join the brigades in the Madrid defence, reminding them all as he left that they were communists. They stayed, wrapped up in the revolutionary fervour and camaraderie, and, slightly amazed, got drunk.

"I think I'm in love," the Geordie added.

"For how long this time," Jack enquired. "Piss off, Tyneside. Your affairs of the heart are as profound and long-lasting as a Charlie Chaplin film. Almost to the minute, in fact."

"Latent anti-Semitism right there," William butted in, pointing with his glass of Hierbas, the Ibiza liquor, which he spilled. "That does it. It's you and I for Mary then, Alan. Two horse race. Jack's knackered."

Alan belched loudly. "What, she's a Jew? No way. I thought this country had them all purged in..." he clicked his fingers impatiently, swaying. "...1666. Torquemada, and all that."

Jack and William shared a look, suppressing grins.

"Yeah, that's right," Jack added wryly. "It got pretty hot for them."

William raised his little tin cup. "A *toast*, to the victims of the Spanish Inquisition... all of Spain's Jews who burned to death in England... in the Great Fire of London."

Alan went to join in the toast with a spontaneous little cheer, before comprehension dawned on him.

"Oh *howay* you pair of bastards. Whatever bloody year it was, then. Too bad for your cockneys, Jack, though there's not enough fires in London if you ask me."

He knocked his drink back, and called for a refill mid-conversation. "Anyway, *Mary*. She's completely changed the way I think about Marx's theories!"

"Aye," William had agreed, stopping to hug a passing Italian militiaman with an eye-patch who was sharing their hotel with them. The man fobbed yet another Hierbas onto the Scot, and kissed his cheek, yelling '*No pasarán! Fascista maricones!*' William yelled it back, roaring with laughter, and the little café took up the chant with gusto.

"These POUM fellows are great people!" William added, once the haiku died down.

Jack had weighed in, and the consequences would change all their lives for good. "Well, I was going to suggest we join the CNT… our communists are working for centralism and efficiency of state, and from what we can tell, anarchy definitely cares more about total liberty and equality. That's more what we've been looking for! But it will never catch on in Britain – imagine it!"

They'd all agreed, laughing, a little sadly. And then Jack continued, fatefully, "But the POUM… that *is* Marxism and liberty… that *is equality*. Look at Mary!"

"I think I will!" Alan roared, slapping him on the back, and spilling the rest of his own newly acquired drink over a Spaniard militiaman behind him, whom he embraced fondly without missing a beat. The Spaniard replaced Alan's drink, calling him *hermano*.

And they had stormed out into the thronging Barcelona streets to join the POUM. The headquarters was not far away, down the bottom of the Ramblas towards the Columbus monument, and there was no scarcity of drinks, songs and camaraderie in the POUM section to reinforce their confidence in the defection.

Before long, they shipped out on a packed train, and found themselves sharing a trench with Mary and a battalion of mostly Catalans. A handful of other odds and sods from all over Europe made up the numbers, from Frenchies to Italians, even a few Jerries who'd similarly defected from the International Brigades and allied to the Catalan Marxists' cause; wanted exiles who had fled Hitler's Germany before being extended the legendary Gestapo hospitality at Prinz Albrecht-Strasse.

For them, even more so than the Italians and Spanish it seemed, the war in Spain was deeply personal and irreconcilable, with fervent Nazis on the other side, and the chance to fight the mortal enemy of their own country in a way that was impossible in Germany itself. Their fate was sealed, parallel with the foreign Republic they fought for. They would win, and live, or lose and die.

Good people.

"Babe," William murmured in the present as he lay with his lover, thoughts lingering in the arid climate of blood-drenched Spain. "Do you remember Willi? German Willi?"

If he expected a smile, or laugh of recognition and warmth, he was left disappointed. She wriggled a little in bed beside him, and her tone was flat.

"I remember him."

And so she did. Young Wilhelm, they called him, or *Heini Villi*. He'd been older than they by several years, but had retained the boyish face of an unshaven child yet to sprout his first chin hairs. Willi was from Nuremberg, which nobody could quite believe; it being a heartland of National Socialism, after all, and they put him through lengthy mock interrogations as a Fifth Columnist. Once he'd stood with the Hitler salute for a rendition of *Deutschland Über Alles*, while they roundly booed him and threw pebbles from all sides of the trench.

Prone to wild mood swings, his cheerfulness and gentle nature suddenly gave way to bouts of brooding and anger, and in combat he fought as though driven by some bad memory of darkness past. Wilhelm died in the May Days, back in Barcelona. He'd been killed by a communist – it was safe to assume – who shot him from an upstairs window as he walked down one of the Ramblas side streets on which they'd all sang together; anarchist, Marxist and Stalinist alike, only seven months prior. No division then; comrades, brothers all. William had shed tears at the news, that terrible night, as they traversed the outer town to find shelter elsewhere, away from the bitter intrigues of the Ramblas and the 'political' quarters.

"We've been fucking betrayed," Alan screamed, grabbing at the gun that had been taken from him by a white-faced William. Jack steered them down an alleyway, from doorway to doorway, until eventually they stole out to non-politically tainted territory and marched northwest, Alan's vile muttered curses the only sound from a shell-shocked group.

Jack expended great energy dissuading Alan from tearing up their CPGB cards, which they knew could prove to be, quite literally, lifesaving. They reached a neutral hotel, miles from the Ramblas and booked a room, in which they stewed quietly, bile rising in their throats. Willi had twisted, wriggled, contorted on the cobblestones; choking out his last breaths in the dust. Mary, for the first time, just stayed quiet. She was numb with shock.

At least, the Catalan thought now, *he never saw it coming. Wilhelm was lucky in a way – he missed 1939. Nor did he see the POUM members rounded up, shot or imprisoned. Nor the fascist tanks rolling through the streets. Nor the rapes, the tortures, the evil. Nor did he live to see the Nazis invading the very country to which they fled their nightmare.*

"He's dead, William," she whispered, sadly. "Another dead boy *en un sueño loco...*" and with that, her voice trailed off.

She kissed his chest again, fighting back tears and he held her, tightly, as though he'd never let her go.

That first day... a dream. It seemed like a lifetime, some kind of bizarre and distant hallucinatory dreamworld; like a shamanic peyote cactus trip experience that transcended them to some Quixotic, far-flung fantasy, in which everything good and true and honest and *just* that could possibly happen to humanity, every beautiful feeling and acceptance of solidarity and love, *did* happen. So distant, yet still there on their skin, on their hands and tongues and in their eyes and thoughts and dreams... nothing could possibly express how it felt; no words or storytelling could begin to encapsulate how special it was, excitement palpable, riding into the horizon of change and inventing history as they went along; how *invigorating* it was that there was no concept of class, or man-made constructs like money or status, neither barriers and divisions, nor race, how none of them were British or Jews or Italians or even Spaniards and Catalans, simply *human beings* all, and all equal...

There was no question of what it meant for all of us, William thought with deep pride and sorrow. It was the sense of destiny, of belonging; for the first time in *history*, The People had risen together and triumphed over the forces of tyranny; institutions of evil and suppression, the church, the state and all central authorities and ruling elites. Catalonia was the nuclei of some kind of elemental force that had triumphed over the worst instincts in humanity and kicked them screaming to the curb. A central authority still reigned in Madrid, holding the rest of Spain together in its democratic social paradigm – even with the rebels under Franco and Mola securing huge swathes of land across the peninsula – but it was liberal; it was accepting, even *supportive*. Catalonia's own people broke free and reigned in true anarchy; the real meaning of 'no man left behind', not military jargon, but the real belief that human beings of that land could live in *egalitarian peace*.

Such cathartic times... walking through Barcelona the first day, singing and dancing, shouting, chanting slogans, hugged and embraced by everyone. Strong smells of tobacco and cannabis smoke; unwashed bodies, energy, excitement, emotions at fever-pitch. Meeting Mary, hearing this beautiful Spanish girl – they didn't know yet to distinguish – outpouring her passions and the triumph of solidarity which to them had only been a pipedream in their English pubs and bedrooms and walks through the park. To their surprise and delight, Alan, completely overcome and drunk, embracing them both with tears in his eyes, "this is how life is supposed to be! *This* is how life is supposed to be!"

Now, it didn't matter what your beliefs were, what vantage point you gazed from or what your role in this brave new world was, or how it viewed *you*; from catharsis of the soul to the crushing of it; in little over four years, the world had turned the other cheek, or looked and watched and then fought too late, to stop merciless power from unleashing its tyranny of racial and ideological persecution, treacherous diplomacy and military aggression, pitiless malice, blasting the libertarian goodness into oblivion with the roar of bombs and bullets.

Naomi's day could not have been better, up until that point.

Leeds was radiant, glowing green. The bomb damage at the Woodpecker Pub on her tram line leading into the city centre had ceased to be of interest to anyone, let alone a saddening sight, and it seemed people were finally beginning to see light at the end of the tunnel. Even Naomi was hopeful. She'd been teaching unimpeded for five weeks without interference, and the sight of German uniforms was a rarity.

With the resistance underground, and the sparse battles – more isolated ambushes now, was the rumour – were situated so far past the city's northern outskirts that by this stage, nobody in Leeds could hear the sounds of bombardment. Nothing of the wartime reality existed in this present, and the sun, bizarrely, continued to shine with a continental European summer's heat, with the English autumnal chill having not yet struck.

So it was with a spring in her step that she skipped into the headmaster's office to see Mr Clifford, who had summoned her for a meet after the day's lessons were at an end.

The old dandy of a headmaster was perusing some notes at his desk; a sheaf of some quality, thick paper that looked bizarrely out of place in the immediate aftermath of wartime. Naomi couldn't make out the unfamiliar seal. Though she rapped the door before entering, Mr Clifford took his time as he leisurely inspected his papers before deigning to raise his head to the striking young woman he'd summoned. When he finally did, she noticed the distracted, discomfited look in his eyes. He was unsettled. The man's usual steely composure had been affected in some way.

"Do come in, Naomi, and take a seat..." his voice trailed off, uncertain.

"Thanks."

Mr Clifford sighed. Young for a head at 41, his eyes were only just beginning to betray his age, with crow's feet adoring the smooth skin around them that he'd managed to carry into his late thirties. A thick but sleek mop of wavy hair split in a centre-parting so equidistant she suspected it had been measured with a ruler, and high cheekbones set on a stern but boyish face, Clifford was a dandy, though he could quickly become a rather forbidding figure. But the older man had always had a good rapport with the amiable, witty Naomi, and his deep, stentorian voice was softer than usual when he addressed her, though he quickly recovered and maintained his typical lack of any modicum of hesitance.

"Look Naomi, I'm going to get straight to the point. We've received a letter from something called the *Race & Resettlement* office, of all things... what that office has to do with employment or the education system in this country, I have no idea, but unfortunately it seems to supersede any existing legal framework and our dear friends from the continent seem to have enforced it with some success from London."

She continued to look puzzled. Noting it, he hurried to explain.

"In the letter – *this* letter," he said, holding one of the pages aloft of the high quality paper, so she could see the two hated lightning runes at its base. The seal had been an eagle, she saw now, with the swastika held in its talons. "They have made a direct enquiry about, well... I'm very sorry to say this, but they've highlighted your *ethnic* background... which in the system to be imposed... *hopefully* only while the governments arrange a deal, but nonetheless in the *here and now*... means that your presence in this school in itself contravenes these new rulings."

Naomi's mouth fell open. After all these weeks, just as things were starting to look up, her world was to fall apart like a paper shack in a storm. She had been waking up and enjoying the pale sun on her face again, walking through the park filling her lungs with fresh air, relishing the continuance of some semblance of *normal life*. That was now over. Mr Clifford made no effort to provide her with a honeyed explanation, but his voice was notably tinged with regret.

"As you can imagine, Naomi, I'm not in a position to lie about such matters. This race office is part of the SS machine; teachers and educational authorities start lying to them and all hell's liable to break loose. So…" for the first time, he dropped his gaze, absentmindedly shuffling the sheaf of stacked papers. "After serious deliberation, I have concluded that the only way forward is – and it really does pain me to say this, it *pains* me to say this – I'm going to have to ask you to leave St Mary's. *For the time being*, at the very least, just until this thing clears. Which it hopefully will, sooner than later. I am so sorry, but I really have no choice."

Naomi was stunned. After all the initial fears, time had deadened her senses and the comparative calm of the period had led to her believe that things were on the way up. The outrageous anti-Semitic materials had been quietly shelved by the teachers, and no one had bothered to check them. Even the persecution of her people, if you could call them that, now seemed abstract, a distant nightmare. Something *other than real*, like an urban myth or a bedtime horror story to teach children; a grotesque cautionary tale, to be sanitised and packaged as future entertainment. But now it touched *her*. This madness, whatever it was.

She found her voice, which to her surprise had a choked quality.

"But… how can they? How? They've only been here a matter of weeks?

"I know, they're awfully efficient aren't they?" He chuckled without humour. "On things such as war and matters of race and ethnicity, this new breed of German seems to be quite formidable organisers. They're more robot than human.

"They're not human," Naomi said lowly. He nodded in sympathy, but evaded the point.

"I believe they are working with the Inland Revenue. Unfortunately, with a Jewish name such as yours you stick out like a sore thumb. It's a perishing shame… you have been an excellent member of our team."

"What, and that's it?" she cried, suddenly flaring up. "I'm meant to just grab my stuff and leave? Who'll take my classes? What about my kids?"

But Mr Clifford's face lost its increasingly avuncular look, and in his more familiar deadpan expression Naomi saw no hope for pleas to prevail upon his better nature. Nor could she charm him, she knew; he alone of the male staff had never so much as cast an admiring glance in her direction. He was utterly devoid of lust, it seemed. And in this case, of true empathy.

"We'll manage, Naomi. You've not had them for half a term, anyway, children can cope. I really *am* sorry. We will of course pay you until the end of term, and provide you with a small settlement – off the record – but alas, beyond that, I really must insist on your resignation."

She left his office in a daze.

Outside, the walked outside the school gates, fighting the urge to throw up, until finally she succumbed, half-stumbling into one of the rhododendron bushes on a grass verge at the edge of the school grounds. She got back to a level-footing, shakily, and began tottering away in the direction of Hyde Park for the tram.

"Naomi, Naomi wait!"

Paul ran several hundred feet to catch up with her. Naomi was embarrassed to be seen in a state, and would have preferred to lick her wounds privately. But Paul was Paul.

He reached her, not yet out of breath but with a slight catch in his voice.

"I've just heard the news. It's awful Naomi, simply awful."

She murmured something indistinct. He shrugged, helplessly, and then added with vehemence.

"No, it's *bloody* awful. Jerry *bastards*." He bit into the latter word with venom, the Leeds accent spitting it in the phonetically blunt Yorkshire style.

"I feel like I'm dreaming, Paul," she said weakly. A gust of wind blew a great tuft of hair over her face as she looked around, as though panicking. "What have I done? What is it with these people? Who are they?"

"Come 'ere, you," he told her gently.

He held her tightly to him, and despite her best efforts, tears welled up in her dark eyes. She blinked furiously.

"What am I to do?" she asked quietly, from his armpit. He felt, more than heard her sigh, and quickly suppressed the resulting train of thought.

"Well... first thing is to get you somewhere safe. I know this might sound off, but you shouldn't go back to your parents. If they need help I'll get it 'em, if they need a new roof over their 'eads. You shouldn't stay at yours, either, just in case. If—" and as his voice rose, she looked up at him in alarm as the words sank in, her eyes pleading for clarification. He spoke soothingly. "Relax… relax. I just mean, in case this got worse, if they were trying to slowly tighten the noose without drawing attention to it, gradually…"

She started to sob again, and he cursed himself inwardly. *Bloody* hell, *Paul. Think man.*

"We just don't know enough yet to feel completely secure, do we? So it's best to play things safe. You can stay at mine until we think of something more long term."

He wondered if it sounded vulgar, even – God forbid – opportunistic, like some kind of perverted act upon her recently increased tenderness towards him. But to his relief, some happiness shone through the misery in her eyes.

"Of course."

~

They took the car Paul shared with his increasingly frail old father, and drove east to Chapeltown North Street where Naomi had decamped; ironically enough, more part of the Jewish community than was her parent's house in the terraces towards Harehills. Paul chose the inner-city route, avoiding the city centre due to the possibility of random German stop and search. Not that either of them were actively working against the Reich's fragile – or was it? – hold on Great Britain, at least north of the capital. But with the onset of anti-Semitic laws reaching the north of England, neither trusted in blind optimism any longer. Clearly, it was Quixotic and foolish to believe in any collective altruism in the near-future.

The people were eating as well as they had two years prior. The resistance was stubbornly clinging on, in hidden countryside bunkers and fortified zones;

without foreign support their supplies, and then time, would run out. The rest were either in factories, foreign POW camps or living quietly. They had all suffered, to some degree. No one would wage further war for the sake of a few unemployed Jews.

They reached Naomi's flat, and she kicked off her shoes, mental exhaustion showing as she fell into the couch. Paul took the armchair, looking around.

"Well, to finally reach your inner sanctum. Not the best circumstances, mind."

She smiled weakly in response. They sat in companionable silence for some time.

Finally, she sighed. "It's like a bad dream. It doesn't feel real."

"All that we see or seem, is but a dream within a dream..." Paul murmured smoothly and she smiled, recognising Poe.

"Dark path to go down. I wonder what Hitler would make of old Edgar Allan?"

Paul snorted. "Love the bastard. A yank mongrel, racially impure and all that, but exempted as an *Aryan descendent* somewhere along the way, hundreds of years back." He snorted, and began to tick an invisible list with his fingers. "Wears a 'tache. Neurotic. Morbidly obsessed with death. A morphine addict, like the Führer's own beloved Prime Minister. Yeah, Poe is fine for Hitler."

"There are moments when even to the sober eye of reason, the world of our sad humanity may assume the semblance of Hell..." Naomi offered. He grinned, a little forced.

"Right, old girl," he said loudly, rising to his feet. "Time we move thy bloody stuff, eh? No use moping about."

"I know."

He hesitated.

"Go on," she exhorted.

"Well... I'm just thinking, this is a pre-emptive measure. A precaution, like. You don't have to, y'know... sell this place, or anything. Or, it's only rented, eh? Even better. Just leave it empty. Don't worry about money on it, or anything... if you wanted, I could stay here while you stay at mine. And I'll keep for both places, put my name down on this place... and mine's only small it's not much at all, no trouble..."

Embarrassed, Paul started arranging items for his friend to bring with her. She spared his feelings by leaping to it, nudging him playfully, and she set about collecting that which she could not bear to leave behind. Within a minute, she had all she needed. Bare essentials, and some items of sentimental value, enough to fit between one bag and a single box.

"I'll come back book for your books," he offered, lamely. She shrugged.

"Not much to show for a life on the run, is it?" she tried to laugh. "Bonnie Parker probably had a more exciting inventory for her travels."

"Charming. That would make me Clyde, a murderous nihilist." Paul did a parody of mock-celebration. "From lowly teacher to *dangerous romantic felon* of international renown. Today marks an advancement up the social ladder, aye?"

Naomi laughed, as she always did at the way Paul's words often sat at odds with the Yorkshire accent. While herself born and bred of Leeds, her own was tinged with family heritage. As with all wanderers and descendants of the diaspora, the slight Semitic bite of Hebrew still edged its way into the pronunciation of the adopted tongue.

"And a harbourer of a *partisan of assimilation* and *enemy of the German Reich*," she quoted, even managing a genuine grin to accompany it. He whistled.

"My credentials are through the roof. I'll be on wanted posters next; Paul Heggerty a.k.a Clyde, *Dead or Alive*. Now then, let's be 'aving you, Bonnie. To the criminal lair."

They drove back west, the route through the estates of Chapel Allerton, Meanwood and Headingley interspersed with leafy lanes and several quiet public parks and squares. On Woodhouse Lane they passed the road to St. Mary's, and continued down towards Hyde Park to the north of the city centre where Paul's flat was.

Entering was a furtive affair. Once inside, they both relaxed.

The flat was converted from one of the newer two-up-two-down terraced houses in the Hyde Park area, many of which had been converted for use as student digs, and were equipped with indoors bathrooms. The house was four floors overall; Paul's apartment essentially consisted of the intended kitchen and ground storey indoors toilet, and a large basement bedroom underneath. The stairs to the first and second floors, and the ground floor bedroom had been partitioned with a wall that made a loud, resonating sound when knocked, and which gave very little in the way of privacy.

Naomi looked around the kitchen. The small room, with its sofa couch and small dining table, would be her world for much of the time. Down the straight, wide wooden steps, Naomi found a surprisingly roomy basement, whose bathroom subdivision she suspected Paul had himself installed.

"Oh, Paul."

She turned to him, as his footsteps echoed on the wood behind her.

"It's not much, I know," he said quickly. "Just an easy place to live for a single teacher near his school. Somewhere to read at night, and not too far from the pubs."

He winked, after the rather flat endorsement of his accommodation. Naomi looked around, seeing it anew. Well-leafed old paperbacks, thick tomes and heavy hardback copies of novels, poetry, philosophy, theology, jurisprudence, and every other conceivable subject and field of interest.

Her liking for the place swelled. It was a suitable underground den for Paul, and his strange, studious ways juxtaposed with a slightly Bohemian nature.

She turned to him, beaming, to find him leaning against the wooden beam by the foot of the stairs, a slight smile on his face.

"Come on, you," he chuckled. "Time we had a drink, lass."

~

The Hyde Park pub was barely four minutes' walk away.

Entering into the smoky atmosphere, Naomi winced. It was not so much the cigarette fumes that bothered her, it was the returning memory that drifted up of the Leeds Blitz.

The terrible scream of the 'Jericho Siren' – a German Stuka bomber unloading in the centre of town. The fire watchers had called it in, and her Auxiliary Fire Unit had headed for the roaring blaze that engulfed the old Woodpecker Pub.

Curious Leeds folk thronged the street to survey the damage. Some were children. Even now, Naomi had a vivid sense of the surreal atmosphere; her own incredulity at the acrid smoke and the visual horror of a military attack, and the complete absence of fear from the populace. Hours later, with daylight two hours old, the firemen and women had considered it a job well done, and the old publican of the 'New' Woodpecker had opened his doors to serve them all a few ales on the house. The camaraderie had been as warm as she'd known it, in those months serving. Even now, she remembered the genuine laughter and happiness following the fire. The spirit of *overcoming*.

Little did Leeds know that the horrors of war would shatter its peace beyond the tiny forewarning of those bombs. A pub here, a house there. Nothing on the terrible scenes of the following months.

They sat down, Paul clinking two glasses down on the round wooden table. Smoke hung in the air above them.

"Do you mind?" Paul asked, pulling out a Woodbine. Naomi responded by leaning forwards coquettishly, and snatching the packet from him, before retrieving two and using Paul's lighter to spark them both. Maintaining the steady, flirtatious eye contact with him throughout, she silkily extended one of the lit fags to an amused Paul with her right index and middle fingers, which she then twirled theatrically.

"By all means, Clyde."

He laughed.

"Dangerous girl. You'll tempt me to more scallywag behaviour before this occupation is through, I'll wager. Bet the house on it. Perhaps," he leaned forwards, eyes widening comically, "we could become black marketeers. Have our pick of the cigarettes. Trade playing cards with naked ladies on 'em. Bootlegged moonshine, like the yanks in the '20s."

"Careful. Already hoarding illicit goods, remember."

Her tone was still playful, and he seized on it.

"That's the point; a stashed Jew will be more dangerous than a few black market smokes and a pistol, eh? More risk, more reward. In for a penny..." he said, winking.

She smiled back, but it was transparently false, and he saw the creeping doubt cloud her eyes.

Bloody hell, Paul. What's the bleedin' matter with you lad?

"On a serious note," he said quickly, seeking to limit the damage. "Whatever is best for you, I will do it. This week we'll get your name off the other place, and I'll stop there and all that. Put your Mam and Dad in with mine... whatever it takes."

He took a mighty swig of the pint to cover for his painful awareness of the clumsy approach, and was immensely gratified when she laid a hand gently on his.

"You're not going anywhere. And I won't forget what you're doing for me."

They drank three pints of mild each, complete with the extravagance of smoking three cigarettes each, and then returned to the flat. Given the larger space, they went straight down to the basement.

Paul strolled in, trying to act as naturally as he could, and deposited himself on one of the small chintzy sofa's he'd placed next to each other along one wall of the room. Naomi stood awkwardly by the stairs, ill at ease. He looked at her confused.

"This is your room. Don't worry. I'm sleeping upstairs."

Beats of silence passed, and she drifted over and laid down on the bed, flopping out as though suddenly drained of energy. Paul grabbed a book, and a spare blanket from the sideboard, and decided it was time to leave her to it.

"Hey. I'm going to head up. You relax, settle in and unwind. Remember I'm just upstairs."

"Paul, I can't take your room."

But he was firm. He'd decided that the hesitation and idiotic throwaway comments had to be ruthlessly eradicated. These were times that called for decisiveness.

"I'm sleeping upstairs. Tomorrow I'll go settle in your apartment if you like, make you as comfortable as possible. We'll get through this."

 He successfully resisted the almost instinctive urge to make a facetious remark, something along the lines of being quite glad she was a Jew, as her apartment was far the superior to his. Moving up the first steps, he half-turned back.

"Good night, lass. Sleep tight and try not to worry about all this, eh? Could all come to nothing. This isn't Germany."

Wasn't it, Naomi thought. Ten years ago, Jewish teachers, doctors and lawyers practised and worked in Germany. German Jews contributed to science, philosophy and literature in a Germany not ruled by fascist militarists and Nazi racial theory. Who knows what's going on anymore? *Anywhere.* Or what Germany, and France and England, *are*, or *are not*.

"Hey, Paul?"

She called him back, softly, just as he reached the top step where the threshold back into his makeshift kitchen and living room was. He came down four steps, and ducked beneath the beam, craning his neck to see her.

"Yeah?"

"Bonnie and Clyde, I referenced earlier. But what happened to them in the end? Did they get away? Go underground? Or get caught?"

He chuckled; a little sadly, she thought.

"They were shot and killed by the police."

She looked at him, framed in the half-light. *The police.* In this country; operating under German laws, ruled from Berlin, manned by SS.

"And they died?" she asked, her voice steady.

Paul began walking back up the stairs. "Yeah. They died. Sad story, eh?"

"Drink up Jerry!" Tommy screamed, his young face flushed a violent crimson. Hoffman roared at him.

"Insolent private! I am a Lieutenant of the Führer's personal army! You'll be whipped for this!"

There was an immediate chorus of gibberish from the mouths of twenty drunken Englishmen. "*Unteroberschlieffenhofferzollerbeckerführer Hoffman! Heil!*"

Hoffman tried repeating it, failing miserably, and laughingly downed his portion of the Scotch. The sharp taste almost made him retch, and there was a cheer from the men.

"OK, again!"

They played the same stupid hand-slapping game, whereby both would, in turn, try to slap the other's hands, which were held together fingertip to fingertip as though clasped in prayer. Tommy won again, and Hoffman downed yet another short of whiskey, his face bunching up afterwards. He looked around the hut, seeing James Wilkinson sat stoically at the back, on his own, reading. Several others had opted out of the alcohol-fuelled merriments, but James' closest friends had enthusiastically joined in. He was aloof.

"Private Wilkinson!"

At once, with a mocking air, the Yorkshireman leapt to his feet and said in monotone, "Ja, mein SS-Lieutenantführer Hoffman."

Hoffman snorted. "Don't be silly. Come join us."

At once Tommy began entreating him, as did several others:

"Come on, old boy! Whiskey is whiskey."

"Hoffman don't bite, son!"

"Don't worry about Jerry he's all right, it's his gift!"

Ultimately, the whiskey proved too alluring, and the disgruntled private finally stormed down the aisle, as the cheers grew louder. Perching himself on the end bunk, James downed a prodigious gulp of Scotch, and grudgingly smiled as Tommy clapped him on the back.

"Good job, northern monkey!"

Hoffman fixed his gaze on the Yorkshireman, and the smile melted from James' face. The German wasn't hostile, he seemed curious. James was as inexpressive as ever.

"You've avoided drinking with me for weeks and weeks," Hoffman asked, quietly. "A drink here or there, but you never stay to talk. Every time I bring beer or whiskey, you prefer to remain separate." The gaiety died down. Some men looked at the floor.

"I know it's me that you have the problem with," he continued. Not the Scotch. *No* real man has a problem with Scotch."

There was some titters, but mostly nervous anticipation.

Hoffman affected mock-sadness. "Well, private?"

"I just don't think it's right to declare you lot enemies, go to war, then t'next thing we're all bloody pals drinking Scotch. It's either a bit daft, or it's just not right at all."

There were some muttered agreements; guiltily from a couple sat drinking the booze brought by the lieutenant, and more vigorously by the handful that had abstained. Tommy looked down at the floor. Brian and the Sarge shared a worried glance, and did likewise. Hoffman noted the reactions quietly, and raised his hands up, facing James.

"Again, I am not your enemy. Just a *Jerry* who got transferred here due to speaking good English, and given the role to liaise. Of course, I was eager to take it. It involved no real work, simply an effort to interact with other people, like a human. To share drinks," he said, raising his glass. "Like there is no war. Senior officers think it is not only acceptable, but a *good* idea. I take advantage. Thus, we sit here, happy, drinking fine Scotch and smoking better cigarettes than the public in Berlin or London do. We wear different uniforms, and I don't know, Private Wilkinson, perhaps you and I have different views. I would hope you're not a communist. But I know you're not a freemason, or Jew. So under the uniform, we're the same. We can drink."

James looked back at him, thoughtfully. He let it all sink in. *I know you're not a freemason or a Jew.* That was interesting. From the sound of it, they had all been checked. And if Hoffman was lying in his ingratiating approach, he was an uncommonly good actor. Impossibly good. Potentially a psychopath the likes of which had never before even been imaginable.

"All right. So you want to be best pals with me and the boys, do you?"

There was a hint of a sneer that Hoffman did not pick up on. Tommy tried catching his eye to warn him off. James ignored him.

"Friends don't lie."

Silence. Hoffman nodded, urging him to elaborate. He did, but like a truculent Yorkshireman, refusing to be rushed, in his own time.

"I want you to tell us honestly... judging by the fact you're not an army man, with those little 'S' lightning bolt things on your collar... why do you love Hitler so bloody much?"

For a split second, you could cut the silence with a knife, and then Tommy let out a roar.

"*Ohhh*!!! That's a money question right there!"

The others regained their semi-drunken merriment, and heckled along. Even Hoffman was forced to grin.

Tommy interjected again, grinning. He'd made the bond with Hoffman, and knew that he could force home the advantage with less chance of finding himself in bother, unlike James.

"Right, Lieutenant. That's a good question. Why are you in the SS? You've got to tell us."

Hoffman's own smile faded again, and the room waited with baited breath. All were unashamedly curious, as though they were about to have an alien descended from Mars explain itself and its species. The excitement at the booze, and Hoffman's easy manner and language skills had helped greatly obscure the conflict of interests and beliefs. But, as James had never lost sight of, he wore the SS runes.

"Very well. You feel you must know?" Hoffman asked. James nodded, and a murmur of assent rumbled through the men.

With the silent room listening intently, SS-Obersturmführer Hoffman quietly began.

"I am 26. I cannot explain to you what that means as a German. Twenty-six years ago, the Fatherland was embroiled in a Great War on two fronts, against Britain and France to our west, and Russia to the east. Facing the world's largest empire, the world's largest army and the world's largest country, all at once. That was how strong, how great Germany was. My father sired me just before signing up to the army. He told my mother he would either return victorious, or in a box. I never even saw him."

A few faces softened at that. There were other orphans in that room from the same war, possibly the same battles, and several men nodded in grudging solidarity. Hoffman continued:

"My mother took on his job in a Munich armaments factory. She caught jaundice sometime after I was born – likely when I was still breastfeeding. Her health overall was not too good. But she survived the war. My father did not. He died on the Black Day of the German Army. August 8th 1918... five hundred and fifty tanks, two thousand aeroplanes, twenty British Empire divisions, twelve French, one American. All against Germany. We had eight divisions, three hundred aircraft."

He shook his head in wonder. "How could the Fatherland fight for four years against the entire world – conquering Russia in the east, facing the British, French and Americans in the west! Overcoming even the Black Day, making advances again weeks later, holding firm on foreign soil, fifty miles from Paris! Only to be stabbed in the back by the coward government, our money flow cut and our country signed away by a Jew as our boys fought in the mud..."

Total silence, as Hans bitterly recounted his understanding of the Great War and his country's political situation. His voice had trailed as he gave way to anger. Then his usual composure returned.

"After the war, shame. *Humiliation.* I was too young to truly understand, but I remember the confused aftermath five years later, aged 10; the shame and degradation! Hyperinflation. Unemployment, poverty; families losing their life savings overnight. Decadence, prostitutes, filth everywhere. Germany was in terminal decay... infected by sickness, persecuted by the Great War victors and a shell of its former self. We recovered, and then a few years later, the Depression put us right back there..." He shook his head sorrowfully, at the memories. All watched him quietly.

"Oh, Tommies, you cannot imagine the horror. Banknotes in shopping bags; wheelbarrows filled with money just to buy their children's milk. Millions of marks for a loaf of bread; people's savings wiped out and made useless. We were lost, with nowhere to turn... every young son of the Fatherland was in despair. I was on my knees, bleeding to death."

Hoffman's face transformed, and he gave off a manic, reverent glow. His voice grew soft, shaking with scarcely suppressed emotion.

"But then, *I heard a man speak in Munich.* A night at the Bürgerbräukeller that will live with us forever... he *spoke* to me. He understood, and *shared my pain.* He felt my grief."

The lieutenant's eyes shone. Everyone listened, rapt, and there was not a flicker of movement in the silent barracks as the German resumed his reminiscence:

"I didn't even know what the party *was*. I'd tried the communists, and heard Soviet slogans about the workers revolution. But this man... he understood. He felt it too. All the suffering that the Fatherland was going through, he felt more keenly than anyone. He felt what we all felt, in that beer hall, but he wouldn't laugh, or joke, or grin and bear it. This man would fight it, purge Germany of its weakness and enemies, and make us strong again. And we all knew that night, that our Führer had been sent from God. It was the hand of Providence, to save Germany, to build a new Reich and free our people from their chains. To free all of Europe, and destroy those that would destroy us. For him, we gave our oath, and he delivered us..."

No one spoke for a long time. Hoffman's eyes still glowed, as he visibly fought back the tears, and with utter reverence, he held aloft a glass of Scotch, and murmured in a loving croon, "to my Führer. Adolf *Hitler*."

The young Bavarian tipped it back, eyes wet.

~

The next day had been a quieter affair than usual, mostly due to the collective hangover that the other barracks seemed to be sharing with them, all benefactors of similar SS benevolence. There were no classes, and after roll call the men spent the day smoking, relaxing and reading the materials provided – most of which was translated from German newspapers and magazines, literary classics from Goethe and a collection of English novels.

The routine wore on. Early the next week, the daily lesson was attended by every single man in the Stanley's Boys barrack. The class encouraged debate and argument, as opposed to school-style droning of 'facts' and figures, and many of the soldiers present engaged in the debate. The talking shop focused on the role played by Jewish financiers in the Great War, and 'The System of Debt Slavery Imposed On The Gentile Peoples'. James was uncomfortable, having had Jewish friends from the Leeds community in Chapeltown and a few scattered around his home base of east Bradford, not to mention a half-Jewish pal from the training school, but some of the others took great interest in the class. Only after an hour had elapsed, when the neat makeshift lecturer in his ceremonial black SS tunic – they were no longer officially used, Hoffman had told them – brought out copies of 'The Protocols' for use as a reference point did the men heckle and bray, tiring of the lecture.

"Next time, gentlemen," he smiled, completely unfazed.

They trudged out, barely squinting in the weak late-Autumn sunlight, giving mixed reviews of the session. James overheard some men from the next barrack along, who were not in their original platoon.

"They have a point though. Bleedin' Jews, didn't see any serving with us did we? But my old Ma was working for 'em back home, where they'll still be, rich as you bloody like!"

"Ah, bollocks," his Liverpudlian friend retorted, in his thick, distinct and nasal accent. Typical for a Scouser, the pronunciation was 'bollixx', his speech laced with many suffixes and words oddly emphasised at random. The Scouser spat a prodigious blob of green phlegm onto the asphalt. "It's all a load of *bollocks*. Bloody bankers *this*, lawyers *that*, newspapers the *other*, they run the *world* and forced the gentiles into *war. Bollocks* man. I used to *work* in a *factory* with a pair of bleedin' *Jews* who barely even *knew* they *were* Jews."

"They would when they took a piss," someone else chortled.

"Who gives a flyin' *fuck* about their *foreskins* though, *la*?" the Scouser replied, baffled.

"They made money off t' rest of us in Wakey, I tell thee that bloody much," a strong Yorkshire accent loudly chuntered. His belligerence met with several murmurs of approval.

James sighed. They could all say what they liked, believe what they wanted, but these Nazis in their pretty SS uniforms and their fancy insignia and sinister cap badges could tell him the sky was blue and the grass was green, and something about them still compelled him to argue. No matter how nice they decided to be, there was still something missing there, something essential. Like warmth. A *true* warmth. However capably communicative they were, underlying it; most of them seemed hard without sentiment.

They all separated after the meal at dinner – the usual excellent fare, with meat and potatoes – to spent time writing letters, reading and smoking quietly. In the camp, there was an unspoken system that allowed each man his private time, alone with his thoughts. It was a collective conscious will to coexist as comfortably as possible, with each other as much as The Jerries, and it worked a treat.

That night, Brian quietly approached James Wilkinson's bunk, and tapped his foot. The Yorkshireman glanced up, internally debating whether or not to make an issue of his quiet time being disturbed, but affection won out. He put his book down.

"Go on."

Brian said nothing, his expression troubled. James sat up, checking around them. The others were sat around the room chatting in small groups on various bunks, but none were in earshot.

"Speak up lad. Tell me."

Brian whispered, "There's going to be an escape attempt."

"What?"

Brian spoke hurriedly, as though guilty and wishing to rid himself of a burden. The words came tumbling out, an outpouring of equal enthusiasm and defence:

"A few of the others were on about it last week the night Hoffman started bleating on about how much he loved Hitler and all that. A few of the boys are convinced that what Wolf said about the 'undred of our lads shot after surrender was bollocks, and *they all got done in*. Reckon we're in a camp run by liars and murderers. They're pretty serious about it. Reckon the towers are no good for getting us if we head over the far corner at the back, over the grass. Barbed wire but a few cuts are no problem. Once we're over, it's forest! And... if enough of them do it, I think we should. And I don't want to leave you, mate." He collected his breath, as though his burden had been expunged.

James considered it. He didn't much care for the situation they were in. On a more pragmatic level, though, he wasn't sure if a real alternative existed other than riding it out.

"Thing is, Bri... what's the alternative mate? Assuming escape *was* that easy, and this lot are so *slack*? If the empire was still at war with Adolf we might have a reason to escape and join the fight. But what are we going to do, stumble through the French forests and make for the sea? Where do we go? Even if we got a boat, we couldn't go home. Jerry's there. Belgium? Holland? Luxembourg? Or perhaps a border dash to Baden Baden... escape these krauts in Germany itself. That'd throw 'em, eh?" He snorted, scornfully.

Brian looked thoroughly put out. James regretted his sardonic approach, but knew it would be dangerous to concede the initiative he'd seized with such scorn.

"We can't turn anywhere, Bri. Heading south is no good either. Even if we made it, Spain would arrest us and send us back. They're fascists. And assuming we could make it that far, Italy would be no good either. They bloody *invented* fascism, the pricks. No mate, every direction, same situation, fascists everywhere. On all sides. Switzerland would be our only bet, and I don't see how it's possible."

"Why not mate?" Brian asked.

He tried to be casual, but James detected the desperation in his voice. Brian wanted out; the unrest was getting to him, and all he wanted was for his friend to offer a glimmer of hope for some plan or other, just to validate the possibility of success and thus vindicate the attempt. But James couldn't. He sighed again.

 "Because from where we are, Bri, it would take *weeks* to reach the Swiss border. You're talking about travelling six hundred miles, mate. *Limping* six hundred, in your case. To its north, both Switzerland and France border Germany, and there'll be patrols up and down the Rhine. Assuming we managed to head the right way, and actually reach Basel – by which time it will be Nineteen-Forty-Bloody-Eight – it's a border town, some of it's in bastard *Germany*!"

He looked around, having raised his voice. Satisfied no one had heard, James sat back, and lit a cigarette. The first puff was thoughtful, and then he continued. "They speak German, mate. Kraut soldiers will be everywhere, in a semi-circular ring closing it off. In the event of a border-crossing, army-crossing miracle, and we got inside, Kraut spies would be inside it too. And French, for that matter; this lot have hated Jews longer than the Germans have. They're already dancing about in swastikas, with a cooperating government, chucking commies into labour camps. Hell, they had camps for commies and lefties *before* the fucking Krauts got here... everyone who fled Spain got interned by the frogs. And you think *we'll* be all right?"

"So there's not even a possibility of success?" Brian asked, crestfallen. James wanted to cheer his good-natured friend up, but realised it was kinder to give him the honest truth.

"There's more chance o' Major Wolf coming in here dressed as Charlie Chaplin in a skull cap."

Offering him a cigarette to sweeten the bitter facts, James winked at him. "Cheer up. Like Tommy and the Sarge are always bleatin' on about, could be a lot worse."

Brian accepted the smoke. "Suppose so, aye." He took a few leisurely drags. James could see he was still troubled. After a while he got up, looking vacant.

"I'll leave you to it, big lad. Just thought I'd get your opinions. Now I guess I've gotta go moderate the rabble, make sure no one is daft enough to bunk off on their own on a six hundred mile circum-bleedin'-navigation eh?"

He wandered off, and sat down with James Fletcher and several others who, James noticed for the first time, had a plotter's air about them. James shook his head, and resumed reading, a new cigarette clenched between his lips. "Gormless southern bastards," he muttered, grumpily.

~

In his room that same night in the officers' building, Lieutenant Hoffman gazed at his own reflection in the mirror, set into a toilette cabinet in his tiny box of a bathroom. He preferred to shave himself, rather than trust his neck to a barber. His mother, herself half-English, had told him the story of Sweeney Todd when he was a child, the demon barber of Fleet Street, and it somehow stayed with him vividly. He also preferred to shave at night, in the quiet, no rush. Even drunk, as he was now, he had never cut himself. SS Obersturmführer Walther Hoffman used a brush to spread the creamy soap lather across his face, filling each patch of skin carefully, like thickly buttered bread. Methodically, he began to gently scrape his face with the sharpened razor, smoothly removing the sparse stubble.

He stared at the naked blade.

"Hold still," the man – Dietrich? Dieter? – had laughed, cruelly twisting the Jew's arms up behind his back, making him scream as a bone snapped. Hoffman grabbed his sidelocks, drew his own razor and sliced the plaited locks from his head. The Jew fell, writhing in pain and degradation. Hoffman felt no pity. Pity was weakness for the enemy that made Germany weak. The Jew bled host nations dry. The Führer merely ensured we destroy them before they destroy us.

This is a war of annihilation against the Judeo-Bolshevik racial and ideological enemy. One day it will be Russia, too. Either we will destroy them, *or they will destroy* us.

Walther Hoffman remembered the Jewish Action, entrusted to the fledgling SS Totenkopf division of which he'd been part, drafted voluntarily from the *Totenkopfverbände.* He signed up in August 1939, with twelve other SS-TV guards from Dachau.

The wooden houses on the outskirts of Włocławek on the Vistula had already been set ablaze by air raids during the Wehrmacht advance, and the Totenkopf 'Brandenburg' outfit had followed in their wake for the clean-up. Hoffman stared at the mirror, seeing only carnage where his own reflection should be.

"This has been long overdue," Standartenführer Paul Nostitz said grimly beside him. All the suffering of our people, the parasitic infestation of European nations for a millennium..."

Włocławek. Despite himself, Walther sometimes saw it in his dreams.

It had been easy enough to find, simply by following the smoke plumes from the blackened husks of burnt out buildings. The city had not escaped the Luftwaffe – none could. The wrecked debris of human settlement was scattered around in smouldering piles all around, the acrid stench almost suffocating. Frightened civilians were stood here and there, watching the panzer unit pass through the city streets, but by and large the ominous spectacle of a war-ravaged ghost town was more evident.

The Death's Head had set up shop, billeted comfortably. Hoffman was an Untersturmführer, pending promotion. Nostitz had read his recommendation with cool approval, and Hoffman had known that to become an SS-Lieutenant proper he must perform well in the initial Jewish actions in Poland. He had to marshal men, and take a leading role directing the vengeance. He'd done it coolly. *This is war. They are the enemy. They are Jews. It is them or us.*

He had led by example.

The convoy rolled through a street on the outskirts that had been relatively untouched by the chaos. The road was paved smooth, not cobbled, and wide, spacious gardens were separated by wicket fences. Each house was detached. Hoffman had sneered, as had every man in each panzer tank, each armoured car, and the troops' truck. Of course, the Jews would be out of the way. Safe. Secure. Probably sat back earning money from facilitating arms deals and loans to finance the Polish resistance to the Reich.

Heydrich's SD had prepared booklets for them. A black list. Names of the doomed. The intellectuals, commissars and Jews of Poland. None were safe. The Jewish elders of the city would be killed as an example. The rest would be ghettoised.

Hoffman stopped the convoy. This was it.

Waffen-SS troops poured out of the trucks. They wore the skull and bones on collar and cap; men of the Totenkopf; The Death's Head Unit, comprising of combat troops from the Totenkopfverbände concentration camp guards. Now their cruelty was turned outwards, to the Reich's external enemies. From jailors to hunters.

Hoffman himself marched down the middle of the street. "Two in there," he barked, pointing to the houses of the damned. "Two in there! That house! And that house!"

Cradling the sub-machine gun strung around his neck, and drawing his long-nosed Mauser in his left hand for effect, he'd taken one house for himself, feeling the thrill of the chase, the exhilaration of battle. The door being cheap and wooden, inexpensive after all. Kicked through with ease. Bursting in to find a terrified Jewish family. Huddled in the corner, two girls and a women crouching. Crying in terror. A father, protecting his daughters. Hoffman stepped forwards and brought the officer's Mauser down across the little man's nose, breaking the bone with a sickening crunch.

"Get out!" He roared at them in Polish. "Get the fuck out!"

Screaming a haiku of German curses, he kicked the old man out, flailing as he sprawled on the gravel; his wife begging and pleading in a hysterical hybrid of Polish and Yiddish. Hoffman seized her in a strong grip, and threw her out bodily onto the path to her front door that cut through the neat square of the garden. Seething, his nerves on fire, he slung the children out onto the grass himself where the huddled to their stricken parents, paralysed in shock.

One house along, ear-splitting child shrieks from a child cowered in the kitchen corner. The little boy stood metres from where a woman was wailing over the prone body of her husband, who had quite clearly been battered senseless. The family had been eating; the evidence of an interrupted dinner lay on the table. Half-eaten, the family meal would never be enjoyed in quiet; it was their last moment of peaceful normality, before a terrible whirlwind from elsewhere sucked their lives, and so many others up into its path.

The Jewish father had been beaten to the brink of death. The sight of a bread knife in the man's hand had driven the SS men apoplectic with rage. Or something other than rage... a bestial frenzy of wild hatred.

"Don't worry, the kike is still alive," Hoffman sneered, on witnessing the scene.

The Jewish woman wailed, which intensified as she was hit flush in the face by a stream of urine from one of the Death's Head troops. He made sure the prone Jew was covered too, and mocking laughter rang out, joining the cacophony of misery echoing around the small, stone-floored kitchen with its meagre collection of trinkets and ornaments.

The larger houses on the street were being ransacked. Loot was piled into vehicles, for the war effort; each man careful to show that he was not in breach of the Himmler order forbidding loot taken for personal profit. *The SS must remain decent.* No, this was simply a pragmatic policy; the Jews must pay for the cost of security police work.

"Get them in the trucks," Hoffman called out. He patrolled the street, observing, directing, flushed with his responsibility. All the months of diplomatic hardball with Poland, and now, as the Führer of the Greater German Reich himself said, they were taking no more provocations, their peoples were being freed, and *bomb was met by bomb.*

After the Jewish elders and their families were in the trucks – some ninety of them – the destruction order came. Flamethrowers and grenades lit the sky with an incendiary offering to the Gods. Houses crumbled, melting like max. Some still had their occupants inside them; one Jew had been nailed to his front door by one overzealous trooper, and the body burned like an effigy as the lapping flames engulfed the building. The whole street, even the houses not occupied by blacklisted 'Jewish elders', was a raging inferno. The inferno heated their skin, the stench of its smoke clinging to them. Hoffman had smiled at the street aflame, as they drove away, haunted screams echoing across the devastation. It looked like Hell. No more than they deserved.

Two further large-scale raids took place that day alone. More arrests, beatings, and burnings.

They took one hundred and seventy blacklisted Jews who had been seized from their homes to the nearest ready-made, large anti-tank ditch, and riddled them with bullets. Blood flew through the air and spattered the ground around the ditches, creating a charnel-house of mud, awful, thick red blood and slaughter.

A handful of others, they lined up against walls in the town and filled them full of lead. Bullets cracked through the cold air, and people fell. Some of the Totenkopf troops had been laughing as they did it, swigging from pilfered vodka or the standard-issue schnapps. Onlookers were silent and soon quietly slunk away, keeping their downcast eyes to the ground. The most prominent of the captured elders were hanged with piano wire in the central square of Włocławek, and left there as a warning. The city's surviving Jews were silent. Nostitz ordered the burning of all the synagogues, and they tortured five Jews into claiming responsibility for the arson. Payment to the Reich was fixed at 100,000 zloty, and the Jewish community collectively paid it. The SS Death's Head war machine rolled on.

~

Hoffman struggled with himself, looking into the spotless mirror in his little private bathroom in the staff building of St. George no.5. Such conduct was wrong… barbaric, even. Not fit for the Germany of Goethe, Beethoven, Mozart, even Nietzsche. It was extreme cruelty. Hoffman knew that, and the hard reflection in the mirror seemed to know it too.

Hoffman remembered the little girl in the black parka. How old was she; 8, 9?

A tiny figure, still unable to walk without betraying a lack of basic equilibrium in her fledgling little legs; the girl had turned her back to the SS men levelling guns at her family, who were part of a larger group of blacklisted pro-Bolshevik Jews who'd been lined up against a wall in the town. She just held her father's hand; her sobbing mother embraced the little ones, whispering words of comfort, but the father had been completely undemonstrative. Silent, as though in shock. Uncomprehending of his family's fate. The little girl, ludicrously small in her big parka coat, reached out and held her father's adult sausage fingers between her own tiny hands, before a volley of gunshots cut them all down.

How could Goethe and Bismarck approve of this? Even the arch-anti-Semite Wagner couldn't condone such coldblooded *slaughter...* but, Hoffman reasoned, clenched in combat with himself – this is *war*. A fight for survival. For the SS officer to show remorse, even *pity* for the enemy, was also wrong. The Jew had corrupted and weakened Germany in the days before National Socialism. The freemasonry of the Jewish financiers, merchants and petit bourgeois had undermined the Fatherland; their politicking had caused defeat in the Great War. The decadence of the Weimar Republic and its filth, its sex shows and debauchery and drugs and negro music... and the depression. Hoffman's memory of the Jewish girl subsided into reminiscence of the deprivations and frustrations of Weimar years, and his eyes narrowed. The Jew had continued poisoning Germany until Hitler's rise, and even now they continued their provocations abroad. He *could not* show pity. He *could* not. He *must* not.

As bright as that day in London was, Field Marshal Walther von Brauchitsch stormed into the meeting of *Oberkommando des Heeres* High Command and brought only rainstorms, cloud and thunder with him, lined in the contours of his face.

None present needed to ask why.

"Heil Hitler!" The Field Marshal brayed.

"Heil Hitler!" returned twelve unenthusiastic voices of the high command. Quickly dropping the salute, they all dropped into the great wooden chairs with studded leather armrests, and settled themselves at the great mahogany table that dominated the wide room.

Every officer present was a general; the lowest ranked being a brace of Generalmajors, to several Generalleutnants, a group ranked at Generaloberst, and lastly two Field Marshals present, both of whom were promoted in the great wave of Hitler awards following the rapid collapse of France. All generals present bore the gold epaulettes, and wore trousers striped with red to distinguish them in   their   rank. General Halder looked around the room, thrilled in the show of military might in the heart of London, great capital of the world's foremost Empire.

"Greetings, Generals," von Brauchitsch said, settling himself into his seat.

This was a meeting of the Oberkommando des Heeres, High Command of the German Army; today marking the second great conference of its kind since the invasion, and once more held in the former British 'War Rooms' of Churchill's War Cabinet in Whitehall. The man whom Hitler appointed Military Commander of Britain formally opened the dialogue, though it was not with the confident air of authority that he had previously possessed. That was due largely to his title becoming a pyrrhic victory, if not altogether obsolete. But where his confidence lagged, the commander countered with volume.

"Herr Generals & Officers, the next phase in the incorporation of England into the Greater German Reich is about to begin," von Brauchitsch barked. "New directives from Berlin and the Party suggest that while our important public relations work must continue, contemporaneously with the continued crushing of organised armed resistance in the northern theatres."

He sighed, and some of the men nodded in solidarity. They knew what his next point would address.

"As some of you are already aware, along with the SD & Gestapo units operating as Security Police here already, the latest development is that the SS-Reich Security Main Office leadership itself will be arriving in Great Britain tomorrow." He winced, visibly, and while those already aware of the recent Führer Order merely grimaced, the other officers blanched in open shock.

Field Marshal von Brauchitsch continued, in a pained voice.

"SS-*Ober*gruppenführer und *General der Polizei* Reinhard Heydrich, our beloved hangman in Berlin will not only spearhead intensified *Sicherheitspolizei* operations, but the Führer has bestowed significantly more jurisdiction on him than was previously granted in Poland."

There were murmurings of unease, and looks were exchanged around the table.

"Military command remains with me and Army High Command, but as Oberkommando des Wehrmacht chief Keitel–"

"*Lakeitel*," one of the other generals muttered, which inspired several agreements and sneering remarks. The pun on Wilhelm Keitel's name meant 'poodle', or 'lackey', which is how many within the German Army viewed his attitude towards the Führer.

Britain's nominal military commander smiled, and continued. "Keitel signed an order with the SS-RSHA that no impediment is to be given to Herr *Reichsprotektor* Heydrich's work by decree..." he drew on the title for effect, noting that the generals present were as uncomfortable as he himself was with it. They'd all witnessed the horrors wrought by the Einsatzgruppen of SiPo and SD that Heydrich had set up in Poland. Mass-executions, villages and whole towns left in flames, anti-tank ditches filled with bullet-strewn corpses, blood, shell casings and broken vodka bottles had followed the Heydrich death squads like an incriminating and particularly sinister trail in the wake of their almost wanton destruction.

It had chilled even some of the Wehrmacht High Command, all of whom had served in the charnel-house of the Great War and its bloody trenches. Yet this was new horror; the Einsatzgruppen defied description. Thankfully, thus far in England they had been restrained, for the most part. The insane burnings – villages and towns razed in the style of Genghis Khan's savage Mongol armies, with all the inhabitants butchered heedless of sex or age – were, thankfully, not standard SS practise in a land of 'racial brothers.'

Yet, it was whispered by some. *Not yet.*

"On top of the decree," von Brauchitsch explained flatly, "Reichsführer-SS Himmler himself will be arriving with Heydrich. Obviously, this means the country is to be swept and cleansed of any undesirable elements, and police measures will intensify that, we are told, do not concern the Wehrmacht."

The sneer in his voice was unmistakeable. General Halder wondered why he kept it out of his voice during meetings with Hitler. The commander continued:

"The order from Keitel, you can find in front of you, if you'll permit me to read the pertinent parts…" he cleared his throat, and in a tone that clearly emphasised the disagreeable parts, shared with his fellow generals the orders concerning the Wehrmacht in Britain:

"Subject: Regulation on Commitment of the *Security Police and SD in units of the army.* The execution of special Security Police missions outside the unit makes the commitment of special detachments of the Security Police and Security Service in the Wehrmacht's operational area necessary, as well as unoccupied and civilian zones. In agreement… et cetera, et cetera… with the chief of the Security Police and the Security Service, SS-Obergruppenführer Reinhard Heydrich, Reichsprotektor of Great Britain, the commitment of the Security Police and the SD in the operational area is regulated as follows:

1. Missions. A: In the army rear area: Before the start of operations, securing of tangible objects (material, archives, card indexes of state organisations and/or organisations hostile to the state, units, groups, etc.) as well as especially important individuals (leading emigrants, saboteurs, terrorists, etc.)."

Field Marshal von Brauchitsch turned his face up to the table, his contempt palpable. He was gratified to see his feelings mirrored in the men before him.

"On this note, where the SiPo and SD actions may disrupt an ongoing army operation, the *commander of the army and the Chief of the Security Police and SD are to reach an agreement on the individual action*, or if this is not possible in the given timeframe, *the Security Police commander* in question must *use his own initiative* to determine expediency of accomplishing the mission in question, and the possibility of doing such without jeopardising army operations."

Again, several generals made derisive noises. The document was cancer to their eyes.

The commander, sickened, continued his reading *ad nauseum*. "1b. In the army group rear area: Discovering and combating endeavours inimical to the state and Reich, insofar as they are not incorporated in the enemy armed forces, as well as generally informing the commanders of the army group rear areas about the political situation. Et cetera, et cetera..." the Field Marshal paused to gulp some water before continuing, his voice clearer. "2. Collaboration between the Einsatzkommandos of SiPo and SD, and the military commanding authorities in the Army Rear Area (to 1a). *The special detachments of the Security Police and Security Service carry out their missions upon their own authority.* In the zones of armed conflict, and when attached to the army for coordinated operations, they are subordinate to the armies as far as marching orders, rations, and quarters are concerned. *However, outside of conflict zones, they hold complete jurisdiction to operate in civilian areas and behind the army frontlines in non-combat zones.* Disciplinary and legal subordination under the Chief of the Security Police and Security Service is *applicable in all areas*, outside of adhering to army operations in active areas of conflict. *They receive their technical instructions from the Chief of the Security Police and Security Service*, although if occasion should arise are subordinated to restrictive orders of the armies in conflict zones with reference to their activity. (See No. 1a.).”

And for the last line, Commander von Brauchitsch, cursing his pyrrhic title and the siphoning of his power away to the bastard upstart Heydrich, and the bastard’s clever language and politicking, spat:

“*With this in mind*, a commissioner *of the Chief of the Security Police and of the Security Service will be employed in the area of each army for the central direction of these detachments*. He is required to bring to the attention of the Commander in Chief of the Army promptly the instructions sent to him by the *Chief of the Security Police and Security Service*, who in cases of grave importance for Reich Security and that of occupied Britain has *jurisdiction to decide in his power as Reichsprotektor...* the direction of such coordinated or overlapping actions, and *to issue the necessary orders determining the course of action taken.*”

Silence met the last proclamation. The implications were clear enough; the Military Commander of England did not hold even complete military sway in England, let alone civilian administration. No, the Hangman of Berlin had extended his empire west, and in the process, snatched away the hard-won victory of the Wehrmacht.

He pressed on, sensing that his diatribe had run its course. “We have been... instructed, as in Poland, as the army of the nation not to impede the... *noble historic tasks on behalf of the Fatherland* that our SS comrades are to perform. But we have our own tasks; the stability of the incorporation of England into the Greater German Reich... now, I want updates. General Halder?”

General Franz Halder, his Chief of Staff readjusted the pince-nez on his nose and answered in clear, clipped tones, casting his gaze around the table as he did so:

"Nothing new to report on the military situation, Herr Feldmarschall. The two Scottish cities remain secure; organised resistance in Scotland has been pushed south, and in any case much of it joined the bandit groups of northern England. As to the northern zone; resistance continues; we have secured the cities in the east-west Ludendorff Line: Hull, Leeds, Manchester, Liverpool, and we are established between twenty and thirty miles north of all those cities."

Lieutenant-General Kritzinger pitched in; "And of the cities themselves, General? Have there been any instances of further terrorism or organised revolt?"

"There has not. Organised resistance remains exiled to the unoccupied pockets, mostly following the part of the underground auxiliary situation. Quite ingenious, I must say; a snowball effect from the small groups set up, as those who fled our troops were recruited en masse into collectives. But their hideaways are limited, and many remain hiding at home, with friends or sympathetic locals in villages, towns and whatnot." Halder looked around impressively. "Commendable, but they cannot hold out through winter."

"Excellent, General. What of continuing resistance in northern cities and townships, and policies enacted?"

Halder cleared his throat. "No. Army Group Centre was not been badly affected. The bulk of its reserves remain in the cities and major towns, but only individual acts of desperation or madness occur. Near Sheffield, three hundred partisans were shot for resistance that led to the death of nearly eighty soldiers. There is a complete press blanket on this story and the sharing of this incident was minimal."

"Any others? Full report."

Some of the generals began to make notes.

"In Leeds, the hanging of the mayor from the Town Hall seemed to be most effective. Two hundred were shot in City Square in reprisal for continued incidents in the weeks after Group North: Army Group B initially took the city. It was not an SS style reprisal," he added smoothly, letting the statement sink in. "The General here was most specific in his report; the two hundred condemned had all been involved in active armed resistance to us. As to the rest... most of those willing to fight were flushed out along in the uprising, and either joined the partisans or were picked off retreating. All subsequent actions were individual acts of desperation or fear, and dealt with at the police level. Imprisonment, or quiet executions, nothing loud. The general populace got the message from the shooting in the square."

"Not to mention the mayor," another general chortled, and the men laughed.

"Everything in the path of AGB from Sheffield, Rotherham and Leeds was crushed. All the swine were pushed north. Things are quiet *now*," Generalleutnant Walter Model cut in, irritated to have had the Yorkshire front laid out by Halder so peremptorily covered by Halder when his Panzer division had led the Army Group B spearhead in the fast blitzkrieg through Sheffield, Rotherham, Barnsley, Huddersfield and the Leeds offensive that had taken only three days. Army Group B had been the fastest among Army Group Centre to establish their section of the Ludendorff Line, despite Leeds being further north than were Liverpool and Manchester on the west.

He lit a cigarette, despite every other general having abstained in the meeting room. "The surviving swine fled north, the rest are settling in to the new way of life," Model concluded with gusto. The Generalleutnant sat back, pleased to have offered his piece. Model had no love for the Prussian aristocratic class of general, and hated the OKH and OKW General Staff as much as they despised him.

Halder shared a glance with von Brauchitsch; Model's presence in reporting to OKH was the reason they were relatively restrained in their criticisms of the Führer's policy, even regarding the SS. Model was a Nazi.

Unfortunately, though only in command of one motorised division of Army Group Centre, his input on the current conflict zones was necessary for the continuation of the 'sweep and cleanse' winter policy for north of the Ludendorff Line.

"Does that hold true elsewhere?" the commander asked Halder, trying to delay Model's coarse contribution as long as he could. There were some murmurs of affirmation from several generals to the question, but Chief of Staff Halder offered the formal report.

"Roughly the same situation for Group C in Manchester. Prominent shootings in Piccadilly Square of armed resisters, and some hangings of the more prominent. The Einsatzgruppen under Six," Halder said with audible distaste, "… were more zealous in Manchester, where they set up their major HQ for the northern zone. The Security Police executions were public, and graphic. Resistance crumbled fast."

Halder checked the notes on the table in front of him, before continuing. "Hull at the far east of the line, secure. Manchester, Liverpool, secure. South of the big cities' belt; Bristol, Birmingham, Wolverhampton, Coventry, Sheffield, Rotherham, Barnsley, all secure. West of Manchester and the final part of the great defensive line was volatile, but the Security Police groups secured the area after the army had pushed through. No continuing organised resistance south of the Wehrmacht's Ludendorff Line. Group D that took Liverpool..." he hesitated, cleaning his glasses, and then resumed, "... Group D encountered some truly disgusting occurrences on the west coast." Halder's nose wrinkled in distaste. "But resistance there was soon quelled. Most tried to escape, rather than join the partisans or reach Scotland. Many set off across the sea for Ireland. No doubt we shall catch up with them soon enough."

"Regardless of which zone," a burly major-general boomed, and the assembled banged their knuckles on the table in approval.

Halder concluded. "So all in all, the major northern cities across the 'Ludendorff Line' and within one hundred miles south have been cleared.

The Commander nodded in approval. "Eight weeks and *All Quiet on the Western Front*?"

Halder grinned. "Like Paul could have only dreamed of. And we shall not be reaching for any fledgling birds, Herr Feldmarschall."

"What of Scotland and the major cities?" Brauchitsch asked.

Halder glanced to Field Marshal Ritter von Leeb, one of those twelve generals promoted along with von Brauchitsch in the aftermath of the fall of France, not long before Operation Sealion had begun. Göring had become Reichsmarschall, a six-star general of the German Armed Forces in combination with his political roles of Reichstag President, Prime Minister of Prussia and the virtual economic and social dictator of Germany.

Ritter von Leeb had been assured by the Führer that becoming Commander of the Scotland theatre was befitting of his recent elevation, and he sweetened the pill by issuing the title of Acting Deputy-Military Commander of North Britain. But, given how von Brauchitsch's own title was now largely worthless, his fellow Field Marshal was content to be known simply by his rank.

"Rebels have fled the occupied zone," he began. "Fighting was, as you well know, extremely fierce in every township we encountered, though Army Group North's progress was irresistible. After the initial hostilities we were quick to reach an arrangement with the suitable authorities. To all intents and purposes, we are not treating it as an occupation. Independence from England is the currency on our lips, as per the Führer directive, and as such we have forsaken reprisal policies.

The commander nodded without enthusiasm. "Mass-executions avoided. No reprisals. But what of resistance?"

"None remaining in the cities, despite our relative lack of size compared to the South and Centre Groups. It must be said, though, a great number of Scottish males of military and non-military age alike fled south to ally with the northern rebels of England."

"They are doomed. What of the situation in Scotland itself," von Brauchitsch demanded impatiently.

"The demarcation line has been drawn just north of Glasgow and Edinburgh, from Kirkcaldy in the east stretching down to Paisley in the west. Nothing of any strategic importance for the army exists north of those cities anyway, and the use of existing military bases in future or the building of new ones is a purely political issue, and unrelated to our current operations."

Halder interjected. "As the Führer said, once things settle down we can just give the Scots independence at the price of naval and air bases in the north, and simply have done with them. As long as Germany controls the waters north of Britain, there is no reason for troops to be held down there just like there is no reason for Scots to fight and die for England."

"Or for Saxon English to fight Aryan Germans," von Leeb observed.

Every officer at the table murmured assent, even those with fiercely anti-National Socialist views. Much like the Party command, the largely aristocratic General Staff could not understand England's war against Germany either. Not with communist Slavs to the east.

Every one of them, that is, except for von Brauchitsch.

Now, the military commander took point. "Discussions are ongoing between Berlin and the Scottish fascists. We will send someone from Mosley's lot to help things along if there's no one in Edinburgh capable enough. As for Wales, no resistance whatsoever outside the major towns. They will get the same deal. And as per Führer Directive no.32 for England, we are to leave Northern Ireland alone. The Irish can deal with their own affairs. Right? Good. On to less troublesome matters; public opinion. Generalleutnant Kritzinger?"

The stern Kritzinger spoke with militaristic Prussian austerity. "As per Dr Goebbels' orders, the Hearts and Minds campaign is ongoing. Public forums are being arranged; we're using educated English speakers for the task." He checked the sheaf of notes neatly set before him on the great mahogany table. "Men of said calibre also encouraged to drink in public houses and integrate with the working class male population."

"Good," von Brauchitsch said, somewhat unenthusiastically. "Of course, use your most educated and diplomat junior officers to lead these public relations exercises, with the pick of any enlisted men with a good grasp of English and a good head. Try and keep any loose cannons out of that line of work. We need them to be on their best behaviour; God knows, once the Gestapo leadership gets here there will be incidents and rumours that could turn this whole place back into an explosive cinder keg and ruin the Führer's plans. No army excesses; no SS behaviour. This isn't the east. Anyone in the rank and file stepping too far out of line gets sent to Poland or the north of Norway, got it?"

"Yes, Herr Generalfeldmarschall," all the Germans barring Halder intoned. They hid their amusement; the commander's own instructions prior to Sealion had instructed the Wehrmacht to forcibly deport all males between the ages of 17-45, unless there were 'extraordinary circumstances' involved. And now, not only had suppression and security matters in the civilian zones been handed over to Heydrich, but the Führer had decreed that he, the military, the Wehrmacht, were responsible for the fostering of good relations between the populace and Germany. And Hitler wanted an England agreeable to the Reich, embraced into the fold with Italy, Vichy France and Spain. No wonder von Brauchitsch was miserable.

Not foreseeing political developments, he had submitted a proposal for mass-deportations of males for enforced labour. Just his luck that for once, the extreme option was not the one Hitler appreciated. And the most extreme paladin of all, Heydrich, now held sway.

Walther von Brauchitsch now tried to endorse such gentle occupational policy with genuine magnanimity, and as his grim tone and reference suggested, the Field Marshal truly had experienced a change of heart.

"Good. Let's ensure the good work is maintained in improving the relationship between the Reich and Great Britain." He snorted, openly. "It will be more important than ever for the Army to create a good impression and maintain the stability of the country, now that Himmler, Heydrich and the killing squads are en route."

No one contradicted him to observe that the Security Police of all SS branches had been in Britain for all the weeks they had been there. The imminent arrival of a Reich Protector nicknamed *The Blond Beast* could only herald change. To what extent, and the form it took, the Army High Command could only imagine.

~

At Hyde Park corner, the crowd continued to grow as Wehrmacht armoured wagons drove around central London, from the City through Covent Garden and Soho, up to Bloomsbury, Camden and Regents Park, down through Mayfair and beyond; braying through loudspeakers and extolling the populace with papers to legitimately access the central district to make their way there. There had been several radio announcements from Joyce asking Londoners to 'participate'. Similar booths were being set up across the capital's non-central districts; nine others in London, and several each in the northern population centres, where they were held outside Town Halls or suitable civic buildings.

Oberleutnant Sebastian Koller was finishing his smooth, polished opening speech extolling 'The Great Friendship Between Nations', and the German desire to improve productivity in Britain and restore pre-war living standards and levels of efficiency. The Hyde Park crowd murmured amongst themselves as he neared his conclusion. There was no applause, but many exchanged surprised glances of approval.

"And of course, if you have any questions at all, please do not hesitate to ask," he smiled. "You there, in the white coat! What is your question?"

"When will rationing be lifted? The woman demanded, to scattered cheers. Sebastian's smile only widened, his white teeth glinting in the autumn sun.

"Rationing will be lifted *very* shortly, I can assure you. The military high command has met to determine the transition, and both the governments of Berlin and London are working to bring about an end to rationing in both countries..." he paused, letting it sink in, before raising his hand to quell the rising torrent of questions that burst at him. "Just to clear up the issue of rationing... let me assure you it is no different in Berlin and Hamburg than here in England. Scotland cannot be compared as there is nowhere quite so cold in the Reich."

A small rumble of laughter erupted from some in the crowd. Others maintained stony expressions, glowering as the German public relations exercise continued with blatant ingratiation.

"But I assure you, there is no reason for rationing to continue for very long, as the situation stabilises and of course, as soon as productivity shifts from military focus to civilian life! It is not required any longer, and regarding the transport of foodstuffs by sea, remember that neither Germany nor Britain will be attacking the food they bring in for us!"

The man stood next to the woman in the white coat who had asked about rationing frowned as more people were won round to the affable German. He bore a visible facial scar, and was shabbily attired, haggard and slow of speech. He was the prototype of a man who had seen more than he should have in the Great War.

"When will the curfew be lifted?" he barked, suddenly animated, which cut through the crowd's laughter and catcalls.

Sebastian sought him out in the crowd, and fixed a stare onto the bedraggled man. He did not speak; the enlisted soldier sat uncomfortably next to him on the raised platform answered the shabby man. "The curfew is only a temporary measure, it will be lifted as soon as Berlin is satisfied things are stable here."

"And when will that be?" another voice called.

Sebastian took point again. "We must wait for the high command to decide. Of course, we would like the curfew lifted too, we would like to spend our nights in a more relaxed manner! But when stability and peace is assured, the curfew will vanish. For now..." he raised his arms wide, in an exaggerated parody of apology. "Sorry, it is out of my hands!"

"My cousin was hung!" A cockney man suddenly screamed.

"Oh?" Sebastian replied pleasantly, into the silence. "Where, when and why?"

"They said he was hoarding food illegally, and resisting. You're fucking liars!"

A shocked murmur passed through the assembled, and those who had been somewhat mollified by the public relations exercise filtered away. Sebastian Koller was utterly unfazed by the confrontation, however, and in his most infuriatingly polite voice, responded to the angered East Ender.

"Yes. Several men in the – I have to assume, you are the East End of London, yes?" He beamed, as though delighted with himself for his cultural awareness. Several titters broke out. "... *Were* indeed hung, but those men fought with the soldiers who sought to apprehend them. Surely," he grinned, holding the gaze of his antagonist, "... innocent men would not fire weapons on the policing forces? Those men were lucky to survive the gun fight. As for subsequent justice, well..."

Sebastian stood up, raising his arms out wide with his palms raised upwards.

"Military courts punished acts of resistance, which firing gunshots most certainly is. I am not to blame for this. But that is over. We are all working towards a future; a strong economy, a strong Empire –"

"Ours, or yours," the cockney interrupted yet again. Sebastian stifled his irritation.

"Both!" he cried. "The British Empire is untouched! Germany dominates European politics, Britain rules the waves. This is what is needed for a strong future. Economy, food, jobs. The Saxon people must work together!"

Failing to suppress a grin of triumph, Sebastian basked in his position for a moment longer, before slowly sinking back into his seat, and accepting the subsequently non-confrontational lines of inquiry from other members of the public. The disgruntled cockney left, snarling at the watching crowd. Sebastian began to talk of trade agreements, and once more reiterated the impending abolition of rationing.

As the hours passed, the enlisted German soldier sank further into his seat, thoroughly bored with the tedious affair, and he was eventually replaced by a junior non-commissioned officer. Sebastian Koller, meanwhile, became more and more animate as the hours passed, periodically repeating his opening speech with relish to the freshly assembling crowds that trickled through, replacing the mixed bag of those departing; the appeased and the sceptics alike.

More sun. It shone without much warmth, but nevertheless glowing in the twilight of the autumnal peak. This was *Führer Weather,* Goebbels assured the people listening to his now once-weekly broadcasts over the radio; a surprisingly high number of listeners tuned in, more out of a misplaced fear that it would be a crime not to than simple curiosity. In unusual circumstances, all people adapt remarkably quick.

"The Reichsmarschall," Lord Haw Haw solemnly broadcast over what was now the most listened to broadcast in Western Europe, "wishes to proclaim to the people of Great Britain that it is a beautiful time to be alive if you are English or German."

Joyce relayed some token friendly statements from the Reichsmarschall about hunting game and enjoying the woods and forests, and a Blake quote about 'England's Green & Pleasant Land'. With the attack on 'asphalt culture' so fresh in the memory, and Goebbels' other choice derisions and condemnations, it was clear where Göring's cheery message was aimed.

An English cartoonist who'd characterised Göring as a hugely fat, ugly Viking caricature wielding a spear in a 1934 cartoon had quietly disappeared. Göring the rotund Viking was depicted next to a demonic Hitler, who was breathing steam and holding a smoking gun, glowering at what were supposed to be a group of disgraced SA leaders. The Night of the Long Knives had been satirised across Europe and America, but this depiction was by far the most famous. The rumour mill whispered and spread its web of tales across an occupied city with more clandestine fervour than one in peace time, it seemed. Unconfirmed reports of a group of trench-coated men wearing hats that covered their faces leading the artist to his car in the dead of night were supplied as a titbit of information, though none could tell if the Reichsmarschall had truly demanded the man be punished, or if he'd simply slipped underground. That had happened a lot, too, and German bureaucratic efficiency did not often stretch to generosity with information regarding just who had escaped and who'd been seized.

Meanwhile, international tensions were being soothed from Berlin, as a reportedly terrified Stalin – "a tiny rabbit mesmerised by a snake," was said to be Goebbels' reiteration of his earlier sneering comment, as word trickled down from German soldiers to collaborating women and thence, the rest of the British populace – was removing more than twenty army divisions from the proximity of the Soviet/German border along occupied Poland and East Prussia, for fear of the 'provocation' that would serve as a pretext for unleashing the blitzkrieg. Already, jokes were springing up about 'the oncoming war' – one in particular was circulating in London:

A jerry Field Marshal informs a colonel that the showdown with Russia is coming, but that Mussolini's Italy is ready to declare war.

'We must keep 10 divisions ready to counter, in that case Herr General', the Colonel said.

'No, he is on our side again,' the General says. They share a deeply concerned look.

'Well, in that case we need 20 divisions.'

Jokes were still being made in the occupied zone about Mussolini, the focus of ridicule having switched from Hitler's imitations of Il Duce to the obvious shift in power between the two; now, the unique, theatrical characteristics of the founder of fascism and his opportunistic sycophancy to the Führer who'd once idolised him were subjected to mockery, but the banter rang hollow. Quips made about

Germans and Hitler were followed by what had already been called 'The German look' in the Reich since 1933; that brief, fearful glance to ensure you weren't being overheard by an informer or law enforcer, or even some young zealot from the Hitler Youth, the generation of children programmed to believe that even familial bonds were subordinate to Party loyalty. War propaganda such as 'carless talk costs lives' had never been so grimly apt.

~

Again, it had not been a good day on Tottenham Court Road for Maisie; another one in which the hours passed by slowly, the custom a mix of irritating, rude or timid, and most of all, her own restlessness. Much to her chagrin, she had found herself thinking about the German boy in uniform, idle thoughts wandering to him from unrelated sights and sounds. She had no smell yet with which to distinguish him, no odour to waft into her nostrils apart from Dunhill cigarettes. *British* cigarettes. Maisie was no fool; she was well-aware that she shared her brother's impulsivity, and had launched into past dalliances with little in the way of concern for the consequences. She was ruled equally by cerebral and emotion thoughts; luckily, this had saved her from the grief of choosing the wrong lovers, with the sharp intelligence and decisiveness to sever all ties instead of becoming bogged down into the neurotic, undignified push-pull of a cruel breakup. For such a warm, loving person she'd done it quite clinically, as would a doctor operating to save a patient by cutting away the cancerous body part with a clean stroke; her mother had marvelled quietly at her poise and will.

But this boy was dangerous, she realised. Something about him suggested danger; there was a coolness in his grey-blue eyes, an assuredness, but he was not cocky. Quite the *opposite*... there was no arrogance or cruelty there. He'd even seemed shy, a sort of confidence bred by the masculinity of the culture overriding a naturally sweet temperament... oh, *God*, she thought, I'm thinking about him again.

This time, she allowed herself a few moments to ruminate. He was definitely not arrogant, or cocky, nor cruel or overbearing. She wasn't sure he was even a patriot, which by now had been a legal prerequisite in his country for almost eight years; punishable by God knows *what* bestial atrocities. Maisie wondered what horrors he'd face, if ever he were betrayed – assuming of course that her assumptions were correct. *Cat'o'nine tails, rubber truncheons, imprisonment, torture, death.* Or perhaps being made to listen to the Führer's speeches for days on end. To those not hypnotised by his particular brand of magnetism and gravitas, he had the air of a particularly menacing escaped lunatic, a carpet-chewing syphilitic madman, and Maisie bitterly longed for the days in which such opinions could be voiced without being fearful of who was in earshot.

Pulling herself out of the umpteenth reverie that day, she got on with the hasty process of shutting the shop up. As she was locking the door, Maisie sensed rather than saw a shadow looming up, and a figure come upon her. She was about to jump, when a hand lightly grasped her shoulder and the double whammy made her involuntarily yell out.

She caught herself quickly, and glowered at the man before her, who gallantly stepped back with head slightly bowed.

"Jesus Christ," she all-but yelled, "what are you playing at?"

Hans was mortified. He backed away slightly, though his tall, lean body was already out of arms reach.

"I'm very sorry," he offered, clumsily. The composure of his approach had been shot to pieces. "It was certainly not my intention to scare you."

She looked at him for a moment, and for the first time in her life, couldn't hold a man's gaze. Noting the somewhat overly careful English, she decided to tease him instead.

"It's ok... *certainly.*"

He looked baffled, which made her cross.

"Well you did. Anyway... never mind. I'm off for the train. I'll see you later." She stumbled over the latter part, sending out mixed signals. *Push, pull*, she thought... silly girl! What am I doing?

She turned with poise and began to walk away, northwards in the direction of Regent's Park, and almost incredulously sensed – again, sensed – his movement. An immediate reaction. Do I make this boy nervous, she wondered, and her own insecurities were instantly banished.

"May I walk with you," he asked her, coming level.

She glanced at him, and almost laughed at his earnest expression. He noted it himself, wryly.

"I'm heading this way anyway, fraulein. I would enjoy your company."

She affected a sigh, which they both knew was false. She made sure it didn't sound too serious.

"Come on then," she chirped.

Hans kept stealing glances at her as they walked along, seeing nothing of Tottenham Court Road, the street, the buildings, passers-by. He didn't register any of it.

She was tall, and well-made, though simultaneously lean; he supposed she had a good bone structure. There was no fat evident in her face, or her legs, which were covered tastefully by the long white dress she wore, with its padded shoulders. Evidently, wartime rationing had affected her and Hans could see that she'd sewed over several patches – with some skill, he noted, as they weren't especially visible – but in the brief moment in which he was in close proximity to the girl, he filled his nostrils with her clean scent. She was washed, which was not always a given in either this country or his, and her dress gave off a freshly washed, clean odour. Her hair – naturally dirty blonde, a sort of light brown that naturally curled at shoulder length, was also clean and flowing. He decided he liked her hair, in contrast to the vast majority of German girls now who were adhering with proper National Socialist discipline to their Aryan roots, and using peroxide to dye their heads blonde.

So they can be as Nordic as our Aryan supermen leading us, Hans had joked in the Tiergarten to his old friend Isi, brother to his lover. This was before laws had forbidden his pal from entering the park; at this point, only the park benches and the Tiergarten Zoo were off-limits. *Nordic as our heroic leadership. Limping Joe, Fat Hermann and the carpet muncher; the ideal German men for a New Age of Warriors.*

Isi had laughed. *Just my luck to be a Yid. An accident of birth; if only I were as blond as Hitler, as tall as Goebbels and as slim as Göring!*

Just my luck too, you Jewish swine. If you'd been all that, I wouldn't be risking my life to be seen with you. To have my pure German mind corrupted by your poisonous words.

Isi had sobered at that, his almost comically stereotypical Jewish face and its hooked nose twitching in the sunlight of a bright Berlin summer day. *Jest or not, you raise a valid point, my Aryan friend. An undeniable point.*

Yes, but Isi my dear yiddo, I'd leave you in a heartbeat for the Hitlerjugend but how could I abandon your sister!

Thinking now of 'Isidor', as Yitzak was known, was painful, and he brought his attention back to the present.

They strolled along – slowly, Hans noticed – for around half a minute. He wondered if she was shy of him. The thought aroused his curiosity; even with Sarah, his only previous lover, he'd never quite understood what she saw in him, how he provoked such feverish passion in her or stirred her to such emotional depths. She gazed into his eyes sometimes with an intensity that confused him. He expressed himself with startling honesty, and had a good eye for, and appreciation of aesthetic beauty and a positive energy, but being prone to bouts of unhappiness despite Germany's Great Awakening surely couldn't be an attractive trait? Plus, he expressed himself clearly, not cleverly. Of course, that was simply practical these days; thinkers and intellectuals were frowned upon; anything Goebbels derided as idealistic or politically unreliable in public had the potential to land you in Dachau.

Thinking about Dachau and Sarah hurt too. In the present, on Tottenham Court Road, he opened his mouth, and then closed it. What was the point? She liked him, or didn't. *Don't get close. Don't form attachments.*

"My name is Maisie". She looked at him for the first time since they'd set off walking from the shop, and she smiled sweetly, her mouth closed. Her toothy grin was a game-winner, and she knew better than to play that card just yet.

He smiled back at her. "Hans."

"Where are you from, Hans?"

He paused, looking around at the buildings lining Tottenham Court Road, as though they reminded him of home.

"Berlin..." he glanced at her, and she held his gaze. "The capital, just like you," he added.

"Is it like London," she asked, innocently. He considered; was it? In style, architecture, the roads... the soul of a place was no longer determined by its buildings, its architecture, its physical monuments to humanity, he'd decided. Not with ideology driving men to extremes, against each other.

He hesitated... "... in a sense, I suppose you would say. There are similarities. Physical similarities. I think even most of the people are the same. But..." he stopped himself. Experience had taught him caution. He used his honesty on a different tack. "I miss home. I love Berlin."

"You miss Germany?"

"I miss *Berlin*," he responded with gusto.

Maisie herself hesitated slightly. "You don't seem to be... a *proud* Nazi soldier."

That was it. She was safe. Probably, at least, and Hans decided to chance it. He glanced to his left, into the road and behind him; The German Glance, *Der Deutsche Blick.*

He decided to trust her.

"I'm not even a German." Smiling at her confusion as she digested this, he added, "I'm a Berliner."

"I'm not sure I understand?"

"Berlin is *Berlin.* There's a reason National Socialism holds its major rallies in Bavaria; Munich, or Nuremberg... troll country. Big-bellied beer hall brawlers, Jew baiters and Neanderthals. They are, like you British say, *cavemen.* Not gentlemen. In my city, as long as they are lucky enough to have blond hair and blue eyes, nobody cares about calling Reichsmarschall Göring fat, or Goebbels a crippled dwarf, as long as there are no *polizei* nearby." Maisie looked at him in surprise, her eyebrows arching high and he laughingly elaborated. "Oh yes! In their own homes, lots of people make fun of Limping Joe and his broadcasts. The *Mahatma Propagandhi.* And everyone hates the local informant – the Gestapo, ah... how do you say?"

"Snitch?"

Hans smirked. "Snitch. Disgusting! But, it is worse in troll country. Berlin has more 'March Violets', or party members who joined in 1933 than anywhere else in the Reich. Lots of social democrats, lots of Kozis – communists. Lots of cynical, sarcastic people, like England. Hitler hates Berlin."

Maisie laughed. "No wonder you are comfortable here."

Hans snorted with mirth. "I guess. *Ja*, Berlin... I know a lot of my old friends were disappointed when we took Paris... and *nobody* likes France."

Now Maisie, against the warning of her inner voice, couldn't help but query this astonishing boy.

"Then why are you a soldier? Why fight for Hitler?"

Hans stopped in his tracks, almost unconsciously. Maisie stopped with him, her eyes full of questions, heart full of hope. If this perfect Aryan model of the Nazi dream could hate the tyranny of her country and its evil government, its pervasive menace and the quietly haunted peoples living under its rule, perhaps there was hope for the world.

Hans, for his part, knew that confessing his true thoughts to this English girl he barely knew was the most foolhardy act imaginable. But almost because of that, he resolved to continue. Speaking freely was, in his opinion, a human right. The British and Americans were right about that, at least, as ridiculous as they were. Not his people. The Deutsche volk. As ridiculous and frightening as *they* were.

"I did not behave," Hans started, cursing inwardly as a slight tremor in his slightly-singsong Berliner's voice betrayed him, "in what you might call a racially desirable way."

"*Racially desirable*," she queried. He elaborated, sadly:

"I fraternised with Jews."

Sweet Sarah. Isidor, who was likely in Dachau, perhaps dead. He was never a fighter; mocking, cynical, essentially sweet tempered, clever; he played the

315

violin. Did they beat him with rubber truncheons before they took him? Did he have all his teeth when he finally reached the camp? And what then? Did the SS break his violinist's fingers, which played Beethoven, Bach and Mozart? Oh, poor Isi.

Maisie was standing beside him, waiting for him to elaborate. He sighed at memories he preferred to shut out of his mind, keeping his eyes averted from her, looking ahead.

"I... fraternised. Visited Jewish shops, used Jewish businesses... The SA men painted stars of David on the windows; I would stroll in to buy items I did not even need. Back then all they did was curse at me, call me *Jude Liebhaber* – 'Jew lover'."

Hans' tone was bitter. His eyebrows contracted in a set frown. He resolved to share the full extent of his past. "To tell you the truth... I had a Jewish lover. Her name was Sarah..." his voice trailed off, as the shadow of sorrow crept over him. As he glanced at her, Hans saw that its bleakness must have shown in his eyes, as she registered his pain. The eye contact was brief, but sufficient to register the shared moment of empathy before he looked away again. Maisie felt a rush of sympathy for her strange companion. He silently hoped that he had not revealed too much. They walked on, each momentarily lost in their thoughts.

"You say, you *had* a Jewish lover?" Maisie asked quietly. Hans nodded glumly. She had indeed noticed the shadow come across his face, and shuddered inwardly, dreading the answer. But she had to ask. She *had* to.

"Yes. She was interned in Lichtenberg *Konzentrationslager*... a concentration camp. Then they built a camp specifically for women. Ravensbrück. That was around two years ago, I think... they do not inform me; after all, I am a rehabilitated soldier of the Fatherland, and she is a Jew. I doubt she is alive..."

Hans stopped. This was the first time he'd spoken about her since the day when, ashen-faced, he'd recounted the whole tale to his Mother, who could only stroke his head, faintly quavering at her son *oh my boy... oh my boy...* embracing the ashen faced teenager in the small apartment, whose world had collapsed around him. *How can I love my Fatherland,* he kept repeating in shock. She'd held him by each strong shoulder, looking up into her son's teary face, stern now. *You must never say that. Speak through a rose. Smile through the pain. Live for tomorrow.*

"I'm sorry." Maisie jerked him back to the present, the sunlit Tottenham Court Road in London. Passing men were casting evil glances at the pair as they strolled along.

"Me too," he said sharply, and instantly regretted it. "*Ja,*" he resumed in a far softer tone, more resembling his own, "... so inevitably, there was a denunciation to the Gestapo, and I was a criminal in the eyes of the law. I signed a consent form called a D-11, the 'Order For Protective Custody'... one of the most laughable things you can imagine, no?"

She shook her head, uncomprehendingly. "House arrest? Or they thought you needed protection from other Germans for fraternising?"

Hans laughed at that. How cruel his world must seem to her. How little she understood of it, even with German soldiers in her country. How right she was.

"'Protective custody' is Nazi custody. It means I signed consent for my own internment, or incarceration, however you say – in a camp. It is not very 'protective'. They call it a guarantee of good behaviour, for the record, but in reality they make you sign it, the Kriminalpolizei officer threatened to beat me until I did – and then they threw me in a cell, and hauled me before a court one week later, after some classic Berlin Kripo hospitality from some thugs who probably want a transfer to the Gestapo. Berlin cops were always tough; I absolve the Nazis of that much."

Maisie marvelled quietly at his grasp of her tongue. His English was impeccable; only the singsong of his accent and some slight twang of hypercorrection identified his upbringing.

"So what happened? You were punished and sent to a camp, or released?"

He grinned, surprising her. "They offered the choice of arrest and internment, or as I was of good Aryan stock, traced back six generations; racially pure and had done well at school – perfect little Aryan boy – father fought for Germany in two wars, Party member from '31 when Hitler got off scot free in court for perjury, and he realised they were the rising force – as such, I could choose military service to defend the Reich and redeem myself in the eyes of my country. As a bearer of the mighty Aryan race, I simply had to do my duty to the Fatherland." The last sentence was undercut with biting sarcasm.

She was undeterred. "And your father?"

Without a hint of regret; "Died in Spain. Fought on the Turkish front in the Great War as a kid, and then stayed in the home army through the madness of the 20s..." Hans paused, and registered one particularly malevolent look from an old man who passed them. "So, still in the army, he was stuck waiting for whatever force took power in the melting pot of insanity. As it would come to be, he was still a military man when the *Nationalsozialisten* came to power. Then he got sent to help our glorious fascist *kameraden* destroy democracy in Spain. *Communism*, they called it. He got transferred to the Flying Corps, took part in the bombing raid on Guernica, and then later died in a crash during take-off. A pointless death in a pointless war... for Germany, at least. And for Spain," he added.

They strolled on for a while longer, nearing the Euston Road area close to Regent's Park and the London Zoo. He'd noticed that they'd already passed an underground stop en route, and Maisie had continued walking up the length of Tottenham Court Road in its entirety. He knew too, that the road's eponymous tube station was nearby to her shop, less than a minute's walk in the other direction. He chose not to pass comment.

"Is it really so bad for Jews over there?" Maisie blurted. It was the burning question on her lips. She'd had Jewish friends herself, as had her older brother. Until their mid-teens and the rise of Hitler in Germany, Jewishness had not been something she or it seemed, anyone else she knew gave any thought to. It was just there, or *not* there; like trees in a street, or leaves on the ground. Their apparent importance, influence and evil had baffled her, as she was sure it had the Jewish shopkeepers, students and assorted others she'd known. One was a librarian.

Hans sighed. Sweet girl – she had it all to come; the grim realities of life under Hitler, the realisation that life was cruel... or rather, just how cruel it could be, when viewed through the lens used by his country's rulers. It would be a rude awakening.

"Germany is bad for everyone but Aryan Germans who believe in Nazism. Even the racially pure who do not have to speak through a rose at all times."

"Is there no real opposition? Music, politics, literature?" She asked as though the very idea was utterly ludicrous. Even after weeks, *months* of occupation here, Jewish authors could be read in libraries. The wireless radio had been playing Mendelssohn the night before.

But Hans shook his head. "They burned subversive literature. Goebbels organised fires in the State Opera Square and made speeches about Jewish intellectuals. Un-German books were burned."

"Music?" She was incredulous; a touch of anger bit her deep. Artistry was expression of the soul... censoring it was the ugliest, stupidest thing Maisie could imagine.

She shared that opinion with Hans, who enthusiastically agreed.

"So they even censor music?"

Hans answered, warming even more to her. So few girls in Germany had their own ideas now. So few had independent spirit, opinions... *passion*. Real passion. Anger and hatred is only pseudo-passion.

"Banned," he affirmed. "Some *kinder* listen to, ah... *negro jazz.*"

Despite herself, Maisie gave a great snort of laughter at that. Hans looked bemused, and then shrugged good-naturedly.

"Sorry about my English."

"No, it's fantastic," she sniggered, sobering. "Where did you learn?"

"Un-German literature was not always banned. I like police detective stories. I read Arthur Conan Doyle."

Maisie was delighted, a blush appearing in her pale, smooth cheek. "Sherlock Holmes!"

"*Ja*. I like him. It's why I kept coming back to speak to you; I saw your reading *Hound of the Baskervilles*. There were books in English with German translations, too."

She flushed, slightly. Apart from her brother and his near-fanatical friends, she'd never met a boy who liked to read; who actively *enjoyed* reading, for *fun*, and to learn.

Whatever it is that I do, Hans thought, *they react to it*. He recognised a similar reaction to when he'd first gotten to know Sarah. *Some kind of positive quality. Perhaps honesty. Or simplicity. Something they seem to respond to.*

"Anyway…" he continued, "Germany is not good for opinions. We too are occupied in a certain way, although with the Kaiser we had a similar system that nobody could criticise. I feel we had the same ideas about different peoples then, too. I hear stories of the African colonies. Killings, forced starvations… Now though, it is far worse; even at home people are afraid of being denounced to the SS and the Gestapo. Nobody…" he spread his hands wide, and let them fall, as though world-weary. Hans shook his head in exasperation, blond hair swinging in short tufts on the crown of his head. *How to explain the madness*?

"Nobody is willing to share their opinions freely," he said finally. "They all fear internment, questioning, torture. Even before we were at war, many people disappeared. All the time. Especially in Berlin. I think police can kill with impunity, as long as it is not a party member."

"Scary," Maisie shuddered. "Psychotic policeman with the legal right to kill you."

Hans winced, nodding in agreement with the stark remark.

"It is terrible to live in fear."

Never before had he spoken with such bleak frankness. Not even with Isidor, steeped as their rebellion was in humour, Semitism and love. Neither boy had ever expressed much in the way of weakness or insecurity. But with this English girl, and her compassionate eyes? *It is terrible to live in fear.*

What a treasure trove of information he was, Maisie thought, with his knowledge, and beautiful ease with the complexities of the English tongue. Smoothly crafting sentences, conveying emotion; fear, sorrow, regret – perhaps hope? She felt a vague guilt at her selfish motives in questioning him, and a distinct unease at the looks that bypassers were casting her way for being seen with a German soldier. The glances were brief and furtive – none dared direct opposition, with Hans in uniform – but she recognised the quick stab of hate in their eyes. *Collaborator,* they spat, silently seething. *Whore. Wench. Vixen.*

"People are afraid," Hans added, himself once more oblivious to the negative attention. Perhaps he is used to it, in a conqueror's uniform, Maisie mused.

"Christ. An awful way to live."

"The Hitler way. *Heil Hitler!*"

Hans grinned again; dimples spreading under the soft flesh of his cheek, a wide smile splitting his face and the perfect form of white teeth ringed by red lips. Maisie liked his sudden expressions of... amusement? Happiness? She sensed his mischievous side; the schoolboy, constantly in trouble for unlawful consorting and a refusal to kowtow. An impish side, lurking dormant beneath his adult, soldierly surface.

"Of course, Maisie, you could report me for saying this..." the grin faded. "and men in SS field grey would haul me away, discipline me, throw me in prison and then, send me out east to wait in an East Prussian forest for the signal to cross the temporary Soviet border..." Hans held his hands up, in a parody of wonder, "And I'd be lucky enough to receive the ultimate German honour, freezing in the snow for lebensraum; crazy Bolsheviks shooting bullets at me... explosions, gunshots, massacres..."

Hans considered, all semblance of humour gone. "Or performing my heroic, *historic German tasks* such as rounding Jews up into ghettoes... or in some punishment battalion, clearing mines... either that, or just Dachau. They have my D-11 after all..."

He had no real fear of that happening, but part of him had wanted the vindication of her verbalising their bond. He regretted his transparent subterfuge of a joke, but Maisie was wide-eyed, and did not disappoint.

"Never, Hans." As he looked at her, surprised at her earnestness, she winked.

"It's been a while since I spoke this unpatriotically," he confessed, suddenly embarrassed.

He couldn't express it, but while the raging nationalism of the present system was abhorrent to him, he did love Germany. He *loved* Berlin, and the cynical, sardonic, mocking people of his beautiful city, and happy summer days on the nearby lake at Plötzensee. He just couldn't express love without hate. He couldn't verbalise the juxtaposition of the things that he, and others like him, *loved*, without justifications and recriminations and explanations and focus on all that was bad. It was a confusing position to be in; ideology, he'd realised, was the easy way out for the majority. It did your thinking for you. Life was made easy.

Enemies were provided. Solutions were offered. Questions discouraged. Advancement described. Greatness narrated.

Frowning in concentration, Hans tried to explain it to her, knowing that her mind was unsullied and fertile, and she listened – still as wide-eyed as she had been during the description of an imagined Russia – and when he'd finished, she reassured him that he was a credit to his family. He had nothing to worry about. He was a thoroughly decent person. His soul was untarnished.

Maisie's kindness almost overwhelmed him. She had such soft skin. This clean, wholesome girl who thought, and cared. This beautiful, funny, gentle English girl.

They'd reached the end of the great, wide Tottenham Court Road, at the junction where the main Euston Road thoroughfare sent the tube commuters north and east, into Bloomsbury. Hans stopped. The second tube station was now unavoidable. He looked over at Warren Street station, and back at Maisie expectantly; she merely smiled, coyly.

"Actually I walk up this way because... I like the park. After work I like to reconnect with the actual world, not just... stone. Buildings, and metal, and brick. To hear birds and see water and flowers. Regent's Park is just over that way."

She pointed over Hans' shoulder, past a slovenly, unshaven man in an overcoat bearing the distinguishing hallmarks of Great War trauma, to where the next Tube station was situated on Marylebone Road and beyond it, the lush park.

"Oh... beautiful. I often walk in the Tiergarten. We have a zoo. This is the park where your zoo is, yes?" He gestured up the road.

"Yes."

They held each other's gaze, uncommonly comfortable.

"May I walk with you in the park, until you decide to leave?" he asked finally. She smiled for the umpteenth time at him and, registered the distaste of yet another disgruntled passer-by, took his arm and with a burst of self-assuredness that comes with an unalterable impulse backed by will, steered him towards the lovely green that rose pleasantly in the distance, past the man-made stone and brick.

"There are rose gardens there," she purred happily. The words took a split-second to register, as Hans internally translated them into German, before almost shouting in laughter. It startled her, and she laughed along.

"Rose gardens," he repeated happily. "In such times, there are still rose gardens."

He felt her squeeze his arm, almost imperceptibly but a pressure nonetheless, between her linked arm and the flank of her torso. His nostrils caught another waft of her fresh, clean smell; wholesome, and innocent. He wondered if he deserved her.

She led him into the park, and they found a spot by the water where a foliage overhand formed a tunnel of the waterside path. Water lilies swayed slightly in the still pond. To their right was a green bush; the opposite bank was covered in rhododendron bushes of bright purple loderi and bell-shaped flowers of pink and blue. The smell was not of cloying water, but fresh, of grass and flowers, drifting lightly, unobtrusively, into their nostrils. Hans marvelled quietly at the scenery. This, too, was a great city, to foster nature and not forget it in the massive drive to erect monuments to humanity's self-awareness and changing of environment and destiny, apotheosis, visible everywhere.

Daisy sat shoulder to shoulder with the young man lost in his thoughts. This time, she squeezed him to her hard enough for there to be no doubt. He was almost stiffened with surprise, and his heart-rate quickened. Her soft voice rose sweetly, in a world of green:

"There'll be rose gardens after Hitler too, you know. And Göring, and all your nasty politicians and generals and policemen... There'll still be rose gardens to sit in and read Sherlock Holmes by the lakeside."

The thought made him dizzy.

Armed SS units fought ferociously alongside the Wehrmacht during the war in Poland, later becoming the "Waffen-SS". One section of it bore the Death's Head symbol on their collar tabs, as well as their caps, as they were formed from the Totenkopfverbände organisation of SS camp personnel, the perfect breeding ground of brutality. What was officially named the Waffen-SS Totenkopf "Death's Head" division in October 1939 fought as three regiments in Poland, consisting of voluntary enlistments of concentration camp guards drafted from the SS-Totenkopfverbände, proudly sporting the sinister skull and crossbones insignia they had made their own.

The morning after his application to join the armed SS military unit being formed, Walther Hoffman, Untersturmführer of the SS-Totenkopfverbände had been summoned to the Dachau Commandant's office to meet the camp's first real commander, now Chief Inspector of The Concentration Camps and SS-Gruppenführer Theodor Eicke.

"*Heil Hitler*!" Hoffman shouted, raising his arm. The Inspector-General had nodded in austere approval as Hoffman clicked his heel.

"Heil Hitler. Take a seat, Hoffman." The voice was as Bavarian as Hoffman's was, though not Munich. Still, the accent was so strong, every syllable was dripping with malt beer and clad in lederhosen.

Hoffman did so, and Eicke sat perched on the edge of the commandant's desk in front of him. Commandant SS-Oberführer Hans Loritz was not present.

"Untersturmführer Hoffman… you wish to join the SS-Totenkopf armed unit, and serve your fatherland. We know war with the Poles is coming. You wish to fight for Germany. That is good. You are a good candidate."

Eicke surveyed him, like a stern old schoolmaster. Hoffman had seen him on previous visits, but had never spoken to him. He'd noted the former commandant had a good rapport with the rank and file guards there, remembering names and details with a quick familiarity. The man was a huge figure in their world. A hefty frame, great hams for fists and a wide, flat nose in the middle of a lined and fleshy face, slick black hair neatly parted at the side and clad in an SS-General's uniform; Theodor Eicke had a large physical presence. It was said even Heydrich could not dislodge him from his position as SS-*Gruppenführer und Inspector der Konzentrationslager,* and that Himmler personally protected his rule over the Reich's vast internment system, successfully preventing an SD-Gestapo coup.

Eicke fixed his gaze on Hoffman; one eye was slightly larger than the other, which gave him the discomfiting appearance of intensely peering at the younger man with some kind of stern, inexplicable anger.

"So, *Hoffman,* as I look to gather good, young, committed officers for the formation of this division in a new armed force of Germany, bearers of the Führer's political will, it is to people of your calibre I must turn."

Hoffman accepted the plaudits patiently. Already he began to sense where this was headed.

Eicke folded his arms, settling a lengthy gaze on the young officer.

"You are a committed National Socialist. Model Aryan, perfect German, young, strong. This is an ideal candidacy, I thought to myself. Then I checked your file."

Eicke briskly rounded the wooden counter, and sat down behind his old desk. He did not seem to notice the curious position he was occupying. A worried Hoffman tried appealing to the SS camaraderie he'd seen Eicke freely display with the guards.

"Back in the old chair, mein Gruppenführer. Good memories I hope." Eicke looked up from the sheaf of papers, and Hoffman quickly added "Sir."

The general grinned. "Dachau is still mine. Not even the Prinz-Albrecht Palais could take the camps from me."

The Prinz-Albrecht Palais was headquarters of Heydrich's *Sicherheitdienst*, the SS Security Service and party intelligence agency. A garden at the back of the SD offices connected them to their sister organisation the Gestapo, housed in the old art college on Prinz-Albrecht Strasse. Heydrich had monopolised all security and police branches of the Reich into his SS Security Main Office, with the sole exception of the Totenkopfverbände. The concentration camps were the one area that 'The Hangman' in Berlin had not somehow managed to gain administrative control over, constantly pressuring Himmler to add it to his personal empire as per Heydrich's rulership of all manner of policing and suppression in the Reich. Hoffman had no strong feelings about the Reichsführer-SS, but he'd heard many jokes from the rank and file about 'Heini der Wimmler' and how he should watch his back, as Heydrich would one day outgrow him, or tire of using the Reichsführer as a battering ram to power one of these days. If Ernst Röhm and Gregor Strasser, Hitler's two chief party rivals weren't safe from Heydrich, they said, then nor was Himmler. Nor anyone else who got in his way.

The powerful general grinning across the desk at Hoffman did not seem an opponent to take lightly, however, nor one easily rolled over. Even by 'The Blond Beast'.

"Things were different when *I* started," that man boomed. "The TV didn't exist. We were not even a separate branch of the SS. And I didn't wear the Death's Head on my collar tab, when I was here, nor did any of the others."

"The TV wore SS runes?"

"No. A small 'D' for Dachau. I was Commandant – most of the rank and file had blank tabs. '34 I left here to become Reich Inspector, the SA cancer was cut from the National Socialist body, and the SS-TV became its own beast."

Eicke's grin widened as he spoke, lighting himself a cigarette carelessly. Hoffman silently noted the absence of an ashtray.

"Now, your file, Hoffman. Joined the party, 1930. The year I joined the SS, *Untersturmführer*," he said, adding slight emphasis to the rank as though to question the disparity between his considerable seniority and the 2nd class lieutenant's far lowlier status. Then he seemed mollified. "Ah, took three years to join the SS. However, excellent record with regards to your political reliability and upholding of German honour. Married 1935, Claudia Hoffman née von Kahr."

Eicke's eyes widened in alarm, and shot up to Hoffman questioningly. Hostile.

"No, different family," Hoffman reassured him firmly.

Gustav Ritter von Kahr had been Bavarian Minister-President, and a 'traitor' in the failed 1923 *putsch* that led to Hitler's arrest and imprisonment. Revenge had been savage. It came eleven years later, during the Night of the Long Knives purge of '34, masterminded by Heydrich and with Göring and Himmler's unholy alliance to sway the Führer. Gustav von Kahr had been hacked to death with axes by SS men, even as the SA leadership was being murdered en masse. And as

Hoffman was well aware, Ernst Röhm had been shot by none other than Theodor Eicke.

Röhm's executioner continued reading, mollified from his brief apprehension. "Transferred to Totenkopfverbände under Gruppenführer *Eicke*, 1936; began duties at Dachau September of that year. Promoted Untersturmführer September '38. Of course, superiors and comrades have offered their assessments, for the file. Allow me to read."

He cleared his throat. Hoffman watched, apprehensive.

"Untersturmführer Hoffman is dedicated National Socialist, boasting excellent recollection of key passages from the Führer's book, and a readiness to extoll the Party virtues. He is a diligent administrator, an ideal representative of the SS and one of the more reliable of Konzentrationslager personnel. He is hardworking, efficient, capable... sparing with punishment... humane... stern without cruelty." Eicke's nose wrinkled with distaste. He reeled off the latter observations like one would identify particularly insidious forms of a disgusting breed of parasitic insect.

Hoffman was quiet. Eicke leaned forwards.

"That all sounds well and good," he said, with barely concealed disdain, "but only the *best* of our young generation may represent the Fatherland in the Führer's personal guard. You want to be a member of the elite order? You have to show it, through loyalty and action. SS man; *your honour is loyalty.*"

Eicke stood, casting a shadow over Hoffman as his frame blocked the light streaming through an exposed gap in the cheap curtains. He cast a brief look of frustration at the junior officer, and he turned to look out of the single-paned window at pyjama-clad prisoners circling the yard.

"Here behind the barbed-wire lurks the enemy of National Socialism and the German people, Hoffman. He watches everything you do. Your diligence and administrative capabilities are all well and good. But we need men of iron. Words must be supported by actions. Do you follow?"

Hoffman nodded, mute. Eicke turned to look at him, and the Untersturmführer nodded again.

"Your enemy will try to help himself by using all your weaknesses. Don't leave yourself open in any way. Show these 'Enemies of the State' your teeth. Anyone who shows even the smallest sign of compassion for the enemies of the state must disappear from our ranks. I can only use hard men who are determined to do anything to purge the enemies of the Fatherland. We have no use for weaklings."

He leaned in, a fierce look in his eyes. "I hope you see things as I do, Untersturmführer Hoffman."

"*Jawohl*, mein Gruppenführer!" the young officer barked back. For the second time, Eicke grinned; this one a little churlish, even menacing.

"Good. Follow me. Let's see if you can *truly* serve in the SS order against Germany's *enemies...*"

Baring his chest proudly, apeing the body language of an alpha male mountain gorilla, the big officer briskly walked out of the office, Hoffman in hurried pursuit. The young officer's stomach lurched. He knew that if push came to shove, he would be equal to performing whatever task General Eicke had in mind for him, for Führer and Fatherland, but Hoffman could not entirely suppress the small, internal voice that suggested his conscience may not be completely clean after it.

Hoffman tried in vain to suppress the bourgeois value system that had been instilled in him, and he focused on Germany's troubled past, the pride of the present and the promise of its future.

They marched through to the prison block, a narrow corridor, poorly lit by flickering yellow light. The cell doors were narrow, with serving slits. Some of them were standing cells – offering only enough room for the unfortunate prisoner to stand, often for weeks on end with a six-hour sleep break on a wooden cot allowed once every three days. They were fed one single piece of bread during the break. Hoffman had witnessed its results. Emaciated skeletons with bloodshot eyes, unable to walk, pulled half-alive out of a pit of their own filth. It was uncommon, but not unheard of, and the broken men duly died 'of natural causes' in the course of their return to forced labour. The camp crematorium incinerated all evidence of their existence.

Eicke led down to the end, where a waiting guard opened the rusty steel door of the cell. As they drew level, a middle aged man came into sight that Hoffman had never seen before, clad in an inmates striped pyjama bottoms and grey-white top, stood at the far end of the room under the light streaming in through a tiny arch above his head. Hoffman blanched as he saw the man's death sentence; a red triangle inverted within a yellow triangle. He was not only a Jew, which was not as yet legally criminal, per se, but he combined the hated race with political subversion. A *Jewish political* prisoner. Worse still, a pink triangle stood next to the red and yellow makeshift Star of David. The man was homosexual.

Eicke beckoned Hoffman to enter the cell. He did so, staring at the prisoner, and taking care to stay inexpressive as he took in the Jew's haggard appearance; burn marks and cuts evident, a haunted, knowing look in his eyes. Hoffman hid his emotions behind The Cold Face. The general leaned in to his ear, and hissed:

"This degenerate piece of dog shit is a pink triangle, a *Jew* and a fucking *Kozi*. Doesn't it boil your blood just to look at him, *SS-Untersturmführer* Hoffman? Or does it provoke *humane feelings*? Are you a National Socialist, and a true son of the Fatherland? You must decide, as you look at the Führer's enemy; a Jew, and a communist pervert. *Deutschland Erwache!*"

Germany Awake.

The last line was all that was needed. Though the SA style Jew beatings and public persecutions held no appeal for the relatively mild-mannered Hoffman – despite his dislike of the parasitic people who had profited from the misery of honest, decent Germans – the sight of one such Jew stood before him as a *sodomite,* and a political criminal against the Führer assailed his senses. It was sickening to be around such vermin. Sickening.

'Germany Awake', the Führer had proclaimed, and piece by piece, it was reclaiming its own land and people from the scum like the one before him in this dingy, dank little cell. And now Hoffman, and people like him, could fight back, and contribute to the awakening. No longer would swinish filth like this disgusting man be free to persecute and mock them. To extort them, and corrupt their systems. No longer would degenerates like this piece of garbage be allowed to poison the Fatherland with such sick disease. They could purge their enemies together, led by the Führer, bound by their blood and destiny.

Hoffman unsheathed his truncheon, and slowly approached the trembling captive. Knowing that Eicke expected punishment as well as justice, he brought the club down in a vicious, curving arc into the side of the prisoner's knee. Cries rang out, and he spat in response, releasing a contemptuous gobbet of mucus that spattered the stricken man's neck. The young man circled his helpless prey. It was not the savagery of the natural world, but beyond animalistic; a lingering, spiteful pleasure in the act. Lightly tapping the doomed Jew's head with the baton for a sadist's touch, Hoffman heard an approving chuckle behind him, and even before the methodical blows reigned down, he knew he was going to Poland.

The silver cigarette holder gratefully accepted its seventeenth Dunhill of the day, and was quickly clamped between the teeth of its beleaguered owner.

Simon sat ill-at-ease, trying to relax, as he reclined in his smoking gown of burgundy velvet and silk; a favourite item, not inherited from his father, but one that he himself had procured at considerable expense, along with a large, curved wooden calabash. It was a favourite little eccentricity of his, and though he rejected high society almost as a whole, this was one private quirk of the well-to-do that he relished. Enjoying the leisurely smoke, the journalist considered switching the holder fastened-Dunhill for his calabash; an act that never failed to give him a thrilling sense of kinship with Arthur Conan Doyle as he wrote. He quickly abandoned the idea. Not yet. The calabash drew his attention, and sat heavy, cumbersome. Sherlock merely pondered with it. The beautiful, marvellous thing was utterly incompatible with writing.

It was evening; his appointed time of reflection. Having completed all professional work, and private dissidence for the public eye alike, he set about recording his private thoughts in the leather journal for posterity, hoping that this work would be seen by future eyes; those seeking to understand.

Dear Diary,

Is it narcissistic madness to aspire to become the Samuel Pepys of this age? It is not entirely self-serving, I assure you – assuming 'you', whoever you may be, will one day read this work, should it survive, and that your heart is pure.

Future generations need to understand the madness of this time.

Yesterday, I strolled through Hyde Park, and it was truly joyous to see some of my leaflets scattered about. Some from Eric, some from myself. German soldiers were making manacled prisoners collect them. From the averted eyes and occasional glances, even smirks, I know that many of the people I passed in the park have been reading my materials. I was thrilled, and it would be dishonest and unbecoming to pretend otherwise.

I am likely a doomed man. How long can this be maintained? Perhaps, more so than Pepys, I am more likely to become... the Chartist printer they hung in the mid-1800s... or William Carter. Or perhaps even a William Tyndale, if I actually achieve anyway significant with this malarkey, beyond a two-finger salute and a few raspberries blown at the krauts.

I should not call them krauts. The term is almost fond. It thoroughly – and unfairly – diminishes the overwhelming menace and evil of their actions. Theirs is an apotheosis I struggle to contemplate; a tyrannical idea of the supremacy of blood and race over people and individual lives, which may yet choke the world with its own innards. Such scientific racism is so malevolently wicked, the old post-war German concept of 'life unworthy of life' has been allowed to re-enter the public consciousness, immunised and dulled as Europe has become to the awful brutality of National Socialist theory, and the violence of putting it into practice.

The leaders of this movement are almost godlike. Human lives are a shabby irrelevance in contrast with their great Movement of Blood and Race, which shall shape history, or so they tell us, while destroying the past. Immortality beckons, to them; a standard empathy for human suffering is beneath their wild thinking from on high. Hitler is a psychotic; his paladins soothe and stir the passions of his soul, and the more coldly rational amongst them manage to transform his visions into actions that provide them with enormous power over life and death.

It makes sense that Nietzsche is held aloft as one of their philosophical masters. Why would he not be; the breaker from Schopenhauer, the man to whom life was a Darwinian struggle within oneself as well as externally; true victory being to conquer oneself and abandon the abstract; the concept of God, and the quixotic notions of morality and justice... it is their own path. They have used blood and race as the conduit to bind their mindless masses as a people, while they themselves broke from traditional values to become Gods.

To some extent, these people represent the Napoleon, or the Emperor or the Pharaohs of human history dating back as far as was recorded. Their sense of right and true ends with the threat of an equal, or one of similar power, and then destruction or assimilation supersedes any notion of decency. Their benevolence can only stretch as far as kindness to underlings, and at that, only those of acceptable, similar blood. To rise against them was our crime; the mere suggestion that an opposing sentiment or way of life could be as worthy or more worthy than theirs was our ultimate sin in their eyes. But now, to us, the implication is clear; the Gods have spared us. They have shown mercy, and history will record their greatness.

But this is not theirs alone. This Nietzschean value is the same of all great men throughout history. The human herd is destined to be led by psychotic dreamers and morally questionable shysters; evidently, this breed of superman is the only type of person capable of seizing power, driven as they are by insatiable hunger; alas, our contemporary times further prove it. The age of the omnipotent ruler is far from over; Emperor, Pharaoh, Führer.

Simon paused. The cigarette had burned out, and on seeing its ash, he was grateful for the smoking jacket. He replaced it, choosing what looked like a Turkish cigarette from the wooden box – those poor people, reliant on black market smokes of tea and God knows what else – and, vaguely pondering how unfair was his position in comparison, continued to write.

You cannot imagine the disgust with which the prior paragraph was written.

Here is an insight into the machine minds of such a system, and its marshals:

Out of sheer curiosity, I went to Speakers Corner, to see if any still dared use its privilege afforded as per the civil rights of an Englishman; that to speak, and speak freely. To my disbelief, it was. A small crowd of good-natured hecklers were gathered around a scruffy cockney lad of about 19. The young man was giving mock-Hitler speeches, twisting them for comedy; two fingers pointing in the air, screaming, frothing at the mouth. He was really good, truth be told.

"English... English people... listen up..." he cried.

"...Only when the people of England and Germany rise up, and unshackle themselves from the rationing, will unlimited sausage and sauerkraut be available to the Aryan peoples... the Jews have destroyed our sausage making capabilities, but only a people with cultural creativity maintain true cultural performance. We will rise up, and a new order of sausage making will emerge triumphant from the ruins of the old world – any person or group opposing our people and the historic making of sausage can do so quite calmly, for they have never even for one single hour been on the battlefield! But our sausages will prevail! England Awake!"

Two Wehrmacht soldiers were laughing at him openly from a distance. Almost hysterically, in fact, which certainly added to the moment. And then the car pulled up; armed SS got out, with the blank collar tab. Everyone knows what that means now. Heydrich's shadow army – SD/Gestapo. The boy tried to run, and was brought down with coshes and hauled away, still yelling. I doubt the man will see Christmas.

Despite incidents of this nature, the Germans are playing a clever game. Most of this seems to be from the army. It's a sort of velvet fascism.

Simon paused. *Velvet fascism.* That is a good one. He made note of it, for the next leaflets and pamphlets. A good warning for the people only too inclined to believe the best, to harbour optimism for this future.

The Jerries staged public talking shops. Junior officers and enlisted men took up the brunt of it. I expected political language, euphemisms and veiled threats. Instead, we got reassurances and a promise that rationing is not long for this world. They boxed clever. Some beastly, abhorrent, smug little snake oil salesman called Sebastian was speaking at the one I saw, in Hyde Park; by all accounts he carried on for hours. There was no end to him, the man went on like blood gushing from an opened vein, an air raid couldn't have stopped him... the man was a protégé of Goebbels himself; wasted in a Wehrmacht tunic.

Curfew; also soon-to-end, or so they say. Rationing to be entirely lifted; equal as in Berlin, and indeed, slightly better than was in Britain.

But meanwhile, they have killed democracy, executed dissidents and conducted shadowy, clandestine police operations in the thick of night; obscured by the fogs of war and the mindless optimism of the masses. If this diary survives; let the menace of the time be remembered.

Sinking back into his chair, Simon sighed. Optimism was something he begrudged in every living soul he saw. Placing the silver holder in the right-breast pocket of the smoking jacket, he pulled out the calabash, and having emptied tobacco into it, began to puff away, thoughtfully, basking in his private sanctuary of comfort.

Bormann's quiet rise had interested Heydrich. While Hess remained Deputy to the Führer, his Chief of Staff Bormann was the power leading the Party brownshirts and bureaucrats, as well as partly living in a house above the Berghof in the Obersalzburg complex that he'd designed, and more recently, sliding effortlessly from *de facto* Party leader into the simultaneous role of Hitler's secretary. Bormann built the mountaintop complex; Bormann made the Führer rich from stamp royalties; Bormann, not Hess, never left the Führer's side, during long, idle days on the mountain. While Goebbels ran Berlin and the national propaganda, Göring's legendary energy waned as his waist widened and morphine addiction increased; Bormann, meanwhile, was by the Führer's side. With Göring and Goebbels long established in their roles, only Himmler and Heydrich had seized as much tangible power since Hitler's appointment as Chancellor as had the sly, fleshy, brutal Bormann. Heydrich had recognised his machinations for what they were, almost admiringly. It amazed him that the Göring who'd once been so politically ruthless was now content to sit idly by at Karinhall, wildly enjoying the trappings of power while a Bormann existed in the shadows – or rather, in the glaring spotlight, in Heydrich's eyes – quietly manoeuvring himself into position by virtue of never leaving the Führer's side. Göring the recluse; Prime Minister, Reichsmarschall and all his other titles and accolades aside, even beyond being the chosen successor; Heydrich still couldn't understand the fat man's withdrawal. That sort of inactivity at the heart of power was an anathema to the Reich Security Chief.

So he'd put his SD to work. On the outbreak of war, Heydrich switched jurisdiction of Codename "Brown" to Gestapo agents; incredibly, as luck would have it, one of whom was conducting an affair with a close confidant of Martin Bormann's wife. Gerda Bormann visited this friend, often in tears, showing visible signs of abuse and outpouring her marital misery. The Reich's Security

Police chief was delighted. By the spring of 1940, when he had collected sufficient material to strike, Heydrich made his move. Unannounced, he paid Herr Bormann a visit at the Party Chancellery in Munich, also known as the Brown House; heart of the National Socialist movement and home to its hardliners. Bormann, 'The Brown Eminence', had stayed on alone an extra day on urgent business before joining his Führer at Obersalzburg, a rare separation. Heydrich, tipped off and as calculating as ever, had quickly seized his chance.

This was the heartland of the Party, and it was from here that Heydrich had planned his and Himmler's own rise, simultaneously intriguing *against* and being indispensable *to* Hermann Göring in Berlin; castrating the rival SA before wresting away Göring's control of the German criminal and political police, known as the Kripo and Gestapo.

Bormann was a different beast.

Unlike Göring – who simply thought little of Himmler, to whom he'd entrusted his Gestapo, the operational control of which was promptly handed to Heydrich – Bormann had never been inclined to use Heydrich to weaken the SS chief's position, or to dispose of some other rival in the Party, police or army. He had passed the law that granted total jurisdiction as the Party's intelligence service to Heydrich's SD, but officially in the name of Hess, as his Chief of Staff. No, Bormann had not yet moved on Himmler, despite marginalising his own chief the Deputy-Führer, and given his proximity to Hitler, had not yet called on the services of General Heydrich.

Heydrich had needed the leverage of intelligence. As ever, it had worked. *Knowledge is power*, he thought wryly, remembering Bormann squirm.

Heydrich had been warmly welcomed, and ushered in to the Führer's office; a move which was telling in itself. Göring and Himmler had offices here that the Reich Security Chief could use, but he chose not to, preferring the conjoined SD and Gestapo headquarters in Berlin. But Bormann commandeered the old man's office, which none but 'dear Bormann' would have been willing to do – Speer was intimate but lacked the seniority in rank; Göring, SS chief Himmler and Reich Chancellery head Lammers all lacked the ability to view Hitler as a mortal man. Heydrich would put his dirty boots up on the desk, when it was his, and invite compliant Bavarian girls to join him in his working hours. He found the possibility Bormann was sending out a message by his chosen workspace quite humorous.

Heydrich entered the great wooden room with a powerful stride.

"Heil Hitler! Greetings, *Sicherheitsleiter, Gruppenführer der SS und polizei*." Bormann had stood, at least. Had he remained seated behind his desk, the Reich security chief would have twisted the knife with even more malice. Interesting, thought Heydrich. Although he was *de facto* a general and leader of the criminal and political police forces, he held no such legal title as that used by Bormann.

"Heil Hitler, Reichsleiter." Heydrich sat down without waiting to be asked.

After some token small talk regarding the situation in France and victory, impending operations against England and the SS role, without further ado Heydrich pushed on with the purpose of his visit.

"Yes, England. That is most definitely something you can help me with, Herr Reichsleiter. With the planned military administrations being a possible curtailment of SS and Party policy in the occupied areas, as they were in Poland – no doubt our goals are aligned on this most important matter."

Bormann's face remained cool, which Heydrich quietly admired. "Indeed, Gruppenführer, a smooth path to achieving goals would be most expedient. Perhaps I can speak to the Führer about this matter of security and stability? Or arrange a meeting for the Reichsführer-SS?"

Aha. Heydrich smiled inwardly. That was crude of Bormann. Reinhard Heydrich was not one to be marginalised behind the inner circle; particularly as he'd been instrumental in helping Himmler achieve that lofty status, not to mention a history of tearing others down from equal heights.

He did not dally. "No. As director of Einsatzgruppen and the Security Police operations of the Reich and territories, I want immunity from army interference and a clear hand to deal quickly and effectively with the problems faced in Britain."

Bormann stared. Course, brutal, he was not polished. But his secretarial role demanded concessions in subtlety, and he'd perfected the art of agreeability in the Führer's presence. In contrast with his own professional modus operandi, at least, Heydrich's directness was shocking. And presumptuous.

"Herr Reich... *sicherheitsführer und polizeidirektor*, this is perhaps a matter best discussed between yourself and the Führer, and perhaps Reichsführer-SS Himmler and the Wehrmacht–"

"There was talk of capture from the Bolsheviks in 1920," Heydrich loudly interrupted, with relish. "And a secret deal. Some kind of pact signed, and a promise of information if the young Freikorps man ever manoeuvred his way into a position of power in a major right-wing, nationalistic German *party*. A written pact, connecting the *young Freikorps man* with the *Bolshevik enemies of the*

Fatherland. You have an unregistered, personal shortwave radio transmitter, Martin, do you not?"

Bormann's eyes widened, bulging grotesquely in his fleshy face until he resembled a manic frog. Heydrich allowed a thin smile to curl his cruel, delicate lips. His high voice purred.

"And of course, Gerda. The lovely Frau Bormann. Such troubles... her woes, that tragic figure, fallen Rhinemaiden of German womanhood. Her pain. Of course, there is the stenographer at Obersalzburg. But Gerda... her woes..."

Bormann opened, and then closed his mouth, a shrewd expression on his face. Already, the alarm was gone, and Heydrich recognised the cool glint of calculation in his eyes. He could see that Bormann realised he was not in immediate danger, otherwise he'd have been arrested, and the slippery intriguer was weighing up his options. He would come to see that a pact, of sorts, was his best and only course of action. But still, Heydrich pressed the point home.

"I know what you are thinking, Martin. It would be no tragedy for SS-Gruppenführer, Chief of the Reich Main Security Office, its criminal and political police and the SD, and INTERPOL President Reinhard Heydrich to disappear..." Heydrich reeled off his titles lazily, enjoying himself. He'd noted Bormann invented two for him earlier, a truly crude ploy that he nonetheless approved of. "But rest assured, the Führer's *dear Bormann*," he sneered. "If I were to meet with an unfortunate accident, there are those within the Reich police forces that would ensure certain facts about Martin Bormann found their way to the Führer. And Himmler, Göring, Goebbels – many copies, in fact, for dissemination amongst the staff of the good Doctor's Ministry. Or perhaps just to discredit me in the eyes of the Führer? Alas, thou remembers *not* the *Führer's* own words regarding the necessity of mobilising Reinhard Heydrich against the Reich's enemies. Göring and Goebbels would agree. And of *course*, the last people who tried to remove me were Gregor Strasser and Ernst Röhm. You remember their fate, Herr Reichsleiter? And they were both the two men most exalted in the Party behind only *the Führer himself*. The same Führer who exonerated me of the ludicrous Jew rumours circulated by the *late* Strasser, although of course, beyond *Führerprinzip*, multiple investigations proved my blood is as German as Wagnerian opera."

Bormann broke his silence. "There's no need for fucking threats, Heydrich. I know your calibre. That Bolshevik business was laughable bullshit. You're a powerful policeman and national security chief. I'm the Führer's executive arm. Gregor Strasser was a cunt. Röhm was a faggot, a pervert. Himmler got an independent SS. You got the police, even Göring's Gestapo. We're neither of us fools. So what is your point?" The informal, course Bormann was out; all shades of the quiet, measured secretary and chief-of-staff gone. The party hardliner so despised in Berlin was nakedly on display, his pragmatism superseding his distaste at being cornered.

Heydrich simply ignored him.

"So perhaps, instead of the *late* Strasser and the other *dead* Party bigshot Röhm, who came to oppose me after the early years of comradeship... you should take after Göring and Goebbels, the ministers who essentially replaced them? Synergies between the leaders will make our government strong. Do *you*... like *they*... see my *usefulness* as the judge, jury and executioner of all Enemies of the Reich?"

A curling smirk played at Heydrich's mouth, and an incensed Bormann fought hard to stay calm. The police leader continued with open enjoyment, smiling. "I would think, Martin, it is beneficial to you to smoothen *my* path, not least because the more administrative jurisdiction I wield over European policing and security, the less... *burden*, shall we say, on the Reichsführer's remit? Himmler has many *historic German tasks* to fulfil, as the Führer says. The *high priest* of National Socialism cannot be burdened with the policing and administrative problems of an entire *continent...*"

As his voice trailed off, Heydrich mocked Bormann with his eyes, sneering at him for his intrigues and his permanent place at the Führer's side, while being utterly fallible to the man who'd been labelled 'Moses Handel' – 'Heydrich The Jew.'

Bormann stared impassively, the eyes still bulging, but patiently hearing out the cocksure monologue of the Reich's police leader. The Blond Beast was silently impressed with his restraint, though utterly contemptuous of his helplessness in the face of internecine intrigue. Bormann was stuck in a game of cat and mouse, maintaining eye contact as the vein on his forehead throbbed. Time passed slowly, like a knife.

In time, Heydrich continued.

"Göring of course entrusted the Jewish Question to *me*, and gave the Gestapo to Himmler *on the basis* that *I* would run it. He threw a party for me at Karinhall, did you know? After Röhm's death. When we purged the SA, I sat with him at the chancellery – the *Reich* chancellery that is – and we laughed all day in the command post, with sandwiches, wine and beer. Prime Minister Göring is *excellent* company, Martin, although I realise you and he have no relationship to speak of. But Göring is not politically sentimental, nor in regards to power. The fat man is utterly ruthless. He rewarded my ability and work, and always in a way that advantaged him. As for Goebbels, the good Doctor sees fit to coordinate his cultural enlightenment campaigns with Reich policing policy, and he benefits from intelligence *I* feed him. Which leads me to *you*."

Bormann nodded. He knew a dangerous adversary when he saw one. This policeman would not dare to challenge – to *attack* – the man closest to the Führer if his own position were not absolutely infallible. Bormann recognised much truth in the younger man's arrogant bluster. Much like Hess in the party for Bormann, in the SS, Himmler was clearly a kind of human shield for this tall, handsome young devil sat in front of him, basking in his triumphs. Aged 36, he had the world in his hands. Machiavellian to his rotten core.

Martin Bormann realised, then, that any realm of power he wished to build would have to accommodate the current chief of Reich Security. He could well be the future leader.

Heydrich continued. "The Reichsführer-SS is a busy man. The chief of SS-Reich Security, in my own personage is similarly busy, but unlike dear Himmler, my duty concerns only the suppression of enemies and security of the Reich. England is to be a nominal part of the Reich now, yes? *The British Empire, glorious Aryan allies of the German Fatherland,*" he said, with a trace of his sneer lingering in the air. "And the Führer needs both security, and a strong leader to marshal the integration of England into the new Saxon order in Europe."

"So what do you want," Bormann asked again, quietly. His tormentor finally saw that the man's patience would endure the lengthy haranguing, so he got to the point.

"In the event of resistance, I need to be more than just SS-Commander England – the Security Police leader is already that, to all intents and purposes. I can appoint myself or my own subordinates to that role, and the international jurisdiction of INTERPOL could be used to further that aim. No, true governance requires civil authority. Not merely a police role. I mean a *viceroy*, with political sway. A Reichsprotektor of Great Britain."

"Reichsprotektor," Bormann repeated doubtfully.

"Yes," he replied firmly. "And I shall want your assurances that outside of SS hierarchy that my personal contact with the Führer is maintained at all times. No more burdening the Reichsführer with reports and orders through the two-way chain of command. Direct. And I shall require from you, *assurances* that no army, party, police branch, Gau, commission, commissariat or whatever other ludicrous fiefdom wants to stick its nose in Reich Security business shall try to do so, nor can they legally... as a *Reichsprotektor* and – what did you call me, Martin? – Reich *Sicherheitsführer und Polizeidirektor...* is answerable *only* to the Führer."

Bormann scratched his chin, scowling as he considered the practicalities. "With Göring – one of your benefactors of course – I could persuade the Führer of your worth in position with a free hand in Britain in the interests of bringing a quicker peace and stability. Any man with the confidence of *both* his chosen successor and his right-hand man will have the backing of the Führer. But 'Reichsprotektor?' England is to be neither an occupied Commissariat nor a Protectorate. And Scotland and Ireland are ultimately to have their independence. Wales, too, if they want it. Every Aryan nation gets what they want, as long as they play nicely alongside Germany. Führerprinzip."

But Heydrich shook his head. "It is fitting. The same role as Neurath in Bohemia and Moravia, but with operational jurisdiction in my joint-role as SS and security police chief. No more inefficient chain-of-command rigmaroles to disrupt expediency. No army interference. Explain to the Führer, he will understand. Göring will approve. 'Protector' carries the necessary administrative sway, allows for control without restraints regarding the implementation of SS operations, and besides – it sounds comforting." He grinned. "'Protector'. How *avuncular*. It's the kind of sentimental name the British would find comforting, Martin. Don't you agree?"

As Bormann's doubtful expression turned to one of deep resentment, Heydrich couldn't help but throw his long, blond head back and laugh uproariously. What a day. Another triumph.

Leaving Bormann fuming at the Fuhrer's desk, the sniggering Heydrich left, without even bothering to salute the all-powerful Party boss.

He flew himself back to Berlin that same day, after several further meetings with Party higher-ups and the chiefs of the Munich police. As the sun slowly set, his personal plane landed at the Luftwaffe airfield to the north of Wannsee, whereupon the Reich's Security Chief stopped by INTERPOL headquarters and then drove his open-top "SS-3" Mercedes into central Berlin, making straight for the Salon Kitty. Heydrich marched in to his honey-trap brothel, and after the most perfunctory of greetings, promptly ordered a large Scotch, and a petite blonde. In the luxuriant room upstairs, which was covered in brightly coloured drapes and hangings of purple and red silk, he ripped her clothes off with violent lust, chuckling manically. The small girl squealed as Heydrich lifted her bodily and threw her down, spreading her legs and seizing her swollen clitoris between his teeth, still sniggering as he bit the bloated, sensitive flesh, making her cry out in pain. Next, his spidery fingers wrapped around her head, and he forced her to fellate him as he stood with arms outstretched, thrusting his body into her face with considerable force, before eventually ejaculating with a loud aggression. It did not, however, signal the end of his lust, and the girl was pushed back onto the bed, resignedly settling back on the silk sheets in the knowledge that her ordeals were not yet through. The Reich security chief didn't even bother to check if any of his own microphones were still bugging the room. Flushed with alcohol and victory, Heydrich was on top of the world.

Four days later, he was summoned to the Berghof with the Reichsführer-SS to see Hitler.

It is remarkable how quickly things change.

The most remarkable transformations often happen in such a bizarrely short space of time it can leave your head spinning; an almost cruel, jolting improperness to the British sensibility. Death, incarceration, arrest in the dead of night, a loved one dying on the battlefield, an air raid attack – all manner and means of miseries and misfortunes can come at any moment with indecent swiftness; a life changed forever, or broken, or transcended. The abrupt dropping of a bomb that obliterates all in the path of its damage radius, leaving behind nothing but a crater and its collateral damage, the splintered remains of what was once human life; so grossly indecent to the ideal of a gentleman's agreement for 'Marquis of Queensbury' rules – a wicked abuse and a low blow, foul play. Those raised to believe in correctness and a sort of unifying code of decency are often shocked by the unnatural state of war, the volatile unpredictability it brings and the confusion that comes from that the muddied waters of morality and properness in such situations. Love blooms fast; secrecy and furtiveness replace transparent dealings, and the all-enveloping mist of intrigue covers all, those that want it to, and the unwilling alike.

In such times, drastic changes occur in milliseconds.

In the saloon bar of the Royal Oak, the low sound of *Elsa's Procession to the Cathedral* from *Lohengrin* could just be heard; its delicate legato drifting through the air in the open space behind Arthur's bar, through which the old landlord could scuttle to and fro to serve both rooms. Even with the smooth melody of a familiar menace – associated with field grey uniforms and impassive, stony faces – Alan and William were regaling each other as Mary giggled to herself, struggling to follow the distinctly northern dialect from the pair but intensely amused by their childish enthusiasm. It was moments such as these that she reminisced on fondly, at night; the moments of warmth when war was forgotten.

But in such a world of extreme political systems, war cannot be forgotten for too long, and it returned to them in the form of the three pints of ale and a worried expression on Jack's face – however much they tried to delay the obvious.

"I've got news."

Even now, Alan tried a joke. "Hitler's dead."

"No."

"Franco's dead?" Alan and William hopefully asked in unison. Jack smiled at the Geordie and Scot combination, despite himself. His insides churned inside him.

"No. Sadly."

"Bastard will never die," Alan mused, in deep regret. Mary spat on the floor. Even with Spain's nominal neutrality or 'non-aggression' in Hitler's war, Spanish volunteer divisions had fought in the Wehrmacht and SS, fascist support was still evident, and they viewed *El Caudillo* with visceral, undying hatred.

William agreed. "He'll outlive us by thirty years at least, the little bastard. And his friends." He pointed at Alan, suddenly animate. "You think Sanjurjo and Mola *both* died in *accidental* plane crashes? I'm telling you, Hitler and Mussolini will explode in a Focke-Wolf one day, mark my w–"

"Art's just passed me a message," Jack stated firmly. That shut them up.

He slipped the note into Alan's hand, covertly, breathing "dispose of it." The lithe figure smartly stepped out, heading to the toilets. Even with the room to themselves, the possibility of being seen reading from a note was a foolish risk to take. In dangerous times, they'd learned that even eliminating the smallest risks could be vital.

"Looks like this is it," Jack told them redundantly.

This time, Mary took his hand, squeezing in a firm pinch while snatching William's in her left.

"No going back."

"Is everyone ready? Not," Jack quickly added, seeing his friends' eyebrows raise, "that I need to ask."

"To pending news!" William smiled wryly, raising his pint. They clinked glasses, in an enforced jollity that none of them felt.

"That old feeling, eh?"

"That old feeling."

They drank to that. Presently, Alan returned, but to their instant dismay he wore an ashen look, palpable worry showing in eyes that darted here and there, unable to focus on anything for longer than a second. He slid into the booth, and downed two thirds of his pint with a mighty swig.

"Well?" Jack queried.

Alan gave a small snort of laughter, humourlessly. He took a moment to compose himself, fixing his eyes on the table in front of him.

"Well... now it begins."

"What begins?"

"The SS," the Geordie muttered.

"Will you fucking well tell us what the SS is bloody beginning?" Jack exploded, quickly hushed by the others. Alan looked shaken.

"France and Holland are obviously pacified, with resistance raging here. Hitler's Praetorian Guard and high priests are coming over to oversee an SS consolidation of German power in England. At least, I'm assuming England – Wales and Scotland will be cut off at this rate, aye? Volunteer units and all that, probably, membership to the BUF, puppet governments and all that, aye?"

He was babbling, eyes moving laterally, and when his vision finally focused ahead of him, he saw that the other three were staring at him uncomprehendingly. Composing himself, Alan sighed.

"Major players are coming. Rumour has it one is setting up shop here permanently. But they're both coming, from a source in the SS itself."

"Who, Alan? Bleeding hell!" Jack cried out, exasperated. The anticipation was wearing on nerves and patience that were already strained thin.

Again, that deep sigh. Alan hadn't sighed – or even so much as *grimaced* – when they attacked a Spanish village held by fascists and Catholics in early '37. He'd been laughing during the battle, even after his hand was shot.

"Heinrich Himmler... and Reinhard Heydrich."

The ensuing silence was deafening; Mary imagined that the only sound heard in that room was the furious beating of their hearts, hammering heavily. Her own thudded in her ribcage, and she distractedly pressed a hand to it, trying to control her breathing.

Jack exhaled slowly. He'd been unconsciously holding his breath so long he felt dizzy. William sat with his heads clasped behind the great mane of his head, looking up at the cracked ceiling. Jack didn't move, but every muscle in his body was tensed.

"Himmler... AND Heydrich?"

To his relief, his voice was strong.

"The two most dangerous men in Europe," William muttered, unnecessarily.

Jack stared at Alan. "They're sending both of them? Why is the police and Gestapo chief coming here with Himmler? How can they both just bunk off?"

"I don't know."

"What's so bloody important about them coming here? All these months later? Ninety percent of the country's just getting on with it. As long as they're fed, no one gives a damn now about the armistice, they just wish Jerry would piss off back to mainland Europe and leave us in peace."

"I don't know," Alan repeated tensely.

William hugged Mary, who smiled bravely. "They are not very nice men," she said, which lightened the mood somewhat with its profound understatement.

Her lover, smiling now, queried Alan.

"What are you thinking, big lad?"

Alan didn't answer, and the smile was wiped off William's face. He and Jack had the same dawning realisation, and their eyes met in quiet horror. They were a special group of saboteurs from the off; veterans of Spain, and from what they could tell, they hadn't even been recruited conventionally by the *unconventional* standards of the auxiliaries. Based in *London*. Not a village, or up in Coventry, or Liverpool, Leeds, York, Sunderland, Glasgow. London. The island capital, heart of the Empire.

Alan noted their reaction, and snorted mirthlessly, supping his pint.

"So," William declared, a little too loudly into the silence. "What do we know? Göring supposedly said 'Himmler's brain is called Heydrich'. So the wee blond fellow is a bit of a nasty little man. Organised most of the purges, pogroms, persecution measures and police actions in kraut-land since Hitler's rise."

Alan snorted again. They ignored him, knowing he would overcome his pessimistic lethargy. He always did.

William continued, "Himmler is the overlord. Heydrich is the cold steel of the SS that unifies and runs the SD, Gestapo and German police. These guys created and maintain the system of fear that we swore to stamp out. While Hitler's swanning around his mountain or his great chancellery, these guys are running the police state, midnight callers, internment camps, the whole death machine. They are the greatest menace on earth."

"What difference does Heydrich make?" Mary asked curiously.

They knew why. For her, from what she'd seen of both political extremes in her ravaged country, it was the system that trapped them. Even Franco had only been part of a junta of generals, before Sanjurjo's plane crash that led to a vote for unified command. Even then, it had taken Mola's plane crash to bring the Generalísimo to total authority. And the systems she had believed in were huge collectives, with less in the way of individual drive.

"A lot," Jack said darkly.

"Germany is different. After the first purges and the Nuremberg Laws they might have toned things down," William explained. "The economy improved, all other parties had been wiped out, the Jews–" he stopped, horrified with himself. "...ah... well, it was *these* two centralising the German police forces and merging them into the SS that maintained the police state. And stirring things up year after year, along with Goebbels and Streicher, to keep things at fever pitch. Not to mention they kept the camps going..."

Alan finally piped up.

"Heydrich matters a lot. They call him "the Blond Beast," or "The Hangman." He keeps the SS Empire ruling Europe, the evil genius behind their schemes. Apparently he's the most switched on of the entire bunch of rotten apples, and the most ruthless. Some say they're all scared of him – Göring, Goebbels, Hess... even Hitler and Himmler."

"The perfect guest," Jack observed. "Brilliant."

"He's obviously here to take the reins on suppression. Perhaps send in his Security Police instead of the army, to flush 'em out. Or to work the cities. Or set camps up, who knows?"

"Camps, oh God," Jack muttered, shaking his head. "Savages."

"Animals," Mary spat, with feeling.

They empathised. Only after leaving France did they realise how close they – in particular, she – had come to internment there. Other fleeing Republicans had not been so lucky. Many were still there.

"They'll be setting camps up for sure," Jack mused, morosely. Alan shrugged.

"We don't know that."

"Why else would they both be coming here?" William pointed out.

They argued the toss and theorised for several minutes longer, until Mary started viewing them with suspicion. There was something a little too conversationally blasé about the debate, and she coughed, pointedly at Alan. He nodded, resignedly.

"It's all on us," he confirmed.

"¿Que?" she scowled.

"We've got to kill Himmler. Heydrich too, if we can."

Jack had been absorbing the implications of the note for several minutes, and so retained his faculties on hearing it. While Mary gave way to shock, his composure was intact.

"Why *Himmler*? If Heydrich's so bloody dangerous?"

"Just going on the instructions. Makes sense on paper I suppose – get the top dog. Kill Himmler, and if possible, take out his chief gangster."

They shared a look.

"Ho*way*, that would be smarter, if you ask me," Alan forced a laugh. "I reckon taking out the blond one would be smarter. But specifically, orders are 'kill the chief'. Take out the SS leader and we strike a real blow to Berlin."

Silence fell on them. "I feel sick," William admitted. It helped destroy the dramatic effect of the previous statement, but did little to assuage the tension.

An ugly, black tension hung in the air at St George camp no.5.

Total silence was being observed, and the psychological torture of ignorance to one's fate was allowed to work its evil spell on the group of thoroughly dispirited men. They stood lined in nervous rows at the roll call position, but no shouts were heard. The absences in their ranks were only too apparent. Things had been going *so well*, you could almost see them thinking. But the minority group of whisperers were insistent; they drew their lines in the sand. Escape was duty. Obedience was treachery. The SS was enemy.

There was no free England to return to. But the compulsion to flee was too strong.

And these SS, if they needed further illustration after May 1940, were not the fanatical Anglophile detritus of Nazi pseudo-soldiers they'd believed them to be.

Tommy raised his eyes from the floor, the position and pose that the majority of the internees in the yard had determinedly stuck to for the twenty-five minutes they'd been stood there. Impatience wore his nerves down. He stared with equal determination at Lieutenant Hoffman, whose downcast eyes told the same tale as that feared by the assembled British men. Tommy stared at him desperately in something between anger and pleading, until the big German sensed his plaintive gaze and looked up. Hoffman offered only an imperceptible shake of the head, and looked away again.

The mood was as black as the jackboots of stern SS troopers, gazing unsmiling at the Brits from the parade ground, with several silhouetted up in the watchtowers overlooking the camp yard. None wore Waffen-SS military jackets; all were now clad in close-fitting tunics, the sleek, silvery *feldgrau* of Hugo Boss. It was the same transformation that Major Wolf and Hoffman had made so soon into the internment period; a subtle morphing into glossy parade ground soldiers from rugged men of war.

Eventually, the approach of a distant car could be heard, and some men jolted unpleasantly with the reports from the exhaust. Those men who had been under heavy barrage in the frenzied retreat along the Pas-du-Calais in particular winced, flinching in unpleasant recognition of the ugly mechanical sounds, distant as they were. Stanley, who'd served in the Great War, moved not a muscle; the Sergeant's chin and chest were out, maintaining the quintessentially British stiff upper lip, a proud stance.

They'd expected a truck; it was a cattle cart. First easing in through the main gateway of the outer compound – a horseshoe passage in the wire from the watchtowers standing sentient – in and past the long building, and then finally, the cart shuddered to a halt and stopped at the barbed wire gates leading into the furthest corner of the compound; the barrack huts of three companies of the British Expeditionary Force interned at camp no.5.

The cattle cart disgorged its weary cargo; men, whose faces were spattered with blood, limping tiredly in a pitiful group through the gates. The soldiers escorted them in followed, and lastly, with a brisk march that made his jackboots clip-clop across the asphalt ominously came the hostile presence of Major Jochen Wolf.

The German officer *gleamed* black. The portentous contours of his dark expression were perfectly reflected in the perfect black cloud, and everything the colour represented was embodied by his menace. Though the ceremonial all-black SS uniform was still absent – to the continuing confusion of some of the British lads, to whom the 'blackshirts' of Moseley, the originals of Mussolini and then the SS were the embodiment of fascism itself – however, the suave, custom-fitted field grey tunic clung to him inside the outer black layer of leather trench coat that descended over a foot past the top of his black jackboot.

The captured men stood in a line, facing their own comrades from the companies. Major Wolf suddenly threw his long coat off with a quick, singular movement, flinging it back to his aide. Now grey from the kneecaps up, he was no less impressive for it; the Iron Cross dangled from his left breast pocket, and the space between his fastened collar, in pride of place over the Adam's apple.

His tone was superficially pleasant, but it was glaringly obvious that the officer's severe demeanour was beyond cold. He exuded an icy demeanour that would not have been out of place in the Antarctic. Major Wolf could have frozen the Serengeti.

"Gentlemen, I spoke to each platoon separately, but I shared the same sentiments to each. My instructions were clear. This is not imprisonment per se, simply a temporary measure before the next order of the Greater Reich and the British Empire in Europe and the world is made clear. In the meantime, there are to be no escapes. *None*. Was this not clearly expressed? Yet these men... unlawfully, without permission, and against my *explicit* orders and those of the SS and the Führer himself... they left St George no.5, in a regrettable attempt to flee SS hospitality. This is a severe breach of the *clearly – defined – rules...*"

The silence that greeted this was ugly; tension palpable. Those few who doubted the sincerity of SS denials of 'no prisoners taken' orders were dismayed. For the captured escapees' part, most were resigned to their fate. Resistance had, in any case, been beaten out of them.

Wolf continued, with the same awful calm. "I was explicit in my wishes. In lieu of a suitable British commanding officer for the companies as a whole, Sergeant

Stanley Hitchman; as NCO and the platoon leader of some of these men, what do you suggest I do?"

Stanley was taken aback. "Well, I say… ah, the best course of action in this particular case…"

"Answer the question, Sergeant." Wolf was blunt.

"There will be no further escape attempts, Major. You have my word of honour on that," came Stanley's firm reply. He'd recognised the hopelessness of appealing, but the SS man clearly despised indecision; one of the new breed of clear-thinking militarised Germans whose paths were laid out so clear. Mercy was weakness. Pity was treachery. *Your honour is loyalty.*

"I understand. So in this predicament, you are requesting leniency on my part towards these captured transgressors, Sergeant Hitchman?"

"I am, Major."

"Then I must shoot *you*, as leader, if you are responsible for their lives and actions?"

Hitchman's eyes grew wide, as the cold, steely statement from Major Wolf sank in. To his credit, Stanley mastered his reaction, though a slight panicked dissent was voiced in the ranks. The German voice that screamed at them to be quiet came from Hoffman.

Wolf's eyes never left Stanley's face. Not yet thirty, the major possessed an almost demonic confidence and will that shook Stanley to his core, just as wholly and terribly as did the death sentence those pitiless blue eyes had pronounced, boring into him.

"If you are fully responsible for these men and their criminal actions, you are to be shot, yes?"

The level, even tone only added callousness to the dire threat.

"Major…" Stanley began weakly, faltering; stuttering the lost, half-formed words as noise. He knew it was hopeless. Wolf, for his part, was horribly calm and clear.

"As platoon leader, you are *responsible* for your men. Either I take it upon myself to shoot them all for *desertion*, dereliction of *duty* and breaching the rules of both the British Expeditionary Force and the Waffen-SS… or…" and Wolf smiled an awful, cold smile, "I will shoot *you* to penalise this transgression."

Wolf was entirely still. Tommy, from the second row, was afforded a ten o'clock view of the man's face, and despite himself, he was awed by the spectacle. Wolf betrayed not a single twitch or muscle spasm, despite the electricity crackling in the air from the terrible drama of the moment.

Stanley, too, was awed. His tormentor's merciless blue eyes and his utterly controlled poise had an almost elemental power.

It was another sunny day, and the Sarge felt the sun's heat on his face. It calmed him. Unlike so many Englishmen, he would not die in the rain. And unlike so many millions in the last war, he would not die in the mud.

In for a penny, in for a pound I say, Stanley thought. He straightened up, sticking his chin and chest back out, like the proud British officer he'd been entitled to be.

"So be it, *Sturmbannführer Volf.*"

Tommy's mouth hung open. With the sergeant's defiance came mockery. The tone was obvious, the pronunciation blatant. Silence hung in the air like filthy smog, lingering in the evil atmosphere of that fine, clear day.

"Spare the men," Stanley called, proudly. "I shall take full responsibility for their brave but misguided actions. If the German Reich wishes to punish a British soldier for that, let it be me."

Wolf held his gaze, searching for any semblance of fear or disingenuity and then, as though satisfied, the SS officer smiled, beckoning the British soldier over to the front, to stand before the row of the thirteen would-be escapees. The Sergeant obliged and marched as proudly as he had spoken, betraying not a quiver of fear. He nodded to the captives before turning to face the rest of the company; his boys, and a combined seven hundred other British soldiers of the empire.

"Be calm, men," he called out, his voice steady. "Rather one life than twelve, of course. I will go out with a smile on my face, doing my *duty*. For King and Country. Godspeed, lads."

Hitchman clicked his heels, and the men saluted him, some with tears streaming down their cheeks. James Wilkinson's face was bunched up. Tommy and Brian wept quietly. They all put three fingers to their temples, to a man.

Stanley saluted them back.

Major Wolf, still smiling, raised his Mauser to the spot between the Sergeant's eyes. Stanley tried to smile, his trembling lips pinching together, and he looked up to the glowing sun as the major pulled the trigger.

Click.

A spontaneous yell erupted from the men, and then silence. The only sound came from Stanley, whose brave façade had been destroyed by the trigger click, his power instantly gone, as though an electric light switch had been flicked. The greying Norfolk soldier's face had bunched together and his whole body seized up entirely as the Mauser mechanism noise echoed through the silence. The gun was empty.

Major Wolf nodded approvingly to the British sergeant, whose face was turning red from not breathing. Finally he gasped, and sucked in some fresh, clean air, sinking to his knees, wheezing, at last betrayed by his body, having maintained control of it to the point of an expected death that never came. The men looked at him in horror, totally shocked by the scene, before relief flooded through them like a warm electric current. He was alive. James, though, felt a rush of hatred towards the smug, intolerable officer that held command of the camp. Looking at Major Wolf, James imagined sending a bullet of his own through the icy, chiselled features; smashing through the angular, strong jaw, tearing through flesh and coming to rest in the pulsing grey matter of a brain that lacked something human.

Wolf was gazing at Hitchman with a mixture of admiration and amusement. Some sense alerted him to the hatred he elicited, and he turned to meet James' gaze instantly, without so much as seeking him out. The Yorkshireman detected a slight wink, before Wolf turned sharply and surveyed the stricken Hitchman again. Never before had he hated a man with such intensity as he did Wolf; as Stanley gasped on the dusty ground, James envisioned cold-blooded murder with relish. Stanley had lived through two years in the trenches as an enlisted man. Shell shock had ended as many lives as sniper's bullets for Stanley's generation.

And here he was, all these years later, hyperventilating after the cruellest shock imaginable.

Major Wolf turned to the ranks, spinning the pistol around his right index finger like the parody of a western cowboy. The movie star face and those piercing eyes betrayed nothing. He holstered the impotent weapon, thoroughly unruffled, his composure astonishing. Through drying tears that had given way to enormous relief, Tommy could not help but retain a grudging admiration for the SS Sturmbannführer. His was an unchallengeable power, and a rare forcefulness. Major Jochen Wolf's gravitas was undeniable.

"You are lucky to have such a brave platoon leader," Wolf began pleasantly. "He's worth much, much more than Sergeant-Major, or some other NCO rank. More like Stanley Hitchman, and you gentlemen would have undoubtedly lasted more than four weeks against us, even with our Ardennes surprise." His eyes twinkled. Most seemed too relieved to fully take on board his speech.

He resumed it less congenially; a trace of steel unmistakeable in his tone. "The next time there is a breach of the rules, I *will* personally shoot everyone involved, him, and anyone else in the platoon in question. There will be no speeches, no gestures, no warnings and no empty guns; no chance for the bravest and best of you to show your honour like the sergeant just did, in such *admirable* style, like a true British gentleman. I hope that is fully understood; *crystal clear*, as you English say. Do like the other companies in similar camps, and follow the rules here. I am mortified that in camp no.5 alone there has been a breach of this severity. There will *not* be again. In time, all will become clear and bullets will not be wasted on brothers of Aryan blood – as the Reichsführer-SS Himmler and SS-Obergruppenführer Heydrich are so fond of telling us, our bullets are better served elsewhere. Please don't make me regretfully waste them on you, and the brave Sergeant Hitchman."

Turning one final time to the kneeling, dazed Hitchman, Wolf offered his hand. Stanley had stopped gasping, and magnanimously took the proffered arm of the man he'd fully expected to end his life not fifty seconds before, recovering his poise and rising to his feet. The older German clapped him warmly on either shoulder, grasping him in brotherhood, as though holding him upright.

"You are worth more than an NCO, *Sarge*. Much more. If you were an SS man I'd promote you to junior officer rank on the spot. Sturm...bannführer... *Volf* will hereby refer to you as Untersturmführer Hitchman. When Britain is truly threatened by external enemies, *real* enemies, alien civilisations that long for her demise, and *you* are compelled to defend her, I assure you it will be as a Lieutenant at the least."

At this, Wolf reached over with his right arm, thrice patting the discombobulated soldier on his shoulder before turning to walk away; his trademark brisk march taking him out of the barracks area, followed by the aide that was still holding the major's great leather coat, hurrying in his wake.

"Naomi? Are you *decent*?"

The young Jewess chuckled at the falsity of his affected tone, and responded in kind.

"One is quite very well decent, *wouldn't you know* dear."

"Jolly good, jolly good," he cried, clunking down the wooden steps to his room.

Paul marched straight over to the sofas, and deposited himself into the most comfortable place with gusto. He went to pick up his weathered paperback copy of Dumas' *The Count of Monte Cristo,* and then thought better of it; caught between decisions he dithered, hands fidgeting as he settled restlessly in the seat. Finally looking over at Naomi, he saw she wore a weary, if amused look on tired, puffy features that betrayed that she was freshly awoken from sleep.

"Hello, Paul."

"Aye, afternoon. Some sleeping pattern you're keepin'."

"Don't nag," she implored.

"All *right*. Anyway…" Paul picked up Dumas absentmindedly, lightly tapping the book against his knees. "I've 'ad an idea. Instead of being a half-hearted bloody night-scribe, with half a mind on eighteen unfinished novels stuck in desk drawers… I'm writing something now. A *serious* one."

She held his gaze, encouraging him to elaborate.

"I'm g'na write about how we beat the Nazis."

"How's that work, then?" She asked, confused. Lighting up a cigarette, he tossed her the packet, and grinned.

"I make it bloody *up*. Anyway, I'll tell you more in the pub. Hold that fag for now; get up, do what you need to do and then come for a pint before they close for dinner."

Pubs in England shut for several hours mid-afternoon, for a lunch break of sorts, before reopening three hours later in time for those who were finishing work shifts. It was an unquestioned system.

"Give me five," she told him, leaping out of bed.

He waited upstairs for her to get ready. She quickly washed with a wet flannel, hurriedly dried with a towel, tied a headscarf around her thick, flowing dark locks of hair and threw on her favourite long, red dress. Sliding into her green coat, fastened with buttons and a belt, she was upstairs in four minutes flat; a figure of gravitas, utterly transformed. Paul looked up from his book and whistled, softly.

"Bloody hell, Naomi."

"Fast, eh?" She winked at him.

"I don't mean that..." he nodded at her dress, and looked her up and down.

"What?"

Paul chuckled. "Nothing, lass. You just... well, you scrub up well for a pint at dinnertime."

She grinned at him. "That's the loveliest thing you've ever said to me. What a *gentleman*."

Smirking, he opened the door with a mock-gesture for her to go through it.

"Opens doors, helps old ladies across the street – the works, dear girl," he told her solemnly, feigning a pompous air. She curtseyed.

"*Mon cher, thou art indeed* a *gentle*man and a scholar."

That made him snort, almost without mirth. "Don't speak that frog language. That's the same mouth you kiss your mother with."

Easily matching his snort in volume, she scoffed at him as they exited the house, strolling out into a day pricked by stabs of that quintessential northern English sunlight that, while occasionally bright, lacks warmth and can be entirely redundant with regards to clothing requirements. It illuminated the parklands, an open area ringed with trees that served as a dividing line between the city centre and the northern districts of Leeds; aesthetic in the aftermath of autumn's effect on the trees. It was the final period in which most British people actually enjoyed their homeland for some months to come, barring Christmas. As he glanced around, taking in the visual scope of their environment, Paul mused that many months down the line, the onset of spring was unlikely to stir the soul, optimism facing extinction as it was.

An absence of hope was a minor death in life. Paul had the vague sense that he was superficially keeping it together, balancing his emotions with his responsibilities with difficulty while merely smiling through the disturbing days. Individual occurrences, too many to name, had privately disquieted the humorous Paul and he suspected that beyond the superficial, he was barely hanging on to his control and poise, an underlying rising sensation of suppressed tension building to fever pitch.

Sarcasm, the Yorkshireman's great ally and weapon, helped him and countless others to mask the gamut of concurrent feelings that as-yet, he could not properly label or name.

He did not share with Naomi the savage beating he'd witnessed that day. Three soldiers, filing out of a restaurant in a manner that suggested to Paul that obnoxiousness combined with a refusal to pay was most likely their modus operandi – the arrogance of a conqueror – had momentarily paused for thought as they passed an older black man.

No Jew, perhaps, but somehow Paul doubted the streets of Berlin and Hamburg were awash with too many dark-skinned faces. Or arms, legs, torsos, heads, feet and hands either, for that matter. This man looked like one of the hell-enduring slaves of the 19th century, and it was not hard to imagine his great or great-great-grandfather's arrival in the west being the conclusion of a forced and torturous journey.

"You insult Deutschland?" Paul remembered a red-faced army soldier screaming at the man, using his country's endonymic name in the tentative dual-communication style that was already nicknamed 'Krautglish'.

Utterly exposed, and unable to avoid their attention, it was clear the black man had known that once the initial surprise wore off, the Germans would react to his appearance with hostility; the pack mentality of wild animals. Quicker to regain his wits, the local man pre-empted their introduction, but it was not placatory. "Shalom," Paul heard him say, barely able to register it himself. That's when the gigantic Jerry began to bawl.

Was it black humour? Paul wondered, before further registering the double entendre. Why would the man aggravate them; a nationalistic people ruled and governed by institutional racism. Did he hope to shock them into non-action? Or does he simply not care about the consequences of provocation anymore?

Either way, the man's choice of words had a very distinct effect. The soldiers were snapped back to life, reanimated by the Jewish greeting. And they crowded him, visibly bristling. Shock and composed disdain transfigured instantly into naked aggression and loathing.

"Answer me! Did you just insult the Fatherland!"

"You insult us? You insult the Führer?" this voice came from a smaller, calmer soldier, with the dangerous air of a clinical sadist. Such men deliver persecution and punishment with a lethal precision, protracted; club-wielding thugs had given way to the new breed of Nazi. Those who as adolescents or adults had no experience of a world not run by Hitler. Those unaware of the crimes committed for his system. And those who thrilled in creating it.

Paul knew the man was in trouble. Invoking the name of Hitler justified any and all actions in the eyes of his believers – just like God. A religious devotion to either celestial dictators or living, breathing men was a warrant for wickedness; claiming attack on the unchallengeable was the common denominator for all.

"I greeted you," the man said calmly, a hint of West African patois in his leodensian voice. "That's no insult."

Yelling in German, the large, blond man brought the back of his hand up from his bulging waist with considerable force, smacking across the face of the black unfortunate and sending him reeling back into the smaller, wiry soldier. That man wasted no time in redirecting their victim's momentum, using the loss of equilibrium to hip-toss the unresisting figure, using the man's own shirt lapels to twist and slam the back of his head into the concrete cobbles.

A sickening beating had taken place; Paul had to turn and leave, nauseated, by the sight of the martial artist-cum-sadist methodically breaking the now-stricken African fellow's fingers, snapping them like brittle biscuits covered in chocolate, and attacking with the insatiable hunger of a fat child; malevolent in their violence. The third German, a large pudding of a man but less in size and stature than the huge pig that was his *kameraden*, had his gun trained on Paul and the other bystanders who, by chance, happened to be in that particular part of Headingley at the time. The message was clear; interfere, and you die.

Only after leaving did Paul realise that such moments demonstrated exactly *why* fascism had triumphed. 'Enemies of The State' are obscenely punished, yet everyone else walks free; the classic case of divide and rule. *Self-preservation.* Even as one *individual* instance of capricious, callous behaviour and abuse-of-power from a gang of possibly uneducated, socially inept soldiers, Paul knew the awful battering that was meted out to the ethnically-exposed unfortunate represented the new world *whole*. The idea snowballed, until Paul began to contemplate if he now bore some of the collective guilt, and it was with some difficulty that he finally repressed it.

If we all resisted, totalitarianism would never succeed.

In the present, that cruel beating seemed like a distant dream as he strolled in the open air with Naomi. They used the park-side road that ran alongside Woodhouse Moor to reach the pub. As they stepped in, Naomi attracted the same stares as ever from the pub's patrons. Paul wondered if she genuinely did not notice, or if she simply didn't care.

They took a seat in the far corner, and clinked glasses.

"Cheers!"

"Cheers, Paul."

Both enjoyed the taste of the Tetley's ale, smacking their lips, exaggerating a little in the style that both their grandparents' did. It amused them that both of their families seemed to share the same silly quirks.

"Right, Paul. You didn't come yesterday. I'm kicking my heels. I want to know what's going on. School, everything. What's up with thee?" she began, sweetening it by mocking the ultra-Yorkshireism he sometimes used.

He looked away, sipping his Tetley's, but as his gaze drifted back her eyes were still firmly boring into him. Paul sighed.

"Well..."

Almost one week prior, it had been announced – on notices, billboards, and on radio by both Goebbels and William Joyce, in their usual sensitive manner – that all Jews must register with the authorities, and bring their passports to get stamped. That was a quarter of a million people in Britain. Naomi had felt weak with the news. All non-registered Jews would be subject to severe penalties, they were warned. An unregistered Jew is an enemy alien, parasite, *partisan of assimilation.*

Trips out had therefore been limited to the local pub. Naomi found herself longing for these moments of normality, and her heart burst with love for Paul every time they stepped out together into the fresh, clean air.

"Please."

"You sure you want to hear it?" he asked her, scratching his chin.

"A *minute*, Paul. Christ. Then neither of us have to mention the Boche and the Quislings again today."

"Christ? There you are now, see..." Paul sat forwards, wagging his finger at her. "That's it. If you lot hadn't bloody killed 'im, we wouldn't be in this predicament would we?"

He cast her a look of deep disapproval, and sipped his pint again, snorting some of it back out as they both erupted in laughter.

"That, and stabbing Germany in the back during the Great War," she reminded him primly, turning her nose up in the air as though superior. "We planned it all."

"Oh, aye. Forgot about that. You pissed off the Spanish, too. And it's not like the Catholics to pursue violent crusades against other peoples. Your lot *must* be wicked."

"You're awful, you are," she laughed.

"I know."

"We also control your banks, press and Parliament too, why do you think Hitler had invaded all these countries? Liberation, Paul."

"I knew I liked 'im, deep down." He took a deep swig of his pint. "To 'itler!"

"At least I can rely on you for some gallows humour when they finally make it illegal for me to be alive."

At that, he sobered. "Well, that's it. Since this registration business... now they're *enforcing* the teaching of the Protocols in schools."

She gave in to her genuine horror, momentarily, and then shrugged, unnecessarily rearranging her hair, which was more-than effectively wrapped, while trying to disguise how deeply shook she was.

"Well, that's a turn up. Bloody vicious bastards."

Despite himself, Paul suppressed a little smile. He liked it when she swore. Naomi Rosenberg was the only girl – woman – he knew that used profanity, as well as frequenting pubs to drink pints. But it never sounded ugly from her; she was too sweet-natured, with too nice a temperament. And God knows, he thought, *she has every reason to swear with these buggers here.*

"Don't worry. No one is too inspired. And cops – *our* cops – will hardly be breaking down doors to check passports will they? People aren't buying it. That screaming Austrian charisma just doesn't translate into English. As for the Protocols, it will bore the kids to death."

She was only slightly mollified. He pressed on, trying to cheer her up.

"It won't catch on, lass. 'Germany Awake' and 'Hail Victory' aren't exactly '*Liberté, Egalité, Fraternité*' are they? You reckon we'll go Nazi mad? Have you *seen* the goons coming out of the woodwork in BUF clobber?"

Naomi opted to not answer, taking a lengthy swig of her Tetley's while brooding over the hated Protocols, the hated registration, the hated Nazis. Paul tried to catch her eye with a smile.

"I read it funny. In class, like... Make a real show of it, complete with theatrics. Act it like Fagin the Jew, with his gang of boy thieves..." Seeing how little impact the jokes had, Paul's smile faded, and he sobered his tone. "Come on, lass; everyone knows it's a load of old bollocks. The kids laugh."

"And the younger kids, Paul? The next generation of kids? The ones that follow?"

He hesitated. "It won't last that long."

She forced a laugh. "Oh, that's right, Mr Writer. Your novel explains exactly how we defeat the forces of evil. Like a Winston bloody Churchill speech."

"Shh..."

Paul glanced around, nervously. There were only a few local drunks in the pub, sat smoking pipes in their Sunday best. Paul always wondered about them. They had the air of defeat, of suppression and melancholy, which he understood as most had fought in the Great War. But these forlorn figures wore their Sunday best to the pub. Their demeanour of being broken men was masked; misery clad with the outward appearance of respectability. It confused him.

Some hated him. One old man had approached him once at his table in the far corner, at the height of the Blitz, tottering over unsteadily as Paul sat reading quietly, drinking his fourth Tetley's. "More like you, and we wouldn't have held out even this long..." the man had said. "Bleedin' *coward*."

"I'm a fireman," Paul told him shortly. And when the man shouted at him again, he added a little less reservedly, "I'm a fireman, and a *conscientious objector* to war. I'll *help* victims, not create them. I'll do my bit for my country, but not by agreeing to what every other stupid bugger did, including those at the top who think war's such a great pastime. *All right*? And I've not slept either, and I'm tired, and reading, so kindly piss off."

"You're a ruddy coward, you bastard *shirker*," the old man told Paul, utterly impervious to his irate counter.

To his astonishment, the old man had spat on him, and then left. He'd never returned to the pub thereafter. Paul hoped he hadn't killed himself in grief. He sometimes wondered.

Now, Paul leaned in to Naomi.

"Yeah. Well, about that... I figure it might help, it might not."

"So what's the deal?"

"Well, I write about England victorious."

She shook her head. "Impossible."

"Aha!" he cried. "That's only *retrospect* convincing you of that. Really, things could, and probably *should* have gone differently."

Now he had her attention. He leaned in, suddenly animated.

"The navy *repulse* an invasion. Obviously a few thousand Boche initially land, the Luftwaffe cause some mayhem, *yada* yada, but then the Navy, *our* lads, arrive in force. Churchill..." he leaned in closer, and his voice went even lower. Naomi could smell the cheap aftershave perfume he used on his neck. "... Churchill *never got deposed*. No armistice. No defeatism. *Tell Jerry to go stick it up his arse.* Fight to the last man. They know the SS won't actually *harm* a single POW, or the yanks and maybe Stalin, the empire en masse; *every* other bugger will come in on our side... they call the bluff, hold their nerve. Whitehall stabilises. They rally together..."

He was speaking faster than she'd ever heard him, bubbling with enthusiasm.

"The Navy blocks further kraut supplies, support and troops sent from the coasts of France, Belgium and Holland. The air force didn't overextend and get battered in May and early June, and the Germans delayed their planned invasion to mid-September at the earliest. By that time the RAF had recovered its losses. Then Jerry focuses only on bombing the cities, only uses the Messerschmitts for *guarding bombers*, instead of knocking out Spitfires faster than we can build new 'uns. They *can't support the divisions that landed*. The rest of the Wehrmacht are stuck in France. The Boche navy can't clear ours. The RAF holds out. The Jerries who landed run out of supplies. *The invasion collapses*."

Speaking quickly at barely more than a whisper, Naomi allowed herself to be taken in by the passion of Paul and she pondered, musing on the possibility. It seemed an insane concept, yet something about it rang true. *Imagine*, she thought. The Germans beaten back from British shores. *Imagine*.

"If only," she said wistfully. "I might still be a teacher. Thousands of others might still have their jobs. Thousands would still be alive," she quickly added, catching herself lest Paul notice the unintended callousness.

Paul scratched his chin, eyebrows raised. "Not be rain on the parade, but..." beats of hesitation. "loss of employment may not be the worst of this grim tale."

She smiled coldly, which was unnatural for her, and he shivered to see it.

"When a madman appears sane, it is high time to put him in a strait-jacket," she observed, once more reverting to Poe, one of the few favoured poets of Paul.

"Even for those to whom life and death are equal jests, there are some things that are still held in respect," he replied with his own, noting that it was inadequate in the face of such nihilism.

"German blood, blond hair and wars of aggression seem to cover it," she deadpanned back, ticking the three on her fingers.

"Including *Saxon* blood, which miraculously and stupidly includes Britain. In reality we're all as mongrel as each other, but who's to tell Hitler that? Hopefully once the dust settles the issue fades instead of being focused on."

She smiled with warmth, now. "I'm confused. So you think I should stay the course, or go back to my place or leave the country or..." she shrugged, feigning indecision.

His eyes held hers for millisecond too long; just enough time lapsed for him to see the question form in her mind, through her inquisitive eyes, dark brown and Semitic against his Celtic green.

"Stay the course. We'll ride through this storm," he said smoothly.

"You seem very sure about that, mister..." Naomi asked, half-hoping for reassurance. It came in the form of a churlish grin, as Paul raised his glass to her.

"*In vino veritas*, missus," he chuckled, and despite herself, Naomi let an understated giggle escape her lips as their pints met in silent toast. *In wine there is truth.*

The bell tinkled, signalling last orders. There was a time when boos and jeers would greet this noise; that day in the Hyde Park Pub there was barely a stir. Naomi and Paul finished up, ordered a second pint which they drank at a leisurely pace, as Paul briefly, sadly described the unsightly scene he'd witnessed earlier in the day, before leaving for a nearby café that had peeling paper on the walls, furniture that seemed chintzy even for a greasy spoon, and a dumpy little woman with the disposition of a bulldog with venereal disease.

They ordered two coffees, both winning their silent game of suppressing the urge to stare at the woman's unsightly boils, and asked for two bacon butties. Paul regretted sharing the story of random German violence, and hoped it would not unsettle his friend. But her mind was elsewhere. Sitting down at the thick table of what felt like plastic, Naomi resumed questioning him about the book.

"How are you going to get it printed? Assuming that's what you're after...?"

"Don't worry about that," he replied breezily, trying to dissuade her from the conversation.

"So how does this book end, if the invasion fails at the start?"

Paul's eyes lit up as he warmed to the subject, that of his creative juices flowing; basking in the product of his imagination. His animated demeanour was unforced and balanced, which she found endearing, and a yet-more intrusive feeling.

"They come back the next year – mid-to-late 1941 – having rebuilt the Luftwaffe and created a load more U-boats for the wolfpacks. Spain, France, Italy all join the hunt, so our Navy gets tied down fighting off four major powers simultaneously. *Stretched*, fighting for our lives. The air force can't hold out. They land en masse; stabilise their position, and reinforcements flood in. Their stronghold widens; the advance begins. London capitulates, declared an open city..."

"That's more bloody like it," she said darkly. He grimaced in reluctant agreement.

"They execute Churchill. Neither he nor the Royals get out."

"My heart bleeds for Churchill and the royals," she said again, bitterly. "Wish I was in bloody Canada."

He blanched, and she felt ashamed of herself.

"I'm *sorry*, sorry," she cooed hurriedly, a half-smile fixed on her pursed mouth. "You know I didn't mean that. It's the beer talking. Canada's even colder than here. And there's French people there. *Frenchies.*"

He smiled widely at her. That was more like it.

"Don't worry. Ride it out, this registration bollocks will die a death. *Anyway...* well, yeah... *viva le revolution.* We rebel. The Scots come down to the northern cities, kind of like what happened but more of them, and the whole populace fights back. Eventually the Germans pull out, because it's too costly and they cannot occupy England, let alone Britain. *We win.*"

She considered the possibilities.

"Paul..." she said slowly. "That's not entertainment. That's a bloody incitement to riot."

He didn't respond, fixing her with a sudden look of intent. She recognised it for what it was.

"Oh, bloody hell, Paul."

"Let's just see how things turn out."

"Paul, even owning the paper you *write* that thing on will be a death sentence."

He shook a young head of slicked

"Don't worry."

She folded her arms, crossly.

"I know you will anyway, because you're bloody-minded and stubborn. And for what you've done for me, and my family, I can't disagree with you. But I think you're daft."

He leaned in, something sombre, sorrowful, in the smooth contours of his boyish face.

"Naomi… I'm not a fighter. I never was. Never will be."

Her eyes searched his. There was fire in them as she'd never seen, and the hair on the back of her neck prickled.

"But we can't just let the ideals of this country *die*. Even if those at the top are comfortable with that happening, and the classes who flourish regardless of system. I mean the intangibles. The sense of fair play and good conduct. Democracy, even. Civil rights. Everything that wasn't represented in that scene I witnessed, and the countless others that have happened and *are* happening and *will* happen… And this is how I can help. If I muster people up to fight, at least it would be for the right cause."

"Plenty of people die for the right cause," she observed sadly.

He nodded in silent acknowledgment, but in this thoughtful expression, Naomi saw no crisis of confidence, and knew that he'd go ahead with his plan.

~

The pale light faded as the afternoon wore on; obscured by clouds, the sun pierced through with less frequency as a chilly breeze bit the young teachers with sudden force. They returned to Paul's flat after a lengthy stroll around the park, by which time the sun had fully set, and darkness descended on England's north.

Neither had acknowledged it, but the sight of Blackshirts marching in Woodhouse Moor – known to most as Hyde Park – had deeply disturbed them. It seemed so raw, so visceral; to celebrate a foreign triumph over countrymen. And why the park? The very centre of the city centre was barely a mile down the road.

"Perhaps they've marched here from the city centre barracks. An evening break from licking German boots," Paul joked. The responding chuckle had been hollow.

Sunlight had pierced the red-brick estate street at intervals, thinly pricked beams of light forcing through the gaps in the park trees. Were it not for the serious, marching men in the park, the leafy parkside lane, nestled away to the far-corner of the wide open space, would look for all the world like a late-summer day in the north of England. Unoccupied, with no antagonistic political force present, nor unwelcome foreign visitors.

And no grieving families. Brothers, sons, nephews and cousins lost. And for what?

"A lad I used to be friends with at school signed up," Paul found himself blurting.

She looked at him in surprise. Despite some slight crossovers, Naomi and her younger friend had different social circles, but while she had to admit that Paul's friends were an eclectic mixed bag – an assorted bunch of aspiring artists, writers and fellow teachers with creative ambition – with odd quirks and traits, none of them were particularly disagreeable, let alone malevolent. It was hard to imagine Paul associating with a man who would sign with the British Fascists. Even Oswald Moseley, it was now thought, had supposedly renounced support for a foreign occupier and had been resultingly praised, appeased, publicly elevated and then marginalised.

He caught her look and nodded, glumly. "Tony. Lost touch after school. Used to want to be a fireman. Christ, I wonder what happened to him? The kid's from t' Rookwoods, was just an estate kid without a farthing to scratch his arse with. Knew nothing, but he were pretty 'appy. Nice lad in fact. Used to play football together on Sundays; he had no prejudice, no politics, only one or two phrases he'd picked up from his daft old man. Now..." he said bitterly, gesturing to the field, "he's *that*."

Paul's head slowly shook from side-to-side, surreptitiously watching the fascist demonstration in the park – almost detached from his own movements, bemused. How had Tony ended up a fascist? How had these people? How had so many in Europe done likewise?

The Fascist Blackshirts, or BUF party members, had all taken to walking with newfound arrogance in general, which was received with widespread disgust. Paul had commented on his previous visit two days prior that he'd seen a march in the city centre, some kind of asinine SA mimicry. They were yet to wield clubs, thankfully, and their overall insolence was tempered by a more British approach.

Of course, Paul realised even as he observed their restraint, Britain had not had to deal with the frantic revolutions and bloody mutinies on the home front after defeat in the Great War, nor economic collapse. Germany had, until recently at least, lived through an altogether more dramatic 20th century within its own borders than had Britain. Yet still, as war-games, it was sinister to see the emergence of that blackshirted street dominance. There was something animal about its visage; the alpha behaviour as exhibited in the world of primates, along with the threat of violence as the ultimate victory; reason and restraint dismissed as an all-too *human* quality, representing decadence to the hard young men of the new, strong, fascist continent. A scientific regression, almost religious; the belligerent disdain of softening principles and glory inherent in abandoning one's own mind to a cult. Fledgling as it may be, neither of the studious young Brits had any doubts that it would not take long for the proud, raw recruits to the cause to evolve from man to machine; violence comes naturally in the right circumstances. Göring, for one, had voiced public approval and praise for the BUF, though Hitler was yet to comment.

And as it was wryly pointed out through Chinese whispers of the knowing, it had been Göring who seized control of the police force in 1933, set up concentration camps and turned the SA loose. Don't trust the fat man, they said. Fat and jolly men too can do terrible, wicked things. So can bank clerks, and bus conductors. Create the machinery of tribalism and fuel it with fear; enough people will soon embrace it through self-interest. Incalculable suffering and calculated pragmatism often go hand-in-hand.

~

In the end, Paul was too tired to bother leaving, and he once more took a blanket upstairs to the sofa. He bade a swift exit, refusing to hear of her protestations, and in the ensuing silence of the dark underground room, tiredness descended on Naomi. To her surprise, despite only having been awake several hours, sleep came naturally.

She awoke to his knocking on the wooden beam.

"Come in, Paul, it's your room," she murmured sleepily, wriggling with pleasure as she stretched her limbs, still in a dozing state.

"*Top o' the mornin'.* I've brought you some breakfast."

That woke her up fast. She sat up, dumbly rubbing sleep out of her gummy eyes with her knuckles, to see that he carried a tray on which sat a plate of buttered toast and eggs, a biscuit and a cup of tea.

"You're a star, you know that?" Naomi shook her head in wonder.

"Nonsense, it's a pleasure."

Bloody hell, she's beautiful, he thought. Even with her hair now tousled and hanging in knotty clumps, freshly awoken from slumber in a basement. She was *radiant.*

"You shouldn't waste your rations, Paul. I don't know if I can eat," she confessed, expecting him to break into his usual repertoire of teasing jokes and silly puns. He didn't.

"Try, lass. Try."

And he looked so earnest that she gulped down one of the toast slices.

Paul consciously avoided her with his eyes, after the first bite; feigning interest in one of the discarded books on the couch, he retreated to its distant sanctuary and as casually as he could, tried to read. Her morning presence in his bed, a visage of strange vitality, had shaken him with a visceral quality, and simultaneously filled him with lust and attacked his fragile self-belief. Somewhere in his mind, he was dimly aware that a barrier of sorts in his mind had broken down; a lessened inhibition, or just an epiphany? Or was he simply scared and listless, and twisted by the occupation? He couldn't be sure, but wired as he was, Paul conceded – almost relieved – that he was definitely not powered, at least primarily, by lust.

Whatever the outcome, Paul was certain that his quality of intent was pure.

Naomi sat calmly, comfortable in his presence. The disorientation of awakening passed in her mind, and the awareness of how life can change drastically in an obscenely short space of time suddenly struck the young teacher again. It was a recurring thought, but instead of dismissing it, Naomi found herself ruminating on the positives of an altogether grim and foreboding situation. Hope stole at her fears like an infusion of energy; a sick, empowering confidence that was inexplicable yet transcending.

In high great humour she tried the tea, expecting the usual ersatz that had been the norm for weeks now, and periodically since the war began. Yet she was rewarded with the sweet taste of sugared, *proper* Yorkshire tea. It was overwhelming, but before she could gush her gratitude to her host, Paul's voice piped up from across the underground room.

"How did you sleep?" he asked.

"Like a baby," she admitted. "I've had, what, sixteen hours of shuteye in the last calendar day. Not 'alf out of synch."

He laughed. "Think I'm rubbing off on you, you're sounding more and more Leeds every day. A right little Leodensian."

Not Yorkshire, she thought to herself, smiling inwardly. Paul had harangued her about it before, over a drink. He loved his city. Leeds, I'm a *loiner. Or tyke.* Or *Leodensian.*

It's a Leodensian accent, he always insisted, not bog standard farmer's Yorkshire. A Leodensian family stretching back generations made his appreciation of the place manifest more militantly than her own family. *Do I sound like I'm from bloody Barnsley,* he'd protested. *Or Ilkley? I've never* seen *a bloody farm*!

He watched her as she sipped the tea gratefully, admiring her beauty despite being wrapped up in a night gown and pyjamas, puffy-eyed and in bed, having just awoken in a basement room. Her pale skin was perfect; the dark eyes, lashes and cascades of thickly-flowing hair seemed Mediterranean; of western variety, as opposed to its coasts to the east from whence her roots came. The exotic quality only made her more conspicuous; other women seemed drab and colourless compared to her aura. She looked more like a Spanish princess than a Semite. Paul wondered what kind of idiotic master race would exclude this woman from its exclusive ranks. Was this the face of a Jew? The eyes, ears, nose, the perfect profile of a parasite, a destroyer of nations? She was heavenly. He watched her, *drinking her in,* every fibre of her being.

Naomi swelled with affection for Paul. She felt at a loss, embarrassed by his kindness, and sat clenched with inner combat. Then, as though in weary trepidation, she suddenly decided. Her course of action was clear. She was laying low from potential persecution. Stripped of her normal life, Naomi had no dignity left with which to worry about losing if she asked. What was the worst that could happen? There had been enough time wasted on shyness, yielding to conventions, her passions repressed. How long could her unbearable tension go on for?

"I felt terrible knowing you were on the settee, Paul," she began. "It's hardly big enough for a child."

"I don't mind, silly. To be honest, I was knackered, lass. Really couldn't face driving to yours."

"There's no need," she said, blushing. *Hold it together*, she told herself.

He waved a hand dismissively. "Wouldn't hear of it. And there's a lot of ugly rumours, not to mention 'em cracking down on the teaching syllabus with that old forged rag of Zion. If they care about that, they really *do* care. Hang tight, Naomi. You're a mile better off 'ere."

"No Paul, there's *no need*..." Naomi's voice caught, and she cleared her throat to speak clearly. "Because I want you to stay with me."

Again, she half-expected a joke, and self-consciously ruffled in bed with her puffy eyes and tousled hair, she stared at him unwaveringly, in defiance of any rejection he could make. The young lady had never tried to live by her passion before, and was poised, fragile, hoping against hope. Passion in lust was a socially stigmatised form of verve for the female, emancipated or not; Emmeline Pankhurst was not so far removed from the public eye. But Naomi was outside the realm of what was considered normal. When Paul failed to respond, pokerfaced, a sense of flat dejection came over her until his mouth opened and closed and she registered his profound, palpable shock. Relief flooded through her.

"Oh... uh... well..."

"There are chords in the hearts of the most reckless which cannot be touched without emotion," she offered quietly, and in his confusion, again, the quoted words dusted the surface of his recognition.

His questioning eyes searched hers; two shining pinpricks of brown flame, yet still he could not believe her, and she threw off the bed cover, diving forwards to seize him by the face and kiss the stunned young man hard on his mouth.

PART II

The buzzing roar of the Focke-Wolf whirred down to the airstrip, touching down at the heavily defended makeshift air base established on the Thames southwest of central London's boundaries. With the perimeter lined with Feldgendarmerie 'chain dogs' drafted from the Wehrmacht, and an honour guard of their own SS forces, the leader of the Schutzstaffel and his chief of Security Police and intelligence, the new Reichsprotektor of Great Britain, marched smartly down the base. A ship awaited; Hitler's promised entrance as conquerors and a clear message to the people, and no doubt, Heydrich thought, a knowing smirk at Admiral Raeder's expense, having a former dismissed Navy lieutenant in the Reich Security Chief be allocated the finest ship of the force as his vessel to carry him into the heart of the land he was now 'Protector' of.

~

"When are these buggers going to show up?" Alan muttered restlessly to William, who merely shook his head. The Geordie and Mary were finding it hard to stand still, and were not helping the tensions William and Jack shared equally. The Catalonian in particular was murmuring obscenities under her breath, despite William's constant whispered entreaties for her to shut up. Being overheard speaking 'foreign' was hardly going to be of help, and was a problem quite easily avoided.

"For shite's sake, man," Alan hissed.

"Well all this lot aren't here for jollies, are they?" Jack pointed out, reasonably, keeping his tone calm.

He was referring to the greatcoat-clad military figures in what looked like SS regalia who were lining the Embankment. Either side of the river, they could see the same *feldgrau* figures, and Wehrmacht armoured cars were patrolling the

Strand, through Covent Garden and all the way down Whitehall, which was more heavily guarded than had been seen since the invasion. There were even four Panzers in the middle of the Waterloo Bridge.

It was the first time in months that the exhaust fumes of motorised traffic could be detected. After the quiet lull, the hullabaloo was a strange change of tempo, and not an entirely welcome one. Familiar though it was, the return to noise and pollution for central London did little to change the swastika flags that flew at random intervals from flagpoles, nor the sight of Wehrmacht troops manning oddly scattered checkpoints, nor the knowledge that odious men of the SS, and the unspoken word – Gestapo – were operating in plain clothes through the city.

Jack, Alan, William and Mary absorbed the scene, carefully surveying the area and its concentration of German personnel.

They were part of the gathering crowds near the Savoy. The hotel that had been commandeered by the SS.

"Right," Jack breathed, wary of being overheard as the Strand became too densely packed to be safely out of earshot of others. "When they dock, we split up and get absolute confirmation they are staying here, take note of their security and how easy it will be to get a clear shot at them."

William rolled his eyes. "Take a look around."

"Do you think the inside of the hotel will be any different," Mary erupted loudly, and they all hissed at her in unison, with varying degrees of profanity.

"We should have done it here on arrival... at least had a pop," William murmured into Jack's ear.

But he shook his head firmly.

"For all we know it would be impossible. And look *how many* of the buggers there are. At least we know Heydrich is blasé about security."

"Ironic, eh?" William grinned back with enforced coolness.

After that, they waited in silence for the coming of two men whose careers had already marked them as two of the century's notable villains.

~

Kriegsmarine *Kondor* sailed around the corner as the Thames curved up to Whitehall, gliding evilly through the dark water like a black, amphibious pterodactyl.

An ostentatious honour guard of planes flew overheard. One of the black-clad men standing on the prow grinned. Heydrich knew that Göring was certainly not responsible for the gesture, Air Force chief or not. His file at Prinz Albrecht-Strasse was filled with juicy titbits of the Reichsmarschall's choice words for Himmler; 'mentally deranged schoolmaster' and 'stupid, talentless chicken farmer' were his personal favourites, along with the more widely known 'Himmler's Brain is Called Heydrich'.

That man had never looked so in his element.

Heinrich Himmler had always avoided the flamboyance of Göring, preferring to live frugally, scorning the vulgar demonstrations of National Socialist favour from the fat man and various Party big shots. But now, the Führer's own self-professed Ignatius Loyola stood resplendent in his all-black classic SS attire; black trench coat, black pirate's cap, black jackboots. Heydrich, himself clad in the same uniform but with the old formal black great coat, was impressed, despite himself. The weak-chinned, schoolmasterly Reichsführer-SS had never looked so imposing. *Fitting*, he thought. *Good boy, Heini.*

Heydrich had of course upstaged him; service medals prominent.

The ship sliced through the water, and onwards to the Embankment.

"Makes one feel like Napoleon, Heydrich does it not?" Himmler smiled.

Heydrich glanced at him. The SS chief's face was fixed staring ahead; only his eyes moved as he glanced at either bank. His motionless poise was curious. Like a still cat, observing with wary, shifty eyes.

"Indeed, Herr Reichsführer," he intoned smoothly. "We enter London as conquerors. That goes beyond Napoleon. We were undaunted by the bitter weeds of England he mentioned…"

"Indeed, Herr Obergruppenführer," Himmler replied haughtily.

Heydrich held back his pleasure. His SS chief was hiding his discomfort at the new promotion, and vast power bestowed to him by the old man; Himmler was steadfastly refusing to use the Reichsprotektor title, continuing to state SS rank which was, of course, subordinate to his own. At least, Heydrich mused, Himmler had seen fit to promote him to *SS-Obergruppenführer* and *General der Polizei…* though to all intents and purposes, he had, *de facto*, effectively been that anyway. Accumulating titles meant little to him, now; only tangible power mattered.

"There are *many bitter weeds in England,*" Heydrich pronounced, imitating Winston Churchill. "And the Reich trimmed them. And now, millions of Jews and freemasons are trembling – I can hear them."

The wind that had threatened to remove the SS leaders' caps suddenly died down, and patches of cloud which sullied the sky dispersed somewhat. The sun, while weak, bore down on them, which Heydrich knew the superstitious Himmler would appreciate.

The Reichsführer finally broke his still pose, and patted Heydrich, somewhat approvingly, like a pervert attempting to be avuncular.

"Excellent."

Heydrich smiled at him. Himmler gazed at the west bank, which the ship drew towards; the crowds visibly deepened and they drew level with Whitehall Palace; the Parliament building and Big Ben.

Heydrich felt a spine-tingling thrill. Even his legendary poise was almost broken, and he worked hard to maintain 'the cold face'.

Himmler was shaking. "We stand poised for historic tasks of the German order. It will be our life work. The form is harsh, but in our harshness we are kind to our blood. The necessity of cleansing England is a shame, these men too are of our blood, but just as in the Reich we must purify. That is SS duty; I am no more a murderer than was Arjuna, a loyal servant of the Aryan people and Krishna."

Heydrich winced in irritation. Himmler *would* have to spoil the moment with his idiotic bluster.

"Quaintly expressed, Herr Reichsführer," he responded sarcastically.

The silent crowds watched as the Kondor cruised by; Heydrich could distinguish faces at the distance. The SS guards lining the Embankment clicked their heels to attention as the boat passed; one in three stood facing the river, and gave the salute. Himmler and Heydrich both returned the straight-wristed gesture in the style of the Führer.

Heydrich, having enjoyed it for some moments, spoke again.

"Yes, *quaintly* expressed. Not that these tasks are to be written of with *quaint expressions*. It must be *unwritten*.

"Indeed, Obergruppenführer," Himmler said uncertainly.

"It will never be written, but our tasks will be done for the greater good. Like the Germ Theory of Disease; we remove a cancer to save the body of our civilisation."

Himmler smiled at that.

"Your logic again, General."

"National Socialism's world vision is as logical as it is idealistic. You say are Arjuna, Reichsführer? I am a policeman, restoring order in the pursuit of a German sphere of influence in Europe. The Jews are a people of assimilation; thus, too, have we absorbed their best qualities and vilified them for the worst. Our hatred of their nuances only strengthens our racial bond."

Himmler was shocked, though he masked it. Heydrich let him digest that, before moving to assure him as the ship slowed, approaching the small port at which they were to disembark at the Strand.

"Enemies of the Reich are to be exterminated, and there is no shortage of bullets with which to accomplish this. The times of Jewish intellectualism is over; we have absorbed their cleverness and incorporated their determination, now, the Teutonic peoples; Aryan, Nordic, Saxon, will overcome through purity of blood and the hardness to create a real future for our race."

Himmler glowed, thoroughly reassured. "My dear Heydrich... Obergruppenführer, General; you are a shining light of our race."

Fool, Heydrich thought. All the years of rising together with Himmler, through setbacks and triumphs, the ease with which he could manipulate the prim, puritanical pedant was still a source of irritation for Heydrich, though useful. Even the casual mention of 'race' was a crude reminder of the old Jew rumours from Heydrich's grandmother remarrying with a man named Süss. Despite the name, the man was no Israelite, though Gregor Strasser had tried in vain to bring the 'Hebrew' Heydrich down with it. Since then, Himmler had foolishly believed it to be some kind of leverage, despite a full Gestapo investigation and the Führer himself exonerating Heydrich after an hour alone with him.

Even more idiotic considering when Himmler had showed him the Süss dossier, trying to mask his delight, the superior smile had been instantly wiped off his pallid face the minute Heydrich planted his own, much bulkier folder on the desk the SD had compiled on the Reichsführer's Jewish cousin, David.

Stupid, spineless desk warrior.

"What we do here will be unwritten," Heydrich told Himmler.

Himmler glanced at him, but Britain's Reichsprotektor neither spoke nor acknowledged his enquiring gaze.

The ship gently anchored at the Savoy Wharf; German photographers snapped for posterity the twin figures of black, standing proud on the prow, and then, disembarking, in front of the great cross on the ship's side, framed with *Kondor*, The Thames, Big Ben and Parliament to their backs.

Swastikas bedecked the wharf, and a band struck up *Deutschland Über Alles*.

They were both thrilled. Typically, the *Horst Wessel Lied* would play as they arrived at state functions, with the national anthem reserved for the high Party members; typically Hitler, Göring, Goebbels, Hess and on state visits, the ambassador or Foreign Minister.

Heydrich was now that man. For the first time ever, he stepped nimbly around the Reichsführer-SS, and marched forwards past the honour guard to the Embankment Gardens, a sea of SS black standing sentinel to mark his route, and with Himmler striding powerfully to catch up, he barged over the road and in to the Savoy Hotel, the flashing bulbs of the cameras capturing the moment for the annals of human history.

SD-Foreign Intelligence officer Walter Schellenberg was ushered in to the Royal suite of the Savoy, and upon entering, his eyes grew wide. Large windows, thick carpets, valuable tapestries, ornate chairs... unlike Himmler, the Reichsprotektor had furnished his rooms in the style of the Führer. Across the table in the living room, where Heydrich stood adjusting his immaculate uniform in a suitably large mirror, was huge buffet of wines, champagne, a selection of fine meats and cheese, chocolate, even caviar... Schellenberg was stunned.

His boss had become a viceroy of Germany in the style of Frank in Poland, Neurath in the former Czecho-Slovakia... even akin to Göring in the Reich itself... resplendent, surrounded by luxury, intoxicated by his own power.

Heydrich's face split into a rare, wide grin in the mirror on seeing his foremost SD deputy.

"Schellenberg."

"Herr *Reichsprotektor*."

Heydrich turned to face him, standing tall; his chest jutted out proudly like a black peacock. The Führer's new Viceroy of Britain still wore the black ensemble that he and Himmler had chosen for their entrance – purely dress attire, having been discontinued for active service use some years before – but without the black great coat with its white lapels, revealing a formal black tunic, belted with white, service medals dangling.

The Warrior-Minister, Schellenberg noted wryly. A typically brilliant contrast; the man looked set for an elegant ball, rather than a trench, but with obvious signs of valour visible. A peacock, perhaps, but a courageous, clever, nihilistic and dangerous one.

"How was your journey?" the nasal voice asked him.

"Fine, Herr General."

"Any women en route? The usual Schellenberg magic?"

"No, Herr Obergruppenführer it was a straight flight and drive here. Far less dramatic than your arrival, sir."

At that, Heydrich looked gratified. "Quite. And good, I cannot report success of that kind of my own journey here, and I'd frankly be outraged if you had outperformed me to that degree."

Britain's Protector strolled to the table, as relaxed as his deputy had ever seen him, and casually opened a gold cigarette box, carelessly selecting one before propping it into his mouth. He smoked undemonstratively, but with such obvious pleasure that Schellenberg could not help but stare. The intense man who so bowled him over in their professional lives more resembled the man in private; stripped of his uniform and away from the office, the man with the voracious sexual appetite, who demanded Schellenberg's presence at all hours in the nightclubs of Berlin; whose ungovernable proclivities were displayed with such boozy metanoia. But here, he was calm. There was no hint of self-destruction, merely... shockingly, to Schellenberg... *ease*. Incredibly, Heydrich was *relaxed*.

Schellenberg knew better than to drop professional formality. The memory of Heydrich's eyes boring coldly into his own, and the words 'you just drank poison. If you wish to live, tell me everything' were still fresh in his mind.

Heydrich, for his part, was in great spirits after the grand arrival. Skipping in ahead of Himmler had been the crowning point, not to mention acquisitioning nothing less than the Royal Suite of the Savoy for *The Office of the*

Reichsprotektor of Great Britain and Supreme Headquarters of the SS and Security Police and SD. No doubt Himmler would struggle to swallow that particular mouthful.

And dear Schellenberg here, newly humbled.

"Have Müller, Eichmann and the police commanders arrived?" the Reichsprotektor asked presently.

"Yes Obergru.... Reichsprotektor. They are here."

"Are you hungry, thirsty? Have a drink."

"Thank you, Herr Reichsprotektor, but I—"

"Have a drink Schellenberg, and make it a good one. Try the champagne, you may as well get used to it before I assign you to Paris, where no doubt you'll spread your wings a little more than you've allowed yourself to in Berlin for some time. And for God's sake, while we are at it, it is just you and I alone here, and 'Sir' or 'General' will suffice."

"Yes, sir."

"Has Ribbentrop finished bothering you with his asinine plans regarding the Duke of Windsor?"

"No, sir."

"Don't worry; I'll get rid of him. The man's an idiot; anyone can see the Duke will come to us of his own accord. Being restored to the throne will satisfy his vanity. Göring and I will get rid of Ribbentrop as soon as the Führer finally realises the man's colossal stupidity, and lack of any semblance of talent or intelligence..."

Satisfied with his pronouncements, Heydrich nodded assuredly to Schellenberg, and turned back to the mirror, self-consciously examining himself.

Schellenberg drank in silence, deciding against making a quip about poison. When Heydrich was good and ready, having satisfied his various personal vanities and collected his thoughts, he turned to the SD Major, noting with satisfaction the files and dossiers in preparation.

"Well then... shall we proceed, Walther?"

They descended from the lofty heights of the Royal rooms to the designated conference suite booked for the conference. Fifteen attendees. The power of life and death in all of continental Western Europe and Britain held between them.

~

The young rebels were sombre and tired as they traipsed down the Mall from the Strand towards Buckingham Palace; the flags and pomp of the tree-lined street being a sad, flat irony. It was almost self-conscious; the stiff-upper lipped British maintaining 'Rule Britannia, Britannia Rules The Waves' with the Union Jack and the magnificent approach from Trafalgar Square and the Marble Arch to the palace home of the royals.

Yet the King was in exile, along with Churchill. It was a great illusion of imperial majesty. It was empty.

Alan was cross, and having already mentally given up on the plan, had ceased looking out for the best sniper's spot along the expected route.

"Look, this plan's bloody daft if you ask me. How do we even know he'll bloody come this way?"

Jack's patience was wearing thin.

"What do you expect, Himmler on the tube?"

"No, but—"

"I somehow can't see Heinrich Himmler getting off at Hyde Park corner in his pirate clobber, me old mucker."

"We don't know for sure he'll come down here," William observed reasonably. "Hell they could leave the Savoy north to Leicester Square, down through Piccadilly—"

"Swing by the Ritz for tea and crumpets on the way?" Jack was scornful.

"Jack," Mary said, in an uncharacteristically relaxed tone. "We are ready to do this. There is no doubt. But is *muy* importante we do not miss them."

He softened, as always with her.

"I know, love. But if Göring is there, or even if he's not... look at the way those bastards just entered..." they approached the palace. Jack gestured at its locked gates – Wehrmacht troops stood sentinel, alongside members of the King's Guard, for a truly farcical touch.

Occupation was not normality; in such a world, as all is tipped upside down, these are the kind of half-measures and half-hearted compromises that make a mockery of the whole thing. The concept of countries and realms.

"This," Jack pointed out, gesturing at the palace, then back down the Mall, at the whole magnificent spectacle at the heart of Britain's Imperial Might. "You think there's even 'alf a chance these bastards will pass *this* route up?"

"Fair point," William agreed.

"After the two hotels themselves, this bit will be the most heavily defended, though." Alan observed.

"True. So let's find a spot."

They strolled down, alongside the great palace and cut off at Green Park, which ran parallel to the Constitution Hill road and palace gardens, leading towards the Wellington Arch.

"Well…" Jack considered. "It's pretty sparse. There's nowhere in reach from this side you could sort out a proper Eagle's Nest. There's no hide site here, and chances are they'll have a second lot further back in the park waiting. Looks hopeless, old boy."

"I agree," Alan nodded. "Terrible job for a marksman, with the right security positioning. Trees offer no protection, crowds could be blocking the road, no higher ground, this would be a tough call."

They looked at William and Mary expectantly, the two most opinionated when it came to political or military matters, despite their markedly different means of expression. Yet they both nodded too, reluctantly. It was a tough call.

They marched past Wellington Arch, and round to Hyde Park corner itself, where the nervous would-be-assassins stood gazing across the green. They briefly debated commandeering an office from one of the surrounding buildings, but quickly rejected the idea. Buildings so close to the palace and en route to the apparently Göring-commandeered Dorchester would be vetted, perhaps crawling with krauts. As if to highlight this, their slow meander had taken them past more Wehrmacht troops than they had previously seen in all of London at any stage over the previous twelve weeks, and they knew, at once, that their suspicions about the route were correct.

"*Right*, then…" Alan breathed.

"Then left, then right again, that's walking, mate," Jack smiled. But Alan was focused on the task at hand.

"I've got a plan. We'll get these bastards. One minute."

A further minute up the road, they stood at the southernmost point of the dual carriageway that ran alongside London's Hyde Park, with The Dorchester several hundred metres further north on the right hand side, by the lane that led traffic south. But here, Alan stopped, a gleam in his eye.

"Do you see it, lads? And you," he conceded, to Mary, who was not listening. She understood at once.

"That!"

They all stared at the statue that Mary pointed at; stood on a great concrete base, and on slightly raised ground as the park rose to a mound, the eighteen foot high sculpture offered a clear shot at the road from no more than twenty-to-thirty paces away. It was the Wellington Monument. Should the roundabout section not be properly guarded, this was the perfect place from which to strike.

"Achilles, eh?" William whistled. "Bloody hell, Geordie, that might just be the bastard ticket. That might just be it."

They all stared at the famous statue of Achilles.

"Very fitting," chuckled William. "The Achilles heel of these shysters is pride. And whoever is not safely inside an armoured car is going to get a Paris arrow."

"In London," Jack quipped, grinning. "A London arrow. Don't think old Homer figured 'Cockney' as much of a heroic name though, do you?"

"Or Artful Dodger," Alan laughed.

"Imagine if he was called 'Scouser' – would *Liverpool* be the city of love?"

"Thirty thousand extra Scouse birds named Helen," William snorted, and was pinched by Mary, who understood enough to recognise the strange English term for girls.

Even as they sniggered along with him, the realisation of the mission's nature dawned on them all at once. Alan, sobering, followed their eyes to the statue and nodded.

"If any can honestly say they're a better marksman than I, say the word now and I will happily run at those bastards emptying my pistol." He patted his pocket, where lay his trusty Star, which he still lovingly tended, two years after last firing it in anger on Spanish soil.

But Jack and William shook their heads, gravely. They all knew he was the man to do it. The mission's success superseded any instinct for self-preservation.

"We know, mate. And yeah, we have more chance of surviving a firing squad than rushing the car. But it has to be done."

"We know," Mary said. "This mission is worth it."

But they all rounded on her, and told her it was out of the question. After several minutes of heated arguments, she finally relented, quietening down to a resentful sulk.

It was a death mission. Alan alone had a chance of escaping it.

"Look, I already know what you'll say, but you know I could do this mission alone, right? Without you lot chucking Molotovs."

Molotovs was their term for grenades, based on the homemade incendiary bombs or 'Molotov cocktails' the Finns used against Russian soldiers earlier that year.

"Can't do it from further back," he continued, considering, "... *but,* if I come up close, get up on the plinth with Achilles, or even just stand next to it, and quickly fire one off as the car approaches–"

Jack told him to forget it.

"No. You're the man for it. And that's a damn good spot; it's just high enough to get a clear shot over the crowd, but unless they're everywhere it will probably be unguarded. Why guard a statue? It's not even high. But it's literally perfect. Hell, it's barely thirty-five metres, Alan, you could get him with a regular rifle from there."

"Aye, but we all could. That's the point. And my job's safest."

But Jack was firm.

"No. *You*. Besides, if your first shot rings true, abandon ship. If there's enough people, the panic will be massive; drop and run with the crowd. You can stash your bike towards the back of the park, maybe up towards the tube stop on Bayswater Road... it's still a long shot, but perhaps–"

But Jack's words died on his tongue. As they continued up the Park Lane, reaching level with the Dorchester Hotel across the way, their attention on the surroundings for the next day had blinded them to the present danger of today. It came in the shape of two scowling, sauntering BUF members.

"Right, the four of you," the larger of the two boomed. "I want your papers."

~

Heydrich accepted the salutes of the two guards standing sentinel, exulting as he strode into the meeting.

Seven *Einsatzgruppe* commanders and a Wehrmacht liaison officer were in the process of settling themselves round the great oak table in the room's centre, chatting informally, and the Reichsprotektor was immensely gratified to see them all rise to salute him. Alas, Himmler was not yet there. *Smart boy, Heini. Either that, or you are sulking.*

Heydrich took a seat at the head of the table, and several of the SS exchanged knowing glances.

"A shame the table is not round," Heydrich boomed with as much authority as his nasal voice would allow. "We would be like King Arthur and the knights."

The SS men chuckled politely, and looked around, having only just arrived themselves. The opulence of the room drew impressed murmurs from the assembled; many of whom themselves were hardly strangers to the trappings of ostentatious government in the centralised agencies, after Albert Speer's influence in Berlin had started to make itself felt. An ornate chandelier hung low at what was just above head height for a person seated at the polished oak table that served as the room's point of gravitas. At Adolf Eichmann's discretion, ornate chairs had replaced the straight-backed wooden chairs that had seemed oddly out of place with the rest of the room; its thick, velvety carpet on which footsteps could hardly be heard; its thick beamed walls with their gleaming shine; its portraits, which had fittingly been replaced with that of the Führer in pride of place; smaller portraits were hung on the walls around; one of Göring, one of Himmler, and one of Heydrich. The latter picture was noticed by the assembled commanders, and their surprise had been briefly visible. Of those professionally closest to Heydrich, Müller, Lange and Eichmann smiled wryly at the portrait.

Presently, the Reichsführer-SS entered with Joachim Peiper, and the large, looming presence of an Austrian SS and Police leader of Poland, whom Heydrich had drafted to Britain. The group rose, and to a man, saluted the supreme chief of the *Schwarze Korps*.

"Heil, heil," Himmler said sternly, pausing briefly to take in the seating arrangement and, barely hiding his distaste, chose the empty seat directly facing Heydrich. That man, however, quickly began the debate, seizing the initiative, to the surprise of those in the Reich Security Main Office whom had seen nothing but outwardly subordinate deference from Heydrich to Himmler in the years they had worked beneath them.

"Herr Gentlemen, thank you for coming to this gravely important meeting," Heydrich began smoothly. "Please note that we have Field Marshal von Brauchitsch's personal adjutant here in Major General *Siewer*, so the *Oberkommando des Heeres* and the Military Commander are kept fully abreast of administrative proceedings and official directives from the office of the Reichsprotektor of Great Britain, and Chief of the *Sicherheitspolizei* and *Sicherheitsdienst*."

Heydrich's chief deputies noted the relish in his voice, to varying levels of approval. Gestapo general Müller openly nodded his own, being a strong advocate of assertive leadership and of Heydrich's qualities being better served as the Führer's chief paladin; a view Heydrich himself shared.

The Reichsprotektor looked over to Himmler, smiling.

"Regarding SS affairs, the Reichsführer-SS has been assigned to Great Britain for the time being to oversee and accomplish various tasks on behalf of the Führer."

He waited, expectantly, and Himmler found his voice. His customarily prim demeanour and rather superior manner had surfaced, overcoming the initial disorientation of his subordinate's uncharacteristic approach. Himmler worded his introduction carefully, ill-at-ease with the concurrent power chains at work and the subtle intricacies of his SS subordinate. As such, he tried to take the lead.

"Gentlemen... This is an important discussion, so let us not waste time. The briefing is as follows, as per Führer directive no.2 for England, as expressed in his mandate to me which you will find in the folder that SS-*Obergruppenführer* Heydrich has prepared; this will not be further recorded in print. You each have copies of Information G.B and Special Wanted List G.B. compiled extremely well

I must say by SD foreign intelligence chief Herr Major Schellenberg – excellent work for which we can thank the Major here."

Schellenberg bowed to him, ingratiatingly.

"Thank you, Reichsführer."

Several of the officers banged the table in approval.

"The Herr *Obergruppen*führer," Himmler resumed, nodding at Heydrich – rather pointedly, Schellenberg thought – "has spoken to you at length regarding security operations; beyond which, we can pass on to the army the responsibility of winning public opinion, maintaining a well-oiled social machine."

He gestured with false courtesy to Major-General Siewer.

"The Führer's will at that the army and its commander von Brauchitsch are to run civil and social matters with a firm but fair hand, in order to peacefully incorporate the British Empire and our Saxon blood brothers into the Greater Reich and establish a Germanic order in Europe and the world. But in order to do that, antisocial elements and enemies must first be dealt with, and this book..." the Special Arrest Lists handbook was raised aloft, "is our handbook, our manual to cut away the cancers afflicting England and the British society."

Good God, thought Heydrich. *Enough. Within five years, you are a dead man. You and your awful wife, and your Jewish cousin alike.*

Himmler concluded his brief introduction.

"Obergruppenführer Heydrich and the SD have been preparing for this over the course of several months, and from the reports sent to me for the Führer's eyes you have all performed well thus far in suppressing hostility. As I am myself not aware of the extent of our intelligence, I will hereby pass on to our Reich Security chief, Herr Heydrich."

Heydrich filled his cup from the water jug, taking his time before reassuming the leading role.

"Gentlemen, first and foremost thank you to Gruppenführer Müller and Sturmbannführer Eichmann of the Gestapo main office, for coming from Berlin to the heart of the largest Empire on Earth... for now."

The group thumped the table to a man. Müller nodded unsmilingly. Eichmann cursorily reacted to the General's mention, before returning to the sheaf of notes he was scanning intently.

"And the Brigadeführer here, the SS and Police leader from Lublin, with a special task reserved for him here in Britain, thank you Odilo."

The fleshy, brutal features of the Austrian that Heydrich gestured towards broke into a smile that looked like it pained him.

Heydrich resumed. "I will say, with respect to Major General Siewer, cooperation between the army and *my office* in all civil matters is paramount so as to not disturb the peaceful integration of Great Britain into the Greater German Reich; I will further and assist with all army policy, excepting cases where we feel their decisions and mandate, when not *personally* directed by the Führer are clearly *counter-productive*, and of course, when it is a matter of security, concerning action towards undesirables or enemies of the Reich."

Siewer assented, looking as though it was the last thing he felt like doing. Heydrich loftily accepted his concurrence, but pressed home the point, to send a message to his subordinates present... and to Himmler.

"Herr Major General, as adjutant and liaison to Army commander von Brauchitsch, might I just ask for confirmation that Army High Command accepts wholly the wishes of the Führer, Herr Göring and the Party as to our close cooperation, and with regards to *my* express authority over security matters and prosecution of National Socialist policy in Great Britain?"

All eyes turned to the Wehrmacht man, whose tone was rather flat in response.

"Field Marshal von Brauchitsch is perfectly aware from where policy emanates."

"Excellent," Heydrich said, without further ado. "And to the rest of you, commanders of *Einsatzgruppen Britain*; Dr Six, and the *Einsatzgruppe England* leaders, welcome."

Seven nods. Heydrich had briefed Commander Six, with Müller and Nebe, and each of the other leaders personally in Berlin at the end of May, even prior to the surrender of France and the attack on this isle. They were intently waiting to find out what this particular meeting would entail; up to now, their roles and remits were perfectly clear.

Heydrich gazed around the room, taking in the tapestries and portraits, the pleasing aesthetics and general ambience, before turning his attention to the Kripo chief of Germany.

"And Gruppenführer Nebe, good to see you. You are missed in Berlin."

Nebe replied with equal courtesy, "And you, Obergruppenführer, and you. Welcome to England."

Eichmann and Schellenberg watched him for a sign of weakness, but Nebe, a police commissioner even before the Nazi takeover of power, was far too slippery to show his hand. A perfect façade of a smile played over his face, beneath the enormous nose that could have been a death sentence for one of lower prestige in Nazi Germany. However, perhaps his star was on the wane. Heydrich, chief of the Reich Security Office to which Kripo was part of – department V – had appointed Nebe commander of *Einsatzgruppe Manchester*; an obvious snub, with the subordinately ranked SS-Brigadeführer Franz Six of the SD in overall operational command in Britain, and head of the more prestigious London *gruppe*.

With Nebe in the north of England, Bernhard Wehner was deputising as Acting Chief of Kripo, RSHA Dept. V, and Friedrich Wilhelm Lüdtke was the Acting Commissioner of Kripo Berlin.

On top of his Action Group leadership Nebe was left with a transparent sop; *Deputy-Commander of SiPo and SD in Britain of the Reichsprotektor* and *Police Leader in the Northern Zone* – a meaningless title, threefold, and deliberately so; it was Dr Six who officially commanded the *Einsatzgruppen GB*, the absent Oberführer Schöngarth had been drafted from Poland as Heydrich's *SD Chief of the Northern Zone*, and Nebe was an SS-Lieutenant General and Kripo police chief already who outranked both. There were no SS men superior in either rank, position or executive police power than Nebe in the entire country, save for the Blond Beast himself.

Heydrich smiled to himself, as Nebe smoothly parried his taunt. *You are a cool one, Arthur. Always were. Even now your hands are dirty and your pride is hurt.*

The Reichsprotektor continued, playing his trump card, speaking with greater speed and force. His tone made abundantly clear that he was not to be interrupted.

"In addition to the mandate the Führer gave the Reichsführer-SS as a broad scope as to the implementation and direction of his aims here in Great Britain and territories, I, in my role as the *Minister Responsible for the Reich Central Agency For Jewish Emigration*, have been given an authorisation from Reichsmarschall Göring in the form of this document which you will see in your folders; if you will open the file..."

Eichmann noticeably smirked, as did Müller. Schellenberg glanced at Himmler, his suspicions that the Reichsführer was unaware of such a document confirmed by the steely glint in Himmler's eyes, which were locked on Heydrich resolutely.

Heydrich retrieved his own copy of the file. "I hereby charge *you*, Obergruppenführer Reinhard Heydrich, SS-Reich Security Chief, Head of the SiPo and SD, and so on, *and so on*, and in your concurrent capacity as Minister Responsible for Jewish Emigration et cetera, et cetera, with *all necessary executive authority* to find, dispel and remove all acting and potentially dangerous or unsuitable elements within Germany, Great Britain and territories; the necessary police organisations of your office being the determining agency, reporting..."

Heydrich barely suppressed a grin at this point; the laughter in his voice was unmistakeable.

"... *Directly* to myself and to the Führer on such matters with no impedance from, and with the full cooperation *of, all other military and executive branches of the Reich...* henceforth assuming responsibility for all matters of 'internal political security' within the National Socialist Empire, not merely for matters of 'police security' and with regards to the total subjugation of hostile elements, seizing and combating organisations and elements working against Germany, and working towards a Final Solution to the Jewish Question, and so on, and so on... signed Hermann Göring, *Reichsmarschall* of the Greater German Reich, Prime Minister of Prussia, President of the Reichstag and so on, *and so on*, to Chief of Security Police and SD, Heydrich, Reichsprotektor, President of INTERPOL, et cetera, et *cetera*..."

He looked up, briefly, unable to resist seeing the effect it had on the men present, they being some of the most powerful men in Europe. The sight overjoyed him.

~

Neither Jack, Alan, William nor Mary moved. The two fascists exchanged an oddly joyful look that exhibited the pretence of exasperation, and they began to flex their newfound social weight.

"Papers," the smaller man glared; a distinctly Jewish looking weasel of a man.

The group paused. None had brought their identification, despite the strict illegality to the Germans of such a move, purely in the event that this happened, in order to plead ignorance. But while they would have been forced to face arrest at the hands of Wehrmacht or – God help them – SS, and more pertinently SD or Gestapo, they certainly couldn't face having their plans derailed by a pair of Englishmen.

Even two English scum wielding coshes, in the employ of the Germans.

"Papers," the weasel demanded again, more forcefully.

"Why, do you need a smoke, Jakob?" William sneered.

"Oh, a funny bugger are we?" The rat-like fascist leered at his larger, somewhat more intimidating friend. "This one's a funny bugger, isn't 'e."

"Since when do we have to do what you bastards say?" Alan demanded.

Jack grinned. "Yeah, you aint ever had any say in London, guv'nor. Us three were here when your lot got your heads kicked in up the East End."

"Yeah," William joined in, "... and when my Geordie friend here says 'you bastards', I should point out that he means *fascists*, not yids."

They all roared with laughter, despite amusement being the last thing they felt. There were Wehrmacht and SS men stood idly smoking, or alternately, patrolling across the road at the hotel. Things were going badly awry for the group.

"Well," rat-face began, slowly, enjoying himself. "I don't know about yids, as it should be obvious neither of us are dirty kikes. You'll find that things are changing around here... what with the new Viceroy of 'itler being an SS and police general and all. BUF men of a *certain standing* have been asked to deputise as a sort of auxiliary *peace-keeping* security force, until things settle. So with that being said–"

He never finished his sentence. Jack feinted, pretending to crouch before head-butting the fascist would-be copper, his hard skull driving upwards and through the brittle man's chin with all the weight and force that Jack possessed. He was unconscious before the back of his head hit the ground, blood leaking out of it onto the pavement. Alan immediately leapt in, planting a big left hook on the larger man's chin, almost spinning him. A second punch that glanced clumsily off his boulder of a head was supplemented by William, who sprang in to stamp down hard on the disorientated fascist's kneecap, sending him twisting to the ground. Alan kicked, and then stomped the stricken giant's head for good measure, sending it thudding into the concrete with a horrible shudder of impact.

The whole attack lasted no longer than ten seconds.

They all heard a great shout from across the street in German, and instantly fled into the park. Two SS men with the SD sleeve diamond sprinted across Park Lane, with the shouts of Wehrmacht laughter ringing out behind them.

"Bayswater Road," Alan shouted, in a great pant. "Get to the Tube."

The only German they could now hear behind them were guttural, threatening yells.

Fleeing across the grass past the first row of yellowing trees, Mary began to sprint out into the open expanse of grass, westwards into the heart of the park.

"*Mary*!" William yelled in high panic.

Thankfully the cry registered even in flight, and with the nimble feet of a girl whose childhood was spent outdoors in the Catalonian countryside beyond Barcelona, Mary turned on her heel and darted back into the tree-lined route along which they sprinted northwards towards Speaker's Corner. There was no noise behind them, but from the stares of the park stragglers they passed, all were sure that the chase was still ongoing.

They cut northwest, navigating the northeast park lanes at Cumberland Gate and to their relief, found themselves on the main road which was near-empty, and free of German patrols. Disregarding their safety, they unhesitatingly tore across the lanes without checking for traffic, and having made it across to the cobbled pavements north, they turned east, passing the Marble Arch junction at the northeast corner of the park. The tube station was in sight.

A warning shout in German rang out behind them, guttural and harsh.

"Hurry," Alan urged, and they sprinted across, bitterly regretting their tobacco habits.

They all rounded the corner and in to the station, slipping on the shiny floor as they cut in from the street, and hurled themselves down the stairs three at a time, William falling at the bottom. There was a train at the platform heading eastwards – three stops to Tottenham Court Road, from whence they could walk – its grimy white side had opened its doors, and confused passengers were staring out.

Jack and Alan reached the train with a final burst of energy, and almost fell through its doors in relief. But Mary stopped at the door, in horror.

"William," she screamed.

The young Scot had badly twisted his ankle in the fall, and was limping along painfully towards the open doors.

Frantically, Mary ran back to her lover, and dragged him along furiously. The bemused conductor, for whom people running to catch trains was no uncommon sight, had dismissed both the sight of Jack and Alan tearing across the platform, and the spectacle of the young man's fall, but the shrill Latin scream of Mary had been too much for him. It was too panicked and emotional to be related to the train, which in any case would be followed in ten minutes by another. The old conductor didn't know *why* she screamed, but his curiosity was tempered as he knew that he didn't *want* to know.

His whistle blew, and the doors began to close.

~

Heydrich gazed around a room of men who were still stunned by his far-reaching proclamations regarding the further power bestowed on him, this time by Hermann Göring. And none were more amazed than the putative master of the SS himself, in Reichsführer Himmler.

"Gentlemen," he said gruffly, minimising the nasal qualities of his high voice. "*This* is the directive, and that which the Reichsführer-SS has himself discussed with our Führer and briefly explained to you, is clear – in Germany itself, we will soon begin major resettlement operations, and at present, here in England and the British Isles… which are to be cleared of undesirable elements in order to procure peace in a German Europe, and for the British Empire to become our allies and partners in the great racial struggle of our people against ideological and racial enemies in the East, and elsewhere."

His eyes bored into the men seated on either side of the great table. The silence was deafening.

"This is to be achieved by *force* if necessary – it likely will be – and with all the experience our Gestapo and SD have earned within Germany itself, for that to be turned on England in order to set the course for a New European Order in the world."

The ensuing silence was broken by Eichmann and Müller.

"*Jawohl*, Reichsprotektor!"

All others apart from Himmler and the Austrian followed suit, banging the table in support. The Reichsführer-SS took the liberty of interjecting, anxious to rein Heydrich in and assert his own supreme SS authority.

"Very well said, Herr Obergruppenführer. As to the removal of those threats, you have all done a fine job thus far, a *fine job* thus far. Herr Schellenberg has provided exceptionally clear details in the books that show how to appropriately deal with *all manner* of issues pertaining to gaining control over Great Britain. They are quite thorough and include lists of prominent Jews and freemasons, all masonic lodges and those within the nobility who are involved in that criminal organisation, as well as fugitives from Germany..."

Heydrich himself interjected, as the little speech of Himmler's paused momentarily.

"*Indeed*, Reichsführer, perhaps the finest work of the SD thus far; it will provide all necessary and relevant information. Masonic lodges to be crushed as and where they crop up in their new form, this dangerous Hydra. Like Vishnu, one hundred arms and limbs to this beast. I want them smashed, *defiled, ransacked* and their members hauled in for Gestapo questioning and subsequent execution, regardless of rank!" Heydrich's voice rose to a high-pitched cry of excitement, and he rose to his feet, aware of his voice, and quickly composing himself. "They will be hung publicly, with piano wire like *cattle,* as something of a deterrent and a just punishment."

Heydrich gazed at them each in turn.

"And with the meeting that myself, the Reichsführer and Herr Göring are to have tomorrow, it is *paramount* that each *Einsatzgruppe* speeds up the departure of many enemies of National Socialism that we would first like to acquaint with Gestapo hospitality, or SS bullets."

Again, the Einsatzgruppe commanders nodded their assent. Heydrich paced, calmly.

"Moving on; beyond freemasons and prominent Jews – the two are often the same – we have listed the believed whereabouts of influential financiers, and while I doubt we'll find Mayor Rothschild or his close family on this side of the world, it should be expressed to the men of our action groups – as in Poland – any key figures who have or had any control over economy or string-pulling on Downing Street must be captured and hung from meat-hooks as a matter of the most urgent priority of Germany."

Himmler nodded gravely from his seat.

"Absolute top priority, yes... absolute top priority... prominent Jews and communist party members, freemasons and influential financiers."

"There are also subversive writers and so-called scientists, political thinkers and others of some prominence; Jew and human alike..."

Heydrich's voice trailed, and some sycophantic laughter pealed out from his obedient acolytes.

"... and while unfortunately Sigmund Freud is no longer in the land of the living, many more remain here who it could be said, should not be. I should like to add that, if Eric Blair, better known as *George Orwell*, or Aldous Huxley be discovered in England, that they be held free of special interrogation. I would like to deal with them myself."

He turned to Dr Six. "No sign, I assume?"

The *Einsatzgruppen Britain* commander shook his bald head gravely.

"There is no word or sign of either Orwell or Huxley, Herr Reichsprotektor."

Schellenberg and Eichmann shared a silent look, wryly noted by Nebe. The three of them were each aware of the current situation with Orwell, and equally that Huxley on the other hand was long gone.

Himmler's adjutant, Waffen-SS captain Joachim Peiper enquired of Heydrich; "Are there any new additions to the list, Herr Obergruppenführer, or Herr Schellenberg?"

"No, on the contrary the list was significantly shortened at the highest levels of government," Heydrich quickly answered, lowering himself back into his seat. "Some key ministers smoothened the process of the move towards a new order, and helped facilitate the overthrowal of the old. Thus, I spared them."

Himmler interjected; quite unnecessarily, Schellenberg thought.

"Captain Peiper here will liaise between myself and the Obergruppenführer, and through him I will keep abreast of your actions, gentlemen, for my reports to the Führer. As Reichsführer-SS *I* am here on the Führer's orders to ensure these visions of Saxon order come to fruition. Reich Security Chief Heydrich is tasked with accomplishing the racial and political cleansing of undesirable elements, and it is vital that such work is successful."

Himmler looked extremely satisfied as he concluded his pronouncement. Heydrich exchanged a quick glance with his Gestapo chief Heinrich Müller, knowing the Bavarian would be struggling to contain his derision, before resuming the lead.

"At Prinz-Albrecht Strasse I along with Gestapo Müller here, laid out the foundations of this operation. Now, it must be escalated, in each sector. There is a meeting arranged later this week, based on the Reichsmarschall's directive to combine the efforts of all necessary executive agencies of the Party and State to consolidate SS power over matters of the Jewish Question, social cleansing and occupational policy; fittingly the conference will be held at Downing Street. Several of you will be in attendance; a strong SS presence will help show our friends in the Party bureaucracy the direction from which power emanates."

"Here, here," Müller said approvingly in his coarse rasp, banging his fist on the table, to which the others followed suit.

"Herr General," Dr Six began in a clipped, slightly reedy voice, "what levels of continued partisan action do you personally expect from Great Britain as a whole, given that resistance thus far has been less than anticipated..."

But Heydrich brushed him aside.

"On the contrary, Six; England's system of resistance was far more sophisticated and planned out than had been expected, up until the reports stemming from SD infiltration of the organised resistance in late spring. The Reich would have encountered many more serious and severe difficulties in England had our agentur not come through. Our favourite freemason and agentur of international *Jewry,* Winston *Churchill* is somewhat cunning, for an obnoxious old drunk."

The men laughed, even Himmler, the grim Gestapo pair, and the brutal Austrian SS and Police Leader.

"Do elaborate, my dear Heydrich," Himmler asked.

"Certainly Reichsführer; auxiliary partisan units were arranged across villages and towns the length and breadth of South and South-East England; churches with cellars were fitted with radio equipment with which to communicate with other villages and the underground in London, Leeds, Birmingham, Manchester and Edinburgh..."

Heydrich rose from his seat, and began pacing. The Führer's gaze bore down on his back, from the painting behind him. Schellenberg wondered if it was intended. *Probably*, he decided.

"... Villages in the south, and the larger towns and cities such as Portsmouth, Brighton, Southampton and Exeter, were equipped with radios and caches of weapons and ammunition, smaller villages had trained weapons and intelligence experts planted amongst the villagers to observe and report German troops movements, convey numbers and armour, identify any high ranking officers, et cetera..."

Peiper whistled. "More than we can say for France and the rest."

Heydrich agreed; he rather admired the devious planning of the British.

"Indeed. And if the opportunity presented itself, they would have attacked and coordinated attacks through direct assault or incidents of sabotage behind what would be called the front line if indeed, a frontline had been established in our rapid advance to London."

The men banged the table again.

Heydrich added. "Of course, in the period afterwards this resistance did rear its head, as you gentlemen well know. But your work has been phenomenal."

"I had no idea a sophisticated network was in place..." Himmler began, before trailing off.

Heydrich mused, sitting back down.

"All across the south and southeast; there were sufficient sniper rifles, pistols and grenades, radios, partisan units and by all accounts, *fire* in their Anglo-Saxon bellies to make life difficult for we invaders and to keep this sort of guerrilla campaign going for a while, complete with assassinations and total disregard for German reprisals against the populace. These English are so *feisty*... I don't quite understand how it is they cannot see the reality of the Jew and this cabal of aristocratic and masonic Jewry that controls them when they could be a proud ally of the German Reich and retain the largest Empire in the world – a world run by Saxon blood, triumphant over Jewish printing presses and the Slavic Jewish contagion of communism."

More murmured agreements.

"Gruppenführer Nebe, perhaps you'd like to report on the results of these actions in the north."

Nebe cleared his throat, before his calm assessment. "Cellars were destroyed with grenades, whole groups of men and women alike were quietly liquidated, radio equipment was sabotaged with a quite remarkable 70% estimated success rate, Gestapo agents were able to, *extract*, information from a great deal of the by all accounts very courageous would-be partisans that led to the almost total collapse of the whole resistance movement as a concerted, organised and coordinated effort... at least, in the wake of Army Group Centre, Group C, and as far north as Manchester."

Having noted one particular Heydrich omittance, Nebe shrewdly tailored his planned report to correspond with the Einsatzgruppen founder's apparent preference, and made no mention of that day's operation. The two SS chiefs seemed reassured by his report. Heydrich smiled at his erstwhile Kripo head. Himmler nodded in approval. Schellenberg privately wondered if the Reichsführer's neck was capable of soreness.

"And *Einsatzgruppe Leeds*, Major Lange?" Heydrich inquired.

"Much the same report as the Gruppenführer," the newly promoted Sturmbannführer Dr Rudolf Lange reported. "Complete subjugation and liquidation; all the way up Army Group B of AG Centre; as far north as Leeds and right up to the line of occupation."

Heydrich began to question them in turn.

"*Einsatzgruppe Liverpool*?"

A bleary-eyed Standartenführer Paul Blobel answered, knowing better than to lie.

"All cleared up to Liverpool; a truly horrible state of affairs in the city but things have quietened down. We had our own sick murderer; like that fellow in France, Pettiot... he was killing Jews and hideaways in his basement. Garrotting, strangling, stabbing..." the rapidly ageing Potsdam colonel breathlessly explained, wiping sweat from his brows with a dirty knitted handkerchief. "We got him, though, and then blocked the story. The area is stable. For the most part, all arrests assigned to us as per the *Sonderfahndungsliste G.B* in our sphere of operations have been carried out, although I report that some known dissidents still remain at large."

"See to it that they're carried out in the coming days, and pull yourself together," Heydrich snapped.

"Yes sir, Herr Reichsprotektor," Blobel mumbled, his eyes shifting downwards.

Heydrich scowled at him, and then turned away.

"*Einsatzgruppe Birmingham*?"

"Thoroughly covered, no resistance remaining whatsoever," Sturmbannführer Martin Sandberger reported, his enormously wide-head and square jaw having pride of place as the most menacing visage in the room. In a room that contained the sinister sadist Odilo the Austrian, not to mention Gestapo Müller and Dr Rudolf Lange who had tortured more people to death than Tomas de Torquemada, that was some accomplishment.

Sandberger though, much like Lange, was an educated man, and as the son of an IG Farben director he had provided Heydrich – and thus Himmler and Hitler – with excellent links to that company. Large projects were in the offing, between the SS and the giant corporation. Himmler nodded his approval of Sandberger.

"*Einsatzkommando* 2 of my *Einsatzgruppe* operated in Birmingham during our journey along the west coast, which likely helped placate the city," Blobel offered, and Sandberger looked at him with open distaste. Nebe wrinkled his nose up at the crude attempt to win back favour.

Heydrich simply ignored him. "*Einsatzgruppe Bristol*?"

"Not a shot fired in anger for some time," Standartenführer Otto Ohlendorf replied, in his quiet, agreeable manner. "Every arrest on Herr Schellenberg's lists in my operational area carried out, only seventy-four executions following the initial Wehrmacht entry, and the surrounding zone entirely secure."

"Excellent work," Heydrich boomed, his voice dropping several notches lower.

He turned to Karl Jäger. "I assume you have a full report on Edinburgh and Glasgow?"

"I do, Reichsprotektor. Four months of *Einsatzgruppe Edinburgh* operations." He held his report aloft. Eichmann, sat beside him, took the file from him and began poring over it.

"Excellent."

"Herr Reichsprotektor," Jäger began, hesitantly, "... With respect, I would like to ask as to the plans to establish further action groups in Edinburgh and Glasgow to combat Scottish resistance? With respect."

"With respect *indeed*, Herr Jäger. There has been a new development in Great British policy, in that to kill as many birds as possible with one stone, the Führer has deemed it acceptable to grant Scotland her independence from the Empire's historical capital and power, London. As we incorporate England or rather, as England incorporates herself with our assistance into the new order in the world, Scotland's people will be pacified by their longed for *freedom*, while we ensure that a government amenable to the Reich and with Scottish nationalist support is quietly installed there."

Einsatzgruppe Leeds commander Rudolf Lange banged the table, thrice.

"A very welcome development on the whole for the Reich and for our actions here, Herr Reichsprotektor. I'm sure we're all appreciative of our Führer's ability to secure peace as well as conquer."

"Indeed, you should be pleased as your own tasks in the north will be made more logistically efficient, Sturmbannführer Lange... which I might add for the group's benefit, is your new rank to which I am promoting you, in agreement with the Reichsführer. Regarding Scotland; SS action is best concentrated across the north of England where more people dwell, is part of England and in any case, is where the more aggressive Scottish rebels stupidly fighting for the old idea of Great Britain are to be found resisting and needlessly putting their necks in the noose."

They banged the table again; Lange thanked Heydrich and then Himmler, almost as an afterthought.

"I was not made aware of SS involvement in commando actions on British soil..." Himmler interjected again, rather pointedly. Some men looked down in embarrassment; Heydrich stifled his irritation. They had long since moved on from that particular point.

"Reichsführer, you are referring to the aforementioned Fifth Columnist work in pacifying organised resistance, yes? As I understand it, you were not informed of the use of Waffen-SS commandos and this Gestapo/SiPo and SD operation as in light of your enormously far-ranging duties in the Reich and its territories; it was at a time when your personal direction of crucial continental and internal actions was required; bearing in mind your great cultural tasks and indeed, overseeing of SS matters in other newly acquired territories such as France, Belgium, Luxembourg and the Netherlands. The details of execution were being worked out when you toured the lowlands and France, Herr Reichsführer."

Now be quiet, you pedantic fool, Heydrich thought venomously; his face a smiling mask.

Himmler smiled. "Of course, you have my complete and full authorisation with regards to security matters, Herr Obergruppenführer."

"Excellent," Heydrich sneered, smile still in place. "And on that note, gentlemen, there is to be a buffet; we shall be served with wine and some indigenous cuisine which I must say I'm surprisingly fond of..."

With that, he rose, as did the rest of the table, and they bustled in to the adjacent room, where the sight of a sumptuous buffet brought open gasps and delight from the collection of the hardest, cruellest men of the Reich.

~

"No, you bastard."

Alan sprang into the gap where the door closed, holding it open with his foot. Jack grabbed the metal-plates that held the glass, and pulled with all his might, as Mary and William made an ungainly rush towards the door.

Behind them, two SS men came clattering down the stairs.

The Scot and his Barceloniña clattered through Alan and Jack, and they all collapsed in an undignified heap on the floor, seconds before the train started to take off. The SS men yelled at the train in German, but with all the authority of their foreign tongue, such screams were impotent to stop the train as it inexorably pulled away from the station and disappeared into the blackness of the tunnel.

Panting, exhilarated, the group disentangled themselves from the twisted pile of human limbs they had created on the ground, and registering the confused shock of their fellow passengers, they collapsed again in uproarious laughter, flooding with relief.

~

The train stopped at Tottenham Court Road, and the four friends disembarked, still chuckling, and out into the still-strong light of a day that harkened back to the strangest of those shared on Mary's native soil.

Alan commented on it, for what William decided was the seventh time or so.

"Bloody hell, man... that was a close one eh?"

"Yes, Alan."

"German bastards. *As if* they chased us like that over a cheeky head-butt and stomp on the BUF? It's an all-English affair."

"Yes, Alan."

He snorted. "Aye, bugger off, Jock, it's not my fault you almost got bloody left behind you daft slow clumsy bastard like."

William winced, still limping somewhat. "Thanks for your touching concern. I thought I'd had it there too, for a minute. Christ, I need to smoke less."

Even as he said it, the reality of their situation dawned on him, and he could tell from the silence that ensued that the rest of them thought the same. Tomorrow. The mission. Their smoking habits were an irrelevance.

In conscious irony, William retrieved his cigarettes, lit one and passed them around, grateful of the others' humorous treatment of the gesture.

They slowly progressed through the Bloomsbury Streets, reaching the final square nearest the Royal Oak. Two familiar old figures were sat smoking pipes on the bench. Alan nudged Jack, nodding over to them with a grin.

"Old boys are there."

They cut through the square, and the cracked, slightly wheezing voices came into focus, drifting through the silence of the cold air of early evening.

"These *bloody* Germans."

All four of them suppressed a snort of laughter.

"Aye... it's a bloody joke, I tell you. No free speech anymore, I heard old Ted got arrested and a stern tellin' off, I tell you, more than a slap on the wrist what our old Bobbies would give. Bleedin' terrified, he was."

"Aye, buggers the lot of 'em. Weren't like this when we was kids, Jerries or no Jerries. Coppers gave you a tellin' off, and if you played up again you got a clip, and that were bloody that. But I'm tellin' you, you don't threaten someone what don't 'ave it comin'."

"Aye. Buggers they are, buggers. Our coppers too, playing along with these bloody Jerries. Even enforcing the Jerries' curfew! Enforcing the curfew! I tell you, did we fight in bloody France for four years, and our lads die, to *beat* those bastards, only for their bloody sons to enforce a Boche curfew in England twenty years later?"

"Aye… set of buggers."

Jack and Alan were besides themselves. The near-escape with the German security police had put them both in high spirits, compounded by their underlying nerves, and they were in high humour. Mary was struggling to understand the heavily pronounced pseudo-cockney drawl of the old men, but she was giggling at her friends. William took it upon himself to speak.

"All right, old boys?"

They both looked around in surprise, although the group had been no further than twenty feet away for a fair while.

"Aye. All right son. How are you lot gettin' on?"

"Just getting on with it, old bean, you know how it is," Jack shrugged.

"Aye well, it weren't like this in my bloody day I tell you…"

Jack and Alan half-turned away as a bubbling hiss of laughter escaped them. Their attempt to mask their amusement with bursts of coughing failed to convince the two older men, the oldest of whom glared with sudden spite.

"Well, in my day we all bloody *fought*, of course. That's why these Jerries never came here when us lot were younger. Oh, we was too old to enlist, in proper terms, I were what, 41 in '14, not in me early 20s. *That's* the age they wanted, proper fighting age. Like you lot."

"Aye," his friend agreed darkly. "You lot are the right age to fight."

"It's a bleedin' shame more of our lot didn't go fight 'em this time 'round, i'n'it?"

"Aye, bunch of fucking ginger beers and nancies this time around, lost the fucking country to Jerries..."

The young men felt their good spirits evaporate in the toxic atmosphere of the scorn of the bitter old men, whose nostalgic chuntering was no longer funny. On the contrary, they felt assaulted. Dishonoured, and degraded.

"We fought fascism, old man–" Alan began hotly.

"That's enough. Take care, old boys." Jack interrupted, nodding to the old men on the bench.

"–We fought fascists for *years* in the trenches and never quit."

Jack grabbed Alan's arm, and began steering him away towards the road, and thence the pub. William and Mary followed behind, sombrely. The Scot laced his arm around his lover's shoulders, squeezing her to him.

"We fought you old bastard, and always will," Alan shouted over his shoulder, at which Jack slapped across the back of his head, hard. It didn't further rile the Geordie, but rather calmed him, as he knew he had gone too far.

"All right, all right."

They entered the pub, and under Jack's steely gaze, Alan offered to get the round in.

"Three pints of ale and a special whiskey, I assume gents," Arthur smiled, winking at the red-faced Geordie who managed to return it. The barman silently queried him, and Alan shook his head slightly, winking again, ignoring Jack who was still casting dark glances at him in irritation.

They took up seats in the saloon bar; usually an order would be made from in there, costing more than a pint in the public bar, but with the lack of customers such ceremony was redundant. Alan, having controlled his breathing, glanced over to his right, where the pub's sole other occupant was brooding alone, staring into the dregs of his near-empty pint glass.

"All right, Bill. Can I refill your glass mate?"

Bloodshot, watery eyes sunken in an unshaven face slowly turned to the wiry Geordie at the bar, on whom they rested calmly. Alan shuddered inwardly, keeping his face still. Bill looked as though he had neither washed nor slept for days.

"I'm sorry?"

"I said, like…" Alan began uncertainly. Bill had a strange quality of putting him on his guard. The tone of that deep, cultured voice was clear, even though the man looked, smelled and generally staggered like a wreck of a human. His voice was clear. Even his gaze was level.

"Ah… let me get you a pint. As an apology for before?"

Bill nodded to him. "Thanks. Much appreciated."

Alan bought him a beer, placing it down on the wooden table in front of him with good grace. "Very decent of you," Bill said quietly, without moving. Alan watched him uncertainly for a moment, before turning to take his own pints to the saloon room. As the door swung shut on the Geordie's disappearing back, Bill finally reached forwards and slowly brought the glass up to his cracked lips.

Alan set the glasses down at their table.

"Well, I reckon we've got time for just the one or two..." he scratched his chin.

"Let's meet back here tonight when they've reopened," Jack said, assuredly. "We need to properly plan, after all."

"Yeah, yeah. Plan. And, well..."

"What?"

"It might be nice to have a drink or two. Just enough to get merry. I mean... who knows when we next will, eh?"

His tone was breezy, and they all reacted with similarly breezy, fleeting agreements. Smiles masked fear.

~

Seating back at the great table, Heydrich once more led off to the assembled SS commanders.

"It seems we shall continue without the Reichsführer-SS present, which should pose no problem because with *no disrespect intended towards the Reichsführer of the SS...*" Heydrich cleared his throat noisily, "... his *cultural tasks* involve the study and documentation of *historically sacred German blood* and its influence in England, mysticism and of Teutonic tradition…"

There was a silence, which suited Heydrich fine.

"Our tasks are different. For the record; my idea of the cultural blending of England and Germany is the combination of the two great historical nations of Saxon blood, with our advances in the arts, in science, music, philosophy, poetry and literature – *decadent Jewish materials excepted*; in music and philosophy, likewise. Psychology especially – the pain of any Jewish psychologist of note or those included in our special search lists G.B is to be immeasurable even by Gestapo standards."

"Here, here," Müller snarled, in a low, deep growl. "The Jewish intelligentsia should be packed into a mine and blown sky high."

"Thank you, Gruppenführer Müller," Heydrich said patiently.

He rose to his feet.

"Nothing is to stand in the way of this union. We are the great nations and the German-British World Reich will be an age of glory never surpassed in history, of German and English western culture and Saxon blood triumphant."

The SS men all banged the table in strong support.

"Herr Reichsprotektor," Siewer began, "what were you saying regarding the army's delegation of legal enforcement tasks to the SS?"

"Ah, *specifics*. Good. The Field Marshal and I spoke on the phone about this, briefly. *Negro music* and anything decadent, be it Jewish or black, American or from London or Leeds or Liverpool, is *categorically outlawed*; punishable by severity equivalent to that in the Reich."

The *Einsatzgruppe* leaders made notes, and then looked up expectantly.

"Narcotics... including but not limited to opiates – despite unofficial policy even amongst, *alas*, members of the Party Elite..."

Heydrich's tone was delicate, but every officer present guffawed, especially Müller. Army Chief adjutant Siewer laughed openly, too, slightly warming to Heydrich. With his impromptu rise from captain (retired) to first Field Marshal, and then *Reichsmarschall* – all-but Generalissimo – and total command of the Air Force, the supremely confident, enormously ruthless and falsely convivial Göring was not popular amongst the Army High Command at *Oberkommando des Heeres*.

Heydrich smiled. "Yes... opiates shall be *illegal* and possession in any quantities punishable by internment in the *Konzentrationslagers* the Reichsführer and I are installing here, under the direction of our good friend the Brigadeführer," he said, nodding to the Austrian, who again twisted his face into something that vaguely resembled a polite smile.

"While hardly a problem worth tackling in the Reich itself," Britain's viceroy declared, a sudden melodrama allowing the high pitched edge to his voice, "the so-called 'Youth Assassin' of cannabis is rather more prevalent *here,* much as it is in America... and it *will* be held in the same legal category as opiates, and cocaine and the stimulants."

"And if they are Jews, fucking kill them on the spot," Müller grunted. "Or drag them in for special interrogation."

"Thank you for the reminder, Gruppenführer Müller," Heydrich said, patiently. "Yes, any Jews found in possessions *large enough to be classified as for distributary purposes...* or simply, in possession, is to be *summarily executed* in public as a deterrent – no KZ, just SiPo interrogation and then, it's your call; hand them over to an army firing squad or publicly hang them yourselves at the discretion of the SD squad commander in question. Dr Six, if this is to occur in London which is by far the largest population centre and the expected hub of decadence; I would like you to handle such an affair *personally*."

"Understood, Herr Reichsprotektor..." Six nodded, the response Heydrich expected from his unctuous underling.

"Good," Heydrich nodded. "This applies to all present and those you delegate squads' commands to. The rationed Pervitin pills issued to our troops are exempt; all other substances used recreationally however, are *not*. Cannabis, and any psychoactive narcotic, be it mescaline from the peyote cactus, hallucinogenic fungi, all of it; *Napoleon* banned it, and so do *I*. Europe and our peoples will not permit the wholesale descent to lunatic degeneracy; these so-called free-thinking liberal sodomites and Jew-poisoned, pornographic-minded Bacchians..."

Nebe caught Müller's eye across the gleaming table with deliberate, lingering insolence. Heydrich was notorious for alcohol-fuelled orgies, and wild nights out that often resulted in violence, depravity and barbaric retribution arranged for any and all who happened to fatefully cross him. After a long career as a policeman that predated the Nazi rise to power, the grey-haired, hook-nosed Nebe knew more than most the truth regarding such substances and alcohol, and which intoxicant it was that was more likely to render its users amenable to aggression and immoral behaviour, let alone 'degeneracy' and 'decadence.' And, for that matter, he knew all-too-well what Heydrich was like, regardless of what chemical compounds were in his system. Nebe doubted that use of any drug, even the *degenerate Bacchian* ones, would be enough to purge the man's relentless cruelty.

Müller, himself a policeman prior to Gestapo duties, returned the gaze with an amused, knowing malice. Nebe smiled genially, the skin bunching above his huge, hooked nose, and he turned back to face their chief.

"As to the legal framework," Heydrich continued, enjoying himself, "happily the Führer's military command i.e. *the army* will oversee the necessary legislation being passed – at *least* until the new government is formally approved, and arrangements are made with Berlin, i.e. the Führer and the Reichsmarschall. They will also accommodate our 'Mahatma Propagandhi', Reichsminister Goebbels..."

There was sniggering again. Many at the table feared and loathed Heydrich like the Black Death, and avoided him as they would a leper; his Machiavellian, predatory nature was well-known and whispered of. Today, though, held in his relative favour as he basked in new and awesome authority, they were all slowly warming to him. *That*, and the exquisite buffet, of course. Sometimes, it paid to be in such company.

The humour helped mask the ruthlessness of his naked ambition.

Heydrich paused, noting the body language and reactions of the SS commanders, and with the supreme confidence of an unchallenged leader, broke from his speech. A leisurely pause for thought, and the swollen security chief resumed speaking.

"Yes, the good Doctor... and the necessary campaign of public enlightenment on this and other such matters. They will offer the honeyed and veiled words alike, providing the paperwork, and the Reich Security Office will, as ever, serve as the iron fist behind policy. As we are the dustbin of the Reich, we must become the cleansing agent and dustbin of England, the machine into which enemies will be thrown and come out mincemeat. Clear?"

"Clear, Reichsprotektor," several of the men returned. The ones who remained silent were glared at by Müller, each in turn. The Austrian Brigadier held the Gestapo department chief's gaze, and neither looked away for some seconds before Müller grinned. The silent, animalistic challenge was subtle, but Heydrich wryly noted the exchange.

"Hopefully the English don't persist in the folly of opposing the anti-Jewish measures. On a similar note; for tactical reasons, while escalating these important tasks, *we should not be too overt or public at all times* so as to not provoke our natural allies the English into revolt as opposed to alliance, particularly in the event of a prosecution of a final showdown with international Jewry and Judeo-Bolshevism in the east."

Joachim Peiper, who had remained present as Himmler's liaison, broke in.

"Regardless of balance, if I may Herr Reichsprotektor, once undesirables are eliminated their families and friends will be stirred up to a hatred of Germany, if it doesn't already exist—"

"We will not expect to be popular among the populace if our actions are overtly extreme and public in *all* matters, so I would expect a certain amount of discernment and balance, in light of England's place alongside Germany in the new order we are setting in the world..." Heydrich's response was delivered fast and smooth, and he rose to pace the room, intoxicated by his dictatorial power. "No wanton bloodletting; we must let the economy thrive, the populace come to terms with the new order and the establishment of a certain amount of trust as we have found in willing elements in France; let only Jewish, masonic or otherwise overwhelmingly subversive elements that are to be victim of SS justice become public spectacle, the rest dealt with quietly behind closed doors or in the extra-legal framework of the concentration camps. This is how things will be."

Beats of silence. The Reichsprotektor continued.

"One final note on this, however; all two thousand plus entries *remaining* in the Sonderfahndungsliste Great Britain, those not personally exonerated by myself such as Halifax, are to be treated with *extreme prejudice,* and sent the way of the Brigadeführer's camps if not executed in our care... and if resistance is met and arrest made difficult, arbitrary execution is permitted – made as painful for the undesirable as and where is possible."

"Including women, Herr Obergruppenführer?" Peiper asked, frowning.

Heydrich glared at him. "Regarding the latter point, at the discretion of the arresting agents and their command. I don't see any *overwhelming evidence* that Virginia Woolf and her ilk should be... *relentlessly* tortured... but if they meet their end during arrest or en route to detention facilities, I'm sure that neither the Führer will consider anything untoward about the affair, nor will the KZ commandants or guards complain about having one or several less mouths to feed and bunks to watch."

Dr Rudolf Lange suddenly spoke, his deep voice as coarse and brutal as Müller's, belying his education and erudite nature.

"Regardless of gender, extreme prejudice to Jews and subversives. That is the brief, Herr Hauptstürmführer Peiper. We must defeat the better angels of our nature."

Heydrich nodded approvingly at his protégé. "Indeed. Dr Six and Dr Lange here are more than aware of this following our meetings in Berlin, but for those not present at Prinz-Albrecht Strasse, allow me to explain..."

He rose, and began circling the table. "We will encounter many different types of our Saxon brother and enemy alike here in Great Britain. Firstly, the racial equal who is favourably disposed towards National Socialism and the Reich; as is happening with British soldiers and *re-education*, this is to create our true brotherhood and establish the Thousand Year Reich. Secondly, the racial equal who is *not* favourably disposed towards we Germans or the Party and our policies; these are to be quietly eliminated, firstly – if non-violent and uninvolved in partisan action, by internment and re-education, or if otherwise, their violence will meet with a violent end via the SS."

"Just to clarify Herr Reichsprotektor, severity to be determined on a case-by-case basis, following interrogation as and when is possible?" Dr Six asked.

"Yes."

"Can you explain, Herr Reichsprotektor?" Schellenberg asked.

Heydrich looked at him, deeply irritated.

"... *Yes*, Walther. Notable cases, Dr Six is to personally deal with and decide upon; non-significant arrests are purely security police prerogative; cases constituting a *Threat To The Reich* or of otherwise of major significance is *my* remit, to be passed on with immediate effect... moving on... *Thirdly*, with racial inferiors who have infected this island the same as they nested like vipers in our country, the parasitic Jew or otherwise racial *untermensch* who are *favourably* disposed towards the German Reich..."

He cast a disdainful look at the table, and Müller provided him the reaction he was looking for in the form of a disgusted, disbelieving snort. Eichmann, too, paused from studying the varied *Einsatzgruppe* reports to look suitably bemused.

"...These... *people*... I use the term loosely... once registered, and scanned for infractions, are to be used as an auxiliary civil and security sub-service under our watchful eye for the maintenance of stability, much like the racially equal Anglo-Saxon British fascists... assuming they are not guilty of any overt crimes for which we can pass them over to the camp system, or special interrogation.

Heydrich returned to his seat, and for the first time whilst in an important meeting, lit a cigarette. Eichmann and Schellenberg stared at their chief, in something approaching shock. The Reichsprotektor inhaled deeply with pleasure, releasing rings of smoke, and letting the rest out in smaller whisps.

When he spoke, it was with his trademark urgency and forcefulness.

"We can iron out the wrinkles of this issue in *later years,* when the burgeoning New Order has been established in all German and British territories from the Americas to Africa to the Far East. This period is for the establishment of a new system in England that is amenable to the Reich, which will further the aims and goals of our influence in the continents which we cannot occupy by force. The Führer," he said, letting his evocation sink in, "... *explicitly* stated to myself and... to me, at the Berghof, that this is the most pressing issue currently facing the Greater Reich. Understood?"

Murmurs of assent.

"*Fourth*, and last, the racial inferior who looks upon the German Reich as the rat-catcher of European culture that it is, are unfavourably disposed towards us and the elimination of such people is to be the most public and severe meting out of justice seen here in Great Britain as with everywhere else. No mercy, no secrecy, destroy racial enemies with maximal vengeance who are also actively working against the interests of the Reich, from sabotage to resistance, armed or otherwise, through media and black propaganda, economy, whatever it may be. Destroy all cancer without mercy."

"Understood, Herr Reichsprotektor," they cried in unison.

"Our treatment of these four types will be written into lore. In some parts of the world, perhaps in history books – depending who writes them – a certain amount of opprobrium may be attached to our names and our work, but of course, such hypocrisy fails under measured scrutiny. From Britain's Empire builders such as Cecil Rhodes, and the murderous viceroys who bled downtrodden colonies of their resources, to our own Kaiser's imperial policies in Africa, to the French Revolution and beyond; harsh measures of oppression have often been used to further and strengthen the civilisation of the race as a whole. It is social science. Revolutionary times call for revolutionary actions, and in time, the harsh nature is forgotten for the results they bring. *The ends justify the means.* Objectively, there can be no such censure attributed to our work, and the coming generations will vindicate us wholly."

Silence. Heydrich smiled his full-lipped predator's smile.

"Gentlemen, soon we will enjoy the culture, sophistication and charm of this great city without its detritus. A Jew-free London with no racial or political undesirables, can you imagine? There is a true appreciation of culture here; I will greatly enjoy travelling to the finest concertos and operas that the married trio of London, Paris and Berlin have to offer; one of the TRUE achievements of our cause. A Greater German Reich into which Jew-free London, Paris and Berlin are incorporated. And that will be our victory, the total victory of the SS, and of Germany, and of the *Thousand Year Reich*."

He rose to his feet, and this time, every other officer present leapt to theirs. Fourteen right arms shot outwards.

"Heil Hitler!" Heydrich shouted, his long, pale face suddenly flushed.

"Heil Hitler!"

The men trailed towards the door. Heydrich watched them go, armed with his orders, and he thrilled to imagine the role in the world's new order that he now filled. It enraptured him. Logic quickly replaced his daydream, and almost as an afterthought, Heydrich yelled at the receding figures of the SS command, his high-pitched nasal tone returning, stopping them dead in their tracks.

"Memorise any notes you have taken during this meeting, and then before you sleep tonight, make sure they have been destroyed."

10pm. It was unlike operations in Germany, striking at the onset of dawn, or in the blackness of night, enveloped by the darkness of the early hours. The English winter evening was no less dark, but had been chosen.

Cigarette tips glowed in the back of the military trucks; ten men in each. They wore SS field gear, blank patch and SD sleeve diamond in place, submachine guns at their feet. Several inspected their pistols. All were more than acquainted with such raids; some had participated in the great burning raids of Poland, leaving whole villages and towns in flames and shooting the swinish peasantry as and when they decided. The grey platoon was an *Einsatzkommando*; the prospect of wholesale murder did not appal its men.

As they reached the approach to York on the A64 at Askham Bryan, two of the trucks peeled away, heading northwards to the upper districts. The first truck rolled on, smoothly hurtling forwards on its grim mission.

Behind it, a Mercedes Benz followed in the first truck's wake.

"Not far now, Oberführer," Heinz Jost remarked.

"We will arrive in less than five minutes. Guy Fawkes Inn is right next to the York Minster, would you believe, Brigadeführer."

Jost smirked. "Perhaps Heydrich will attach some quasi-religious sentiment to the occasion. Part of the Reich's spiritual crusade against the godless forces that oppose it."

Schöngarth grinned at that. "After all these years attacking the Church, even with its support of fascism throughout Europe... and the meeting tomorrow with Göring and the Tommies! General Hangman will have a smirk on his face tonight like a Cheshire cat that just got the cream."

"Won't he *just*, Oberführer."

"Well anyway, our friend Eric, or 'George' obviously attached some symbolic significance to it, Brigadeführer," Schöngarth observed. Jost murmured an affirmation, pondering the man they were after.

Due to orders from on high, the two men found themselves at the back of an SS Mercedes together, driven by an enlisted trooper from Nebe's outfit, collaborating in a mission as part of the overall crackdown Heydrich announced that day in London, a major clearing up operation for the Einsatzkommandos before personnel could be sent east. Heydrich tasked Nebe, who passed it to his deputy commander Jost, humiliating both with the reminder of their positions, and to add to the ignominy, demanded that SD Chief Northern Zone Schöngarth participate in 'a mission of vital significance.' Jost had to swallow his pride.

While the Brigadier-General and the Senior-Colonel Schöngarth got along well enough, it was another typical Heydrich move, in that while Kripo chief Nebe was stuck in the role of *Gruppe Manchester* commander while the lesser ranked Dr Six ran London and was chief coordinator for Britain, Jost – who shared Six's rank, and held a senior position in the SD – was stuck as a mere deputy-commander of a *Gruppe* under Nebe, a humiliation befitting the long-time associate of Heydrich's estranged former deputy, Werner Best.

Schöngarth was outranked just one notch lower in the SS-SD hierarchy; a senior colonel, having been promoted *thrice* from major in only fifteen months, but he was *Acting SD Chief of the Northern Zone*. The same hand that held Jost down, pushed up the ruthless, clever man sat beside him. And be it one rank inferior, or three; Schöngarth's favoured position was humiliating for the Brigadier nonetheless. Jost had been a Brigadeführer when SD *Kommandant Nord*

Schöngarth was a mere lieutenant. At least, Jost conceded, the man is educated and bearable, like Nebe. Had Heydrich placed one of the more thuggish types from Gestapo or Kripo as their nominal northern overseer, or a foolish INTERPOL bureaucrat, Jost may have been compelled to risk conspiring against the all-powerful policeman.

The small convoy reached the inner city districts, and passed by the ancient city wall.

"*Jorvik*, Brigadeführer," Schöngarth noted. Jost nodded, thoughtfully.

"The Saxons... the Vikings... and now the SD continues the Germanic legacy of Yorkshire."

Schöngarth laughed at that, his voice granular, contrasting with an occasional eloquence. "I'll have to base myself nearer to your commando, Herr Brigadeführer. Outside of Dr Lange and a few assorted SD in Leeds, most of the SS around here would have no idea who the Saxons *were*. Typical slack-jawed Orpo bulls and Kripo sniffers. Even in Gestapo back in '35, I never heard so many banal conversations about fucking *this* woman, torturing *that* Jew. Not that persecuting Hebrews or catching hold of a *schnuckiputzi* lacks merit but Christ... some intelligent conversation should not be too much to expect, no?"

"Quite."

"With Dissident #1 in custody, we'll have earned a drink anyway, Brigadeführer, perhaps you could show me the little after hours drinking hole you boys have got set up in Manchester? I'm in no rush to get back to Leeds and the likes of that Amon Goeth character. Christ, some of these bastards should be in Poland policing the Jew ghettos, the way they are... they're not fit to be in society."

Jost laughed himself, a deep rumble that began in his chest, spilling out through his oesophagus and escaping his long, set mouth. "Sounds like you need the break. Come over, there's no shortage of wine and women in our neck of the woods. And with old Arthur in command, only the most civilised coppers in Kripo and the SS are hanging around our Manchester drinking holes..."

Schöngarth joined in the laughter; his own harsh and guttural, utterly belying his background and education. Outside, it was a familiar picture of nocturnal German operation; the northern English countryside had been a tranquil sea of black, and the human settlements dozing in peaceful slumber. Crickets chirped, in an otherwise eerie still. The convoy stole on through the night.

As they penetrated deeper into the small city, well within the city limits of the old settlement, appreciative murmurs escaped German lips at the sight of the walls. History, in particular that of the 'Aryan' blood groups in northwestern Europe was of course exalted beyond all else in the new German Reich. It was that history that demanded a Germanic present.

The group rounded the narrow corner of St Leonard's Square, which was entirely deserted with the curfew in effect, beyond the fluttering of some pigeons in the shadows. Had there been human life present, it would have disappeared at the approach of motorised vehicles; the sound of vehicles being driven at night meant Germans, or at the outside best, the unfortunate local police, instructed to prowl by their foreign overlords. Special permits were granted to designated drivers on logistical jobs that were deemed necessary, allowing for night travel within set parameters. Beyond that, only the occupiers were to be found in the dark.

Cruising past the square, the SS turned at High Petergate, barely squeezing through the narrow opening in the ancient Roman wall and down the narrow street. Fifty metres along, the road widened into a square, with the great York Minster cathedral planted majestically to their left, its great west front towering over them, a huge colossus of magnesium limestone; gothic spires and grand architectural design drawing appreciative stares from the two SD officers.

A small grass square and Great War memorial stood to their right; and two narrow streets forked out alongside the famed cathedral's southern flank, separated by a small church building in its shadow. They slowed to a halt, adjacent to the smaller building on the open area at the Minster's base.

Jost got out of the car, quick to take lead in the operation.

"Out, boys look lively! This way"

The troops purposefully disembarked, forming something like a phalanx. Schöngarth, watching, mused that the young men had not seen active combat, merely clean-up jobs, and this was their playing warrior in the dark square of the York Minster. He resolved to tell Heydrich, perhaps draw an approving smile from that pale, mocking face.

Jost marched past the small church building to the second street squeezed between the minster's southern base and the War Memorial Square, to what was almost the first doorway of the long terrace row. *Number 27, High Petergate.* A plaque on the window helpfully proclaimed 'Guy Fawkes, Born Here 1570."

Jost went to hammer the door, and then, thinking better of it, stepped aside. One small gesture with his head, and the stormtrooper behind him kicked the door through, the SS men swarming into the building, yelling loud enough to wake the dead.

Jost and Schöngarth, grinning ear-to-ear, entered the building after them, listening as the troops emptied rooms of the lesser dissident's not fitting the description of their great prize.

In one room they found a typewriter, and stacks of dissident leaflets, some of which they had seen before, having been distributed far and wide across the northern zone, ruminating on German atrocities and extolling the populace to rebel. Worse still, in another room they found communist paraphernalia, a Star gun as used by the anti-fascist International Brigades in Spain, and even a CPGB card.

On the second floor, Jost and Schöngarth stomped past the shrieking figures being violently beaten and hauled from the other rooms, their jackboots thumping on the polished wood as they marched to the furthest door back from the stairs. There, sat bolt upright in the four-poster bed with three machine guns trained on him, in a tastefully decorated room, they found their man.

"Eric Blair," Jost demanded, almost triumphantly.

The man sighed, his neatly-parted hair dishevelled but the pencil-moustache and almost schoolmasterly features identified him to his thrilled captors. He saw the hopelessness in his situation, instead lighting a cigarette in response, sucking in the smoke with rueful gusto as though it was his last. "Viva libertad…" he intoned wistfully, as though to himself.

"Take the swine," Jost told the men in German.

Four hands seized hold of George Orwell, and dragged him, still in his nightgown, out to the street, peppering him with vicious shots and cruel blows all the way. The writer refused to cry out in pain; until the multitude of painful blows rendered him all-but senseless, and a series of more methodical, calculated strikes from his tormentors elicited agonised moans through gritted teeth.

Jost took one last, lingering look at the great Minster, framed against the starry sky over England, before unconsciously letting out a small noise of amused triumph, and stepping back into the Mercedes with Schöngarth. They grinned at each other on the backseat, glowing, thrilled with success. Heydrich would be delighted.

~

In Manchester, Nebe's other commando rolled up on a quiet Denton terrace, and field grey stormtroopers quietly disembarked the cross marked trucks to the cobbles. Doors were kicked off hinges at houses 2, 6, 10 and 11, and several inhabitants were hauled out kicking and screaming. SS men in black ran rampant, gurning manically as they tore through the homes of the damned, methamphetamine-wired to an intense, grim focus from the Pervitin pills. Terrified civilians were dragged from their beds and savagely beaten. One man spat at his SD tormentor; a brute drafted from the Hamburg Gestapo into the Action Groups, who responded instantly by firing into both kneecaps of the Mancunian. The gunshots and resulting screams of pain saw the rest of the street's curtains open, and the shocked and horrified eyes of the estate looked out, watching the grim spectacle as their neighbours were hauled away.

A lieutenant approached the enlisted Gestapo thug, bristling in his own rage, and he slapped the furious trooper hard across his face.

"Idiot! This isn't Poland! Put him in the truck, Fritz."

The surly Gestapo man complied, unkindly hauling the bleeding man up and into captivity. All resistance, however, had been knocked out of his fellow arrestees on the loud reports from the Walther PP, and the agonised yells of his thrashing anguish.

With business concluded at all four addresses, the men of *EK1 Manchester* rolled westwards to the next street on their list, in Moss Side, south of the centre. Further west, the men of EK3M were on a silent prowl of intent in a hunt through Salford and Trafford. Terraced streets became herding grounds of the terrified, as scared civilians were seized and frogmarched into whatever hell the Germans had that awaited them.

Close to headquarters, one truck deposited a group of frightened women in the building, where clinically efficient office staff took charge of them, leading the terrified, pleading group down to the holding cells. Bloodstained floors and chains only heightened the abject terror they felt.

Elsewhere, designated anti-tank ditches were located in the usual places – fields on the city outskirts and beyond – and machine gun fire spelled the end of hundreds more designated Enemies of the Reich; resistance real, false and imagined alike. Men, women and children, cut from the prime of their youth and sent crashing to the cold earth, spilling crimson as the life blood freely flowed.

"Halt," Amon Goeth shouted, stomping through undergrowth that bordered the back of a field near the northern outskirts of Leeds. The ditch behind it explained his presence, along with another group of unfortunates whose luck and time were out. Goeth's men lowered their weapons, wondering what crazed impulse had taken the lieutenant now. Denied his favourite part of the job, the recently demoted Unterscharführer Beckenbaur scowled.

"It is a pleasure, and a privilege," Goeth called out smoothly, his jaw bunching as he stepped over the boggy ground to the edge of the ditch, "... to personally deal with such filth, in the name of the Führer."

He peered at the girl, the first of twelve people stood shivering at the pit's edge, glancing fearfully between the cold mud of their soon-to-be resting place and the cold faces of the men who would put them there. The eye contact was so cruel it burned, but the girl's nerve withstood it. She was a girl of perhaps 21, not long since removed from teenage years. Black hair cascaded untidily down her shoulders, and some was stuck to her tear-streaked face. Her bright eyes were now relatively clear of water, but their piercing energy, and pleading entreaty had no effect whatsoever on the Austrian man who now jutted his brutal face to within inches of hers.

Even through her paralysing terror, she could smell whiskey, and something else unidentifiable on the restlessly aggressive officer's breath; something bitter, yet tinged with a chemical sweetness.

"Say..." Goeth breathed lustily, raising his Luger, "Heil Hitler."

The girl whimpered in fear. Tears trickled down the dirty, streaked flesh of her cheek.

Goeth shrugged, his jaw bunching as he did so, and lowering his officer-issue pistol, the Viennese instead drew a knife with an ostentatious flourish; before she could react, the SS lieutenant began stabbing her repeatedly in the stomach. The cruel blade penetrated her with a sickening sound of metallic blade meeting, and smiting, flesh and bone. As her uncomprehending, terrorised family sank to their knees in a mortified paralysis, utterly gripped by the evil horror, Goeth grinned at them, his teeth bared with churlish, cannibalistic contempt.

"You have the chance for redemption… 'Heil Hitler'… or *that*."

Of the eleven remaining people, four managed to overcome their terror long enough to invoke the name of Germany's leader. Wired on his standard methamphetamine ration, an indecently eager Goeth paced back and forth, revelling in his role as executioner. Having acquiesced to a Hitler salute, the savage Austrian officer shot the poor victims; individual bullets administered between their eyes. Compared to the barbarism suffered by the unfortunate eight, these gunshots were merciful. Even Beckenbaur was relieved each time a shivering, doomed captive managed to blurt out the German salute, instead of simply babbling in fear or mouthing wordlessly in paralysed shock.

In a cold, empty house in the central London district of Bloomsbury, no more than two miles north of Parliament itself, the former Superintendent of the Metropolitan Police John Thomas was sat dumbly in his drab, unclean living room, morosely swigging from a bottle of whiskey that dangled precariously from his swaying right hand.

The rapidly ageing policeman had not been to the Royal Oak in several weeks, leaving the house only to replenish his meagre food supplies, having been in possession of a not-inconsiderable haul of alcoholic liquors and spirits amassed in the days before rationing, in the days before war, in the days of peace. It showed. Two weeks without shaving had seen his stubble grow out into an unkempt mass of straggly hair. The once dashing mop that adorned his head was now a similarly wild, tangled mess that sat without shape above his haggard face and its sunken eyes, the waxy complexion of a vampire. The striking comparison to Bill Wilson was unavoidable, he noted mirthlessly on the sole occasion he had bothered checked a mirror in those empty, long days and weeks.

Almighty was the crash of the door, as a gang of uniformed German thugs tore into the room, but John Thomas did not react. It was a moment he had lived out in his dreams and imagination for as long as he cared to remember, and as the Germans began to discuss the grim spectacle of his ruined, high-smelling home amongst themselves, the Scotland Yard man merely raised the whiskey bottle to his lips to down the last of its pungent contents. He did not even look at them.

In the depths of his drunken stupor, Thomas reflected that he had been a policeman all his life, yet the new form of this role was utterly perplexing. Despite himself, he allowed a sense of gratitude to seep through that while the police of the New Order were here to arrest him, at least he did not have to be part of their system. As a lifelong policeman, he denied them that much.

So weak and malnourished was he – once a strong, powerful man of action – that when the troops grabbed him to haul him away to his fate, the overzealous seizure saw the right arm of John Thomas snap cleanly in the hand of his SS tormentor. The German, youthful in his early twenties, had to hide his disgust from his fiercely amused *kameraden* as they dragged their pitiful prey to the truck.

Any flagged names; any suspected beyond reasonable doubt; all those whom had survived the initial purge, before the Wehrmacht's relative peaceful occupation… all were seized, in the blackness of that evening, vanished from their lives, under *Night and Fog*.

In the French barracks of St George no.5 that night, the men were sat smoking, some tenderly inspecting their wounds from the escape attempt, others merely nursing injured pride. James Wilkinson sat alone, chain-smoking on his bunk in the corner, brooding quietly.

The door opened, and Lieutenant Hoffman entered, with slight hesitance.

Usually, the man's likeable charm had thus far been enough to encourage some kind of good-natured banter being sent his way on arrival, men choosing to overlook his SS uniform. Providing alcohol and cigarettes – good ones – in copious quantities did little to lessen the esteem he was held in. But not on this day. The impotence of the men and their resentment of the day's events repressed all prevailing goodwill they had towards the Obersturmführer from Munich.

The big Bavarian looked to his immediate right at the nearest bunks to him, where the Sergeant, James Fletcher, Brian and Tommy were all propped against the back wall, reading quietly on their bunks. For an hour, none had been inclined to speak.

"Sarge," Hoffman began, using the English phrase. "The major would like to see you, with your permission."

"With his permission," Tommy echoed sarcastically, though his voice was hollow. "*Sarge*? You want to turn him down, Stan. Bollocks to his games."

However, Hitchman nodded. "Very well, Lieutenant. Very well."

Without further ado, he rose to his feet and marched proudly outside, straight-backed, to where two enlisted SS men escorted him away. Hoffman, however, remained behind.

"Tommy…"

The cockney resented being singled out for an entreaty. His eyes did not rise from the book, but he could feel an almost accusatory stare coming from some of the other men in the bunk, whose anti-German feelings were running particularly high after the incident with the escapees, Stanley and Major Wolf.

"Tommy, Brian, James, and you, Wilkinson over there in that corner, and *all* of you, look; this morning was an unfortunate affair but it's just the way things are."

"Just the way things are," Tommy intoned.

He finally looked up from his book, to see Hoffman standing passively with his hands raised. The SS officer looked so earnest that many of the men shelved their hostility towards the man who so constantly replenished their tobacco stores, and brought booze and music to their lives in camp. In hundreds and hundreds of hours spent together, as serving men, they also believed in his genuine nature. Hoffman, they had almost unanimously agreed, was a soldier of their ilk. His honesty was consistent.

Tommy sighed. "Sit on the fucking bed, Lieutenant Jerry."

Hoffman sat down, grinning. "*I* give the orders around here, Private Tommy, or so they tell me. Lieutenant Nonsenseführer Hoffenbaden or whatever you swine say."

That drew some low chortles. The gentle approach made détente possible again, and Hoffman relaxed again in the British room. The SS-Obersturmführer took out his cigarette case, lighting one. He did not need to offer one to Tommy, nor any of the others present; their own supplies were plentiful enough, thanks to him.

"Stanley is a brave man," he volunteered, exhaling smoke.

"Yeah, he is."

Several of the others pitched in, in affirmation. Hoffman noted the pride in their voices.

"Do you Tommies have a code against cowardice in your army?"

James Fletcher opened and closed his mouth, deciding against his own answer. Several murmured answers contradicted each other, and Fletcher shrugged. He looked over to Tommy, who considered.

"I reckon so, yeah. I mean, they shot deserters in the Great War, which only ended twenty-something years ago. And I daresay they'd 'ave shot us lot if we'd bunked off in France."

Hoffman frowned. "Bunked off?"

"Deserted. Had it on our toes. Done a runner. Ran away. Left the war like cowards, against our orders to fight."

"Ah. Retreat without orders. Yes, that does make sense. You cannot conquer half the world if you are cowards."

They all looked at him, uncertain. He had a glint in his eye.

"Meaning the British Empire. That spirit is needed now. Cowards cannot save us from the menace of this world. The terror that threatens western civilisation, and has done since 1917."

James Wilkinson, who had not so much as acknowledged Hoffman's presence in his far corner of the room, audibly snorted at that. He could hear the conversation quite clearly, the room being otherwise completely silent.

Hoffman turned, looking over at the British soldier, his nose wrinkled with distaste. Reclined on his bunk reading Goethe's *Faust*, his ever-lengthening hair now straddling his cheeks and with twirls of cigarette smoke drifting over his head, the Yorkshireman resembled a posing artist or aspiring writer rather than a *bread-and-butter* northern caveman, as he was painted.

"Do you disagree, Wilkinson?" Hoffman asked, with supreme disdain.

The Yorkshireman snuffed out his cigarette, and immediately lit another, all the keeping his eyes fixed on the book.

"Yeah."

"*What* do you disagree *about*, exactly?"

"Communism. Only rich people and Nazis hate it."

"Oh," Hoffman snarled. "So with all the millions dead in Russia, the slaughter of anyone who happened to own something of value, Civil War, the unrest that spread to Germany, riots in our streets, the killing of National Socialists, poisoning Spain, infecting France, the slaughter of Christians, the burning of churches, the Jews at its head leading it, the corruption in Russia, the invasions of the Baltic States from Stalin and the millions of people he has killed... *millions*... and this is not something to hate?"

The German shook his head in genuine wonder. James looked up from the book at him, calmly.

"Yeah. They invaded Poland, too. *With you.*"

"Yes, they invaded Poland," Hoffman stormed. "For no reason. With a stupid pact with us that means–"

But he stopped himself. He would not insult the Führer's decisions, even if he had allied with Russia. It was all part of the plan. Everybody knew that they would have the final showdown with the Judeo-Bolsheviks, if not next year, then the one after it.

"Yes," he said with greater calm. "But they had no reason to fight Poland. We lost soil and blood. We had German people cut off from the Fatherland, we had East Prussia separated, we lost land that had millions of German people still living there, persecuted by the Polish populace."

"Yeah," said James, hardly caring. "And the Jewish communists who run Russia that you've been chelping about are your allies. You'll say owt, you lot."

He glanced up, before returning to his book. "Goethe. He was a good German. Interesting stuff, this, about selling your soul…"

Hoffman scowled, and turned away, ignoring him.

"Regardless of what that *dumkopf* thinks…" he said crossly, thumbing a gesture back towards James Wilkinson, who snorted scornfully. Hoffman sneered back, and then resumed, "They must be stopped at all costs. They are in Lithuania, Latvia, they attacked Finland for no reason, they have troops across the Baltics and Poland… they already border Germany with East Prussia from Lithuania and the Polish separation boundary; they have massive deployments facing the countries they *haven't* invaded yet…"

He shook his head, shuddering with very real revulsion. The English watched him, considering his words.

"Can you imagine what a peasant army with tanks and bombs would do? They are crushing East Poland, purging intellectuals. Millions die in their own country for no reason. In Spain they were burning churches, executing priests. Truly disgusting…" Hoffman grimaced. "Germany is not alone. Other countries see the danger. I only hope that the Wehrmacht, SS and countries allied in the struggle are ready before the Soviet armies are…"

Sucking his cigarette thoughtfully, he lapsed into silence, imagining millions of Russian soldiers pouring into East Prussia and German-occupied Poland, heading straight for Berlin and the vulnerable heart of the Reich. Three hundred Soviet divisions, swarming into Europe like the Vandals; iconoclastic destruction and slaughter to follow.

The door at the end of the long corridor in the main building was open, and Stanley Hitchman was ushered as far as it before Major Wolf strode out from around his desk to greet the man he had held a gun to just a few short hours before.

"Sergeant Hitchman, how wonderful you have come, sir."

"Major," Stanley said, rather stiffly.

Jochen Wolf smiled, something of the wolf still in his handsome, hard face, and he politely gestured towards the large and comfortable sofa that lined one side of the spacious room. Hitchman sat in it, and Wolf took an armchair that faced it, on the other side of a glass table, and at the same eye level as his guest. He had relaxed his usually impeccable SS dress attire; the tunic was unbuttoned, sans medals, and after refusing twice, Hitchman finally relented to the major's insistent offer of coffee. He was privately glad when it came. *Real*, milky coffee with quality beans, not the ersatz typical in wartime, for civilians and soldiers alike. These were real beans. The aroma alone delighted him, and he openly inhaled the rising whiffs of vapour with naked relish.

"Enjoy, Sergeant," Wolf smiled. "You have most certainly earned that drink."

Major Wolf was quite unhesitant, as well as unrepentant, regarding broaching the topic of the incident of the day. Hitchman privately admired his enormous confidence and ease; the unnatural poise with which he carried himself, exuding gravitas. Even in military circles, the man had tremendous dash.

"Thank you, Herr Major," he replied, observing the German title.

Wolf frowned slightly, and then smiled. "That is Wehrmacht, my good man. In the SS we don't use the traditional 'Herr', just rank titles. You will find the SS is the new, less pretentious army of the *new* Germany. The aristocratic East Prussians and cold fish officer corps that make up the Wehrmacht will one day cease to exist as we know it…" he scrutinised Stanley for a moment, and then smiled. "The SS will absorb them. But each man will have to prove himself, as a defender of Saxon, and *European* culture itself…"

Stanley digested this information quietly. He was sure the Wehrmacht High Command would have something to say about that. Not to mention Party members to whom the SS leadership was abhorrent. Would, and could, anyone under Adolf Hitler be truly happy if Heinrich Himmler were granted that much authority?

The earlier incident prevented Stanley from speaking his mind. He had resolved to keep any inflammatory opinions and observations to himself during the long walk to Wolf's office.

"Are you all right," Wolf pressed, affecting concern.

"Well I must say," Stanley began tentatively, ignoring the query and smacking his lips, "it's one hell of a bloody brew you have here, Major. Where on *earth* did you *find* this coffee?"

The major waved his hand, dismissively. "I'll secure you a batch of beans. Feel free to share with your men, as I suspect you would choose to in any case. Obviously you are very much a – what do you say, *team player*? Today proved that beyond a doubt."

Hitchman looked at him curiously. Wolf grinned.

"You are a good man, Untersturmführer Hitchman. I shall call you that now; consider yourself informally promoted, it translates as a lieutenant, second class.

Though there is nothing second class about your sense of duty. You know…" and Major Wolf rose from his seat, waving Hitchman back down as he started to get up too. "Relax, Untersturmführer, sit. *Duty* and kinship with those of your blood is exactly what National Socialism is all about. And I choose to honour you, Lieutenant, with a lofty promotion, albeit honorary, because more so than some Prussian clown pining for the Kaiser or Frederick the Great, or one of your own posh Sandhurst types and *stiff-upper lip King and Country* gentlemen, YOU embody the true officer."

The major stood behind his chair, planting both hands on top of it and gazing with admiration at the thoroughly nonplussed Stanley Hitchman.

"You are an educated man, which is good. But though you speak like one such person, you are not a posh, plutocratic type, or you would not have offered yourself as the sacrifice. *You* are a soldier, a *warrior*, as well as an educated man. You are like me."

"I am an educated man," Stanley conceded. "That much is true."

"And you have a kinship with your men? A sense of *honour* and duty. You fight for what – not for the King, not *you*… for British culture? Western civilisation?"

Frowning, Stanley considered. "You could very well say that, Major, yes. I love my country."

"And western civilisation?" the Major pressed, a slight frown adding small lines to the smooth skin of his younger forehead.

"As opposed *to*?"

Wolf shrugged carelessly. "Militant Islamic regimes and Sharia law. The Japanese Emperor and his military government. Soviet communism under Stalin. Siberian labour camps and collectivisation. Other civilisations, with different systems and different peoples…"

"Yes."

SS-Major Wolf sat back down, an expression of concern playing across his features.

"Then why, Herr Hitchman, would you fight against Germany? Is there not a close kinship between our countries? Your own King and royal family are part German, are they not? Or at least for the most part? Did not Germanic Saxon blood take root on the Britannic isle? Did our tribes not intermingle? Is our white, northern European racial blood type not the same? Are we not the bulwark of the greatest civilisation the world has ever known – from the literature and philosophy of Shakespeare, Goethe, Nietzsche, Smith, Kant, Marlowe… with Kant excepted, perhaps." He smiled. "In science, music…"

"Genocidal imperialism," Stanley observed, and instantly regretted it.

"Genocidal?"

"Mass-murder. Murderous. Destructive."

Wolf's eyes narrowed. "Don't be flippant. An educated man should be more aware than all others regarding the greatness of our civilisation. Do you not agree? Do you not love it? Why would you fight *Germany*?"

Hitchman was thoroughly confused. "I suppose so, yes. And I cannot answer you."

"Be honest," Wolf snapped, firmly.

"I... well, we thought it was right. We appeased you at Munich, and you continued attacking, killing, conquering. Hitler – you – were aggressive. Rhineland, Sudetenland, Prague, Poland – where would it end?"

Wolf smiled. "From a warrior of the world's largest empire, this hypocrisy is invalid. And after Versailles, after French-Algerian occupation of our main industrial area and the degradations and punishment exacted, and the land stolen from us, the chaos and instability inflicted on us... no, *Stanley*."

"Your invasion of Poland was a lie, and a fabrication," Stanley retorted, a little sharper himself now. In the slightly sweet-smelling room, Wolf again smiled his infuriating little grin, eyes narrowing pleasantly, like an avuncular figure with a tolerant twinkle in his eye for an amusing nephew.

"You obeyed orders because we invaded Poland."

"Yes."

"Did the barbarian Russians not invade, also? They are not a western civilisation. They are communists, and millions upon millions of people have died under their system."

"Well..." Stanley began hesitantly, taken aback, "I ah... Major Wolf, I really would not care to comment on that particular development, if that's quite all right sir." Hitchman's tone was unmistakeably disapproving.

Wolf grinned again. "Relax, Stanley, if I may call you Stanley. This is not an interrogation. I have the deepest respect for you as an *officer*, which in my eyes you most certainly are."

Stanley sank back further into his seat, purposefully relaxing his gait. Wolf nodded.

"Good. Now I would like to speak to you on military matters."

Wolf rounded the chair, and once more sank into its comfort. Hitchman watched him recline in it, and cast a lingering look around the office. There were the portraits of Hitler and Göring, but beyond that the walls were bare. Yet the items and furniture displayed a certain taste on the part of the major. A fine silver cigarette case was on the desk, sat next to an expensive looking pen and notepad. An adjacent desk sat with a typewriter upon it, in perfect condition, and various ornaments; one a carved elephant hung with some kind of lapis lazuli decoration. Wolf's medals lay on his desk, immaculately clean and polished. Lastly, but by no means least unusual, on the glass table for couch that Stanley sat on was a copy of Aldous Huxley's *Brave New World*, in English.

All in all, the rather odd room was a fitting den for this strange major of a feared paramilitary armed force.

"Interesting book choice," Stanley noted. "I read Huxley."

"And what are your thoughts on the Brave New World of his imagination?" Wolf asked. "Did it *appal* you, or *excite* you?"

Stanley frowned. "It disturbed me."

At that, Wolf began laughing heartily, slapping his knees. It was not done in an unkind, nor malicious manner to Stanley's eyes and ears, which made it all the more confusing. The man seemed genuinely tickled.

"Oh, Sergeant," he chuckled. "To think you are disturbed by it. That is most incredible to me."

"I can't for the *life of me* see why, coming from a soldier of a totalitarian state like yourself, sir," Stanley said stiffly, abandoning his usual politeness and cross at being a source of amusement to the obscenely relaxed major, who was more than a decade younger than he at the least. But at that, Wolf's smile faded, and his eyes narrowed.

"I can see why you would mistakenly think that, Sergeant-major. You are quite possibly thinking that a man such as myself would be disheartened, perhaps *angered* by a provocative work such as this, detailing the complete subjugation of the human individuality and creative spirit. A world in which the desires of the individual are all provided, of docility and lifeless, passive peace. Is that apt?"

Stanley shuffled in his seat. "That did indeed cross my mind."

"You are also," Wolf continued, a trace of the grin returning as he thumbed a cigarette into his thumb and offered one to Stanley, "… considering if my possession of this book contravenes the blacklist of literature my country deems subversive? If it betrays some dissident leaning of the SS Sturmbannführer you see before you… the educated man who speaks such elegant English?"

Stanley said nothing. Wolf's grin once more split his face.

"My dear Untersturmführer, it's incredible to me that you abhor the *Brave New World* because frankly, you *live* in it."

Wisps of cigarette smoke swirled in lingering clouds between them, and beats of silence passed.

"Stanley, your world was, is, and will be, the *Brave New World*. It is inevitable. You are still an imperial power, but you have debrutalised. You have gone soft. The corporate monsters, the plutocrats, the financial kingpins, whatever you want to call them – the Führer and his paladins tend to rely on the catch-all labels of 'Jews' and 'Freemasons' and the like – they are as dominant as they ever have been. Soon, the rampant consumerism of America will be matched shop for shop, street for street in London. Luxury items will corrupt the youth. The wrong drugs, mindless entertainment and an endless sea of indulgence will numb the mind. Banal trivialities will destroy the creative drive of a people. Distraction and comfort. The people will stop challenging, and questioning the leadership and social values; they will lose their will. You will implode in your own softness."

He leaned forwards again, pointing with his cigarette clenched between the same index and middle finger.

"You think *Brave New World* applies to *my* world? That is not so, Herr Hitchman. Say what you will about Hitler, Göring, Goebbels – National Socialist Germany is *hard*. It is strong. It *is* a brave new world, with no irony on the adjective – incidentally, the book is not a forbidden pleasure, though I believe Obergruppenführer Hangman Heydrich would very much like to offer Mr Huxley his warm hospitality; oh, to be a fly-on-the-wall in *that* room."

Wolf grinned at the prospect, lighting another cigarette as he did so and quite pointedly offering it to his English guest, before resuming. "No, Stanley, I find Huxley an interesting man, and a genius in his way. His book is no condemnation of my world; it is a warning to *yours*." The grin faded. "No, you are wrong. Germany *is* a *real*, brave new order; a *crusade*, if you like. There are scapegoats, undeniably true, and some even deserve to be... but lest we forget 1918 and the following decade of unrest, there are very *real* enemies, and we do not dwell in luxury to attain our utopia; we suffer, we fight, and for a future we ourselves will make... not have it simply placed before us by our rulers. We fight and suffer. And in the end, we will triumph."

Still, Stanley said nothing, the still-unsmoked cigarette eating itself away between his fingers. Just who, and what, was he dealing with here?

Major Wolf smiled, relaxing again. "We have enemies, Stanley, but they will be dealt with coldly, with merciless, pitiless strength. *Brave New World* and your Mr Huxley reminds me what it is to lose the meaning in life, to give in to human weakness and to be subverted into insignificance by malevolent powers. Bolshevism is the enemy of Europe, Stanley, not us. The Bolshevik contagion is spreading. When it does, Europe will need all the good men it can get. Strong men, built to lead. Men like you. Not for stupid, pointless wars such as the one your Brave New World and its criminals inflicted on Germany. A real... war of ideology. A battle for survival. The clashing of civilisations, and a crusade against an evil menace..."

Eyes gleaming, Wolf rose to his feet again, and Stanley rose with him. His head was swimming, and he wanted nothing more now than to be away from this curious, curious man.

Major Wolf held his hand out. Sergeant Stanley Hitchman took it, and with a firm grip, the two men locked eyes and shook. Wolf saluted, the classic military three-fingers to the temple. Stanley, after the slightest pause, returned the gesture.

"Until next time, Herr Hitchman."

"Indeed, Mr Sturmbannführer. Indeed."

In the premature darkness of early evening in winter, one hour before the German curfew would come into effect, the group of young anti-fascist freedom fighters were sat huddled in Jack's living room, situated only five minutes' walk from the Royal Oak, just outside the boundaries of Bloomsbury. The flat had once belonged to his Grandmother, and to all intents and purposes it had been left the way it was. Filled with cheap-looking ornaments and threadbare grey carpet, with the slightly musty smell synonymous with dwellings inhabited by old people whose bodily and homely hygiene and cleanliness had come to be neglected, decorating or even slightly improving the chintzy flat was the least of Jack's worries.

For the group, the flat was ideal; Jack was registered as resident here, and a less obviously innocent place could not have been found. Tools, his prized possessions and anything that could remotely implicate him as either a veteran of the defence of the Spanish Republic, or as being remotely undesirable to the occupying powers that be were left at the house that his mother and sister shared. Weapons – guns, the type that could get you killed – were stashed in a cache ready for collection, upon being given the word.

They were all waiting for a moment of dread; from former figure of fun Lord Haw-Haw's much derided '*Jairmany Calling, Jairmany Calling*" propaganda broadcasts from Berlin, the people of the occupied zone – England and Wales – were about to be addressed by Dr Josef Goebbels himself, 'The Mahatma Propagandhi', the Poison Dwarf.

They passed some time in contemplative silence; jolted from their near-reverie by the announcement that Doctor Goebbels was ready to address England, and Britain.

"I bet the little bastard has a special microphone that hangs low enough for him," Alan sneered.

The others laughed, but it was hollow. The 'limping devil', as Germans they had known in Spain had called him, had too much power to be taken anything other than seriously.

Finally, the familiar voice, speaking perfect English in his distinctive clear and cultivated Rhineland voice came through, to which Mary shuddered visibly. She hated the 'evil little beast.' It was as though he was there in the room; theirs, and every other room in the country.

"Good afternoon, England. This is Germany calling.

I am Dr Josef Goebbels, a Minister of the German Reich. I want to talk to you from the very depths of my heart, and with my deep convictions on the problems that we, as Saxon and Nordic, Aryan peoples of a great history and culture, the driving force in the world from literature to philosophy, poetry, science and the arts, that we must overcome together.

I don't know how many millions of people are listening to me tonight, how many English and German people of our blood and shared culture, but I am addressing you all from the bottom of my heart. We alone are blessed with the sophistication, the history and the revolutionary élan to overcome the difficulties and the enemies attacking our civilisation.

Only four months ago, I was compelled to speak to the German people about England, to rouse them to rise up against their Anglo-Saxon brothers and fight due to the declaration of war from its criminal government – the same Jewish-led criminals who advocated use of mustard gas on our troops, in the event they landed on British soil! Only Churchill's forcible removal stopped that plan, by wiser heads that knew the folly of such war crimes against brother Aryans in a war against Jewry and subversive elements working for the destruction of European civilisation!

So thus, I had the grave and repellent task of addressing the German people with words of war, to drive them against the English. Thankfully, the war was not as long, nor as profoundly bitter as the Great War of 1914-1918, a savage conflict inflicted upon all our people's by the Jewish bankers who profited from both sides in the war, and then refused to continue financing the German government and the economy, leading to our country's collapse. The Jewish financiers, filmmakers, press and media giants, arms dealers, transnational corporations and more in London and New York were the only victors of a war in which millions of Aryans on both sides of that European struggle died, and European civilisation was weakened because of it.

What followed was a tragedy of history. Our peoples, natural and ethnic brothers of Aryan blood, were kept at each other's throats; horrible reparations were demanded of Germany, and later, the Jews in international finance once more personally profited by bankrupting countless countries with the Wall Street Crash and an international Depression. Germany was among the worst hit of our glorious nations which had been subjugated by the Jew.

Thankfully, with the triumph of fascism in Italy, with Spain throwing off the shackles of the communist-friendly republic of Jewish freemasonry, and finally as a united people making the historic choice of Jesus Christ over Barabbas, the tables have turned on our oppressors. In Germany, the National Socialist revolution and its brother fascists and Aryan people's across western Europe have struck back at the parasite, and is in a position to fight back against a Judaea that declared war on our people, on our blood.

Italy, Germany, Spain, France, and now England have all been saved, and restored to their rightful place as the rulers of world and European civilisation, led by a revolutionary soldier, the Führer, Adolf Hitler, who first had the foresight and the courage to stand up to the Jew, and was supported in his quest by the grateful people of a nation under attack.

I ask you, my English brothers, to consider what we all must fight for.

Think, on this criminally vulgar asphalt culture that the Jew has imposed on us. Subverting the economy, controlling our banks and our press, poisoning our youth with their degenerate culture; they are the parasitic people that destroy the foundations of great nations. The court Jews who run England's banks and big business; what know they of William Blake's poetic words, the man who spoke of 'building Jerusalem on England's green and pleasant lands.' The green and pleasant land of England – did he envisage banks, and asphalt, concrete and stone? Blake's poem was a metaphor; he spoke of the mass-industrialisation, the smoke and mills destroying England's living space as a curse. All great men appreciate the beauty of our world, and despise those who deny us our living space and rob our national pride."

It was astonishing. Alan, Jack, William and Mary shared sickened glances across the chintzy living room, looks full of dull forbearing. In the Royal Oak, Bill listened dumbly to the ingratiating spiel of Dr Goebbels, while Art stood rooted to the spot; indifferent to the similarly still gait of his regulars, polishing the same spot on a glass as though transfixed. A dangerous enemy indeed, this poisonous propagandist who was speaking like a native of the country, flawlessly, with just enough plausibility to win over the fickle types to his quietly violent ideology. The velvet glove covering fascism's merciless iron fist.

And neither Italy nor Spain could hold a candle to the cold iron of Hitler's take on fascism, with its added racialist worldview and nationalist fanaticism. The dangerous scapegoating and eugenicist policies only heightened its sinister, black shadow engulfing yet more of the world.

Goebbels' soft words continued to purr from the wireless; it made Mary sick to her stomach. She left the room, blanching, but William could not tear himself away from his white-knuckled attachment to the menacing message of Dr Goebbels' broadcast.

"No... the Jew culture is an asphalt culture. The Jew is a partisan of assimilation in the host country only long enough to subvert its culture and spread across its living space like a parasite. You in the picturesque little English village; you may not know the Jew. You have your land, your beautiful village and you are happy. But you do not know the Jew. The parasite operates from the city; once he controls the city, the Jew controls the land. The Jew controls the village. The Jew controls you.

In Germany, I proposed and later, helped enforce the radicalisation of laws which are to be implemented throughout liberated Europe; beyond removing the Jew from our professions, the Reich further strengthened its core in national defence in the banning of Jews from theatres, cinemas, circuses and the like. They are not to share compartments in sleeping cars with Aryans, nor are they to occupy seats on public transport otherwise intended for the rightfully present Aryan, who is in his own living space. We shall overcome this menace; with the living space of the white Aryan people in jeopardy, and with our cultural grasp slipping away with the infestation of poison and modernist Jewish thinking, of pornography and the feminist movement that allows for women to smoke, drink and behave as men, desecrating the sacred bodies with which they continue the future of our people; with the current climate as it is...–" a trademark pause for effect, "we deemed it necessary – and western Europe as a whole shall come to, as well – to remove the Jew from every area of life in which they may be provocative, or subversive in any way.

Consider the capitalist system they enforced upon you. They wish to infect you all with the raging need to consume; as is seen in America and will be seen in England too; they have brought with them the sickness of consumerism, of an endless cycle of luxury goods, of greed and gluttony at the expense of a nation; of pornography, of vile films, to subvert an entire culture, to distract them, corrupt them and make them soft. They did it in Germany, and we rose up! Now, after the second war that they inflicted on the English and German peoples, we as brothers for our Motherland and Fatherland, for England and Germany and the Anglo-Saxon and the Aryan blood–" Goebbels' voice had risen almost to a scream; William, Jack noted, was almost mesmerised, but in a trance of horror –"... we can save our people, by driving the sickness out of our societies and destroying the poison they wish to inflict upon us!

Sadly, England – under its criminal government that declared war on the Reich, has been so infected by parasitic Jewry that it lost its ability to see the dangers our people face! International world Jewry conceals itself as Bolshevism in the Soviet Union, and plutocratic-capitalism in the Anglo-Saxon states, but wherever it operates, country to country, from parliament buildings to banks to newspaper headquarters to factories to corporations... wherever Jewry operates, covertly, it is a parasite, vermin, working to undermine the national culture.

Consider this…" Again, Goebbels paused for effect, and then his voice returned – back to the persuasive purr, his slight Rhineland 'sch' audible. "All the metal used in pointless, unnecessary items… a few hundred tin cans can be recycled to make a bicycle. Our societies would be sustainable with the sick, destructive need to consume, to have luxury goods and fill our lives and our thoughts with clutter *eliminated*. What does a teenage child need other than friends, books and a bicycle? The National Socialist society which England is now so lucky to enjoy, will see good books and acceptable literature replace the Jewish poison, will see sports replace pornography and idleness; to see my films, and good English films replace the disease of *Juden* Hollywood, and as such, you will see the children learn to have discipline, and grow to be strong, courageous, loyal to their family, their people and their country.

And what, I ask you, is the cause that we must fight for, with revolutionary fanaticism and undying will? It is the prevention of Bolshevism and the Jewish tyranny spreading from the East–" at that, the anti-fascist group gasped aloud. So, with England and France out of the way, the pact with the Soviets was dead; for Goebbels declare it openly to the English and Welsh listeners in the occupied zone, it had to have come from Hitler himself.

"–and while for pragmatic purposes, the Führer allowed for a peace treaty to be signed with the Soviet Union, and for a shared border separating the General Government and East Prussia of Germany from Soviet occupied Poland. And as a race of honour, we will uphold that border, in the interests of defending Europe and our Christian civilisation. Only in the event of gross provocation will the Reich be compelled to act and take defensive measures in order to fulfil the promises we have made to uphold the values and principles of our civilisation."

Jack tried to imagine how many people were sat enraptured by the wireless; perhaps with children on their laps. Was this what it had come to, he thought despairingly? Were our children now having the thoughtful, honeyed words of Josef Goebbels implanted into their impressionable minds? Were the British people – as he saw it, even a Scotland separated from the rest would still have the insidious fascist ideology seeping through the ranks of its children – were they to live in a society whose children grew to love the Party more than their family? Whose children owed loyalty to the state and the Gestapo, yet not the people who raised them to hope, dream and love?

As Mary re-entered the room, white-faced, Goebbels now delivered his finale; the speech had been uncharacteristically short for him, but he was too astute, too deviously cunning to have not catered to the British sensibility.

"The Jewish capitalist in the west – king of the banks, the media, the asphalt culture! – and the Jewish socialist in the East; it is the same creature, joining forces to destroy civilisations and bring European culture under its thumb. The German Reich, Italy, Spain, France and now England are united as one, able to purge the insidious enemy from within, and to tackle the external Bolshevik menace. We will not attack; but if, along the border in the General Government and East Prussia, if Bolshevik formations appear massed across occupied Poland or the Baltic states, ready to invade Europe and spread their sickly, savage disease of communism with its evil ideologies and the horrific mass-slaughter of tens of millions of people that it has caused, by a secret police agency the NKVD led by Jews and controlled by Jews... if this provocation and threat on our Christian civilisation appears, together, the forces of western Europe can combine to pre-emptively strike this menace from the Earth, and prevent the Bolshevisation of Europe from the Judeo-Slavic swine!

In the merciless slaughter of Christians and Slavs alike, tens of millions dead, and the slaughter they spread across continental Europe before the defenders of justice triumphed; Jewry once again reveals itself as the incarnation of evil, as the plastic demon of decay and the bearer of an international culture-destroying chaos. But together, our proud and free nations will stand together to prevent its evil sickness and its murderous footsoldiers from swarming like locusts across our lands.

We will triumph! The Aryan will triumph over the freemasonry of international world Jewry, and the British Empire of England, Scotland, Wales and whatever Irish states wish to be part of it, the Rome-Berlin axis and its allies will all triumph over the evil dangers we face, and if the Jew once more threatens our civilisation, we will rise up and let the storm break loose!

For King and country! For Britain! For Germany! For Christian civilisation and the triumph of our people – *Heil Hitler*!"

The radio crackled for a brief moment, and then promptly cut out, leaving a mesmerising static in his wake. Neither Alan, nor Jack, nor William and Mary shared looks this time, nor could they speak; none could find words to adequately express the quiet horror that had consumed them. A slow chill crept up William's spine, as he fully comprehended the potentially devastating effect that the Goebbels speech had, and he looked at Mary, she whose Jewish blood ran cold in her veins. He expected an outpouring of fiery contempt from her at any moment, as they'd seen so many times in the trench fighting with fascists, or in the treacherous environ of Barcelona as the communists betrayed their POUM allies... but all she could do was stare dumbly back, and a single, silent tear trickled down a cheek drained of colour to the scarlet of lips set in fear.

Eventually, William spoke, and when he did, both the wide-eyed, shaken Alan and equally disquieted Jack's memories were stirred unpleasantly with recognition as he paraphrased a familiar orator, his own voice trembling.

"You know what Goebbels has just done? He just committed psychological mass-murder."

Part III

Paul had just left the grounds of St. Mary's when he was seized. Hands grabbed around his torso, but before he could instinctively lash out he was spun around to face an all-too-familiar face.

"Bloody hell…" but his momentary irritation quickly subsided into amusement.

"Did I make you jump," Naomi asked coquettishly. She leaned in to kiss him deeply, her hot, wet tongue burning in his mouth, and despite himself he felt his desire grow.

"Christ, Naomi…" he exclaimed, breaking free of her. "What are you doing here? Are you crazy? If anyone sees–"

"Then they'll see a young lady kissing a young gentleman," she snapped, fiercely. "Which there is still no law against."

"Are you crazy?" He asked again, softly.

"Crazy about *you*," she breathed lustily, in a manner she had never before employed, and which made her gentile lover privately thrilled and grateful for the consummation of their emotional bond.

Paul pulled her giggling into a copse of trees, and the taller, younger man embraced her fondly.

"Darling, this isn't wise. It's better we're not seen together, remember? It's bad enough the nosey old girl knows."

The day before, as they made a particularly loud racket downstairs, a lady who owned one of the other converted flats had called round. Paul called her 'Old Doris', and on explaining who she was to Naomi, gave way to rare expressions of bitter obscenity and personal loathing. She had knocked, with a loud, maddening rhythmic pattern until he answered, and unbeknownst to him, Naomi had followed behind him, almost resigned to her fate. Her fears were unjustified; it was merely the old gossip of the block. But the old gossip spotted her.

The neighbour asked to be introduced, in a roundabout, impertinent manner. Paul had blocked his doorway, refusal implicit in his body language. Slipping three shillings into her hand, which caused her thick, vulgar eyebrows to shoot up and almost into her hairline, Paul told her that she had best forget she had seen anyone, and to have a good day.

Later that night, the old woman adopted a knowing, lofty air when the ladies knitting together came round to the topic of the handsome young teacher who lived opposite.

"I can't say a word, it would be improper," she said, haughtily. "But alas, my dears, I fear that even if you had seen many less moons, that the place in his heart is occupied by another anyway..."

In the copse of trees, that *other* leaned in to kiss Paul with a fierceness that surprised him.

As she broke free, holding an impossibly unwavering gaze at an uncomfortably close distance, he laughed uneasily.

"You *are* crazy."

"I will be if I stay in that house any longer."

"But it's for your own good, you must understand," he pleaded.

"Shut up and kiss me," she snapped, in false anger.

Despite his playful submission to her act, Paul noted uncomfortably that his kowtowing was entirely genuine. Dangerous, these feelings, and yet more so and more so again in such dangerous times as these.

Suppressing his nagging thoughts, Paul seized her head suddenly and gripped her with a force he had seldom employed in his life. Naomi gasped at first, and then smiled, wilting in love. They entwined in the green copse, clenched in clothed passion and fervently wishing it were otherwise.

As the flustered lovers left the trees and walked towards the direction of Paul's flat, they were spotted by two boys who were playing at the edge of the small wood that was wedged in an estate interregnum that hadn't quite been fully knocked down yet. It was on the opposite side of the road from the pair of teachers, and the boys had no difficulty hiding behind the trees to watch, out-of-sight voyeurs, hardly believing what they saw.

"Look, there's *Miss*! It is her!" One of them said, a ten year old blond boy with fleshy, red cheeks and a lazy eye. Lank hair was plastered over his profusely sweating forehead, and the ample flesh of his frame wobbled with each exertion, however slight. His friend, a taller, bespectacled boy with freckles crowed noisily too, as soon as the teachers had vanished from sight.

"She's with *Heggerty*. I don't believe it, 'Eggy and Miss!"

"Miss Rosenberg and Eyeball Paul, I don't believe it either!" the first boy shouted with laughter, and as his chins wobbled merrily he was touched with a small stab of jealousy, to his vague confusion. His friend sensed their laughter faltering, and misinterpreted it, lapsing into a deep concentration.

"I thought she left because of illness..." the bespectacled boy said thoughtfully.

"What illness ha'she got, there's nowt wrong wi'yer!" the fat child exclaimed, his Yorkshire accent stretching into the realm of parody as he chuntered, failing to control his own emotions.

"You're right. Nothing wrong with her."

"She looks a'right to me!"

"Yeah…"

An Indian summer had well and truly set in for the south of England, and north-central London's wide streets had blissfully returned to their dry and windswept state, yellowed leaves rustling underfoot in the drum roll of feet. In these conditions, an enforced gaiety was possible, even genuine for many of those who had not opportunistically become collaborators in their way, the definitions of which varied greatly. Some maintained that simply operating a business that directly profited from German custom was enough to be labelled a traitor, let alone *fraternisation*, an ugly, whispered taboo, a curse word. But for all, the weather allowed for a fragile collective cheeriness, even happiness, to the delight of children too young to understand the black shadow that had crept across the lives and heart of their elders in recent months who were able to smile in the joy of the Sun's warmth, and to see those smiles reflected back at them. On a sunlit street with happy children, no occupation exists.

Even Charlie was affected. A crippled malcontent, Charlie Lightfoot had left school at 15 just three months before old Neville declared *Peace In Our Time*, and he'd thought it was the start of a great new era; finally, an end to moping about the Great War and a brighter outlook, and a fresh start for a lad with an eye for a bargain and a salesman's touch.

Alas, it had been neither, and with the feverish conscriptions following Hitler's absorption of the rest of Czecho-Slovakia after gaining back the largely ethnic-German Sudetenland where – to general confusion in England – it was now understood that most of the Czech defences were located in the event of military action from the Reich, Charlie had among the first to head down to the recruitment office, certain that with the current predicament facing them the army would be sure to turn a blind eye to his blatant lies; that the gangly, hobbling cockney kid was Of Military Age. But unbeknownst to him, only a handful of divisions were set to be shipped across to France, and by the time Dunkirk was ongoing, it was too little too late.

"Look lad, I'm telling you for the last time. You're unfit for active service in the forces!"

He'd nagged, then begged and pleaded, to no avail. Charlie had caused such a fuss that his friends from Whitechapel had left him there, embarrassed. Eventually the officer who had rejected his application lost his patience.

"Clear off! Pack it in or I'll have you nicked, you 'orrible little prat!"

Thus, deemed "Unsuitable for Military Conscription into His Majesty's British Armed Forces," having failed to meet the physical requirements of soldiery with his leg, Charlie was aimless.

"You'd have been able to slip in with a Pals Battalion in the last war, boy," his bedridden father told him, wheezing. "They let us in as mates. Course, most of us never made it back."

It was their last conversation. Old Ted Lightfoot had died the next day.

Such battalions no longer existed; enthusiasm for them had understandably waned given that most had been decimated by war's end, and, with no home left in any case, the unsuitable and now orphaned Charlie had slunk quietly out of the East End, mortified by the thought of being seen by the people he grew up around as a shirker or a deserter. He shuddered at the thought of a white feather. No guv'nor, he decided, not for all the tea in China.

Central London, however, had not been kind. Untold millions had moved there over the centuries to make their fortunes, or die, unloved, unwanted and unmourned, in the gutters and dirty streets. Only several kilometres to the west, Charlie had felt like he was in a different world, until the day his savings ran down to bare bones. The landlord had been unsympathetic.

"Just one more week," he'd begged. "I'll sort this out."

His landlord leaned close. The huge moustache had quivered across his snarling features, burst blood vessels burning red on his nose. "Clear off. You're just another wrong'un, and we don't need you round here bothering decent folk."

So, that had been that. The onset of darkness and an icy rain had only accentuated the descent of a deep and profound despair that fell on Charlie with the sinking sensation that *this* was that very moment that so many of London's down and outs had experienced; the beginning of the end. He headed north; in a fit of pique and recklessness, he'd decided to have a drink, and the Royal Oak had been a welcome haven from his troubles. A chance meeting with an old acquaintance that had migrated northwest to Camden to start a transport business led to some infrequent work; Charlie saw it as the divine intervention of a God he'd rejected on the death of his father. He had materials to sell. London was occupied, to all intents and purposes, but the dread policing and mass-arrests hadn't come in with the force first feared, as far as most could tell; at any rate, few streets ran red with blood. It could be worse.

Today felt like a new start; Charlie almost even smiled himself as a little girl in a frilly dress came skipping past him, followed by her visibly wearied father. He, at least, bore the marks of the occupation heedless of something as intangible as the weather. That haunted look, that familiar look. Even sunlight could not pierce its caked layers of misery that ran deeper than skin.

Minutes passed, and the traffic of passers-by on the lively road slowly thinned. Charlie began to get impatient. He badly wanted a drink, but with strict priorities, the daily quota must be met before any thoughts of relaxation and beer be allowed to sabotage his efforts. The consequences, then as ever, were dire and occupied or otherwise, London was no place to be down. The cold cobbles and public indifference to the socially ostracised; the beggars, the down and outs, was the same in Berlin, Paris, New York. Once you leave society, acceptance – of self and from others – is difficult, and Charlie, like most others who occupied the place in the social hierarchy lower than underclass, had a heightened sensitivity to rejection.

More waiting. Pigeons fluttered around the quiet street, their wings flapping, a slight rustle in the silence of the street. Clad in a threadbare topcoat that had belonged to his father and which was still, aged 18, too big for his frame, Charlie paced from side to side with growing irritation, allowing himself no more than a few metres from his clumsily erected stall. Should've stayed in the East End, he thought. They'd have at least respected me for ducking and diving, trying to make a bob.

Somewhere, internally, a small voice suggested that he find a way of making himself useful to the Germans, and he quickly silenced it, cursed it, buried it; pacing faster. He'd never sell out. Too many had done that; many the same scavengers who'd made profit from the pre-invasion panic. They were viewed with contempt, though rarely expressed openly. And they were many; men on street corners, accepting the odd muttered curse word as they tried to sell the English language copies of *Der Stürmer* and the *Völkischer Beobachter*; Streicher's outrageous anti-Semitic pornography and Goebbels' effortless switches between hysterical diatribes and honeyed seduction. Bobbies patrolling with Jerries in uniform. *Birds chatting Jerry soldiers up for cigarettes, walking arm in arm. Panting, gasping, sweating under them at night. Fucking disgusting. I'd be no different; a skivvy boy and a traitor. Fuck that for a laugh.*

Charlie's independence was not profitable.

Time passed slowly, like a knife. Finally, the sun's heat began to wane, and the autumnal breeze had an added lingering bitterness to the youth on the street, struggling to contain himself as the minutes crept by. Just as Charlie was beginning to consider spending his meagre daily earnings on a much-needed pint, a familiar figure popped into sight, almost shuffling down the street toward him in the unhurried pace of the unemployed. As he neared, the man gave no indication he saw the boy, who decided to pipe up anyway:

"Wanna buy a scarf, Mister?"

Charlie's somewhat shrill voice, still with the vestiges of childhood, came out in a slight rasp from lack of use, catching slightly in his throat.

The sudden entreaty seemed to awaken the man from his reverie.

"No, thank you," Bill Wilson replied, quietly.

Even in the Royal Oak he'd never spoken to the boy, who was relatively new around these parts, and Bill noted the distinct cockney accent for the first time with interest. Then as though a switch had been flicked, the light of his interest was extinguished, and he shuffled on without further comment. Charlie watched him, confused, as the heavy cotton-lining and collar obscured Bill's head and the older man became a shuffling, great-coated silhouette, leaving him behind in the street. He'd been surprised to hear Bill speak; usually paralytic, rendered insensible from his steady silent diet of whiskey and ale in the pub corner;

another casualty of the Lost Generation. Charlie watched him shuffle away. Anger, sharp and inexplicable, suddenly gripped him.

"Dare not spend your beer money, you draft *dodger*?" He spat impetuously on the ground, the fury of a child's tantrum.

Bill slowly turned, like a man twice his age.

"I am a pacifist," he said calmly. "Do you know what that means?"

"You're a bleeding coward, I know that much!"

Charlie was apoplectic, almost hopping from his good leg to his bad in his pique, pouting venomously at the older man. Bill wondered if he was steeling himself to hobble over and attack.

He smiled pleasantly, to the cockney's confusion.

"OK. Well... good luck with your scarves."

He gestured without malice at the crude stall; a wooden school desk laden with small ornaments, with an inverted ledge on which the scarves were hung; all grey, or black, and thinner than was available in the boutique shops to the north around Camden.

The older man turned again, and shuffled towards the pub.

"Good luck being a fucking radio, you spastic *cunt*," Charlie spat viciously at his back. Such language was unheard of in Bloomsbury; "radio rental" was cockney rhyming slang for one of an imbalanced mental state, and the other phrase was so utterly repugnant to the average London ear that it was rarely heard outside of the East End and dockland pubs. It was a taboo curse that carried significant stigma.

Bill made no sign he'd even heard. Disappearing through the doors of the Royal Oak, he left Charlie stood gormlessly in the street, alone again.

"If it wasn't for my leg I'd be doing my bit, you hear me?"

Silence.

"I'd be doing my *bleedin' bit*!"

But Charlie was shrieking at a building, on an empty street. He reddened, and the anger dissipated as quickly as it had erupted.

"Prat," he muttered to himself. He wasn't entirely sure if it was aimed at Bill.

~

Bill slowly trailed into the comforting familiarity of the Royal Oak's public room, where Arthur was, as customary, polishing a glass behind the bar. Even in comparatively quiet times, the old publican had maintained an immaculate pub; gleaming and clean, with only the smell of smoke and ale betraying the place to olfactory perception as a London public house. Bill took a pipe out of the inside pocket of his heavy coat. He smiled genially, and started pouring a pint of thick ale before Bill had reached him.

In the next room, a rather more intense scene was developing, and pulses were racing somewhat faster than in the gleaming tranquillity of the public bar.

"We've got *one* chance at this. Just one."

Alan was holding court, red-faced from a particularly heroic bout of drinking that had stretched over the previous days – a continuous 'topping up' of the nerves and 'Dutch courage', he claimed – but still largely in control of his faculties. "It's me or Jack to take the sniper shot. Sorry to say it, but has to be the best marksman. You know I'd just as happily kill the bastards with the whites of their eyes showing." He took a mighty swig of his ale, and grimaced. "Which brings me to that point. I'm out of range. At the same time on ground level... there's simply no option other than suicide charges with guns and grenades." He shrugged helplessly.

"For the Emperor – *banzai...*" William intoned.

He hoped that if it came to it, he'd have the courage to kamikaze in the style of a suicide charging a Japanese warrior. He'd seen enough during trench charges in Spain, on the Aragon front, and the results were often grim; lives bled out in the hot dust, an unforgiving sun burning down on them.

"Yes," Jack interjected, shortly. "That's the way. Only we do it for an ideal, not a man."

That settled it, as it so often had before. They had all learned to trust Jack's judgement, his cool and steady head that even by their unnaturally high standards, was remarkable for such a young man.

Jack clasped his hands in front of his face. "I'm trying in vain, at the moment, but..." he opened his hands, expression hopeful, "... if we can get another sniper rifle we double our chances. Doubtful we'd fail, in fact."

William and Mary both chuckled at that; Jack wasn't sure if it was mirthless. "We wouldn't fail." Mary smiled.

"Surviving's another thing. But fail? Nah." William raised his glass to Jack, who winked back. Bickering and tension expended vital energy, and morale was important.

"Touché."

"Can't we get Art to request one?" Alan piped up. He doubted it, but having not contributed to the discussion for several dozens of seconds, he decided it was time to sound proactive. But Jack shook his head.

"Nothing. He's hearing nothing but radio static."

"And you've heard nothing since?" Alan asked William, a little sourly. He'd since been informed of the Colonel's initial approach to his fellow Scot to conscript the group to clandestine action. William shook his head.

"And you have not heard from anybody?" Mary asked. Alan confirmed with a shrug.

Jack explained the mechanics of the enterprise for the umpteenth time, ad nauseum, but in the hope it would help with the Spanish beauty's determination, one way or the other.

"The radio is one-way at the moment, nothing incoming. No idea if any other cells are still out there or if they're enjoying Gestapo hospitality. My guess is with orders to snuff out the local collaborators, choose if they're bobbies, brides or bricklayers, plenty of local folk wouldn't have been so keen to help. Especially after reprisals against the populace."

He shook his head. They still couldn't leave the Greater London area, which had been encircled by Wehrmacht checkpoints and strategically placed companies.

They still had no idea how successful – or otherwise – concerted organised resistance was. Or had been.

"We're stuck with one sniper, one normal. Mary, are you getting on with the floor plans for the Savoy?"

"No joy," she said, adopting the England phrase with her own lilt. "I can *not* get *near*. Everybody working there is *screenéd*, is *watchéd*. And the ho*tel* its*elf* is… unassailable," she said, dredging the old word up from their times in the trenches. Her pronunciation of it was distinctly Spanish. She shrugged, a little sadly. "There is no way we can attack them inside."

She tossed her great wave of thick brown hair, sending it whipping round in a quick circular arc, an impatient gesture they all loved. "I cannot believe how much more…" her voice trailed off. "These Germans. Their secret police is much cleverer than *my* people."

Her soft tone was so bleak, bereft of its usual lilt, that none dared offer a response, even in comfort.

"At the moment, it's impossible, and besides, we were hoping for results from the one person here who is not British," William said protectively. She turned to him with a scowl.

"The *not British* person is perfectly capable of achieving results, not to mention speaking your slow, brutal language, better than you Scottish–"

"I know lass, I know," he quickly replied, grinning despite himself and their unenviable position. Jack and Alan stared at the bickering couple balefully, bemused at the prospect of energy being wasted on pointless quarrels.

"Then the only option left to us is in transit," Jack observed, soberly. "Himmler's car ride from the Savoy to the Dorchester when he meets Göring and von Ribbentrop for this meeting with the puppet government in-waiting."

"Would be ironic if we killed him en route to the full and proper Friendship Pact with England," Alan grinned.

"Britain."

"Whatever," he shrugged back. "You'll get your independence soon, Jock, if they get their wish. *Probably*, like. Then they can seal off the border and wipe out everyone between Hadrian's Wall and the Leeds-Liverpool canal. No soldiers wasted patrolling in Scotland, being shot at by your ugly ginger friends."

William snorted ruefully. "All those centuries, it's all we wanted. Now we're a united nation we'll be split, and all because the Jerries of all people can't be bothered freezing in our snow when they could be freezing in Stalin's…"

Jack turned and spat onto the floor, and an affirming murmur was shared. Spain taught them that the furthest extreme from an ugly extreme can turn out to be just as ugly in its own right; a poisoned mushroom, as Julius Streicher said about the Jews. But Soviet communism was a *real* poisoned mushroom.

"How are we sure they will even take the park road anyway? It would be uh, *more* fast to come via other side." Mary observed. William stole a wink at Jack, who smiled a little. The 'not British' person was a smart girl, and asked a pertinent question while knowing relatively little of the city, compared to the local Jack. Even William and Alan had been there years.

"It's what they do. Always loud, obnoxious, ostentatious." Jack assured her. She looked at him blankly. "*Grande. Magnifico,*" he added quickly, circling his arms. "*Extravagante.*"

"Besides, even if Himmler crept in, chances are if we get in place assuming the Park Road is our best bet, we'll snag Göring or Ribbentrop, or some big leader," Alan offered. But Jack shook his head.

"The instructions were there for a reason. No Himmler – or Heydrich – and we call it off, wait to catch them going back to the Savoy. No use bumping some diplomat or even the fat boy. Besides, we'll be able to tell by the security if that road's in use."

"It will be," William said assuredly.

Alan shrugged again; it was becoming his gesture. "Aye, well... it would be bloody lovely as a little irony if we killed them en route to the Friendship treaty." The grin that followed this was a little perverted for a murder mission, Jack thought. Even on Heinrich Himmler.

"Wouldn't it just," William smiled.

"To friendship! *¡Salud!*" Mary cried.

"Cheers!"

They toasted the thought. Alan cleared his throat.

"By all accounts, Heydrich isn't too concerned with security, he just drives around in his open top Mercedes, reg' plate 'SS-3'."

"Why?"

He snorted. "Evil bastard said that if anyone tried to kill him, it would be the single worst day in the history of their country."

The words slipped out, and he wished they could be unsaid as soon as they escaped his lips.

"Dark clouds over Newcastle today," Jack said darkly.

But William agreed with the Geordie. "These things have to be said. This isn't a game we're playing, and *he's* certainly not bloody *playing*. As to what Heydrich said, judging from the war in Poland he's probably right."

The bell tinkled in the next room, and a silence descended. None of the three seated in their booth in the saloon bar registered the sudden quiet.

"Himmler rides in an armoured car mostly, but you never know," Alan said, the light of hope flickering in his eyes. "They could just take the normal staff car in England. Or even one of Heydrich's, the open-tops he drives," he said, even more hopefully. "From the Savoy to the Dorchester isn't exactly far, and they're going to have SS and Gestapo all over the place. They might get careless – Heydrich is never care*ful*, anyway. Either way if we see Heydrich in the open I'm taking a pot-shot at him regardless of the orders. That's too big a target to ignore."

The low sound of the saloon door swinging shut snapped them out of their focus bubble, and back to the outside world. Footsteps were approaching to William and Mary's back, though the booth obscured them from the rest of the room. Jack, seated opposite Mary and with the room in full view, had wide eyes. Rooted to their seats, the Scot and the Spaniard's hands and jaws clenched, a chill running through them just to see Jack's reaction.

After eight further steps across the thick carpet, a tall man in uniform swung into view for the rest of them. He stood proudly; tall, blond and blue, the young man wore an officer's peaked cap standing high on his head, and the grey field blouse of the Wehrmacht. Shoulder epaulettes of silver-green braid with a stud, and jackbooted to his knees, the confident youngster was a German Army officer. Next to him stood an enlisted man, a soldier in a slightly less decorated uniform and with steel helmet in place of the cap.

"Aye up Mum? Guess wha'?" The blond, fat child screamed from the threshold, by way of announcing his arrival to the family home.

His stern, hawkish mother marched out of the kitchen to see him, the huge thuds of her footsteps on the panelled wood resonating loudly around the large, commodious house.

"What?" She snapped at him; her voice more suitable for the prehistoric beak of some angered bird than all the soft possibilities of a human mouth.

"I just saw Ms Rosenberg kissing Mr Heggerty!"

"What?" This time, the mother's voice was louder.

The boy slapped his knees, in a mock-parody of adult merriment. In truth, he had seen his grandfather do it and hoped it made him appear more grown-up. His chins wobbled with laughter as the story came tumbling out in a verbally incontinent outpouring, worsened by a frequent, compulsive use of glottal stops combined with his abysmally low intelligence and the limited function of his stupid mind.

"Me and Johnny saw 'er! Saw 'er wi' 'eggerty outside t'school and he kissed 'er, they was together, as sure as you like, it were Miss Rosenberg, Mam, and she do'n't look ill at all–"

"Where were they?" His mother demanded, breaking into the stream of babble.

"Well we followed 'em, and they went back to Mr 'eggerty's 'ouse!"

His mother was shocked.

"Is that so? They told us that Jews were not allowed to teach anymore, they've been banned from all the major professions and from *schools*. I thought Rosenberg refused to register as a Jew, and took off?"

The boy looked at her, and shrugged, the great shoulders rolling as his fleshy arms flopped. He didn't think about things like that. His mother considered him, her eyes narrowed, lips pursed.

"Well you be keeping it to yourself, don't be telling tales, d'you hear me?" His mother demanded of him. Then she stepped briskly to the phone, and dialled a familiar number.

~

"Hello," the officer smiled. "Do you mind if we sit with you for a moment?"

They were stunned. Heartbeats, and then Jack recovered his composure, realising that if they were in trouble, evidently it could not be for the reason that by all rights it *should* be.

"Of course, by all means."

"Thank you. We would like to talk with you," smiled the German.

William and Mary scooted along the seat of their booth, until the Scot's left shoulder was pressed up again the plaster of the wall. Jack squeezed a gobsmacked Alan along with his thigh, and the German officer sat down next to him, the enlisted soldier next to Mary. Adding to the disorientation of the group was their age. *They're bloody kids*, Alan thought. It occurred to William that he, Mary and Jack were senior in age to these Germans by at least four years.

"What about?" Alan demanded, gormlessly. The other three groaned inwardly. The time that had elapsed since the German's remark had been such that the Geordie came across as both slow, and belligerent. And aggression was the last thing they could afford.

But the officer smiled. Taking a packet of British Dunhill cigarettes from his packet, he lit once for himself at leisure, and then offered one to his friend.

"Danke," the private said quietly.

The officer, almost as an afterthought, offered the packet round. With a shaking hand, William hastily collected two for himself and Mary. He knew better than to refuse the offer so soon, and besides, they were superior cigarettes to those he himself had been reduced to buying after the stash brought back from the hideaway had been used up.

The officer pointedly offered a cigarette to Alan, who lost the battle of willpower and accepted it. The German beamed.

"Whatever you like," he said brightly, finally deigning to answer.

Nobody spoke. The appearance of the young officer had jolted them horribly. Adding to their confusion was his boyish face; dimples and clear blue eyes, a small pock mark above his left eyebrow the only imperfection on a child's face. His friend, who had removed his helmet, was darker; brown eyes, short brown hair, closely cropped at the sides, and freckles. Both emitted an unusually fragrant scent; lightly perfumed, in their immaculate uniforms, they certainly did not resemble the soldier of both the partisans' imaginations and past. They'd never seen anyone in a trench that even closely resembled these men. The Germans they'd known had been dirty, clad in leather and had not held themselves with military bearing.

The young German tutted, as the silence wore on, seemingly at ease in the discomfiting tension. "Come *come*... you were all talking freely before we arrived. Then again, I have quite clearly neglected to introduce us in the proper manner. I am Sebastian, an officer in the German Army. *Lieutenant* Sebastian Koller. This is Private Helmut.

"Hello," Helmut said unsmilingly. Then, at the drop of a hat, he fixed them each in turn with a grin; his own freckled, schoolboy face unlined. The effect was sinister.

"Come *come*," Sebastian said again. He spoke with exaggerated care, his Received Pronunciation English grating, like an insufferable public schoolboy lecturing proletarian employees, but with the German tint that further twisted the knife. "We are not Gestapo. Our uniforms are on clear show for you people. We are soldiers of the *Wehrmacht*. What is the problem?"

He smiled again, expectantly. Alan, meanwhile, was fondly imagining breaking his glass over the Jerry officer's young face, and the scene he envisioned sent him drifting into a full-blown daydream of prolonged, and excruciating torture. While it relieved his tension, the imaginings gave him a vacant look, which Helmut noticed curiously.

"I am Jack, these are my friends William, Mary and Alan," Jack told Sebastian.

"Hello. My, *my*... what a *pretty* girl you are, Mary. And lovely to meet you Alan, William and Jack. Where are you all from?"

"London. Not far from here," Jack offered, his own pleasant expression fixed firmly in place.

"Edinburgh," said William, gesturing between himself and Mary. Fortunately, neither German pressed her. Sebastian turned instead to Alan, who jerked out of some reverie as though awakening from sleep. It made him look disturbed.

"Newcastle," he grunted.

"Pardon?" Sebastian asked, wrinkling his nose. Helmut snorted loudly.

Jack's right hand quickly gripped Alan's thigh in warning, as his arms lay on the table. Alan knew better than to explode, however, and bit down on his sudden surge of irritation.

"I said New-*castle*. It's up north... *y'know like*, up north in the country."

"Up north in the country..." Sebastian repeatedly, quietly, and taking care to pronounce the words with clearer elocution than had Alan. The German lieutenant had the maddening air of a bureaucrat, or some lower ranking official that used an overly polite syntax and an affected elocution to raise the ire of those they dealt with. A man who took pleasure from inconveniencing people with his authority; the type who grows up dreaming of being a traffic warden.

The pedantic officer looked across to William and Mary. "And you are from Scotland, I believe – yes? Edinburgh, the capital city of Scotland, to the north of England?"

Jack bit down on his own exasperation. All fear had left him. If the officer really did have malicious designs on them, he thought, then surely his tactic was to *bore* them to death with his patronising pedantry. Or, just wind them up to the point of suicide which, Alan considered, might actually come, in the form of a double-glassing incident and the inevitable tender reaction of Heydrich's Gestapo.

"Yes. Edinburgh, the capital city of Scotland, to the north of England," William answered in a dull monotone.

"Then why are you here in London." Sebastian suddenly snapped. As gradually as the tension had left, it returned instantly. The German's eyes burned nastily with sudden caprice.

"We work down here," William replied flatly, betraying no fear. "Have done for many years."

"Aye," Alan offered scornfully.

Sebastian fixed them all a lengthy gaze, and then sipped his malt whiskey. It was rare to see someone drinking whiskey, even in the pubs. Men came to pubs to drink beer – even wine was practically unheard of. In northern cities it was said that only one-in-twelve pubs served anything other than ale; be it bitter, mild or smooth. Alan had once searched Leeds for three hours before finding a pub to drink his favoured whiskey in, having found himself craving irrationally.

But Sebastian was a German. In rationed times, grey uniforms entitled the wearer to many things, and evidently a strong whiskey in a Bloomsbury pub was one of them.

Concluding a rather effeminate sip, Sebastian's eyes roved over Mary with naked hunger, and then he looked to William. Spoke softly.

"I see... what, might I ask, is your profession?"

"I work in a factory with Jack. Mary works in a bookshop in North London."

Even as he spoke, William cursed himself. The old lies. Germans could demand papers. Mary had hers, but his were invalid, and upon inspection he was most certainly not a factory worker. And should they arouse any suspicion, it would not take long to determine Mary was not who she said she was – faking her accent would only go so far.

The German considered them both, with narrowed, questioning eyes.

"What factory?"

"Am I under suspicion?" William demanded sharply. *Fight fire with fire*, his instincts told him. *This kid is pompous, and in the midst of a drink. This is not the real deal. Bluff it.*

The Scot's well-honed instincts paid off.

"No, no..." Sebastian drawled, the infuriating closed-lip smile slowly spreading across his face. It made him seem no less dangerous to either William or Jack, who regarded him warily, trying to ascertain if the Wehrmacht lieutenant was playing a perverse game of cat and mouse. The man resembled a capricious predator that toyed with its food.

Sebastian straightened his immaculate army tunic, unnecessarily.

"You mistake me, William. I am merely asking you about yourself, to find out about you to satisfy my own interest and curiosity, as you would say. Like I assured you previously in this conversation, neither Helmut here nor myself are agents of the Gestapo. I am an officer of the German Army; a *lieutenant*, you would say. I come from Hamburg."

"I am from Munich," Helmut offered.

He spoke louder than his previous terse statements, and in his voice William recognised the distinct Bavarian tones; only four words needed to plant images of lederhosen, mountains and huge jugs of lager in the mind. It certainly explained the pint of ale sat in front of him, that he'd almost polished off already while the rest abstained from their own glasses, absentmindedly distracted by tension. Helmut seemed the more likeable of the two, Jack thought, if such a word could be used for either of them. He doesn't have the same arrogance, perhaps due to rank, or participation in victory. Drinking beer like a man. Not sipping whiskey with his pinkie finger poking outwards like Sebastian, as though anxious to embody one of the effeminate perverts in leather shorts sporting a walrus moustache that British Tommies had jokingly stereotyped 'Jerry' as, on the outbreak of war.

That, and merciless, obedient robots of Hitler's will, he conceded sadly.

Sebastian noticed they all looked with interest on the soldier he'd brought with him.

"Helmut from *Munich*. You would *love* Munich," he said, clapping Jack on the shoulder. "Beer and *beautiful* blonde girls. Of course William, you seem to have a beautiful girl yourself already, so the appeal may not be so high for you."

"Aye," he replied shortly.

If Sebastian was unfazed by their lukewarm reception to his company, or if he truly could not care less, none of the British could tell. He smiled pleasantly, murmured "how lovely for you. A beautiful girl," and then chuckling to himself, stubbed out his cigarette and took out the packet to replace it. This time he did not offer a smoke to the others.

There was a moment's silence; neither the British nor Helmut seemed to know what to say without Sebastian's slightly mocking conversational lead. He seemed content to enjoy the second Dunhill, leaning back against the booth's wall and inhaling the smoke appreciatively. He blew a perfect ring, then another, and a third. Despite themselves, they all watched the rings float lazily across the table, and then vanish into air.

Jack broke first; greatly vexed, he knew that if *his* nerves were wearing thin, then Alan was liable to start making Hitler jokes, or crude puns about 'Hamburg' any minute. All they needed was the time and patience to sit through this ridiculous scenario.

"So uh..." Jack stopped himself asking why they had inflicted their company on seemingly innocuous members of the British public. "Where did you learn to speak English?"

"I studied English, Latin, French, and Italian at university in Heidelberg," Sebastian informed him cheerfully. "Helmut here was not university educated, obviously, hence his lowly military rank as an enlisted man, but nevertheless he taught himself to speak English to a passable degree, with some intermediate French."

To his surprise, Jack felt a small stab of solidarity with Helmut; not merely for being self-educated, from the sounds of it, but for tolerating the snotty remarks of the officer. He wondered why Lieutenant Koller was fraternising, if they called it that, with an enlisted man in his own rank and file, let alone with 'Tommies' in a London pub. Helmut was neither his aide nor adjutant; this was a public house. They were drinking alcohol together, with British civilians no less. Jack was baffled by the whole scene.

"The magic of libraries," the soldier said. "Anyone can learn, if they decide to. I chose to elevate my learning. Nothing special about that, of course. I just wanted to be different from my family, I suppose..." Helmut shrugged.. Jack decided he definitely liked him.

"Well... you certainly speak very well."

"Thank you," Sebastian said, although Jack's answer had been to Helmut, whom he faced. "And I'm sure that all in time, *all* in *time*, there will be plenty of English..." he looked at William and Mary in an exaggerated parody of horror, "... sorry, *British* people, who will be able to speak German just as well!"

At that, both Germans smiled. None of the Brits knew where to look. Through the open section behind the bar, only silence could be heard from the Royal Oak's public room. Even *Lohengrin* had stopped, as though Wagner himself was dismayed by the extent to which Germany had pursued his own dreams of national greatness and anti-Semitic purging, using his name as an ideological standard bearer throughout the years of persecution and blood.

The door violently flew back into the wall, a jackboot appearing in its place, oddly disjointed until the body it was attached to followed it into the room. Six others joined him, and a swarm of SS uniforms poured through the naked opening. Naomi screamed.

"Shut up!" The first man sternly told her. He was quite calm, but the menacing tone silenced her.

Naomi was crouched in the tub, having been interrupted in the process of taking a standing bath with heated water upstairs. Now she cowered in the brackish water, terrified out of her wits. The security police laughed at her discomfort.

The first officer again took charge. Clad in a grey SS uniform – she assumed, at least, as the collar tab where the dreaded lightning runes supposedly were was in fact jet black, and entirely blank – he nonetheless otherwise resembled the part to a horrifying degree. The officer wore the high peaked cap with its Death's Head symbol; a pirate's hat, skull and crossbones, a logo of death. She quickly took in his full appearance; there was a small 'SD' diamond tag on his sleeve, and she noticed three diamond pips on his other collar patch. Tall, slim, jackbooted to the knee; there was no mercy for her in those pitiless eyes, she realised, as she gazed in vain to try to coax some compassion out of the awful young breed of German Supermen.

She took him in, whole, for what felt like minutes. They had stopped laughing, and were stood staring at her with barely concealed loathing.

Finally, the officer cleared his throat. "Naomi Rosenberg?"

Naomi was too frightened to answer the calm German-accented voice, while being utterly unable to formulate a better response. Her usual quick wit deserted her.

"Naomi Rosenberg?" he said louder, his jaw bunching.

"Yes," she quavered.

"Get out, get dressed."

"Leave the room," she tried snapping, but the commanding tone was lost to fright.

As though a spell had been broken, the SD men began laughing. It was a frightening, controlled laughter, and scared her more because of it. There was no frenzied attack, no abuse, no recrimination. Their composure, their total *control* was terrifying.

"What do you think, Beckenbaur?" the officer smirked to the hard-faced man beside him, speaking in German. "Can you control yourself with a naked yid?"

"*Jawohl*, Untersturmführer," Beckenbaur replied sourly.

"We could give you twenty seconds? What do you think; that should be enough for you, village boy?"

The others laughed with a harsh intensity, wired as they were on the rationed amphetamines, and thrilled in the moment of action. Beckenbaur was impotent in the face of their knowledge of his race crime, and the ignominy of his demotion. The sturdy blond clenched his teeth together, muscles bunching in his cheeks as he swallowed his anger. His movements betrayed a slight jerkiness, as did the other grim SS troops in the kommando. Coldly wired, quietly enjoying their power.

Naomi could not understand the words, but the officer's cold amusement was plain to see. Yet so controlled... it was barely human. They seemed joyless, manically intense, taking no real pleasure in their work or betraying any normal human feeling.

Yet theirs was a great suppressed energy. It was psychotic.

"*Please* leave the room," she implored, trying a different tack. It made no change to the stony-faced SD lieutenant.

"We are not interested in your body, you Jewish rat."

The officer's words cut her to the core. A potent mix of fear and anguish threatened to rise up in her, then. His revealing words showed the absolute indifference that they had to her; she was not human. Naomi knew that men desired her. She registered their lust. But here she was, sat naked in a tub and the SS officer barely even acknowledged her nakedness, her physicality, the womanhood of her flesh. Her shame, or sexuality, did not so much as cross their minds.

She tried, one last time, a futile effort at reasoning;

"Look, please listen to–"

Quick as a flash, the SD Untersturmführer leapt forwards to grab her neck with a terrible grip, like a demented rat-catcher, and hurled her sideways. Naomi flew head-first over the top of the metal tub, her wet body hitting the linoleum floor with a sickening slap like raw meat on a slab, before sliding into the wooden counter with a dull thud.

Screamed curses in an unfamiliar tongue began to rain down on her, along with heavy blows. Screaming, Naomi covered her head as she yelled a mixture of pleas, and then apologies, but the strikes of fists and feet rained down, with spittle and phlegm, and lastly, a low, intense haiku of hatred.

"Aye man... you German boys wouldn't be able to handle our Newcastle women. I'm telling you, you'd have never invaded if we'd put them along the coast!"

Sebastian screamed with hysterical laughter, slapping the table in front of him hard enough for beer to spill over the rim of his pint glass. The table was littered with empty glasses. Helmut snorted loudly, and some small fragments of phlegm attempted to liberate themselves from the insides of his nostrils, settled in the minute black hairs that lay inside.

Sebastian made a sort of whooping wheeze, controlling his laughter.

"Oh ho... Alan, I tell you, when we first sat down I couldn't understand a word you were saying. Your accent is so, so difficult! But I understand you now. I would love to meet one of your women."

"Aye... but ah, I think they'd beat you up if you did!" Alan cried back, banging his pint down on the table to more general hysterics.

The laughter did not quite reach his eyes. To William he looked like some sort of deranged comedian, the manic humour an expression of deep depression or mental imbalance. His admiration for Alan was limitless.

William and Mary woodenly played along, though it came easier for Jack.

"Ah... you English," Helmut slurred. "Herr Oberleutnant, is it not time we were heading back now?

Sebastian's laughter petered out to irregular chuckles. Checking his watch, he sorrowfully agreed.

"Yes, I suppose you are right, Helmut."

They stood in unison. Sebastian gave a mock salute.

"Gentlemen... Lady... it has been a pleasure and a privilege to meet you. We will be drinking in this public house for the foreseeable future while we are stationed nearby, so I am sure we will see you soon."

Without further ado, they turned on their heel and with no trace of a stumble, marched out of the saloon bar. All hilarity abandoned, four silent Brits were left stunned in their wake.

"Fucking *hell*, man..." breathed Alan.

"*Fucking* hell..." William agreed almost simultaneously

"My heart was going there."

"I thought we'd had it then.

"Déu meu..." Mary whispered. "I thought the pigs had us."

In the public bar, populated by only six regular drinkers, Sebastian held his arm out at the door, and stopped Helmut in his tracks.

"Actually, private..." he considered in German. "I suppose one more drink will not hurt. We are off duty, after all."

"I agree, Oberleutnant," Helmut replied in English.

They approached the bar, and Arthur, smiling genially, started to pour a brace of pints, the same Westerham pale ale that they'd drank solidly for the past hour or so with the furtive group in the saloon room.

"Two of the same, there you are gentlemen," Arthur smiled.

The oberleutnant took it, carelessly throwing down a mass of food and clothing coupons instead of ¾ 'a shilling, or ninepence, with two Reichsmarks. The value added up to more than the beer's price, but the arrogance of such a gesture was incalculable. The German currency would be a hassle to exchange, too; the process was not far from police interrogation. Arthur's face fell, though he masked his dislike.

"Thank you so much," Sebastian smiled amiably. "One pint of British *bitter*."

The pub's patrons stared at him. He revelled in the attention, an obvious effect of the uniform. While respected in Germany, Sebastian keenly appreciated just how much further his status as a Wehrmacht lieutenant could take him. He intended to see just how far.

Paul hesitated, three doors down from his house. Though there was nothing openly untoward, he knew, with a sudden cold sense of dread that sent chills through his body, that something was very wrong.

The blood ran cold in his veins.

He dropped the bag filled with his meagre remaining coupons' worth of food at the gate. Sensing eyes at his back, Paul turned, his senses tingling, to see Old Doris staring straight at him through the window of the house opposite where she knitted. Unusually, the old gossip made no attempt to look away, and Paul queasily noticed that she was flushed. Not excitement, exactly, nor was there triumph or joy in her face. But she was flushed, as though filled with some recently expressed, or suppressed, emotion.

He turned back and approached his own door. There was woodchip at his feet.

"Oh, no," he closed his eyes, groaning, his head leaning on the door.

Slowly, he opened it, to find the metal bathtub empty. He stepped in, tested it. The water was cold.

"Naomi?" he called, without hope.

He checked the two rooms at ground level, then descended the wooden stairs. One lightbulb was out; the result was the room was dingy. Naomi was not there, and nor were the clothes that she had been wearing, including her green coat.

"Oh, no..." he moaned.

As though in a daze, he walked over to the bed, as unmade as it had been every day since she moved in, and leaned in to the fabric, deeply inhaling her scent.

"My poor girl..."

He broke down, and the sorrow engulfed him; choking on tears and impotence, he wept for the girl who had vanished as though her existence had merely been a dream.

All that we see, and seem, is but a dream within a dream. Had Naomi ever existed outside his imagination? What cruel injustice of fate could possibly see her as a social threat, whose removal was necessary for the continued prosperity of a German-dominated Europe? What threat did the might of Berlin face from his beautiful, harmless leodensian Jew?

After languishing for some minutes, Paul dried his eyes on a woollen sleeve, and looked around the detritus of his room. It had obviously been searched, with no regard to care. Torn paper, clothes and books lay strewn amongst the wreckage of his living space. And it was only then that Paul remembered his novel; some of the pages of which were scattered in pieces around the floor.

Barely able to comprehend Naomi's seizure, he realised that he, too, was in serious peril. Drying his eyes, Paul's mouth opened in sudden horror. Stifling his fear, he collected some of the pages together, and then tottered over to the door that led to his flat's great 1930s luxury; inside facilities, a rarity amongst all but the most modern of houses in England.

The wooden door swung open to reveal the icy blue eyes of an SS man fixed on his. Fear jolted the beating of his hammering heart.

Supreme was the confidence with which the SS officer stepped forwards, and Paul edged back, his eyes wide, body tensed, barely breathing.

"Paul Heggerty," the voice said, quietly. It was not a question.

Almost paralysed by fear, the young Yorkshireman answered anyway.

"Yes?"

"I am Goeth, SS-Untersturmführer."

The man held his hand out, revelling in the cruel parody of the situation. Tremulously, Paul took it with a shaking hand, and felt his knuckles crushed in a powerful, pitiless grip. Goeth held his eyes, grinning malevolently, and after an extended period of silence released the loiner's pained fingers. The Austrian cleared his throat, theatrically, before continuing in a more commanding tone.

"The relationship you have been illicitly conducting is a breach of the German race laws. This is a matter of great concern to the Security Service of the SS, which I represent. But first, I would like to ask you a question. Your answer must be honest, or you will be punished quite severely. You are a creative man, yes?"

A bead of sweat ran down his neck, and Paul felt it slide down his shirt and continue its slippery course down a back that perspiring from fright. He couldn't answer, and his lip shook, along with the rest of him. Paul was paralysed with fear.

"Well?" the soft, terrible voice purred.

"Yes."

"You are writing a book?"

"Yes."

"It is not finished?"

"No."

"There are no other copies of the material found here today?"

"No."

"Do you intend to continue writing… *material* to incite tensions and slander the Führer and Reich?"

"No."

"There will be consequences if you persist."

"I understand," Paul stammered his agreement, trying to control his breathing with considerable effort, and failing.

The officer smiled. "I may not seek to punish you for the offensive materials found here, although the matter will be archived in the files of 'SiPo and SD' – the Security Police and Security Service. The Reichsprotektor of Britain – also the Chief of the *Sicherheitsdienst,* founder of SiPo and SD – bears only *goodwill* towards the Anglo-Saxon people. But regarding the Jew, Naomi Rosenberg, you understand that it is a matter of racial defilement? The legislature enacted in 1935 has been *de jure* British policy for some time. Not to mention her own criminal recklessness in remaining at large as an unregistered, hostile partisan."

Paul could not respond. And now, a definite, malevolent grin spread across the SS officer's face. His tone had remained slow and measured throughout.

"We have taken the Jewess into Protective Custody. There is no chance of properly *redeeming* a Jew, particularly an unruly, insidious partisan and a criminal, but we still remove the more disobedient elements from society into our rehabilitation camps. What I must ask you, regarding this matter of racial defilement is…” and the officer slowly circled the paralysed Paul. “Do you have any objection to the *Sicherheitsdienst’s* removal of the unregistered Jew?”

Paul was mortified. Could this be what it seemed?

“Do you object to the SD’s removal of the criminal Jewess?” he pressed.

Naomi, I’m so, so sorry my lass…

“No,” Paul croaked, his voice breaking.

The SS man nodded slowly.

“Excellent. Then you must sign the following form immediately, stipulating as such.” He produced a sheet of white paper. “This should guarantee your future agreeability to the Reich.”

Paul’s hands shook as he held the paper. At a glance, it was called Form D-11, and specified that the signatory acquiesced to ‘Protective Custody’ in the event that his disposition to the Reich was ever in question. Seeing no alternative, Paul signed his name to the form, and Goeth smiled at him pleasantly.

“Good. That concludes my work here… if you have any further questions, or information, you can call 999… ask for the *Sicherheitspolizei und Sicherheitsdienst*.”

He turned and marched up the stairs with high dignity, as though he was pleased to have concluded business with such class and efficiency. Paul began shivering, and could not stop, even as the SD officer marched upstairs and out of sight. He heard the man hawking up phlegm, which was loudly spat before the door slammed. In his basement, the young teacher sank to his knees, head in his hands, and a salty river of tears formed in his eyes, animal noises escaping him as the great wave of inconsolable grief welled up inside.

"Keep it schtum, anyway," warned Jack. "I can still hear that prick in the other room."

"The whole of London will hear that wee fellow's voice before the krauts leave, I daresay," was William's observation. "I can see him still here in 1942 telling us all he was first off the boats, led the advance on London and raised the flag over the palace."

"Please do not say that," Mary shuddered.

Sebastian's voice grew louder.

"Of *course*, Wehrmacht was simply expediency, to fight for the Fatherland. I could not imagine in late '38 that within two years the SS would be fielding how many combat divisions in France – ten? Twenty? Some of them made up of guards from the lagers. *Unbelievable.*"

"So why did you not join the SS, Herr Oberleutnant?" Helmut asked.

His own hometown was the spiritual home of National Socialism, and it surprised him to find an army officer who was Heidelberg educated and yet strongly in favour of the government.

"I would have, private. Like I said, after my studies I just wanted to *fight*. Educated men became army officers quite easily. With the benefit of hindsight you might be referring to me as 'Hauptstürmführer or Sturmbannführer Koller, as we speak."

Helmut nodded, but noting the self-promotion quietly, he didn't answer. Only agreement with party zealots was wise, particularly when they held military rank over you. But it was the party line he adhered to more than the army rank differential. Anyone could be denounced. And as Helmut's own family were rabid National Socialists, he was immune to such talk. Bluster did not bother him. Throughout his teen years, Hitler's Germany was all he had known. The SS were therefore as natural as the sight of trees or cars or children to him. It was much the same for Sebastian, clearly, but in him Helmut recognised the diehard Hitlerjugend fanatic; the intense child who would have spent his summer days patrolling parks and pools to ensure Jews did not use them, or standing sentinel outside Jewish shops and businesses to intimidate and discourage Germans from entering.

So stupid, such men. For Helmut, National Socialism was about expediency and power, and he was sure that Hitler and Göring would agree. He was a pragmatist, with thankfully pure German blood, and he would use his advantages to get ahead. But for the fanatics such as Sebastian Koller, the revolution was liberation and *Mein Kampf* was The Bible – its words were edicts from on high; unalterable and perfect. The Führer's word was the word of God.

Helmut pondered that it was strange that such educated Nazis as Lieutenant Sebastian Koller would not examine Nietzsche's doctrines and reach important conclusions on the current political movement that embraced them. Scapegoats, patriotism, militarism and nationalism; all tools of power. Not a holy crusade for German Blood.

Sebastian glanced around the pub, sensing that their presence had lost its initial effect. His eyes came to rest on a solitary figure, still wearing his bulging great coat indoors. An unshaven man, a drunken sot slumped in his seat; eyes downward cast and fixed on nothing in particular at all. Even through his instinctive targeting, Sebastian found to his surprise that he was also curious about this man.

He strolled confidently to Bill Wilson's table.

"Hello? How are you, good fellow?"

Bill continued to drink, without acknowledging the German lieutenant's presence. Sebastian lost his triumphant poise, and leaned down to try to force eye contact. As he did so, Bill sat up straight in his chair.

"Fine, thank you." The response was cool.

"What is it that you do, Sir?" Sebastian asked him, a little uncertainly.

Bill met his eyes coolly. "I live."

An awkward pause was broken only by a small noise from Helmut, drawing attention to the smirk he failed to suppress.

Leutnant Koller faltered, and then nodded, his expression grave. "OK... well, we are going to talk to other people. We drink here now. My name is *Lieutenant* Sebastian Koller. You are welcome to join us for a drink whenever you like."

Bill's face was deadpan. "Cheers."

He slowly raised his glass to his wet, bristling lips, and drank deeply.

Sebastian and Helmut shared a glance.

"The man must be a halfwit," the officer sneered in German. The sentence sounded somewhat brutal to uncomprehending English ears. *Der mann müssen schwachkopf sein.*

Behind Sebastian, the door of the pub swung shut, and the bell's tinkle indicated the surreptitious departure of the rest of Arthur's patrons. In the public room, now only one other table was occupied, and Sebastian turned his gaze to it. Towards the piano in the far corner, to Bill's back, a solitary young man was watching the German soldiers pensively. Sebastian approached the table, with Helmut in tow, taking his time. The pint of British pale ale each of them held did little to diminish their outward appearance.

"Hello. How are you young man?" Sebastian asked pleasantly, in his sickliest English voice yet.

Charlie Lightfoot stared into his pint. He'd only just got it as well, tiring of his lonely vigil, squandering a vital ninepence on the ale. And just as he sat down to enjoy his indulgent pleasure, the laughing voices next door turned out to be German. He could've *sworn* it was Alan.

Sebastian cleared his throat unnecessarily loudly.

"Did you hear me, young man? I enquired as to how you are? Why is it your friend left so quickly, with the other gentlemen? We wished to have a drink with the pair of you. With *all* of you, in turn of course." He smiled the sickening sweet grin again.

"I don't drink with the enemy," Charlie almost shouted, looking at his drink. The cockney's face flushed. He bitterly regretted his pint, and just wanted to be left alone.

"The enemy?" Sebastian said, affecting an air of mock surprise. "You're not Jewish are you?"

"No, I'm bleeding well not," Charlie snapped back.

Sebastian exchanged an amused glance with Helmut.

"OK. Well... *as you like.*"

Beckoning to the private to slide along the bar, Sebastian stepped away from the table and leaned on Arthur's side counter, crossing his feet and resting his bodyweight on the left forearm that draped across the wood. Lounging like this, with the pint glass held casually in his other hand; Sebastian Koller continued to smile placidly at the cockney, as though the heavily breathing Charlie was his prey. Ten seconds passed, and the boy remained subject to the German's fascinated gaze. Bill, at the next table along had his back to both of them, and was quite motionless.

Charlie's breathing intensified, and his body language became erratic under the prolonged awkwardness of Koller's composed, leisurely scrutiny. He fidgeted and squirmed, spasming in small wriggling movements until he could take it no longer. Jerkily raising his glass, Charlie downed the two-thirds-full glass of ale in five big gulps. The young lad jumped to his feet, and with no room beside the wall to circumvent his table and bypass Bill's, he had to walk past the watchful Germans. In his own excitement, the boy's gammy leg failed him, numbed as it was from being stood still or sat down for the whole day. Catching against one of the stools, he stumbled into Sebastian, knocking the unprotected pint glass into the German's chest and spilling a measure of its contents down the woollen *feldgrau.*

The cockney boy straightened up in horror and his eyes met Sebastian's, which were equally wide, too stunned to react. Charlie opened his mouth but no words came, and after mouthing a wordless noise at the soldier, he quickly hobbled across the bar and out into the street, moving as quickly as he ever had in his life and puffing with the effort.

The group stepped out into the chill of a late autumnal evening; for the first time, it truly felt like winter. The proper seasonal weather felt like it was finally beginning to assert itself.

Walking some distance to the east of the pub, they stopped, lingering at the entry to one of the leafy public squares, which, deserted, sat forlorn in the middle of the neighbourhood.

Alan finally voiced what they all felt.

"Fuckin' 'ell, man…"

A burst of spontaneous laughter ensued, more than a little hysterical. It was of a nervous, ejaculatory kind, the release of suppressed emotions and fears.

"Did that just really happen?" William asked in genuine amazement.

"Fuck me," said Jack, all ten of whose fingers were snaked through the tousled bush of his hair. "I think it must've done. Either that or I just had the same dream as you lot."

"I'm asking myself the same question," Alan grinned. He took out a small metal flask of whiskey from the inside pocket of his leather coat, which they passed around. "Of all the times we could have sat down and drank with a pair of Jerries!"

"For God's sake, we were sat there talking about killing Himm–"

"*Shut up you twat*," Alan quickly hissed, silencing William. After a second they all snorted in merriment again, due to the irony of the less-than-diplomatic Geordie pleading caution from the studious and careful Scot.

"Touché," William conceded, choking a little on the rough whiskey.

"Let's hope they're as lax tomorrow," Jack pointed out more soberly. They all fell quiet. "Rendezvous at eight o'clock, which gives us plenty of time, and the plan stays the same. William and I, throw the apples, as we try and get some rounds off. We aim under the car. We're lying in wait further along the trail. Agreed?"

"No I do not agree with your plan," Mary snapped, hotly. "The *girl* is going to fight too."

Jack and William protested at once.

"No, Mary we can't allow that."

"No you're bloody well *not*!"

Mary scowled at her lover. "Well sorry, but the *chica* is equal to–"

"The chica is someone I fucking love with all my heart," William stormed, taking her by surprise with his uncharacteristic explosion. "And you're damn well not going to throw your life away on this mission. *If*," he tried to put it lightly, "we fall, then you see what happens next. You will lay low. You can stay with Jack's Mum and sister. If it comes to it, you of all people will be able to sneak out and get a boat west. There's a whole Spanish-speaking continent out there."

"No!" Latin anger danced in her eyes, and from her tongue. "Do not dare patronise me you –"

"I'm sorry Mary," Alan butted in. "I'd give you the sniper rifle, but no offence, you're a rubbish shot. We need to make *sure, 100%* at least one of these bastards fall."

Mary was slightly mollified. "I know, but this is our fight."

"It's not," William said firmly. "We won't allow you a weapon. If you wish to fight, then we refuse to. You will do this alone. We go into hiding... but that won't happen, because we know you believe in this too much to stop us. No, Mary, we care about you too much. And to me, even killing an SS chief isn't worth losing you."

She was stunned into silence.

Jack took advantage of her surrender. "OK, so we stick to the plan? Rendezvous at eight,

And that was that. With purpose, they all clasped hands, knowing as they did so it was their last great pact.

"We did the right thing, didn't we?" William asked. They knew he didn't just mean the assassination plan.

Jack shrugged. "Who knows? Only history can judge us. And who will write our history?"

"We could be a footnote," William suggested.

"Or a chapter," Alan snarled.

"Or a book."

"A long bastard, like *War and Peace*," Alan continued hotly.

"And what will the book say?" Jack asked, cutting him off. "Who knows what history will record, or who records it. But here and now, where we stand and as we see it... yeah, I think we did the right thing. Many people exist who cannot say that."

They all stood in the cold, their hot breath forming vapid mist in front of their eyes.

"Likelihood is that we all die," Jack admitted. "But it will be worth it to get rid of Himmler or Heydrich. It's for the good of humanity."

"We're not strangers to this... but never in the fight against fascism, not even in Spain, did we ever undertake something so important... something certain to kill us."

"We will do it," Mary said clearly. "We will do it."

And then Jack bade them goodnight. "Get a good night's sleep. Tomorrow is... well... it's a big day, isn't it?"

They squeezed their cold hands tightly against each other, and hugged, tightly, as a group, before splitting and heading off into the frosty evening in different directions. Within twenty seconds they had all vanished, and the street was empty, as though they had never been there at all.

The wind whipped Bill Wilson's hair back as he stepped out into the unforgiving cold. A strange, sweet smell hung in the air, and the darkened skies were laced with ominous clouds scattered sparsely in the distance where the fading light still glowed.

Bill set off on the familiar route home. As he cut through the fence opening and into the public square that he used as a shortcut, the grizzled Londoner heard a piteous moaning sound emanating from a particularly thick bush of foliage, where the surrounding shrubbery and trees' overhang produced a small copse of sorts. He had heard enough human pain to know that the sound was not animal. Looking left and right, he took a brief moment to decide his course of action, and then sighing, forced his way through the undergrowth to the small, dark clearing.

A whimpering figure on the ground moaned as he burst through.

"Hey, hey..." Bill said, not unkindly.

The writhing figure stilled, at the sound of a familiar, if rarely heard voice.

"You all right boy?" Bill asked.

"Don't know. I don't think so." The response was a low, wheezing groan.

Bill sighed, his hot breath showing as mist in the frosty night air. He couldn't just leave the boy out in the cold, bleeding and hurt.

"You'd better come with me. Let's get you cleaned up, my lad."

He knelt down, and with a firm grip, gently helped the young man up to his feet. Staggering slightly, the pair made slow progress to Bill's flat, despite its proximity only several streets away. When they got there, Bill rested his injured companion against the wall, and unlocked the door with a steady hand. He helped him inside, through the entrance hall, their feet thudding against the thick wood, and into a living room, whereupon Bill lit one electric light, and started a coal fire.

Straightening up, with the crackle of flames burning, he turned to smile at his guest.

"I'll make us a cup of tea, then we'll have a look at them cuts."

Bill bustled off. His guest rose, and limped over to the mantelpiece, where a framed photograph showed a group of men in military uniform; the standard British Army issue. There, front and centre was none other than Bill Wilson; clean shaven, with short hair, looking fit and strong. A smile split his face; perfect teeth and handsome, sharp features. Several medals lay around the photograph, haphazardly placed.

Presently, Bill shuffled back into the room.

"Here's your tea, lad," he said, offering it. He showed no surprise to see his military photograph had elicited such naked surprise.

"Charlie," the lad mumbled, embarrassed.

"What's that?"

"My name. It's Charlie."

"Oh... right. Yeah, I knew that." He smiled. "My name's Bill. Pleased to formally meet you, Charlie boy."

And his manner was so genial, so obviously genuine that Charlie wanted to cry for what he'd said to him just a few short hours prior. The quiet, slow rumble of Bill's deep voice moved him immensely. Charlie felt tears prick at his eyes, and covered them with his hands, pretending to check the surrounding cuts.

"Right, old bean, let's have a look at you."

He helped the young lad over to the settee, laying him out flat. Bill had a cloth and some vinegar, and he began to treat Charlie's various cuts and scrapes; many of which were a result of being dragged across the pavestones, as well as from fists and feet.

"Ah, Christ!" he moaned. "Stone me; they did a number on me all right."

Bill passed no comment, placing a reassuring hand on the boy, before gently cleaning a large cut over the cockney's left eye. As he winced, tensing up with a sharp intake of breath, Bill patted his shoulder gently.

"Nearly done, boy."

"Bill!" Charlie said through clenched teeth.

Bill Wilson's face melted into the first grin that Charlie had seen in the flesh. It transformed his face; briefly, he looked like the young man of 19 or 20 from the picture.

"OK, that'll do you..." he paused. "They did a good job on you."

"Bastards," Charlie said, with hollow bitterness.

Bill nodded slowly. "Yes. That they are, boy."

He put down his little towel that had been used to dry Charlie, having washed the cuts and covered the poor lad in hotly stinging vinegar. Bill considered him. All the spite seen earlier had been kicked out of him. He looked like a lost boy, in need of a father. Or a friend.

"OK… I'll get some blankets. You're not going to make it home tonight."

Charlie laughed at that, a tad ruefully, which made Bill frown.

"I aint got no home, tell the truth."

Bill stared. "Is that so? Hmm… are you homeless?"

Charlie regretted telling him.

"Yeah… well, I stay at the poorhouse sometimes, but I can't stand the bastards that run it. More often than not I grab my sleep where and when I can, steal it here and there. Got a mate who lets me crash every na'an' again. Sell stuff; treat me self to the odd pint. There's others worse off," he added, defensively.

Bill considered him anew.

"You hungry, lad?"

Charlie grinned; Bill saw he had a canine tooth missing, and blood specked his gums and teeth. "Nah, I can't eat. Thanks though."

He lifted his shirt to inspect the bruising on his black and blue body. Bill whistled on seeing it.

"Christ, boy," he said quietly. "They enjoyed themselves."

"I'll be all right. I'll be out of your way in the morning."

Bill shook his head dismissively. "Don't worry about that, boy, get some rest."

And carelessly grabbing the medals on display, Bill left him to retrieve some blankets from his bedroom, bringing them back and layering them over the stricken Charlie.

"OK, well... good night."

Charlie was already passing out.

"Yeah, good night... oh, and Bill?" he slurred, sleepily.

"Yeah?"

"Thanks mate. Thanks for this..."

Bill's mouth curled into a half-smile.

"Night."

The light turned off, leaving Charlie in the dark warmth, lit by the light of a low, crackling fire; flames flickering patterns against the wall.

Bill went into his own bedroom, turning on a gas light.

On the chest of drawers, he deposited the medals down with the others he'd amassed, and considered the other framed photographs he owned that stood there. There was one of his wife, Maureen. She was smiling, happy. Another of their wedding day. They had married quietly, with a few friends present in a small ceremony in a Whitechapel Church whose name Bill could no longer recall. He gazed at the smooth, unwrinkled photograph. She was beautiful. He himself had a face as unlined as the picture in its cheap frame.

He sighed. Her death in the influenza epidemic that followed the Great War had been as hard a blow as any dealt him in the trenches. He still bitterly missed her.

Not a day passed without his thoughts inevitably drifting to sweet Maureen, like a dull ache.

Something stirred in him.

Bill looked in his wardrobe, where a collection of old, dapper suits of charcoal grey, in a tapered cut rested in pristine condition. Tweed, and bottle blue blazer jackets and coats had been slid to the far right; one garish pinstripe suit had pride of place in the centre, and on the left, Bill's army uniform. He took out the field blouse, slipping into it for the first time since November 1918.

The return from France. The quiet months. A year. Being able to smile again. Songs, laughter. Then Maureen's illness. The sharp, searing pain. Then, alone. Daggers, stabbing, *slicing*. And then, the numbness.

Long months of quiet. *Years*. Two decades. The pain disconnected. Solitude became normality.

Bill stared into his full-length mirror, and felt the flush of long dormant feelings aroused beneath his prickling skin.

Turning back to his chest of drawers cabinet, he raised the picture of Maureen to the light. He remembered singing to her, as she lay stricken, dying. All the confusion of the long years of war, the hatred and death, stuck knee-deep in the mud and blood.

"I'm forever blowing bubbles," he murmured, reliving as he did so his crooning to her, stroking her soft hair as she lay barely moving on her deathbed. He crooned, into her ear. Crooned through her pain. Their favourite new song. *Forever blowing bubbles... Pretty bubbles in the air. They fly so high, they reach the sky, then like my dreams they fade and die...*

At that, the first tears in years trickled down his burning face, sliding inexorably into the unkempt growth of hair that grew so wildly around handsome features.

The shrill ring of the telephone pierced the silent tranquillity of the Savoy's royal suite.

Heydrich started in surprise. Having long-since finished his daily meetings – a repetitive succession of expository projections-of-force, over his SS counterparts and various bureaucrats alike – his explicit instructions were that no calls were to disturb him, unless from the Führer himself. He had even, struggling to contain his laughter, told the Hotel staff to insist even to Reichsmarschall Göring and Reichsführer-SS Himmler that he was resting, and not to be disturbed unless urgent.

This call was significant. With deep concern, Heydrich picked up the phone, his small blue eyes already narrowed in suspicion.

"Reichsprotektor. Hallo?"

Ten seconds later, his face became grave, and then some time after, the smugness returned.

"Tomorrow, yes? And before... yes... that is definite?"

Heydrich lightly picked up a thickly-buttered scone, which he smeared jam over, before demolishing it in four bites, all done whilst listening to the phone call in high good humour. An incredulous smile had curled over his high, horsey features. After another minute of listening keenly, the voice in his ear finally petered out.

"Why, thank you for this call. That is most interesting, my friend. Most interesting indeed..."

Heydrich promptly rang off, and stepped to the window, looking out over the Thames thoughtfully. The electric light of street lamps scattered across the Embankment and Westminster lit up the Houses of Parliament and Big Ben, and he stared across the magnificent vista of London, his eyes filmed with thought.

"Most interesting…" he murmured. In his mind's eye, a plan began to form.

A flash of the dark blackout curtains let a streak of pale light permeate the room, and Charlie awoke instantly, with the instinct of one accustomed to sleeping in hostile environments, instantly alert to danger. His eyes came into focus, to see Bill stood holding a tray, smiling at him.

"Morning Charlie…"

"Morning, Bill…" Charlie groaned, as a wave of soreness from his battering suddenly seized him. "Bloody hell."

"How are you feeling?"

"Like shit," Charlie tried to laugh. "Like a football that has been kicked around for too long, ready for the bin."

"Try to get this down you." Bill told him, offering the breakfast tray. Charlie accepted it gratefully; the older man had prepared tea, a plate of buttered toast and an egg.

"Strewth, Bill… I aint eaten an egg for over a year!"

Bill smiled indulgently. "You must be ravenous."

"Ta, Bill."

Charlie began to scoff the toast and egg greedily, wolfing it down like a starved urchin.

"Bill," he asked, between hefty mouthfuls. "Why you helping me like this? Especially after I sounded off at you like a bleedin' berk."

"What could I do, leave you there?"

Charlie shrugged. "A lesser bloke would have. Can I ask you some'ing, Bill? Are all those medals yours? The ones that was up there."

"Oh," Bill looked embarrassed. "I only took them in... well... I just felt they shouldn't be out on display. Like it's pride. Nothing to do with you being here, lad."

Charlie chuckled at that. "Bloody hell Bill, I wouldn't give a monkey's even if you 'ad taken 'em out cos you thought I was a tea leaf. You put me up, di'n't ya? You gave me a roof, mate."

He finished his meal, and sipped the tea gratefully.

"You still ain't answered though," the boy added with a wink, which stretched the skin of his sore face and made him wince.

Bill sighed. He got up, and stood by the window, looking out.

"Yes."

"You won 'em all?"

"All won for defending *King and Country.*"

Bill shook his head sorrowfully, his back to Charlie, who frowned in slack-jawed amazement. The sardonic tone Bill had answered with was mired in resentment, bitterness and pain. How could he feel that way?

"But... you aint proud of all them medals, Bill? I would be."

The older man continued to stare out of the window. Charlie's tone was pleading, almost begging him to... he didn't know what; admit, confess, change his views... whatever it was...

"But you're an 'ero, Bill. You're a war hero."

Bill Wilson turned to him, with steady gaze, a fire burning in his eyes. Charlie felt a tingling of his senses to look at him. It was as though the old drunk he'd seen staggering out of the pub was now a man of extreme gravitas, from whom emanated an almost elemental power.

His deep, steady voice rumbled with quiet force.

"Medals can't bring your mates back. I didn't receive a medal for holding my brother in my arms, watching him die in the mud; choking his final moments away as his own blood clogged his throat... they gave him a medal for dying, though. *Thanks, boy.* With deepest, heartfelt sympathy from the people who caused the war, profited from the war, then celebrated the war. They gave out medals, but it was our blood spilt in the stinking mud that earned them. And for *what*? You expect me to be proud. You don't understand. No... war is *carnage*. No one wins, not the soldiers anyhow. I don't know why a new generation of idiots have inflicted that hell on us again... led by the two biggest idiots of all, Hitler and Göring, who personally experienced the horrors of the last one and still unleashed it on the world." Bill shook his head, reliving hell in his mind's eye. "Perhaps they cared more about losing than us survivors did about winning. No, I'm not proud. I'm not a hero... I never was. Just a man who was put in hell with a few million other brothers, and told to kill..."

Bill stood motionless, his eyes betraying the horror of some nightmarish reminiscence. Charlie was stunned, stammering.

"You're still an 'ero to me, Bill."

The hazel and yellow eyes rested on him again, steadfastly. Anger burned in them like forest fire.

"I'm no hero. I never was. I'm just an old soldier, whose life was stolen; a tool of the government, thrown in there as a young man and told to kill. It's all an illusion. None of it's valid, son. Don't believe the establishment's lies... rulers rarely love, and those who gain power always do so to *wield it*..."

Memories of noise and gore, gunfire, explosions and screams filled his head, and he let the hellish reel of devilish images play across his mind for another moment in the nightmarish past before forcing himself back into the present.

"Sneak home and *pray you'll never know, the hell where youth and laughter go...*" Bill concluded with quiet bitterness, quoting Siegfried Sassoon.

"Sorry to hear that, Bill," Charlie said, quietly, watching him.

Bill nodded.

"Long time ago, boy," he said with some effort, managing a small smile. "So... what exactly happened to you last night then? I imagine it was our two friends... Arthur's newest regulars."

"Yeah, it were them two Germans that was in the pub yesterday, Bill. They jumped me just before you came along."

"Why did they do that?" he wondered. Charlie already had his answer worked out; the experience had not inspired much in the way of reflection for him, nor had it needed analysis.

"They're pricks, aint they? Just a pair of 'orrible pricks. Enjoyin' 'emselves as Lords of the Manor, in their fancy kraut uniforms like coppers on a power trip.

They were trying to get a rise out of me earlier, and when I left I knocked his drink over. Truth is I didn't mean to do it, it's just this stupid leg of mine."

And Charlie, to his intense embarrassment, found tears stinging his eyes again.

To his surprise, Bill grinned.

"Come on lad. We'll have the last laugh."

"Oh yeah, sure. They'll beat me up every chance they get, the evil bastards. They really enjoyed it. I saw them taking a rise out of you earlier, Bill."

"Who doesn't?" he shrugged, carelessly.

"Why do you take it, Bill?" his guest asked, confused. The man he had seen last night and this morning was so far removed from the drunken wastrel he had imagined Bill to be, it was difficult to reconcile what he remembered with sudden clarity; this man, whose slight East End-accented voice was not so unlike his own, was an overlooked and even mocked figure, who was given precious little respect from his peers.

Bill shrugged, carelessly, but there was still a pained look in his eyes.

"I don't know Charlie, I don't know."

Charlie didn't know what to say. Momentarily, Bill indicated he was ready to take his leave.

"Right, you'd better rest up here until you get well, lad."

"Thank you Bill," he said, with genuine gratitude. "I think you should be proud of yourself, you're a real gentleman."

"Kind of you to say, my boy... right, I've got to get on."

"Going to the pub?"

That grin again. "I think so, boy." And he disappeared.

The two Germans had promised an early return the next day; that meant between late morning and the mid-afternoon shutdown. An idea forming in his mind, Bill strolled into his bedroom, and took out his very best suit; a charcoal grey three piece, with matching tie. At the base of his wardrobe, he found an old fedora ringed with white that matched his best suit. Humming to himself, Bill murmured the words to *Forever Blowing Bubbles* as he finished trimming the last of his beard with a comb and scissors, until only a very short, neat mat of black hair covered the lower half of his face. He inspected his face; it was as though ten years had been removed in an instant. Still humming pleasantly, Bill dressed in his finest clothes, and gazed into the mirror with a mixture of amusement and real surprise. *A real gentleman,* Maureen's voice told him. *You look like a million pounds, my Bill.*

The truck passed a checkpoint filled with guards who looked different to the SS they had thus far seen. Looking out through the bars of a veritable prison transport truck, Naomi saw long-coated grey figures in steel helmets, with sub-machine guns slung over their shoulders. They looked like fighter versions of the SS tormentors she had already, in the space of one night come to know too well.

Barbed wire is a cruel visage. A threatening deterrent to the outside world, and a bald statement of malice to any and all trapped within its confines. As the truck rolled on, and the green countryside began to recede, the perimeter of their destination came into view, and Naomi shuddered to see the spiked barbs. Once within the confines of the outer perimeter, the road stretched on until the grass stopped entirely, and lumpy, ugly military-style buildings loomed into view, behind more fencing topped by evil spikes.

The paddy wagon paused before a closed gate, with *Arbeit Macht Frei* adorning the entry. *Work makes free*, she translated in her mind, and a chill ran down her spine. Her memory was jogged unpleasantly, with little persuasion. It was the same sign as at Dachau.

One of the guards standing sentient came to check the driver's papers. These men were clad in the more familiar SS garb.

An SS man with the blank collar patch grinned at the assembled group of ragged prisoners, most of whom bore some signs of physical abuse.

"Welcome home, asocials. This is your natural habitat."

He glanced out of both windows, at the partitioned sections lined with barrack huts. Around half of them seemed to be populated, Naomi surmised. Thin, unsmiling figures in ashen-grey and black striped pyjamas. It was like a scene from the wartime propaganda newsreel at the cinema; the images seared into her memory, the visions of her darkest dreams.

"Welcome to Catterick Konzentrationslager."

The transport shuddered to a juttering halt.

"Out! Get out, now!" a guard shouted coarsely, banging the floor of the transport as the door swung open. Rough hands shoved the forlorn group out onto the asphalt, including the silent children.

The same guard barked at them, pacing restlessly in his polished jackboots. His uniform, too, slightly differed from the SD.

"It means Death's Head," one of the prisoners had whispered to her. "Those pirate logos they wear at the German camps. If we see the skull and crossbones on their tops we are as good as dead."

But apart from the peaked caps, that insignia was nowhere to be seen. The guards in whose care they were so rudely deposited shared the blank collar patch, or sported the small SS lightning runes. Even in her fear, she noted how perverse it was that she was glad to see that hated symbol.

A tall guard with a duelling scar sliced across his right cheek towered over them, as he grimly led them into internment. The 'SD' diamond was on his sleeve, but all eyes were focused on the riding whip he carried that swung past the holstered luger pistol at his hip. Behind her, Naomi heard the older couple with young children praying quietly for deliverance and guidance from the Lord.

Naomi doubted He was listening.

They passed through a makeshift reception and front office building, where they were signed in and registered at the camp with the correct paperwork, and then led down an obscenely bright corridor that stunk of disinfectant to a shower area. Two guards stood sentinel at the door.

"Get undressed, clothes off!" the guard that had led them from reception barked. His voice echoed in an eerily quiet building.

"Why is this necessary?" came a scared, male voice that Naomi identified as from Barnsley, or south Yorkshire. It was as though fear had made him speak clearly, with no trace of the heavy regional dialect or usual glottal stops. The effect of fear changes people.

"Get undressed," the guard screamed.

"What for!" was the return cry from the family, and the small children began to sob loudly, terrified out of their wits.

Noting the potent mix of fear and despair that could escalate, one of the SS guarding the doors stepped in to pacify the situation.

"Do not worry! You are to be deloused. We must delouse you in order for you to enter the camp. You are to wash, and change into the designated clothing prescribed you as per your entry into Protective Custody!"

The wailing stopped. The first guard quickly seized the initiative over the people in his ward, his red face bulging in turmoil like a swollen puff adder ready to strike.

"Get undressed! And the children! Remove their clothing!"

In a huddle of confusion, the transport of twelve prisoners brought from Leeds of which Naomi was part was soon joined with two others, and almost forty scared, naked and helpless people soon crowded into the showers, with the men separated into an adjacent room.

The buzz of frightened murmurs grew steadily louder.

"What's going on," a scared girl of perhaps twenty whispered to Naomi, who, similarly wide-eyed, had no answer to give.

The horrendous screaming that ensued almost burst their eardrums. Freezing cold water burst from the pipes and drenched the huddle of terrified prisoners, before dying out as quickly as it had started, with several final belching spurts of ejaculated ice water, finally draining away to leave a shivering huddle of frightened women and children, trembling in the metallic, icy room.

The great metal door at the other side of the room swung open with a great groaning creak, to reveal a blonde female guard. Naomi noted the 'pirate's logo' she'd been warned about, and voiced a silent prayer.

"Everybody out! This way!" the small German woman roared, the noise belying her relatively small frame.

They filed out, and were given striped pyjamas in the next room. *How dehumanising*, Naomi thought. A uniform of dirty pyjamas. She noted with horror that hers were stained with what looked horribly like blood, on one of the rough and frayed sleeve hems. It was too small for her, and its cloth quickly irritated her cold, wet skin.

Onwards they marched, through corridors whose smell strongly reminded Naomi of St. James' Hospital. She glanced into the rooms they passed, seeing much the same thing; piles of rings, jewellery, brooches and the like; mounds of valuables and clothes were stacked. The whole building looked like a giant processing unit for personal items. *And what of their owners*, she thought. *What of the people to whom these items once belonged*?

Finally, the disorientated group were frogmarched out back into the sunlight, to a segregated barrack huts area separated by a barbed wire fence. Several makeshift guard towers were dotted along the wire at intervals, obviously designed in a hurry and reachable via ladder cut into the wood.

They approached a large, fleshy figure, built like a bull squeezed into an SS uniform, stood waiting in the area in front of the two accommodation blocks, spaced roughly one hundred metres apart. To his back, miserable prisoners scattered around were watching quietly. That was the scary part, Naomi decided, glumly. How broken they appear. *Inanimate dolls; a parody of human life in all its possibility.*

A black-clad figure, the officer wore standard SS field uniform, but sported the older greatcoat of black wool. It gave him the menacing appearance of the 'Blackshirt' of nightmares; the original SS, the first 'Schwarze Korps' of infamy that came to be feared throughout Germany as the elite armed bearers of Hitler's will. He stood planted, possessed of some great suppressed malevolence, with the predatory air of a vicious carnivore waiting to pounce. The tall guard strode over to him, saluting smartly.

"Heil Hitler!"

The man almost lazily raised his own arm, first into a Hitler salute then, as though he'd changed his mind halfway through the manoeuvre, flicked his wrist back, in the style of the Führer, Adolf Hitler himself, acknowledging cheering crowds.

"Very well, Hauptscharführer. Line them," he ordered in a low growl.

"*Jawohl*, Brigadeführer Globocnik."

Odilo Globocnik nodded, and the junior officer organised the new internees into nine rows of four. *I look forward to returning to Poland*, Globocnik thought. *To be the* leader. *'Jawohl, SS und Polizeiführer'. No chance of being called that here. That bastard Jew Heydrich. Reichsprotektor Moses Handel.* Fucking yid kike bastard.

Still, he knew the prestige of the role in Britain. And as the Jew had promised him, it was all in preparation. *Himmler*, Heydrich assured him, *has a special role for you in the east, Globus. I think it will suit your temperament. Use your time in Britain well. I shall be watching.*

Slippery fucking kike, he mused.

Globocnik raised his hand.

"Jews and criminal subversives," he began, his voice a guttural rasp of coarse German, each syllable steeped in a low, resonating anger, much like Hitler's. The tall guard repeated his sentences in English for the benefit of the prisoners.

"... This is *Konzentrationslager Catterick*. Here you will find out the real meaning of work, and the danger of opposing the Greater Reich. Some of you," he grinned nastily, "will not survive your stay with us. Works makes you free, but redemption does not come easy..."

Globocnik hawked up a great blob of phlegm as the translator repeated his little speech, and spat it into the thin grey dust of the asphalt, only a metre of so from Naomi's feet. He was already bored with the rigmarole; merely trying to lead by example as the new system went through its infancy.

 "Women and children on this side. Men over there," he snapped.

The rows of four were obliged to approach Globocnik, whose pallid face glowered, his great coat billowing in the wind, framed against the sun like a Gothic vampire; a devilish incarnation of Dracula, or some kind of Dickensian villain. The big man oozed thinly veiled malevolence, and Naomi shuddered to the core as she searched his fleshy, brutal face for human qualities. None were evident.

The prisoners were separated as they neared Globocnik, split by gender into the two hut areas. As it came to the family's turn, the screaming mother refused to be parted from her boys, until the SS waded in with their truncheons and forcibly parted them. Even in her own despair, Naomi winced at the screams. She looked down at her own feet as the terrible ordeal was worsened by Globocnik's hungry, lingering gaze as he took her in, as a wolf would a sheep.

The family were separated by a double fence of barbed wire. *The cruellest thing of all*, Naomi thought, as she sized up the segregation boundary *is that it's only just too wide a gap to be able to touch. Agonisingly out of physical reach, by the smallest margin.* The SS were, evidently, masters in psychological torture.

The gates slammed shut. The separation was complete. SS stayed on the outside to guard; Globocnik disappeared towards another building complex, with the exception of the blond female guard, hissing abuse.

Naomi was allocated a bunk in the female hut by the snarling blonde guard, who then left them to it. No guards remained; the new prisoners were left entirely alone.

"Stay strong," a sad-faced girl told her. "Be quiet, and be strong. Things will work out."

She squeezed Naomi's hand, briefly, with a flimsy, bloodless grip before shuffling away and out to the yard; for, as far as she could tell, no discernible reason.

Naomi, in her forlorn, hopeless state, tried engaging some of the other interned women that were present in conversation. But her introduction and entreaties were quietly rebuffed, or lost as tiny mutters and indistinct noises. All had the same hollow, silent air of irreversible loss, and the vaporous demeanour of ghosts.

A resplendent figure of a man strolled out of his bedroom and across the entrance hall to the lounge. Charlie Lightfoot sat bolt upright at the sight of him. A charcoal grey, three piece suit and matching tie and fedora, with his war medals pinned prominently to his chest. Bill Wilson *radiated* power, exuding gravitas.

"Blimey!"

But Bill cut him off, his face set with resolve.

"This is *your* flat now, Charlie. Anyone asks, you rented this place from old John Wilson. That was my father. Or, as you won't have papers, I imagine, if you can sort it out, make sure that the given surname on there is Wilson; you can be my son, and my Maureen's boy. Born 1919, the year before she died, so you'd be about the right age."

"Bill..."

"You'll find some money in a tin in my wardrobe, and my suits. Do what my brother, and my mates couldn't do, and a whole generation or two of lost young men couldn't do. What this generation, from the looks of things, can't do either, with warmongers at the top leadin' 'em. I don't know what the future will look like. But there will be one. And you have the chance to make it a good one, wherever you are, wherever you go. Make something of yourself. Don't be another wasted life in war. Don't serve rulers. Be independent. Be proud of who you are, and be strong. Take care of yourself boy."

"What the hell you talking about, Bill?" Charlie was open-mouthed. "Don't be rash, just... just think about it, all right? Just think about it."

"Remember, *Wilson*. Thank you, Charlie boy."

Bill touched the rim of his hat to the young man, and without another word turned on his heel and left the room. Charlie tried leaping up to pursue him, but was stopped in his tracks by the mutiny his body undertook, not least the bad leg which had plagued him since childhood.

"Bill? *Bill*! Don't be daft now Bill, come on mate, come back and we can–"

The door slammed shut.

PART IV

Swaggering. Sauntering. *Smirking*, almost, with a leering scowl, and a long great coat that swept along with him as he strode to the open-top Mercedes; thus did Reinhard Heydrich leave the Savoy – resplendent in his role as *Reich Protector* of the realm.

Sat alongside him in the backseat was a familiar figure; almost chinless, wearing rimless spectacles and a stern, schoolmasterly expression; a man feared and loathed even more than the 'Blond Beast' beside him, on account of – until recently at least – his far greater fame, and the infamy of his paramilitary army's daring and despicable deeds.

Flanked by two other vehicles, SS-3 set off.

People thronging the main streets running parallel with the Thames River stopped to stare, gazing in a mixture of curiosity and reservation. Birds flocked overheard, flapping together through the cold air, and breath rose in a mist from the mouths of those slowly moving or entirely still figures who were quietly watching proceedings. The convoy purred on, down the Strand and along the Mall, where the sleek black vehicles rolled mercurially past the haunted shell of Buckingham Palace, bomb damage still evident on its flank. With soldiers lining the lane that led to the Wellington Arch, they made their slow progress onwards until curving round to the approach at Hyde Park corner.

~

In the park, Alan peeled away from Jack and William and made straight for the statue. There were no final words or moment of gravitas between them; feelings were clear, the intent was there, and the magnitude of the moment and their deed was not lost on any of them. Sentiment and hesitation had no place now.

"Not as busy as I'd have thought," Jack murmured quietly to the Scot.

"No," he replied thoughtfully. "And not as much in the way of troops either."

William was right. They had expected a heavy line of army, SS or both to stand sentinel along the road and the route, but the troops were sparsely scattered, and inattentive to boot. There was a moderately sizeable crowd of curious passers-by – not as many of they had hoped, but more than enough for Alan to lose himself in after the shot that would change history.

They had no such illusions of their own survival.

Up ahead, the familiar figure in his close-fitting leather jacket slipped in with the figures milling around the Achilles statue known as Wellington Monument. They had decided to spurn the great Winchester sniper rifle in favour of a more subtle weapon – the Sten gun – which Alan concealed with ease beneath the leather of his coat without attracting much suspicion.

The spot was perfect, and oddly undefended. Even had he been firing a 9mm weapon, there was little chance of Alan missing from that range; at twenty-to-thirty paces and from raised ground, he could have hit the two German paramilitary leaders with a stone thrown by hand. As Hitler's two most feared henchmen, it was remarkable that such an opportunity presented itself.

~

SS-3 swung around Wellington Arch, flanked by a convoy of cross-marked cars. Silent crowds watched unsmilingly at the unmistakeable profiles of the two men in its backseat.

Alan loitered, ambling over in as casual manner as he could to the monument, then lingering in place. There were no guards around the Achilles statue; the nearest were stationed at the fence, thirty paces away and keeping no particular eye on his position, their gaze roving across the massing London crowd almost uninterestedly.

Preceded by several others, SS-3 swung into place, and Alan sensed, rather than saw, the two men on the backseat. He surreptitiously hung behind the corner of the statue, spine-tingling chills running through his electrified body, and he noted with an overwhelming rush of recognition that it was the blond Heydrich sat in SS-3, with – incredibly – the familiar figure of a prim, bespectacled, almost-schoolmasterly man. His putative master.

Himmler and Heydrich, sat side-by-side.

Quick as a flash, Alan withdrew his weapon, spurning the monument's base with a clear shot already in sight from his slightly raised vantage. It was a perfect spot for a successful shot, albeit without anything in the way of camouflage and with nowhere to hide. But the mission, Alan knew, outweighed his own life.

He locked on, his line-of-sight passing over Heydrich too quickly for regret or lingering doubt, and settled his sights on the unsuspecting face of Heinrich Himmler.

Alan pulled the trigger, and all hell broke loose.

Dropping the weapon, the Geordie ducked back behind the statue, every fibre of his being electrified with a rush of adrenaline that thrilled his nerves with a fiery charge. Mind racing, he ducked and, making sure to keep low, slipped into the gaggle of screaming people who were breaking for cover in all directions, a mass of flailing limbs and trampled women. German troops yelled out, and several bullets whizzed over in the direction of the Achilles statue, sending several innocent bystanders flying with a great spray of arterial blood. Just then, only seconds into the pandemonium, a great explosion was heard, and without hesitation, Alan scurried out towards the south carriage drive.

Knowing that with German troops further back in the park, the escape route used after the confrontation with the British fascists would not have worked, Alan had kept his bike nearby to Knightsbridge, and in the overwhelming panic of the moment, managed to steal away with the crowd, wincing with every shot he heard fired into the screaming mass of people. No bullets strafed him, and managing to stay on his feet in the mad and frenzied dash of the panicked crowd, Alan fled the southern outskirts of the park and made for his bike, pursued by several Germans who had identified the occasional flash of leather as their man.

William for his part, having seen the shot land, ran forwards from the other side of the road and launched his grenade at the car with an involuntary yell. Incredibly, no German soldier was able to react, distracted as they were by the sniper shot from the other direction; all except the Blond Beast, Reinhard Heydrich. With the innate sixth sense of a cunning predator, he turned to William even as the grenade landed in the car, jumping out and crouching for cover as it exploded, sending horsehair flying from the ruined upholstery of the car, further despoiling the lifeless body of Himmler with its ruined face, a gigantic blotch of red leaking crimson blood like a cascading waterfall framed by dust.

Even as William went to withdraw his weapon, the prepared SS leader had withdrawn his own custom-made Luger pistol and fired twice, rapid-fire shots into the kneecaps of the Scottish partisan. William screamed involuntarily as his legs collapsed from under him, twisting as he crashed into the road, where another bullet from a German soldier entered his left arm.

Moments passed, as Heydrich lowered himself to sit with his back to the wreck of SS-3, breathing heavily. The sound of warning yells in his mother tongue brought him back to life in a millisecond, scrambling around the embattled vehicle as a feminine scream preceded the explosion that sent flame flashing across the car.

Jack had determinedly lobbed his grenade, before firing on the nearest German troops to him and exiting. Hearing the scream that preceded the explosion of his grenade, it occurred to him for a split-second that Mary's war cry had sounded similar in Spain, and he hoped that she had not joined the attack against their wishes. There was no time to find out; firing a third shot at a dazed Wehrmacht man who was blinded by the blast, Jack broke free of the pavement and joined the straggling or injured citizens who, for various reasons, were only just managing to flee the scene. He tore north and east, pursued by a brace of keen-eyed Germans, having been confident that the SS leaders were dead and now thinking only of escape. Firing back over his shoulder, Jack managed to create enough distance between himself and his pursuers, and he sprinted as fast as he could into the nearby maze of avenues, running frantically through the shadows of grey block buildings, adrenaline continuing to pump through his body, more alive than he had ever felt.

Suddenly panicked, Heydrich leapt to his feet and fled towards the next car in the convoy, his long, horsey face contorting in anger as SS-3 exploded in a great ball of flame. A bullet whizzed by the Blond Beast's head, sending the SS chief himself crashing to the concrete as German shots halted another figure that had run forwards screaming. Mary was brought down, swarmed upon instantly by a gaggle of Wehrmacht security troops as they beat her senseless with the butt of their rifles.

Twenty metres away, having seen Heydrich slip away from the impact of Jack's grenade, a frenzied Mary had leapt to action herself, in defiance of the pleas and demands of the others. Her shot had missed Heydrich by inches, before the Spanish beauty was brought down in a hail of bullets too, and she crashed hard to the cobbles in pain and regret. The screams and yells intensified, even as the general pandemonium lessened as the crowds fled in terror. Astoundingly, the Reichsprotektor's orders to the troops to not shoot-to-kill had been obeyed, and the second of four would-be assassinators lay bleeding on the parkside road. The stricken Spaniard tried to swallow the poison capsule she had prepared, but was prevented by the merciless blows that rained down until her resisting hands dropped limply to the ground. Both William and Mary lay prostrate; one agonised by pain and apparent failure, and the other unconscious, bleeding heavily from several open wounds. Yet immobile as they were, both were still very much alive.

Hauling himself to his feet, a dusty, blood-streaked and heavily perspiring Heydrich gazed around the scene of chaos, as the people left in the vicinity of the attacks slowly came out of their hiding spots. He gazed at the burning car, an inferno of flames licking at the supposed body of Heinrich Himmler, terrible brightness and the smell of roasted flesh. Surveying the aftermath of carnage, and with barely a glance at the stricken figures who were being inspected by German troops, Britain's Nazi Viceroy began to laugh a high-pitched, hysterical laugh, swelling with pride as the apotheosis of his own existence occurred to him, and something more elevated than mere pride coursed through the blood in his thrilled veins. Heydrich felt unconquerable, a titan of history, and his proud laughter pealed out amidst fire and blood and death.

The doors of the Royal Oak opened, and sunlight pealed in to the slightly dingy room of polished wood as Bill Wilson strolled in, his footsteps echoing loudly as he marched to the bar with a purposeful stride.

"Good morning, Sir what can I get you–" Arthur began, before the words died on his lips as he realised just whom it was that stood before him. The Royal Oak regular masked his quiet amusement.

"Large whiskey please, Art."

Bill's tone betrayed more of his cockney roots than had been previously allowed, though he retained some refined elocution.

"Oh, it's you Bill. Yes, right away."

Arthur poured a large whiskey out for his dazzlingly dressed regular, stealing glances at Bill as he did so.

"Didn't know you were a military man, Bill."

"Yes. Served through the whole campaign."

"You never said... even when I talked about Passchendaele," Arthur said, curiously. Bill just shrugged.

"No one ever asked, Art."

Winking as the barman, he took an exultant sip of the whiskey, marvelling at the taste. Of all the things this island has contributed to the world, and the advancement of civilisation, Bill decided, whiskey must surely be one of the best.

He voiced as much to Arthur, who was only half-listening, his eyes drawn one particular medal in pride of place on Bill's chest.

"By *Jove*. Is that a Victoria Cross, Bill?"

Bill patted the little gunmetal cross, hanging from his left breast by its crimson ribbon.

"Yes... it is."

Arthur stared at him, open-mouthed. The Victoria Cross was the highest military decoration for an armed forces serviceman in the British Empire, and even in the Great War it was a rarely awarded trinket. Only exceptional courage and performance could be honoured in such a way. It was an award solely intended for those of extreme valour. And this was the man, Arthur noted with astonishment, with whom he'd shared perfunctory small talk every day for nigh on two decades, only infrequently engaging in meaningful, or personal, debates.

"Christ Bill... what did you do to get that?"

The old soldier's rugged, yet striking face, newly exposed by the beard trim, was utterly expressionless. "I did what was necessary."

Bill Wilson downed his whiskey with aplomb.

"Same again, please Art... and have one yourself."

Arthur was still visibly taken aback by the transformation of the handsome, grizzled man who stood so powerfully in front of him, as though reborn. "Don't mind if I do, Bill. And might I add, it will be a pleasure."

He poured them both a whiskey, repressing the consuming urge to query Bill about the remarkable alteration that had transpired in less than a day. With glasses in hand, they toasted each other, warmly. Bill proposed his own; resuming his clipped, cultured tone as he did so:

"To old friends, our *loves*, our *lives*; to comrades lost, to those we've forgotten and those who have forgotten us; to the dead, the living and the yet-to-be; to times gone by, good and bad, and perhaps one day, a better future."

"I'll drink to that, Bill. I will drink to that."

~

Bill was a man of great patience, but as expected, he did not have long to wait. A great clatter of the door, and two Wehrmacht uniforms noisily stomped into the Royal Oak public bar, their exuberance echoing around the wooden room, with two giggling young ladies clutching them as they careered inside. The din they made was more than enough to attract Bill's attention, sat as he was by the piano, unobtrusively, bristling with quiet repugnance.

"Hello, gentlemen," Arthur said, patiently. "Lovely to see you again in the Oak. You certainly seem to get a lot of spare time in the course of duty."

Sebastian's smile faded as the mask slipped, for a moment.

"That is so, yes indeed, Arthur Speakman the landlord. But it is not for you to comment on the workings of the German army, is it?" he chastised, waggled a finger at the man who was almost thrice his age in a parody of pedantic admonition. In his corner, Bill grimaced, quietly seething.

"No, indeed," Arthur managed to say, at his most unctuous. "Now, what can I get you gentlemen and your lady friends?"

And as the self-satisfied German turned to speak to his companions, leaving Arthur waiting patiently, Bill's own patience reached the end of its tether. He rose to his feet, straightening the blazer of his fine suit and strolled to the bar, taking up position behind the arrogant lieutenant.

Eventually, Sebastian Koller deigned to acknowledge his presence, and turned to the older man, not recognising him for a moment. His eyes narrowed as he did, incredulous, before setting on the prominent Victoria Cross.

But Bill did not address him. His eyes were fixed on the Germans' companions.

"Hello girls. I want you to step into the saloon while I talk to these men."

"You what?" one of the girls said uncertainly. She reeked of cheap perfume; Bill hid his distaste, masked with a pleasant smile and an unruffled air.

"Now, *please*... Shift."

Beats of silence, as the girls gave querying looks to the German lieutenant, unsure of themselves. Bill stood proudly, his chest thrust out and his jaw set, like a prize-fighter. The awkward pause grew, and then Sebastian seemed to reach a decision. He nodded at them, curtly, and they promptly disappeared into the saloon, casting uncertain glances back at the dashing, middle-aged British man in his fancy three-piece suit and war medals. Helmut sighed theatrically, taking his elbow off the bar and coming to stand next to the lieutenant, side-by-side, and together they faced down the impertinent Bill.

"That was very rude," Sebastian admonished him quietly, a shark's smile in place.

Bill shook his head. "No, calling me a halfwit is very rude," he told him in perfect German, before smoothly reverting back to English. "Quite an obnoxious insult, after a rude and transparent attempt to intimidate members of the British public, who were peacefully drinking in this pub."

Helmut was open-mouthed.

"Yes… it is you," he said slowly, in English. "From yesterday?"

"I see you are very well decorated," was Sebastian's haughty observation, his eyes now narrowed to slits.

"Oh yes," Bill nodded, taking a step closer to the German. "I did a lot of killing for them. *Dozens* I killed. Dozens of *your* lot."

"Is that so?" Sebastian tried to sneer.

"Yes, it is so. It is *indeed*," Bill breathed, violence in his eyes as he took another step forwards. "I still *see* a lot of them… in my dreams. I see them screaming on the end of my bayonet, or twisting, broken, into the mud in front of me. I once seized a machine gun in a Boche trench… or rather, one of *your* trenches, and turned it on the retreating Jerries. Six of us reached it, of the dozens who charged that section, and your lot died in droves. I remember the hail of bullets, and a line of men being cut down like flies, like grey shadows, falling. This medal," he said, tapping the Victoria Cross, "… was for that, and another time like it, when I alone survived in my whole platoon. The whole company numbered nine out of two hundred and thirty, by the end. *Nine.* Can you imagine? By the Spring of '18 they were sending green kids to make up the numbers. School kids, lying about their age to get sent to France after being taught the *glories* of war; then, terrified by reality, having to run sobbing through the quagmire at machine gun fire, getting shot or blown to pieces, then being eaten by rats. Seventeen year old boys screaming in a muddy trench, bleeding like stuck pigs with their innards hanging out, intestines spilling out into their laps, calling for their mothers as they spluttered and choked to death. *That*, young man, is war. Not very *glamorous*, really. Not a happy time for me, or something to be proud of. Yes, I killed a lot of men. *You* ever killed anyone?"

"No," Sebastian admitted, his face flushing.

"And *you*?" Bill asked Helmut gruffly, turning his burning glare to the Bavarian private.

"Nein."

Helmut looked down at his feet, shamefaced. Bill's contemptuous gaze took them both in.

"No, I *thought* not. Came bloody close though last night didn't you?"

Sebastian stared at him, malevolence returning. "I do not know what you mean."

His tone was dangerous. Bill registered that the German's patience was at an end. He had pushed his luck further than expected. The bully was evidently regretting his own cat and mouse game of toying with the British man, which had spectacularly backfired, and his resulting action would be predictably violent. Only shock had made him defensive; any longer, and the German officer would stop tolerating the importunate, fearless confrontation.

Snick of a pistol action as Bill drew his gun, its loud roar freezing Sebastian as the old British soldier fired a bullet into Helmut's thigh. The impact of its deafening gunshot shuddered through everyone in the pub. The Bavarian screamed, collapsing in a heap as the girls listening from the saloon bar struck up a terrified wailing din. Sebastian's growing anger evaporated with the shock of the moment; he stood open-mouthed, rooted frozen to the spot. Bill trained his gun on the lieutenant; still mindful of the writhing Helmut on the ground, but the younger

German was preoccupied solely with his wounded leg from which dark claret freely flowed.

"There's a clue," Bill remarked calmly to the shocked Sebastian. "The fella had a bad leg."

"What..."

"The boy you nearly killed. He had a bad leg."

"*What*!"

Bill fired a bullet into Sebastian's right leg, where it lodged in the femur, and the Wehrmacht officer fell twisting with an awful, piercing scream, searing pain shooting through him as he howled. A prolonged stream of obscenities and wails erupted from his effervescing mouth, while Helmut grimaced and groaned beside him, wriggling in agony.

"Does that help jog your memory?"

Neither German was able to answer. Bill placed his foot carefully on Helmut's gunshot wound, pressing down mercilessly while he disarmed the young man, before doing the same to Sebastian, pinning him with greater malice. The lieutenant yelled out as Bill's foot crushed his damaged leg, and the cockney calmly unholstered the luger pistol and pocketed it, after appreciatively inspecting its design.

"Art?" Bill called. "Come here, mate."

Arthur hesitantly shuffled out from the stock room. He'd served in the war, and was no stranger to gunshots, but the prospect of a gun battle in his own pub with the occupying Germans had been too much for him to witness.

"Yes Bill?" His voice shook, barely audible over the German cries.

"One for the road please, Art. Best make it a large one."

Arthur inhaled deeply, composing himself, and nodded to his long-time customer. The sheer normality of the drink order helped him recover his wits quickly. He chose his finest glass and filled it with ice, then poured Bill a large Scotch, serving four fingers worth, almost reaching the rim of the glass.

"That's on the house, Bill."

Bill Wilson raised the glass and toasted him, with an approving tilt of the head.

"Very decent of you, Art."

The Victoria Cross recipient took an appreciative sip of the Scotch, smacking his lips. "That's a right touch." Nodding gratefully, Bill tipped his head back and drained the glass in one go, without the trace of a wince, and then turned to the stricken soldiers, trained the gun downwards and fired one last bullet into each.

Drenched in a hot sweat that made his clothes cling to his perspiring flesh, Jack tore through the ginnel, having abandoned the vehicle and pelted out of it, confident that he had shaken his German pursuers. The alley connected two contiguous neighbourhoods, running alongside a long, corrugated iron fence, flanked by a small woodland area enclosed by a wall at its other side. He pelted through, footsteps crunching on the gravel as he evaded litter, branches and leaves, until he burst out into the adjoining neighbourhood and a quiet residential street.

There was nothing but silence in the sleepy suburb. Not even birds could be heard from the small, rectangular woodland of trees, floor matted with the decay of dead leaves.

Jack jogged down the gently sloping road, passing the slew of semi-detached houses... 113, 111, 109... until finally he reached house number 69, and hurriedly extracting a small key from trousers that clung tight to his legs, the frantic young man let himself in to his mother's abode.

He burst through the door, turning to his immediate right to rifle through the cabinet by the threshold. Behind him, curious as to the sudden commotion in the hallway, a young man appeared, perplexed, with questions forming on his lips.

Jack turned, and stared into the blue eyes of a German.

Without hesitation, as though electrified, the young Londoner withdrew his gun, reacting quicker than the unprepared Wehrmacht soldier, and his bullet shot Hans through the neck.

As the young man collapsed to the floor, leaking a spreading pool of dark blood on the polished wooden tiles of the hallway, Jack stared at him uncomprehendingly for a moment, before coming to his senses and racing upstairs. He ran into his old bedroom, flipping the bed over and frantically rooting around for the ready-kit of supplies, ammunition and medical equipment that he had left there. After only seconds of intense searching, Jack grabbed the necessary materials and pelted back downstairs to where a bleary-eyed Maisie was entering the hall, newly awoken by the sound of the shot.

Her eyes opened wide at the sight of her stricken Hans, and then wild-eyed, she turned her gaze to the unexpected sight of her brother, gun in hand, rucksack slung over his shoulder and another large bag in his hand. Her eyes searched his for understanding, as the horror of the moment overwhelmed her senses. He stood frozen, the light of comprehension dawning in his eyes as he bristled at the sight of his sister. Fury took him, and he reached the bottom of the stairs, dumping everything but the gun and turning angrily to the girl.

"You…" he began slowly, shaking his head in tiny, jerky movements, as though begging her to deny the undeniable.

Grief and misery finally welled up in her, after the shock of the moment had dissipated.

"What have you done," she screamed at her brother, dropping to her knees to cradle Hans' head in her arms. The hole in his neck leaked blood, spilling over the white folds of her neat dress, and she pressed her face gently into his, pulling back up as he groaned, choking on the crimson fluids that pulsed through his throat.

Jack stared aghast.

"You are with *him*?!" he screamed, blood vessels bursting in his sweat-soaked face.

His sister continued to sob over Hans' body, holding her own bloodstained hands to her leaking eyes to examine, moaning in horrified disbelief.

"You're with him! A *German soldier*!" Jack roared even louder, infuriated beyond the limits of reason as spittle flew from his enraged mouth.

Maisie turned her tear-streaked face to him.

"Get out of here! Go!"

"But," he stammered, taken aback; his anger instantly dissipating as he held his face in his hands, gripped by utter horror. "Maisie! Come with me! They're after me!"

She continued to cradle Hans' head, and he spluttered blood, spraying her clothes.

"Maisie, they're after me, you're not safe," Jack shouted as loudly as he could, wishing only to get his sister out of the house and away.

"Go!" she screamed, a hysterical, piercing yell.

Jack's face bunched up, running through a gamut of emotions before he focused on Hans, and his eyes grew cold. Without another word, Jack turned on his heel and dashed out into the cold air of the English day.

"Stay with me," his sister sobbed in the hallway, her whole body convulsing with violent spasms. "Stay with me, Hans..."

Outside, Jack looked left and right, ascertaining the road was clear, and then he jogged back up the road as quickly as he could. Hauling his heavy bags across the desolate woodland and its dead trees, the weight of his collected items slowing his progress back to the car, Jack felt tears form in his eyes as the incomprehensible scenario he had just exited registered in his mind. Distracted, he stumbled through the ginnel, only dumbly noting as he neared its end that he was at the car.

Jack reached the vehicle, and – zing! – a bullet whizzed by his head, barely missing, not unlike the one that had almost hit Reinhard Heydrich only thirty minutes before. He yelled out involuntarily, dropping everything but the gun and ducking down, panic-stricken and feverish. With his back pressed against the side of the battered car, Jack faced the ominous woodland, which he peered at until he was certain there were no assailants hidden in its relatively shallow depths. He slid himself over to the front of the car, trying to judge the trajectory of the bullets that were being sent his way. Despite his composure, fear gripped him.

Having escaped the maelstrom of chaos that had been their assassination of Himmler and, he was almost certain, of Heydrich too, this was not the death he had in mind. Had Alan, William or both managed to defy the odds and flee, Jack had nurtured a very real hope that they could link up with Mary and disappear underground, together; victorious.

That quixotic hope was a forlorn one, and having already been dashed by the sight of the German in his mother's house, it had been rekindled by his departure, despite the awful realisation of his sister's fraternisation... only to be sunk yet again, and even more completely, by the sudden shock of this attack.

Jack raised his gun over the car bonnet, letting fly with four shots in the direction of the German troops.

"¡No pasarán!" The revolutionary screamed, partly out of habit, and in order to channel his rising fear into rage. It was an emotive cry, delivered with gusto. *They Shall Not Pass* had been the unifying call to action of the left. Now, it was tainted by tragedy; after Madrid, the city for whom that slogan existed, finally fell to the fascists in '39 the group had vowed never to use it again.

More bullets zinged past the car with a sinister ring, shell-casings landing all around Jack's crouched body, and – perhaps just for good measure – the wall directly opposite him at the ginnel entrance was peppered with shots. His imagination twisting sickly, delirious in the heat of battle, Jack imagined that the soldiers were trying to draw the silhouette of a giant smiley face of bullet holes on the wall for him.

Snapping out of his flight of fancy, he yelled again, spouting more anti-fascist slogans from Spain as he stretched his gun around the side of the car, firing shots at the soldiers or police with whom he battled. It didn't matter to him. They were fascists.

A grenade landed on the pavement by the ginnel entrance; Jack was no more than eight or nine feet away, well within the range of its blast. He scrambled away, flinging himself from a crouched position around the side of the car and rolling away from the detonation, taking care to land behind the vehicle so that he wasn't exposed to the Germans positioned in front. In the ensuing explosion, Jack's brief feeling of relief was shattered as a bullet entered his left quadricep from behind, sending pain shooting through his system and spinning him out into the road.

"Fucks sake!" He screamed, letting out an agonised wordless yell of rage.

Bleeding heavily, Jack wriggled, trying to manoeuvre into position to fire back in the direction of the attackers to his rear, but just as he raised the gun in anger, another bullet passed through the sole of his left foot. The shot shattered nerves, and sent lightning bolts of terrible agony charging through his body with a vicious pulse. Stricken horribly, Jack rolled over and lay screaming in tortured pain, and then a mass of Germans swarmed upon him from both directions like terrible locusts in grey, dragging the shrieking, bloody partisan away to the nearest cross-marked car.

Less than half a mile away, Maisie cradled the head of her lover in her bloodstained lap as he tried to speak.

"I love you," she sobbed, stroking his burning face.

Through his pain, the young German forced his eyes to meet hers, one final exchange of pale blue between them, and then, gurgling as he attempted a final declaration of love, the bubbling blood frothed sickeningly in his mouth and throat, and in gasping agony, Hans choked through his last laboured breaths and finally died.

They hate us because we do not have their thoughts in our heads; we do not think their thoughts. We do not spend every day thinking somebody else's thoughts. We think thoughts, and read books; they burn books, and Goebbels screams at the world the thoughts that they should think. And the part of the world controlled by their army Black Angels, the part of the world enforced by the rule of their guns, their Gestapo, their viciousness, that part of the world has to listen.

They began to think their thoughts, and then acquiesced when they killed and tortured those who did not think these thoughts.

Conformity became patriotic spirit and racial duty; dissent became blasphemous against the Gods of their blood, and their devil held aloft; their Hitler held in place by the jackboots, the truncheons and the guns commanded by the Himmler's and Heydrich's in the shadows.

Simon's quill flashed across the pages of his diary for what he knew would be the last time. Oddly enough, he felt utterly at peace. The fear he had once expected was entirely absent; inevitability brought perspective, which brought calm.

Immanuel Kant wrote regarding morality: 'a means to an end is by definition an immoral approach to take with people, human beings should always be considered an end themselves.' Germany was a nation of philosophers and scientists. These new, coldly logical Germans disagree with Kant; we are all a means to an end, the end always justifies the means, and when their "end" entails a Europe free of blood they deem tainted and 'untermensch' – lesser, inferior – the means with which they achieve it are correspondingly bloody. What of morals now?

The new, cruel Germany took our island. Our whole world, everything we have ever known and loved, the places and people, have fallen under the control of a maniacal anti-Semite who preaches annihilation of his enemies – real and imagined –Europe suffers the bloody tyranny of his bloodthirsty SS private army, and its secret police. His SS chief Himmler, their pet 'Blond Beast' Heydrich and the historic German tasks they oversee that Goebbels tells the German speaking world over the radio is so necessary for the future survival of their people. The Europe they have created lines up dissidents, 'racial enemies' and political opposition against the wall, dressing up mass-murder as the 'liquidation of partisans' – crimes against humanity disguised as actions of war.

"Liquidation"... "Historic tasks"... "Enemies of our blood"...

How can there be racial enemies when underneath our flesh we are all the same people? How did the love of humanity and the horror we all felt at the suffering and destruction caused by the Great War transform into a Nordic blood fetish, into the machinations of sociopaths inciting a lost generation into bloodletting; violent language poisoning the souls of so many good men and setting Europe and our peoples at each other's throats again, like rabid, feral dogs? How did an advanced, cultured nation and people such as the Germans come to view fellow human beings as an inferior sub-species and start to crush them underfoot? How did an entire society come to quietly accept the Gestapo arresting, torturing and murdering thousands of its own people; a few thousand men holding millions in a blood-stained grip of fear?

How, how, how... even as my own probable end approaches, I will never understand...

This is not for publication. I am not writing this to be distributed amongst the people, to stir people up to rebellion or revolt; Christ, I've done enough of that recently, even openly, and still people flock to join the Blackshirts. It is as though I am ranting nonsensically; where are all the people who mocked Hitler the raving anti-Semite, preaching his spiel and frothing at the mouth at every podium he screamed from; victim of the world, the perpetual victim of world Jewry and Karl Marx, despite unlimited power in central Europe? Now I am the undesirable. People are already pragmatically preparing for an endless fascist future, and adjusting their worldviews accordingly. Cynicism and adaptability reign. I am shunned; already the dissident, the one to upset the applecart. In the minds of my neighbours, who avert their eyes, they already see me being hauled away to the van kicking and screaming, handcuffed and black bagged; they already envision the questions that Gestapo men are asking them.

Orwell was arrested last night, and now surely, it is my turn to face their undying hatred of conflicting views, of dissident opinion, of unalterable intellect. We read books, and think thoughts. We write things.

They cannot let us live. They know it, as do we.

If this is to be my final line, I ask nothing of no one. All humans think and act as they see fit. Apathy overwhelms me. Tomorrow belongs to the jackboot; today, my last, I am the king of my own mind, the master of my own realm.

Simon raised his head, acknowledging sadly the lack of absolution and absence of satisfaction that he had expected from the conclusion of his final written entry. Just as he began to add a last line, a new conclusion, hoping to stoke his inner feelings with one final burst of prose, he heard a loud crash from downstairs as the door was kicked in. At that, he dropped a lit match into his calabash, and sat calmly behind the desk, trying to quell the overwhelming violence of his emotions and be calm in the face of the inevitable.

The bedroom door exploded. Three men, in trench coats and fedoras marched in, gazing at him with unfriendly, hostile eyes. The writer took in their visage; noting that they were almost caricatures of the Gestapo of popular imagination. They were cardboard cut-out villains, worthy of a place in one of Britain's great novels of the past century.

"Welcome, brothers," he said quietly.

Simon smiled at them, adding to their bemusement. Before they could act, the writer had raised his father's Great War pistol from his lap, almost triumphantly, and held it to his own temple, breathing heavily. He stared with growing contempt at the cold-faced men facing him, his would-be captors, who to his mind were just as trapped as he was by the unforgiving system.

An old memory of a lakeside afternoon in summer came to mind, calming him, and the half-smile that split his boyish face widened.

"Heil Hitler!"

He clicked the trigger.

Scornful laughter rang out from the Gestapo agents, and the writer pulled the trigger once more, before the useless gun dropped from his grip, and shock seized him. Suddenly, another sensation crept up his spine; the very real, rising panic of fear.

One of the intruders approached the stricken writer, an ugly grin now playing across his own angular features.

"Heil Hitler," he agreed; a sardonic, German-accented voice dripping with savage mockery.

The first swing of the cosh broke Simon's jaw. The second, delivered expertly to the solar plexus took his wind, and with it, removed him from consciousness. Sharp pain cut through the shock and fear, and as he slumped over where he sat, Simon tried to embrace the descending darkness as renewed laughter rang spitefully in his whistling ears.

As though a daze had been lifted, Bill Wilson strolled the streets of his native London with more clear cognition than he had felt since *that* day, years ago, when the teenage boy had set out for France, thrilled with the prospect of battling the Jerries with his pals.

With violent, striking vividity, a series of buried memories resurfaced and flashed through his mind's eye; burned onto the surface of his vision, oddly calming.

Maureen's tears as she waved him goodbye; retreating away up the gangplank, turning, running back to give her one last hug, squeezing tight, squeezing so tightly...

Laughter on the ferry; John dancing in a sort of modified two-step into a tapdance...

Andrew, his brother, wrapping his arm around Bill and saying don't worry kid, we'll be home by Christmas, after we've Given Jerry What For.

Crouched in No Man's Land; bullets whizzing overhead, John lying next to him in the shellhole, his intestines hanging out and innards spilling with the torrents of blood, arterial spray covering Bill's face as he tried in vain to help his friend, frantic, before putting him out of his misery with the bayonet, his first kill, John's eyes dimming, his hand resting on Bill's face, crying, bawling, dying, Bill collapsing against his warm, dead flesh; crying, bawling...

The Battle of the Somme; told to walk slowly, not to run, thousands cut down by Boche machine guns, thousands, twisted and flailing and screaming into the mud, to be eaten by swollen rats the size of small cats...

Looking over to his right; finally breaking into a run as everyone else was cut to ribbons by the monstrous, roaring guns; Andrew to his right trying to cut through the wire that artillery had failed to cut; riddled with bullets, twisting on the wire, trying to reach him and falling into a shellhole, trapped there.

All day, more parts of Andrew's body shot off the wire, until he had no head, no arms, just a bloody stump, a neckhole spurting blood, a lump of torn flesh, stuck in the shellhole watching his brother's body shot to pieces, until the last chunks of it fell from the cruel wire, not enough spattered fragments of gore left to be held up.

The German, pleading for his life, a scared kid of twenty, hesitation, then the memory of their boys being strafed by the machine guns, Andrew's body, his mother's son, the German pleading, begging for his life, Andrew's body in the wire, begging Bill in English, rushing forwards, thrusting the bayonet through his abdomen, the strangled cry, thrusting again, again, again...

Walking down the gangplank in the middle of a trench; sleeping soldiers, some with rats crawling over them, half-dead from exhaustion and stress. How can life continue after this, he thought, how can life continue after this, how can we go on after this, how can we...

A sniper's bullet, slamming into David's temple at the point where a slight step up raised the tall man's head to a point slightly higher than the parapet. He fell sideways into the mud, oozing blood from a neat hole in his skull. Death came to him faster than anything possible.

Announcement; the Germans surrender. As of 11 o'clock, the 11th of the 11th month, November 1918, the guns will fall silent, and the war will be over. Congratulations, men, we have won. Silence.

Christmas, back home. Maureen stricken. I'm Forever Blowing Bubbles, *he sang.* Pretty Bubbles In The Air. *Silence.*

The first day of 1920; his father John, reedy voice crackling with the strain of age, weakened by consumption. Where's your pal John, and Maureen? Why isn't Andrew here? How come you never bring your mates around anymore, Billy? Where's your mother?

His father, dead; a yellow, waxy skeleton.

The memories of those terrible years resurfaced, and Bill smiled to think of them, remembering those faces for the first time without the pain of absence, the sting of regret. He imagined an imminent reunion. Would it happen? *Hope so*, he thought. Bloody well hope so.

Time had passed slowly, like a slug crawling across a razor blade for eternity. Sisyphus. A Heraklean labour. Today, the sun was shining. There was joy in his heart.

Bill made his way through the streets of Bloomsbury, weaving through the Russell Square, attracting curious glances from the handful of people strolling through with their dogs. His chest was puffed out, and he marched proudly, swollen with intent and the glory of mortality.

It occurred to him that while he had survived the Great War, all that followed subsequent had been a proxy life. Now, he was emancipated. Death held no fear for him. The knowledge that all will soon end adds a brightness to each image, a beauty in each visage and a sweetness to each scent.

Exiting the square, he passed the British Museum, glancing almost scornfully at it as he did so, and reaching the alleyway with its quiet, slumbering pub, a more brisk walk took him out onto the Tottenham Court Road.

Bill turned left, and headed south.

A light breeze pleasantly wafted over his face, blowing the newly neatened hair back behind his head as he strolled downwind, nearing the tobacconists, where he sometimes bought cigarettes. The girl there was nice; Maisie, her name was. She was always kind, and spoke warmly and intelligently to him. To his regret, Bill realised that the great majority of the time he had entered to chat to her, alcohol had rendered him somewhat senseless, and he imagined the ordeal for her, dealing with his acrid stench and, quite possibly, drunken rambling; whatever unintelligible, nonsensical gibberish escaped his lips. It simply wouldn't do. Today was a day of change.

Bill decided to go speak to her today, but to his regret, the shop was closed.

Her brother drank in his pub, he remembered suddenly. Obviously the Londoner was the one called Jack, as the fiery one was a Geordie and the one with the pretty girlfriend was Scottish. *Don't call them Scotch*, he noted, *they don't like it*. The Jack lad was a nice enough chap. Bill regretted that he had not made more of an effort to speak to him. They had spoken only a few times, but Jack seemed intelligent, and earnest.

As he passed the shop, Bill realised that what he'd done would be relayed to Jack, so Maisie would in all likelihood hear about it. That was something, at least. He couldn't understand how he had let himself become such a shell of a man.

Sunlight, hidden behind the clouds suddenly burst anew over the London streets, and Bill smiled to feel its rays gently dusting the skin of his face.

It feels good to be trimmed. To feel sunlight on my cheeks. How did I lose the plot?

It doesn't matter, he decided. Today was a great day. A *new chapter*.

Tottenham Court Road ended with the junction at Oxford Street, ringed on all sides by lumpy buildings scarred by polluted air. Grey, of a dirtier shade than charcoal, surrounded them on all sides, assailing the visual sense. This was where Bloomsbury merged southwards into the heart of London; only a mile to the south stood Westminster Palace and its Houses of Parliament, Big Ben and the hallmarks of England and the British Empire. Welcoming the sound, sight and smell of the London traffic, Bill unhesitantly went south, towards the river and Westminster.

It was not long before he saw the first German patrols.

A click of the pistol's cocking mechanism and Bill fired over; two rapid shots that took the Wehrmacht soldiers by surprise. One was caught straight through the throat and collapsed, gurgling a choking death rattle before bleeding out on the cobbles, while the other bullet punched through his comrade's chest. Covert in his strike, Bill had slipped around the corner into the parallel street, and the confused shouts of the other German troops who'd been caught unawares receded as he continued south to where the Wehrmacht checkpoints would undoubtedly be.

Weaving across the lanes that led towards Trafalgar Square, Bill continued to veer away from the increasing volume of audible German activity nearby, and he slipped through grey streets in the silent slumber of occupation, cutting through a blind spot between Piccadilly Circus and Leicester Square. Eventually, back on the wide street and walking southwards, Bill neared the square, passing the statue of Great War nurse Edith Cavell at St Martin's Place, which had been marked off. Evidently, the rumour that either Hitler or Heydrich demanded its removal was true, he thought.

"You and me both, lass," Bill chuckled to himself. "We're both out of time."

In reflective mood, Bill paused by the statue, reading its inscription: "Patriotism is not enough. I must have no bitterness or hatred for anyone."

Fighting back tears, Bill nodded up to her, smiling. He now knew her peace.

Down the road, the German checkpoint at the edge of Trafalgar Square. It was little more than a roadblock manned by three bored looking soldiers, haphazardly checking the identification of the few stragglers passing through. Bill approached them.

"Papers," a bored Wehrmacht soldier intoned. He had a coarse, pockmarked face. Bill surmised him to be thirty-five or so, not much younger than he was. Old enough.

"By all means," the Londoner smiled pleasantly, and withdrew his pistol, firing into the chest of the startled soldier, who died quickly.

Bill was quicker to react than the dying man's *kameraden*; he let off two quick shots that felled the fascist soldiers and sidestepped the roadblock, clinging to the shadows as he stealthily darted into Trafalgar Square. Distant shouts grew louder, and German guns were concentrated towards the area of unrest, but despite three bullets being fired towards the massacred roadblock and the source of their danger, the square's guards were neither close nor quick enough to shoot the exposed British soldier, who reached the centre of the square in the style he had traversed No Man's Land in all those years ago.

Taking refuge behind Nelson's Column, Bill settled himself with the statue as his impediment from the massing Wehrmacht at the Arch; firing off to his right as the several soldiers whose roadblock faced The Strand took position thirty metres south of him, the aged veteran sent one man scrambling away, hit his comrade in the leg and in doing so, he managed to clear his unprotected flank of enemies. The main bulk, he knew, were further south down the road and would be there soon.

Nelson's Column stood in the middle of Trafalgar Square, with no additional cover nearby, and exposed on all sides in a wide public space. Bill had not chosen a spot that he could hold indefinitely; indefensible, at best, it offered a brief haven for a shoot-out.

Bill thought of his dead father, his dead brother and his dead friend, smiling genially as their faces swam before him, before at last settling his mind's eye on sweet Maureen's memory.

I'm Forever Blowin' Bubbles, he crooned to himself, *pretty bubbles in the air...*
They fly so high, they reach the sky,
And like our dreams, they fade and die...
Fortune's always hiding, I looked everywhere,
I'll be blowing bubbles, soon,
And I'm sure I'll see you there...

Bill's piercing eyes crinkled, and a single tear leaked down either cheek to the curved lips of his wide smile. He glanced up to the sun, calmly enjoying the gentle touch of its last kiss on his handsome face as he grinned, silently thanking whatever energy it was that created the cosmos. Drawing the pistol with the cavalier dash of a buccaneer, Bill Wilson yelled out a piercing war cry and sprinted out, firing bullets over to the German positions, too many of them, his wildly inaccurate shots bursting four times from the gun before he was brought down in a hail of bullets, and he crashed hard to the ground, dead, in the shadow of Nelson's Column.

By now the high speed chase was over. A frantic Alan roared out of the boundaries of human settlement and into the kind of tree-lined country road that looks like it migrated to the London area from another part of England; foreign, alien, natural. The motorbike spluttered at its maximum speed, willed on by its frantic rider. He knew there would be army checkpoints on the road ahead; SS-Gestapo, and likely soldiers at his back. Escape had proven difficult; he had reached his bike, using the chaos of the crowds, but not without pursuers. The subsequent mad dash had drained the bike of much of its remaining petrol, and it was a bittersweet moment when he finally broke free of his dogged German followers. His fuel was low, and while he'd escaped the city and the soldiers, it was painfully clear that the ensnarement operation would now be in effect. The enormity of what they'd tried to do, and what they'd done, was too great. *Bikes, cars and trucks. Guns, and evil intent.*

Tears streaking his face – half from the wind whipping unforgivingly into his eyes as the bike screamed away through the streets –Alan raced further out of the city, pushing deeper into the countryside, and he put one final burst into the engine until he saw water. There, down an embankment to his left, some distance from the road and beyond the trees that lined it, he caught a glimpse of water. *Oh God, there's water.* Trees, leaves grass... water.

Veering away off the asphalt, Alan knew he was in contact with the man-made world for the last time.

Good, he thought. *Thank God. Any, all. Or whatever force there is.*

The bike shuddered down the grass embankment, through a gap in the trees that opened up before him. He rolled down the unspoiled turf of the bank to a clearing of undisturbed grassland that surprisingly, given the relative lateness of the year, had seemingly retained all its green splendour. Adrenaline coursed through blood that had run thin in his veins, and he paused, panting on the bike. Trees overlapped above his head, forming a natural enclosure and offering a strange protection from the sky; an enclosed world. His eyes blearily, feverishly, appreciatively absorbed every visual.

Those fucking bastards. Those fucking fascist bastards.

Sunlight pierced the branches with a scattered array of thin beams, almost mockingly bright. After a while, still not hearing the sound of any pursuing vehicles, Alan patted the bike, and shuffled over to the water's edge, beyond the leafy ceiling. The open sky, with nothing human or man-made in sight. Alan stared hungrily around the little lake, before gazing up. The sky, he noticed for the first time, was a lovely blue; somewhere between a deep azure and, in part, a light periwinkle; dotted and specked with clouds. It belied the time of year.

His jaw bunching in a rush of nervous energy, Alan pulled the Star 7.65mm pistol out of his lined black leather jacket; every inch the anti-fascist freedom fighter. The gun had been procured in Barcelona from a member of the CNT anarchist's brigades, not long after their arrival, while the group of friends were all still members of the POUM. Those were the happy days of '36, when all anti-fascists – regardless of party or theorist loyalties – were undisputed comrades in arms, united against fascist tyranny, embracing indiscriminately and singing through the streets. That died, as had, he realised now, the idealistic egalitarian dream itself.

In a moment of quiet regret, Alan conceded that their hopes and dreams had been purely quixotic. If right-wing tyranny had not engulfed them, combined with religion, then the murderous left they had naively believed in would have inflicted a Stalinist hell on the west. If both extremes failed; the ruling classes and financial masters would impose corporatocracy, and perpetuate serfdom. Whatever the form and label, rulers would rule, and the powerful would wield power.

It would never end.

The left extreme had proven as ruthless and obnoxiously, foolishly cruel as that of the right. One had triumphed, the other failed, but the ruling class and corporate plutocrats still sat atop the pyramid either way. *All the bloodshed of young men, ultimately fighting for nothing.* Musing on the cruelties of their lives, the Geordie was suddenly weary, tired of it all. Let them struggle on in their pretentious, blind ostentation. *Let them bow and salute, or fight and fall.* Oddly enough, the cold, clammy metal of his tried and trusted pistol was comforting. Alan's hand shook, but his body was still, a lonely silhouette by the waterside.

The grassy clearing; its wet, fresh smells overpowering the lingering stink of the bike exhaust and of London; damp leaves, the strong smell of grass and of fresh water.... *This is a dream world*, he thought. The pleasant sight calmed the sorrowful agitation of his tortured soul. His eyes wide with wonder, Alan pulled out a cigarette – one left in his pack – and then decided against it, throwing the rolled stick to the ground. He filled his lungs with the clean air, refreshing himself. They could not take this from him. His life and liberty, perhaps, but while he breathed, they could not take the oxygen from him.

Alan had fought against the rising tide of Europe since he'd been eighteen years of age, but he'd always slipped the net, or been under it. Underground, or in the shadows, or faceless in the crowd of dissent. For the first time – and the last, he realised sombrely – he was abolished. Blacklisted. The enemy had finally turned its malevolent gaze onto him. His very existence was a Crime Against People. They'd stripped him of his right to live.

A dissident revolutionary for years of his life, Alan was finally, *officially*, 'Life Unworthy of Life.'

Amidst birdsong, he remembered the American folk song they'd sung in the trenches to keep their spirits up on winter nights. It had been brought over by their comrades from the New World. The song had been reworded; *I Will Overcome, Some Day*. Alan chuckled as he hummed the words to himself, with tears spilling at their ultimate failure; an adult lifetime of fighting against fascist tyranny only to die failing to remove its chief scourge; the Crown Prince of Terror in the horrible Heydrich.

They may well have taken out his only ranked superior in the black order, but Alan could see now that it had been a mistake, even if they'd managed to kill Himmler. What good did removing the lunatic do when a cold, calculating monster like the Reichsprotektor was there to take his place? And if Himmler was indeed dead, the reprisals would be horrible.

How many British people had they condemned to death with their actions?

We Will Overcome... we will overcome... we shall overcome, some day.
If in my heart... I do not yield...
We will overcome, some... day.

The words almost choked him with their grim, forlorn irony.

Alan hoped his friends had escaped. He bent to pick up a stone, skimming it gently across the smooth, shimmering surface of the water... and now he noticed birds, swans and others he did not know, sat serenely in the lake, other smaller types of bird gliding here and there, to and fro.

This is a dream world, he thought furiously, blinking through his tears. This is a dream world. What a beautiful dream world.

Alan looked across the glimmering, shimmering water, its greens and ripples, the lush environ surrounding it, leafy trees with yellowing leaves and the beauty of nature; he thought of the world entrusted to humans – with their endless ingratitude, the wicked malice displayed to each other, the savagery of their deeds – and his heart broke. Then he thought of Jack, and William, and dear, sweet Mary, and – not of the pain – but of their love for each other, the bond they had shared. Blinking back tears of affection, he hoped with all his heart that they had escaped. He thought of his mother, and of his comrades, and a great warm weariness descended upon him. The gleaming, sunlit water and his tree-enclosed vista. *Birdsong.* Alan breathed in the sweet, grassy lakeside fragrance that was lightly dusting his nostrils, savouring it, raising his left hand – the one that wasn't grasping the cold metal of Star 7.65mm and he held it aloft; one last anti-fascist salute as the light faded. He was so, so tired.

This is a dream world. It is a dream world... oh, what a beautiful dream world...

The gunshot sliced through the silent tranquillity like an evil knife, sending a gaggle of panicked birds screeching skyward to the clouds.

Naomi watched with wide eyes through the chain-link fence topped with barbed wire hooks that enclosed her crude barracks, as the sad spectacle played its course.

A group of pathetic prisoners had been brought out for their first roll call; being so new to the Germans' internment system, Naomi watched with understanding sorrow as the hopes of the newest unfortunates were visibly dashed to pieces with each cruel jibe from the foul Austrian bear in command.

One man had been singled out for special treatment. Those who had spent months at the camp already looked on with a resigned air of expectation, having seen such status awarded to earlier transgressors who had spectacularly offended the Nazi leadership. The result was always bloody and vengeful.

This man, it was announced gleefully by the commandant's chief lieutenant, was a writer, guilty of some of the most heinous literary atrocities ever committed, some of the most offensive materials ever seen by the German authorities, and a kinsman to known *Enemies of the Reich* who had actually taken up arms and fought against the European fascist revolution. This degenerate was one of the most notable names amongst the underground collective of *subversive writing perverts*, like George Orwell, who had also been captured and was to be executed publicly in London as a lesson. Unlike Simon, Orwell was destined to be hung with piano wire, along with several resistance members who had attempted to execute the Reichsprotektor, and killed a decoy doppleganger of Heinrich Himmler, the Reichsführer-SS.

In stark contrast, this writer would die here; killed in the camp; no spectacle, no martyrdom, just brutally dispatched as an unmourned dissident. His body would be incinerated, and his ashes thrown into sewage. It was the complete extermination of a human life; body and soul.

This foolish, disgusting man was another outspoken and outdated thinker; spouting redundant ideas of social equality and democracy – *laughable*, they were told. *How ridiculous and toxic*, when the de-brutalisation of British society had proven so weak and ineffective, floundering against *not only* the strength of the Greater Reich, but the insidious poison of Jewry that had eaten Britain alive from within. *With the likes of this writer gone*, they announced, *the British Empire could finally adjust and adapt to regain its pride, and carve out its legacy and authority in the New Order in the World*, as befits a great power and its people.

Simon was to die in the camp.

He was young, Naomi could determine, and sported not inconsiderable sideburns. Dirty blond hair swept across a bloodied face in curled waves, and a somewhat unfortunate, almost Jewish nose stuck out from an otherwise charmingly boyish face. His forehead was stained with blood, however, and the right side of his face was slightly lopsided due to an obviously injured jaw. The bone was visibly broken, and he nursed it tenderly at intervals, several times every minute. Black bruising adorned a misaligned side profile. He looked neither proud, nor defiant, and the body language of this doomed man quite clearly betrayed the depths of his fear.

In high good humour, Commandant Globocnik circled his prey.

"You're a cunt," he told the Englishman, using one of the only insulting phrases in that tongue that he knew.

"If you didn't think that, I would be a cunt," Simon replied, trying to sound defiant but a stammer in his voice countered his intentions horribly. It betrayed his terror, like the frantic flight of a herbivore, bolting before a predator's wrath.

Globocnik paused, considering him. "Whatever you say. You are a swine."

The great whip he carried lashed out, loudly smacking against the wet flesh of the perspiring English writer. Caught unawares, Simon took an open shot to the face and was dropped hard, gurgling a frenzied cry of pain. With only the sound of birds trilling and whistling as a backdrop to the torturous punishment, Globocnik silently watched the writer writhing in agony for several minutes, halting the methodical thrashing to let him recover. Soon after, Simon rose to his feet unsteadily, in the deathly silence of hundreds of observing eyes, and was whipped again, gritting his teeth against the sting as he unwillingly let out a long, whining whimper.

"I would like," Globocnik began, struggling to remember the correct English, "to throw you in a cell and use a submarine engine... to suffocate you like vermin... so you would die like a rat."

Implacable malevolence radiated from Globocnik, as he stared into Simon's watering eyes, grinning as the prisoner proved incapable of holding his gaze. Still beaming toothily, his fleshy face lit with happiness, the big man kicked the writer's legs out from under him and Simon collapsed heavily in a heap. The man's giant fist ploughed into his face, repeatedly. Six subsequent lashes of the whip elicited awful yells; choking in the dust, the journalist screamed at the impact of each blow.

"But killing you like a dog is *fitting*," the Austrian sneered, oblivious to the wound on his own fist from the impact of knuckle on bone.

Simon looked up; birds circled overhead, with his tormentor framed against them and the endless white and grey of the northern English sky. It seemed fitting, somehow, and through the pain he likened the moment to vultures circling symbolically.

At that thought, his courage failed him and he began to sob.

Globocnik thrilled to see the mental disintegration, as his prey slowly but surely broke. He took his truncheon, and lightly stepped in, agile for a man of such a large frame, to viciously club the stricken writer's knees.

"Nobody will care about you tomorrow," he told the sobbing, agonised journalist triumphantly. "The German Reich will never end. Your life and legacy ends here."

With his neural activity heightened by the sharp waves of pain, Simon tried to respond by asking how 'The Thousand Year Reich' could last 'for ever' which was a failed enterprise by definition, though his effort proved impossible. The battered writer could only splutter through blood and the broken stumps of his teeth.

Tiring of his pre-planned insults and mockery, Globocnik smirked before gesturing to one of his aides. They brought forth a prisoner's cap; small and grey, woollen, in the same style of the standard-issue Konzentrationslager pyjamas worn by all internees in Protective Custody.

"Hatred is by far the longest pleasure, men love in haste, but they *detest at leisure*," Naomi murmured sadly, without averting her eyes from the grim, protracted spectacle of Simon's death. The young girl who had been brought to Catterick in the same transport as Naomi, and had been terrified out of her wits, now glanced at the Jewish teacher stood beside her, registering the profound words of Lord Byron. Quietly, she slipped her hand into Naomi's, softly stroking the palm of her hand, and the two young women interlocked their fingers gently, comforted by the human touch of solidarity and love.

Clutching the cap, Globocnik briskly marched away, seemingly heading for an area marked by nothing but a stretch of perimeter fence. Half-carrying Simon, two guards led him over to a section of the fence that was thirty metres beyond the segregated barrack blocks, to where the inner perimeter wire alone separated the camp from the adjacent woodland. An outer perimeter existed further along, past the trees and beyond the line of sight, but from the inner confines of the lager, this particular stretch of fence looked misleadingly like the route to freedom, and the only impediment to the outside world.

Globocnik paused by the chain-link fence. Turning, he held the cap aloft, sneeringly showed it to his tormented prey, and then turned to carelessly throw it up to the barbs lining the top of the enclosure.

"That is yours, Prisoner 1984. Retrieve your hat."

Globocnik pointed menacingly from Simon to the cap, and then walked away without another word. The writer was left with his two grim-faced guards standing sentinel, submachine guns slung over their shoulders and an implacable will to *do their duty* etched firmly into the hard features of their cold, Teutonic faces. The writer stood still, breathing heavily. When he failed to move towards the hat, painfully aware of the obvious outcome, one guard nudged him in one of his injured kidneys with the butt of his gun. There was no way out. Tottering, utterly dejected, he accepted the inevitable and limped forwards to the fence.

Simon tried to speak, tried to sneer with each step, tried to voice and put words to the burning injustices on his tongue; that he was a spiritual *son of Anarchy, and they were sons of Fascism and the two families were fated to eternal enmity as the quintessential forces of light and dark, Set versus Horus, they could kill him but they would Only Be Killing A Man, that his family was stronger and would ultimately prevail; that benevolence was more powerful than malevolence, that hate could never beat love...* the heroic end, he felt it on his lips, his brain begged for the righteous verbal ejaculation of angered defiance but his body betrayed him, head spinning dizzily as the writer fought hard to stay conscious, his knees failing just before the machine guns sprayed a hail of bullets that strafed his broken body and stole his life; a soul released from its earthly torment.

Beneath an imperious Nelson's Column that was rumoured to be destined for Berlin, the hastily erected wooden scaffold creaked under the weight of its occupants, watched by silent crowds.

"A degenerate, criminal writer, guilty of the most perverse subversion… and these reprehensible swine," the German called, a huge vein pulsing on his neck, "… are guilty of one of the most despicable acts of cowardice in modern history. These so-called resistance members did *nothing* but condemn-to-death innocent members of the British public, by brutally murdering several Germans, and endangering the life of the Führer's Reichsprotektor, General Heydrich; a man sent here to preside over a peaceful union between our two nations and to help transition the British Empire into the New Order in the World, as we face external enemies and the threat of world Jewry, communism and disease…"

The German paused. "This writer – a coward, hiding underground like a rat, had partners here in London, and led a network of sabotage and slander. And these so-called resistance members, whose stupid and criminal actions caused the deaths of many British civilians, were joined by another foolish criminal in their sinister Bloomsbury clique; a cold-blooded killer, who murdered several decent German soldiers right here in this square…"

His voice tailed off, stepping away from the public speaker as the words sank in. For effect, the German let the silence lengthen, waiting as he was for the symbolic eleven o'clock execution that Hitler had personally demanded from Berlin.

Sunlight chose that moment to burst through the clouds. Mary, William and Jack all gazed up to it, enjoying the last rays of sunshine on their skin. They were all barely able to stand up, as was the pencil-moustachioed writer alongside them, similarly condemned.

"We have lived in a day of sunshine, and die at the onset of night," George Orwell murmured softly.

The German guards ignored their quiet dialogue, and Jack tried to chuckle through the broken teeth and bloodied, torn lips of his mouth.

"We are out of time, George. It's an honour to die next to you, though."

"And you, brothers and sister. The honour is mine."

"All comrades, eh?" William added softly. "We outlasted the POUM, at least. Killed some fascists and fought the good fight a good while longer…"

Orwell glanced over at the handsome young Scot. "Funny. England was the most class-ridden country under that very sun that we're seeing for the last time," he observed thoughtfully, nodding up to the bright globe of light in the sky. "It was a land of snobbery, privilege and a pyramid hierarchy, ruled by the old and the silly. But compared to this…" he shook his head sadly, "… utopian. Yes… it is time we died, comrades. We are out of time. There is no redeeming spirit left in this age of the jackboot for the likes of us."

The sun petered out and was lost, obscured by the enormous black and grey shape of slow-moving cloud that covered the entire expanse of the London sky. The light faded, and all was grey in the historic Trafalgar Square.

William cried softly to himself, physically and emotionally broken. Somehow, his Scottish nationality had seemed to offend the SS more so than even Mary, the Spanish Jew whom they had simply beaten senseless and left to bleed in her cell. The torture he endured, in comparison, was barbaric.

Laughing amongst themselves, his torturers had given him the choice; his mother, and sole surviving family member, could die in a concentration camp, or they would castrate him, in return for sparing her life. Choosing the latter, the young man blacked out repeatedly through the long torment of his ordeal, hoping to bleed to death, but finally waking up to find his wounds dexterously dealt with by the Gestapo's resident experts in suffering. While the searing pain was unbearable, William had nevertheless felt a strong surge of pride as he woke that morning, comforted by the knowledge that his mother was safe, only to have his world shattered. Given a slab of hard, inedible bread for his breakfast, William was told by his gleeful tormentors that regardless of *their* pact to not kill her, they had passed on his mother's name to the leader of the SS *Einsatzgruppe Edinburgh*.

Informing him that she would likely die within days, the Gestapo interrogators' faces lit up with an astonishing pleasure, as the young Scottish lad tried to ingest the full horror of their cruel revelation.

Tears leaked down Mary's cheeks, out of her reddened, black and bruised eyes. Her lover bore the marks of their brief, yet barbarous captivity, and Jack too was battered and broken, bludgeoned by the limitless rage of fascist aggression. But they all smiled, and nodded, thankful of the way they had spent their lives.

Perhaps, if National Socialism and the fascist movement collapsed, they would be remembered as heroes. All considered it, on the scaffold, but none bothered to verbalise the words. They were beyond self-justification, vindication and fanciful talk of a future that they would not, could not, see.

Suddenly, the German officer entrusted with overseeing the public execution sprang back to life, calling out into a near-silence that was peppered with the occasional piercing shriek of bird cry, as the prehistoric creatures swooped and flapped around the square that stood still, a noiseless, motionless mass of humanity.

"George Orwell, for your crimes you are sentenced to death."

His hands tightly bound, Orwell cut a slender, unbroken figure as the guards approached, to fasten the custom-made noose around his neck. They were to be hung; not with rope, but with piano wire, to maximise the suffering and send a grisly message to those continuing to resist the Everywhere-Triumphant forces of fascism.

"*Viva libert–*" the writer began, but his intended final declaration of solidarity and brotherhood was cut short as the trapdoor gave way beneath his bare feet.

George Orwell kicked and writhed, trapped blood pumping horribly around the swollen veins of his neck, face and head until, after thirty seconds of horrific suffering, the dark crimson finally leaked from his nose and mouth, wire gashing his purple throat. Finally, after the lifeblood cascaded out of him, Orwell's willowy body went limp and the twisted movements stilled.

Jack was next.

"I love you, Jack," Mary called to him.

He nodded, pride in his eyes.

"I love you both. We did what was right. *Viva libertad.*"

Long live freedom.

Jack spoke quickly, to ensure that his final words were not interrupted by his ultimate fate. He had deliberately breathed lightly for several minutes, knowing that shallow inhalation combined with his fear would finish him faster as he thrashed and choked. Several seconds followed, but the drop did not come. Struggling to control his breathing, Jack quickly glanced around the sea of eyes boring into his bloodied face. Oddly enough, he felt calm, caring little how the people of his country viewed him – much less those of fascist persuasion – and though the cruel wire cut painfully into his neck, the young London lad turned to face his two dear friends, grinning as the trapdoor swung open and after a jolt, the light faded.

Mary.

"This swine is the typical Jewish rat, infesting European nations with their diseased poison," the German announcer informed the silent crowds, many of whom were from Bloomsbury and had been forced to bear witness. "Having fought against fascism in Spain, participating in the burning of churches and the killing of priests, this godless communist whore came to England to cause further violence and spread her message of hate..." the silken voice again trailed off, a note of relish audible in his sneering tone.

The Catalan revolutionary was terrified; her beauty somewhat diminished by the ferocity of her captors' force, and scarred by their fists and blades, which had been used so terribly in a single night of awful interrogation. But at least death was waiting for her at the end of this ordeal, she thought heatedly, and then peace at last. The thought placated her somewhat. Her apprehension was solely for the horrific pain of the wire, yet its result no longer appalled. It was almost *worth* dying to never again have to contemplate the prospect of fascism, however excruciating its method. Death held no fear for her. She had been through worse.

Blinking away tears furiously, she turned to William as the savage wire noose was fitted around the soft skin of her shapely, slender neck.

"I love you so much," she gushed. "More than I can say."

Overcome, he nodded as though in a trance, hardly able to see through the watery veil of his own tears of grief. "I know, Mary I love you so–"

The sound of the trapdoor collapsing cut short his affirmations of love and he cried out, in physical pain as her body jerked with the jolt. Piano wire cutting deep into her neck, Mary made sure to turn away from her lover as the blood frothed up into, and then out of, her lovely, ruined face, and as the still-silent crowd watched in hollow fascination, the Spanish freedom fighter choked her last breath. Her body dangled lifelessly from the savage snare of her torment, while her spirit finally found peace.

Alone on the scaffold, and alone in the world, William broke down before the unwavering gaze of the silent British and hostile German onlookers, and the terrible wails of his agony broke free of his body, sending shivers down the spines of the assembled.

Epilogue:

Green countryside flashed past, flecked with the brown of gnarled trees, and looking for all-the world like England. The startling observation occurred to a sombre Maisie, but she kept it to herself, musing quietly.

The young soldier accompanying her was named Johan. He had helped facilitate the journey. It was the same boy that had been with Hans on his first visit to her shop.

"He was against Hitler," Johan said, abruptly.

Caught off-guard, the English girl was startled. Since leaving England, Johan had barely opened his mouth, and she had begun to question his grasp of English. She knew what Hans' feelings towards the National Socialist regime were – all too well, after he had spent weeks educating her about the grim realities of his country – but it was shocking to hear his friend say it so openly, and on German soil. If such statements were overheard, the future for Johan would become very grim indeed.

"He despised Nazis," she muttered back, softly. "They killed his Jewish girlfriend years ago, and her brother."

Johan whistled. "He told you that, eh?"

She scowled at him, in low humour. "Yes. He told me that, *eh...*"

"I'm sorry. I miss him," he replied glumly, and the obvious sincerity of his grief brought Maisie to her feet, and she embraced the German soldier. His body tensed at her touch, but the memory of his old friend came to him, with whom he'd suffered the hell of conscription into the Wehrmacht, the horrors of Poland and the bombs and bullets of France and England. He fought back a tear, with a German soldier's pride instilled in him, but it took a considerable effort to do so.

The countryside flashed past, until finally, they reached Berlin.

Having heard from Hans of the privations of the Reich's capital in wartime, Maisie was astonished at the celebratory atmosphere that pervaded each sphere of German life she saw, as they traversed the sunlit streets.

The fear and repression described to her seemed entirely absent, and she realised with disquiet that with a popular government in power, all the regime's spite and prejudice was being directed outwards; open hatred now the realm of the foreign outposts of National Socialism. Like *Britain*. Germany, she mused, might now be the heart of a Germanic Garden of Eden in the Reich, whose violent depravity had spread afar to more resistant lands.

The media, subordinate as it was to German interests, were circulating endless hyperbole and history-steeped vitriol regarding the deal that Reichsmarschall Göring had brokered with England, the smiling spectre of Heydrich in each photograph. An official 'Peace and Prosperity' arrangement had been made, between German Reich and British Empire, and as a vital economic, trading and – it was rumoured, strictly outside the realm of the press – *military* partner of the Reich, Britain received an immediate ceasefire from all Axis troops on its soil, the removal of all German military – Heydrich's SS security police notwithstanding – from British territory, the continued union of the English and Scottish crowns; the maintenance of de jure control of British legislature – which included the abandonment of the recent German-influenced enactment of the

1935 Nuremberg anti-Semitic laws – and a total amnesty for all those guilty of resistance, sabotage or race. It was, to many, not merely a move away from Nazism, but a return to real *peace*.

And in this climate, Maisie had dared to apply for the travel pass. Aided and abetted by a sympathetic Johan, the sister of the resistance member who had – in their words – murdered in cold-blood an upstanding German soldier – was, to her amazement, granted the pass, for a leave of one week. Though apprehensive, she immediately left for the continent, bound for Berlin, Germany.

The capital city of Adolf Hitler.

After showing Maisie the Tiergarten and its pleasant zoo, Johan dutifully took her to the outskirts of Wedding; a notorious northwestern workers district – formerly a communist stronghold before the rise of Hitler – and as they strolled unmolested down a street that visibly increased in dilapidation with each hundred yards, they eventually came to a tired, detached white house, the paint of which cracked and crumbled as though the squat building had sustained massive damage through the turbulent post-Great War years that Germany had suffered through.

"Red Wedding," he said quietly. "Around here is where the Nazis met their fiercest opposition. Street battles, gunshots, brawls, murders. Hans grew up around it."

"It must have been awful," Maisie replied quietly. He shrugged.

"Those were difficult times for all of us."

"Did you hate them?" She asked him, curious about the reserved young man with whom her lover had shared such a strong bond. He cast a furtive glance around before replying.

"I'm from East Prussia. Hitler isn't popular with us, even after reattaching our exclave to the Reich."

She gazed at him, willing him to say more but he clammed up. It was a common sight in totalitarian states; a sentence started, then stifled, and the sudden descent into unquestioned silence.

"Did Hans fight?"

Johan smiled at that, relaxing. "This was a communist stronghold, so his hatred of Nazis makes sense. But he was *never* a communist. He hated the Reds just as much."

"Hans hated extremism..."

It was as gentle an obituary as her man deserved. Saddening though the prospect was that her own brother – an extremist – had killed him as a symbol of that which he himself despised; Maisie felt a burst of pride for the good-hearted Hans she had fallen for. In a time of such widespread loss and grief, she could at least be glad that her lost Hans had spent the final months of his life in the passion of love.

After her proud, yet glum observation, Maisie registered Johan's silent agreement and pause as a hint and she duly took the lead, ascending the wide stairs to the front door. Lifting the ornate, heavy knocker, Maisie sent three booming thuds reverberating around the old house of her dead lover.

The door was answered by a startlingly young, attractive blonde woman. Her skin was impeccable, but the rings around her pale blue eyes betrayed a stress and grief that Maisie knew all-too-well. Casting a wide-eyed scrutiny over the beautiful skin, Maisie saw Hans' nose, his eyes and his mouth on the gorgeous face of the gracefully ageing German beauty, and though prepared for the moment, she felt hot tears welling up in her own eyes. The German gazed uncomprehendingly at her visitor, bewildered, before taking in the sight of a sombre Johan who doffed his cap, and with that, understanding hit her. Hostility melted away, and she held out her arms, outstretched and welcoming, as Maisie fell into her embrace, sobbing at the bitterness of their shared grief and the cruelty of human love in this world.

The gigantic, awful gates creaked and groaned as they opened, a harsh metallic sound cutting through the lilting, chirping twitter of birdsong. It was a sound that Naomi had feared she would never hear.

Odilo Globocnik had gone. Overnight, the savage Austrian vanished, leaving for some far-flung adventure or role in Reich territory, far from England's *green and pleasant land.* Heydrich had appointed another Austrian, some cold-faced psychopath called Goeth who had apparently been serving in Leeds with the SS Security Police to take charge of the camp. Naomi was mortified to think that the same brute who had arrested her could be placed in command of the camp, but before their new overlord could make his presence felt, her entire barracks had been told to gather their possessions in five minutes flat. Fear had gripped them, until the runty, snarling female SS guard finally deigned to inform them that *alas*, they had nothing to worry about.

They were free.

The ragged group were left to their own devices as the outer perimeter gates swung shut, and Naomi turned back to see her SS persecutors slowly walking back into the bowels of the Konzentrationslager. The women – all Jews – held hands, hardly daring to believe that they were truly free, and still wary of being riddled with machine gun fire as they left. *Shot While Attempting To Escape* had been the fate of many men since their internment began, and in particular, the memory of the poor, scared writer who had been openly murdered all those months prior was still burned onto their memories like a scar.

But no gunshots came.

As the camp began to recede into the distance, Naomi turned back one final time, to see the guards in each tower scurrying along; tiny, the size of ants. And right there, in front of the ragged group of malnourished Jewish internees, was the outer checkpoint, beyond which they saw familiar faces and family waiting for them.

Joy flooded their weakened bodies, almost paralysing them. Completely ignoring the surly SS guards at the checkpoint, the twenty women abandoned all care and ran screaming into the arms of their loved ones. Within seconds, the tearful embraces took on a more concerned, tender nature, as the extent of their physical weakness became all-too apparent; the brief physical contact being enough to demonstrate that their bodies had been reduced to skin and bones. But joyful elation overcame worry, and the ecstasy that lit those twenty gaunt, haggard faces had a magical quality of regeneration to it. One of the younger SS guards had to look away, as he noted an unpleasant, all-too human emotional reaction to the touching scene.

Naomi alone held back. Her haunted eyes met Paul's, and she let him absorb the full visage of her emaciated, skeletal, battered body.

"Let me guess... I've got something on my face," she grinned, her gaunt face suddenly lighting up. She was struggling to contain her emotions.

Paul stared at her, his eyes filled with hot, burning tears.

"I'm so sorry... I'm so sorry."

His hands flailed, as he failed to verbalise the multitude of thoughts he wished to convey to the broken shell of his lover. She smiled; a genuine gesture of concern. "There is nothing to be sorry about."

And almost as though the younger man had been imprisoned in the cruel camp, Naomi gently stepped into him and laid a gentle hand on his cheek, whispering sweet words to him as her thin arms wrapped around his body, holding him to her with a maternal tenderness as they sobbed the bittersweet tears of regret and joy.

Major Jochen Wolf entered the office room, halting before the commanding figure that stood expectantly in the centre of it, whose stern scrutiny was silently fixed on the junior officer. Wolf saluted. The man he faced was SS-Oberstgruppenführer Reinhard Heydrich.

"Heil Hitler!" Wolf snapped.

Heydrich cursorily raised his own paw skywards; imitating the Führer's own straight-wristed version of the salute, as though he, too, was above the usual sacrosanct ritual. He did not verbally respond; the wily Wolf was amused, though equally, impressed by the display of authority shown by this conceited, dangerous man at the height of his powers.

"Excellent work, Wolf. Very well done. Walk with me."

They marched purposefully through the building, saluted on all sides. To the junior officer's surprise, Heydrich lit a cigarette upon exiting out into the Prussian sunlight.

"I'm celebrating the fact that jobs are being well done across the board," Heydrich cheerily informed the inquisitive Wolf. He withheld the answer to the younger man's silent query, and smirked. "Come, Sturmbannführer."

And he marched on, forcing Wolf to meet his stride. The major kept pace, his senses alert to the nuances of the capricious Heydrich, trying to second-guess any tricks or tests that the general might throw in his way. Heading out past the parade grounds and to the surrounding grass fields, Heydrich led them to a small table nestled up the slightly rising slope that afforded a good view of the academy grounds. Courteously gesturing Wolf to take a seat, Heydrich reclined at ease, sucking happily at his cigarette with evident enjoyment. It was a Dunhill, Wolf noted, from England.

"Now..." the SS and Police general began. "To begin."

"I am here to report as you ordered, *Reichsprotektor und Oberstgrupp–*"

"No, no," Heydrich interjected breezily. "General will do."

"Thank you, General," Wolf purred obsequiously. Heydrich's smile glinted at him, as their pale blue eyes clashed. The Major resumed: "I am glad my work in the re-education and conscription of a *whole battalion* of British soldiers for the Reich meets with your approval..."

His eyes lingered on Heydrich's, just long enough for distaste to register through the coolness. Wolf's own Machiavellian nature was valued by Heydrich, he knew, though he wondered if his age – even younger than the youthful general, at 32 – and his comparative good looks *bothered* the Reichsprotektor. Heydrich hated equals, loathed rivalry and despised losing. They were of similar height, and of similar build, but the general had a slightly androgynous quality to his looks, and even the dash of an occasionally effete, effeminate manner; slightly off-putting even to those who were blissfully unaware of his foibles. Of course, the *slightest* awareness of his professional life was enough to cow even the wildest spirits in Berlin in the general's presence. But was it enough? Widely considered to be good-looking, Heydrich's face had strong features but to Wolf, it was somewhat overlong and horsey. The eyes – usually narrowed in suspicion or with the malignant preoccupation of some scheming thought – were slightly too close together, and only on Heydrich's musical performances did their shine appear to be anything other than a superficial mask over an endless frozen tundra of ice.

Wolf, on the other hand, was classically handsome in any sense of the word, and the almost symmetrical shape of his slim face, with its strong jaw and high cheekbones, was perfectly proportioned. Immaculately clad in his SS regalia, Major Wolf embodied the new German male; the high watermark of Aryan masculinity.

He probably could not care less, Wolf surmised, correctly. *Heydrich can take what, and who, he wants, whenever he wants. Outside of Eva Braun and Edda Goebbels, there is not a woman in Europe out of bounds to the Blond Beast.*

That man held Wolf's persistent gaze, and after several seconds, he smiled thinly.

"All right, Wolf. Cut the shit. Your value directly correlates to how well I think you do your job. That is *your life*." Heydrich dropped the smile, staring daggers through the quiet, watchful Wolf. "Stop sizing me up, Jochen, and never think about doing it again or I'll make your life so *terrible* you will think it's a nightmare you can't wake up from, beyond the limits of your imagination. Regarding your job… you did well."

Heydrich spared Wolf his death stare, casting his gaze out to the green hills beyond the academy, his mouth billowing smoke. "Your results – almost a 70% success rate – are significantly higher than camps 1-4, and 6-9 alike. One full *battalion*. For propaganda purposes alone, your work will be instrumental in the eventual deployment of multiple British divisions, along with the volunteer units from France and Spain. I am impressed. Make your final report before Barbarossa."

Their eyes met again, with the hint of a mocking smile playing at Heydrich's lips and one of genuine amusement at Wolf's, before the former St. George no.5 camp commandant detailed in full the year-long operation. Much of what was said, the general had already heard, but Wolf knew better than to omit even the smallest details, lest the predator ever have something to use against him. Heydrich listened keenly, occasionally interjecting to demand clarifications, and as the major laid out his findings in as pedantic a manner as he could, the general absorbed all that he heard.

"Outstanding," Heydrich breathed quietly at the conclusion of his underling's report. "Truly remarkable…"

Abruptly dismissing Wolf, who departed with an impeccably unctuous air, Heydrich remained where he was, the avid athlete and sportsman permitting himself to smoke cigarettes there on the outdoors table, as he surveyed the grounds of the SS Academy at Pretzsch in excellent humour. Such indulgence was rare, but he felt it was merited. As the afternoon breeze gently drifted across his pale, long face, the Reichsprotektor's thick lips curved into their trademark cruel, mocking smile. The encounter with a wily, cunning junior officer had bolstered the fabulous mood he had felt since leaving Britain to finalise the plans to launch the Waffen-SS and the *Einsatzgruppen* deep into Russia, alongside the all-conquering Wehrmacht that now bowed to his decrees.

Having masterminded the initial eastern push into Poland with Operation Himmler, Heydrich had actively served in the Luftwaffe, earned the Iron Cross and then employed an historic stratagem against the British. Then he'd been named Germany's viceroy over the occupied nation home of the world's largest empire. Now, he was a warlord, entrusted with *Generalplan Ost*; measures that would directly affect the lives of seventy million human beings in Soviet territory – most of whom were to be slaughtered – resulting in the complete Germanisation of Polish, Baltic and Russian territories, and forever changing the course of history.

More than ever, Heydrich found that these small moments of private triumph were necessary, as the roaring momentum of his own life careered further and further into the realm of the overwhelming. Even his analytical, devious mind had begun to question the limits, if there were any, on his headlong ascent in an inexorable rise to power.

~

Jochen Wolf, having met with Heydrich, retreated to his quarters, breathing a sigh of relief as he locked the door behind him. He shed the SS tunic and stood to attention in his full-length mirror, staring uncritically at the visage of National Socialist masculinity.

Wolf was an incredibly honest man with himself, and the revelations he produced no longer had the power to shock or surprise him. He was naked under the spotlight of his own introspection. Born into a middle-class family in Hamburg, the younger Joachim 'Jochen' Wolf had been too young to enjoy the decadence of the early 20s, but, initially wide-eyed and soon after, fired up into a fledgling, primal state of bloodlust, he had certainly witnessed the pitched battles and violent street brawls between left and right in the years that followed, with a growing excitement and thirst for action.

The Wolf family had literary aspirations for their son, and enrolled him at the Heidelberg University, Germany's oldest and most prestigious institution for academic study. The boisterous Jochen, however, found his outlet in boxing and wrestling; his martial passions spilled out into street fights and bar brawls when the zest of his bloodlust became too great to contain.

Only in the shattering realisation of his literary limitations, and faced with the reality that he would never be a new Johann Wolfgang von Goethe, was Wolf's mind liberated from the limitations of his upbringing, now free to be anything he wanted.

Questioning his desires and needs, as all young men do, Wolf began to suspect that only in the abandonment of all he had known, and the willpower to make his mark in the world, would his hunger for vindication be sated. But writing, romantic though Wolf found the notion, was clearly not the means with which the younger Jochen was to accomplish this, as minimal practical experience quickly taught him. Adrenaline, danger and violence moved him, stirring his soul, and in that field alone did his quill produce prose filled with interesting or valid observations. In all else, Jochen's written musings were uninspired; a mixture of cheap plagiarisms and half-hearted annotations of his own, that neither rang true with anything other than superficial honesty or substance, nor particularly entertained the dispirited Wolf when he perused them at leisure. Subsequently returning to Goethe was dispiriting. Jochen Wolf became listless with apathy; his academic laziness and newfound arrogance combined to disrupt his studies, and the young narcissist would ultimately leave Heidelberg with an average degree. Even that was achieved only through a last ditch, desperate effort in his final term.

So ended the forgettable tenure of an unexceptional student, whose frustrated yearnings lent bitterness to his view of the world. Wolf was equally arrogant and lethargic; confused by his impulses and fruitlessly searching for his path to progression.

But Jochen Wolf possessed a cunning that many of his fellow students lacked; correctly predicting the rise of Hitler after the 1932 elections, in which thirteen million people voted for the National Socialist demagogue, Wolf – with a cynical pragmatism that astounded his bourgeois parents – embraced the new regime with open enthusiasm, and he signed up for the Party in December of that year. Little more than one month later, Adolf Hitler was named Chancellor of Germany.

The grim realisation that he would never be a new Nietzsche or Goethe in modern Germany had initially plagued him, and an underlying self-doubt from frustrated ambitions had lingering during the course of his Heidelberg studies. But Wolf realised, joyously, that while lacking in original thought and a natural flair, he *did* possess many of the qualities that Nietzsche himself had written were instrumental in the attainment and accumulation of power. Autodidactic and cunning; plots began to form in the shadows of his mind.

The respect and vindication Wolf craved would not, he calculated, come from professional critique or acclaim, but rather as a natural byproduct of the wielding of real, tangible power. He felt reborn. Intoxicated by the limitless possibilities of his aspirations, Wolf felt emancipated from his bourgeois upbringing and the moral constraints placed on him as a child; limitless and fledgling, under the eyes of no creator, bound by no celestial law or earthly sense of morality. He had shed everything, and thus gained everything. He was free.

With joy in his heart, Jochen Wolf joined the SA.

"Lick the pavement," he had screamed at the old, frightened Jew on his first experience of public persecution. "Clean it with your tongue! How *dare* you presume to share the same cobbles as a racially pure German!"

Having alluded to the flimsy pretence of some kind of social sacrilege, Wolf began mercilessly beating the old man, a red mist descending over his frenzied eyes, and he only stopped when he realised the frail old man was lifeless, and the body he was still beating no longer breathed. Blood pooled black beneath him, spreading around the battered animal carcase that only moments before had contained a human life and soul. Yet to his delight, the vigour of his methods met with fierce approval from his fellow thugs in the gang, and Wolf was intoxicated; addicted to this outlet for violent release. He was utterly overjoyed with his new life; a heady combination of conformity with the system and a simultaneous licence to commit violence, meted out with impunity.

The days passed like sweet and gentle dreams, and the literati academic-turned-stormtrooper felt spiritually liberated.

Within one calendar year, Jochen Wolf had casually murdered seven people in the course of the ongoing pogroms conducted by the SA against Jews, which were officially unsanctioned but, it was known, strongly condoned. Wolf's gleeful participation led to seven deaths, all by truncheon. His natural bullying streak found a home in the *Sturmabteilung*, and the more violent urges of his personality were given an avenue of release, legitimised by the endorsements of the state.

Violence had long been a part of the national character – Germany's history dictated it – but for the first time, the forces that glorified military heroism and Germanic racial superiority also happened to be the forces holding political power over the country. In this climate of military mythology and rampant masculinity, Wolf freely abandoned his intellect and acquitted himself with the evil panache matched only by the most brutal of savage, nationalistic anti-Semites who embraced the swastika and marched in jackboots. And in the process, seven lives were snuffed out by his hand, amongst the multitude of lost souls in the maelstrom of blood.

Jochen Wolf felt himself growing with quiet confidence.

Wily as a fox, he defected to the SS only two months before the murderous purge that the Party launched to castrate the SA's boisterous leadership; hundreds died, and the pendulum of power swung in the Reich. Soon after, Wolf managed to attract the attention of the mastermind of the purge himself; an ambitious, ruthless young general of the SS named Reinhard Heydrich. Yet to his chagrin, Wolf found that his earlier affiliations to the discredited SA and in particular, its leadership, proved hard to shake off. It took years of dedication, and a Machiavellian usage of the powers afforded to those Hugo Boss-clad defenders of Hitler's will - *The Black Angels* of the SS – before Wolf came into his own, freed from the shackles of prejudice and with the influence to manoeuvre unimpeded through the ranks, as he sought to advance along the complex hierarchy of the SS. He won over most of his detractors, and discredited the sole grudge-bearing enemy that he couldn't; the man's inability to forgive a drunken bar brawl during inter-party SA and SS tensions led Wolf to falsely implicate him as a Mischling. Buying his witnesses and falsifying the testimonies, Wolf dared to visit an approving Heydrich with the information, and within days his path to advancement had been freed of impediment.

Ultimately, the determined young man rose to the rank of Sturmbannführer by the tender age of 29 – though he privately preferred 'Major', the army and Anglo-Saxon version of the rank– thus reaching a position of relative authority only two years before the outbreak of war.

Wolf *yearned* for war. He possessed tremendous physical courage, tempered though it was by a moral cowardice; not so much a lack of scruples, as an ability to shelve the scruples he had, and relentlessly justify his various excesses and crimes. Under his own critical gaze, naked before his own ruthless scrutiny, Wolf knew that despite his physical courage, he ultimately lacked the courage of his convictions, due to not having any at all. He was philosophically and morally opportunistic, slippery, and nothing more; Wolf had been forced to accept that at heart, he had become a charlatan, and a chameleon by nature. All that mattered, ultimately, was advancement.

Each time he tried to reassess his life's direction, Jochen Wolf reached the conclusion that any critical acclaim he could have received had he tried to promote himself with some thin veneer of literati pretence would ultimately mean far less to him than would seizing some real, tangible *power*.

And now, Wolf had waged war successfully, thrice, and defeated multiple great European nations on the battlefield. Obscured by the fog of war, he could kill with impunity, and he led men to battle. Under Reinhard Heydrich's unsentimental patronage, he was destined to be a general of the Waffen-SS.

Gazing into the mirror in his bathroom, Jochen Wolf surveyed himself with an uncritical eye, and he felt like a god. He could taste the power that years of dedication, strategy and violence had awarded him, and greater still, that which was yet to come.

"So let me get this straight," a heated Tommy snapped, blinking in the Prussian summer sun, "... you're not happy about this but you're only here because of us? And we're traitors?"

The cockney shook his head in disbelief, even as James' mouth opened with typical belligerence.

"Traitors is a tad strong. But yeah, I'm 'ere because o' you."

Tommy shook his head exasperatedly, as the Yorkshireman gave the same pokerfaced explanation that he had repeated relentlessly since the day they signed up for Operation Barbarossa; as usual, sans additional details.

Stanley sighed, casting his gaze around the uncertain men who were lounging around the grass, smoking cigarettes to pass the time. They had free reign in the SS complex, or at least, the parts of the academy that enlisted troopers of any race were permitted to enter.

"Well chaps, you can't very well say we're not fighting for a *cause*. Church burning peasants led by a murderous villain who has caused–"

"Led by a murderous villain, like Hitler," James interjected, snorting derisively.

"*A murderous villain who has caused countless* millions of deaths," Stanley continued doggedly, his tone plaintive. "Starvations, secret police–"

"Like the Gestapo."

"Give it a rest, mate," Tommy asked him wearily. Surprised by the relative pleasantry, the use of 'mate' as opposed to the usual 'twat' or other such derogatory insult, James paid heed and abandoned his sardonic scorn, listening quietly to Stanley's remonstrations.

"Secret police arrests, thousands tortured in the NKVD Moscow HQ every week... collectivisation, killings, minor despots in charge all over the country... no one is safe, not a soul on Russian soil is beyond arrest, and for what, dear chaps?" Stanley gestured to James, bemused. "For absolutely *nothing*... can you imagine the madness..." he shook his own head in disbelief at the wonder of it. "Look, I tell you, the Soviet regime is beastly. They've launched invasions all over the Baltic States and Eastern Europe; they are brutally occupying other countries, and to top it all off they have *millions* of soldiers massing on the border with... with..."

"Germany," James said, quietly. Stanley hesitated.

"Ah... yes. With Germany, in what was Poland. You've got to admit though, my dear fellow, that Europe is under *threat*."

James threw the butt of his cigarette away, and rose to his feet, standing proud before the group of British soldiers. Planting his feet, he knew it would be his last effort to turn the tide and change the inevitable. But, bloody-minded Yorkshireman that he was, James tried one last time:

"Look lads. I'm not gonna deny that Russia's a worthy enemy. Stalin's a twat. But we're fightin' alongside *Germany*. Fucking..." and he hissed at them, keeping his voice down, "fucking *Germany*! Not against the bastards - with 'em! We've actually put our names down to go *fight alongside the fucking same set o' bastards we fucking left to go fight in the first place*!" Behind James' line of sight, Tommy rolled his eyes to Brian, who looked down at his feet. "Now... you all reckon Hoffman and the rest of those krauts at St George were all right, but these bastards are occupying us... *come* on lads..."

James beseeched them, to no avail. Several of the men who had heard his plaintive entreaties several times before simply got up and walked away without a word. James threw his hands up in irritation.

"OK look. You'd rather listen to that half-German prick Tommy *whatever-his-name-is* than me, that's fair enough. But I only came along because we stick together, and I thought I could convince some of you to not do it. So *look*. If any of you lot are 'avin' doubts about all this bollocks, say it now. We can still back out. But once we're in Russia, freezing in that snow, it's a fight to the death."

The half-German was an English born and bred SS officer named Thomas Cooper, from Hammersmith, London. He'd been mingling with the British lads of all the combined St George camps, and many liked him. But James had overheard him speaking with an English anti-Semite from Grimsby, and Cooper had bragged about capriciously killing Jews during his duty as a concentration camp guard.

Having pleaded his case yet again, James looked around expectantly, but then lost his hope, correctly interpreting the pokerfaced expressions he faced. The silence spoke more eloquently than would any rebuttal and his head dropped, snorting derisively before sinking down on the grass besides Tommy and Brian, who both patted his shoulder sympathetically. Shaking his head, wincing slightly as a flock of birds flew overhead; James withdrew his packet of Dunhill and offered his friends a smoke, before inserting one into his own mouth. He lit it, and exhaled slowly.

"We're about to fight a war alongside Hitler," he mused morosely. "I wonder what the history books will say an 'undred years from now." At that, several others rose to their feet and skipped away, quietly talking amongst themselves in the bright light of the Prussian sun.

~

Several days passed, in which the St. George Battalion mingled with other men of the SS. All were remarkably friendly to the British troops, under the strict orders of Heydrich, but much of the interaction was of so earnest and genuine a nature – perhaps by the shared fear and anticipation of the coming campaign – that the St. George boys could not help but feel their decision to fight was reinforced.

James Wilkinson alone remained aloof. Hoffman summoned him formally, within military parameters so that he could not refuse, even by his own country's standard of etiquette.

"I wish you were not so upset about this," he began, immediately abandoning formality.

Hoffman was sat perched on the very same table that Reinhard Heydrich had sat with Jochen Wolf, discussing at length the re-education of the British troops. If the setting, and his instant rejection of formality had wrong-footed the Yorkshireman in any way, Hoffman could not discern it.

James shrugged. "There isn't much I can do, Walther."

"Smoke?" the German asked, offering his pack. James nodded, and Hoffman simply dropped the packet on the table between them, carelessly. Scowling slightly, Private Wilkinson lowered himself onto the sun-tarnished wooden seat, and grudgingly helped himself to the pack. Waving aside the SS officer's lighter, James struck a match, and moments later, with smoke wafting in curled twists over his lips as he gazed skywards, the young soldier looked as though he had already forgotten the German existed.

"We are going to fight Russia, and communism," Hoffman told him frankly, rudely cutting through James' cogitations. "Neither of us can change that now. And," he added, sensing that the Yorkshireman had been on the verge of making one of his trademark dry, sarcastic quips, "... to be honest James, nor would I *wish* to. I'm *glad* we're going to war with the right country and people, this time. I *hate* Stalin. I hate the Soviet Union. I hate communism, and fear it spreading. I even hate the Russian people... cold bastards."

James just stared at him.

"Come on..." Hoffman pressed him. "What do you think of Stalin?"

"He's a twat."

Hoffman laughed uproariously at that.

"Ho, ho... there are many ways both in your language and mine to describe Comrade Stalin, my friend, but you have a definite style. That, I cannot deny you."

The Berliner winked at him, good-naturedly. He genuinely liked the truculent northern English soldier, despite the man's role as an undermining influence in the wider group, ill-disposed as he was towards National Socialism and with – whether genuine or not – a worryingly sympathetic attitude towards Marx. Yet his wit and candour were evident. Hoffman was not sure *what* it was, but much like Tommy, he found a refreshing honesty in James that overcame the difficulties the man's attitude posed him.

"So, my friend, the questions I ask of *you*, you must ask of yourself. And we must find a common answer, as we fight a common enemy."

James sighed, the resistance all-but beat out of him by the collective acquiescence of the platoon. He could not immediately discern the meaning of Hoffman's riddle, but he cared too little to try to mentally readjust.

"You are in SS uniform, technically speaking, but it is *not of Germany*." Hoffman reached over, tracing his fingers over the sleeve of James' uniform, as he spoke with an intense earnestness. "You are not in German uniform. You bear the Three Lions of England. You are British soldiers."

That much was true. The blank SS uniforms were adorned with the lightning runes on the collar patch, but a Three Lions badge had been sewed to the sleeves, and there was no German insignia to be seen. James had inspected his tunic and trousers thrice each, just to be sure.

"What I want to know, James," Hoffman said, suddenly fixing the Yorkshireman with the full extent of his blue eyes' power, "… is if I can trust you in the field. And can our comrades trust you."

James stared back, reverting to his trademark pokerface. "Fuck you."

To his surprise, Hoffman grinned. "Excellent."

"What?"

The German laughed, his humour returning. "James, you just spoke to me as you do your best friend in the platoon. You are an awkward character. But I know that when we line up against Stalin, you will be fighting on our side."

He gazed at him, before letting a semblance of the ice return to his eyes. "But for reference, from now on, I'm afraid it will have to be proper military rank titles, yes? At least, while in uniform and around other SS or Wehrmacht. I am a German officer – they'll have my balls in a bag if they think I'm letting the standards of excellence slip."

Having established the boundaries of a new dynamic, Hoffman reverted to an air of affability, and winked at James who, for his part, was thoroughly puzzled by the bizarre SS man and his unpredictable ways. Weighing up the conversation, he could not help feeling the first tinge of amusement, and he winked back at Hoffman, while drawing a huge inhalation of smoke from the cigarette. Together, the two men smoked and watched the setting sun, speaking of happier times at home with loved ones.

~

Days later, the platoon set off, and on the fateful morning of May 18th, under the bright glare of a newly risen sun, the men who called themselves *Stanley's Boys* were waited with baited breath, on tenterhooks in the fir forests of East Prussia.

To their east, the border with the Soviet Empire could be seen. They could see a small fence of barbed wire, and no checkpoints, pillboxes or bunkers. Aerial reconnaissance had highlighted the extent to which much of the celebrated border, behind which Soviet forces were supposedly massing, were actually poorly defended, to the point of criminal recklessness.

One hundred German divisions stood ready to pour into the vast, near-limitless expanse of territory that was the Soviet Empire. Thirty other divisions, from Italy, Spain, Vichy France and the combined Axis alliance forces were mobilised to supplement German force. It was said that almost five million men had been gathered to repel the threat of Slavic communism from the gates of Europe; it was the most awesome invasion force ever amassed in the history of warfare.

"The World Will Hold Its Breath," Hitler proclaimed, and his pronouncement was relayed to the men of the SS at Pretzsch via an exultant Reinhard Heydrich.

None of the men spoke. Their moods varied from terrified, to nervous anticipation, to thrill, dread and even, in Hoffman's case, excitement. Emotion charged them; the silent, unspoken energies of the moment were felt in each private moment clenched in combat; the bunching of jaws, grinding of teeth, and the restless inability to stand or sit still. War was coming, in all the irreversible ways it assaults the senses, and there was not a man amongst them whose heart did not hammer harder at its approach.

In the distance, the sound of bombardment suddenly cut through the sinister silence of the fir forest, and the men all knew that war had begun.

Tommy sighed; a thrilled shudder of apprehension and excitement shaking his flesh and bones. "Well, this is it boys. Off to make 'istory."

The fir forest of East Prussia through which they had quietly thronged as one huge mass of humanity had been silent; its green beauty a fairy-tale world at the furthest eastern reaches of Greater Germany, admired in awe by the bulk of the troops, most of whom had never seen it. But the silence was finally over; in the distance, the first artillery was heard, and explosions and cries signalled the beginning of something so catastrophically epic in scale that the suffering to follow could not be quantified or fully comprehended by the mind alone.

As one, they followed the explosions, moving with purpose, driven by their passions and the words which fuelled them, onwards to the battle to destroy their human enemy.

They moved with joy in their hearts and adrenaline coursing through the thick crimson blood in their veins; traversing the beautiful green of land that would soon be scarred by man.

THE END

Author's Thanks

Thanks for reading – much appreciated! And my heartfelt thanks to my family in England, and in this paperback edition, I'd like to thank the positive people I'm with in Southeast Asia. *Good energy people* working to achieve goals and enjoying life to the full help to transcend those around them, as I and others were fortunate to discover. Those with whom I've failed to adequately keep in touch; mea culpa – as Vera sang, *we'll meet again*!

Andrew Leone; Anthony Leone; Donny Carlo-Clauss; Lee Haines; Myk Baxter in particular I'll single out to thank for a combination of support and lessons as mates. The rest –the good, the bad and the hideously, grotesquely, despicably ugly – those left behind, by accident or design, and those merely absent by circumstances alike; cheers to each and all of you, you all taught me something too!

~DSF July 15th, Phuket Thailand

Author mailing list: *subscribe for news & offers!* http://eepurl.com/U3QKH

Please do not hesitate to leave feedback on Amazon & Goodreads; both positive reviews and constructive criticism alike is greatly appreciated! Cheers!

https://Goodreads.com/DanielSFletcher

https://Goodreads.com/book/show/22093713-jackboot-britain

https://twitter.com/Daniel_Fletcher

https://SamuraiLife.net

https://facebook.com/SamuraiLife

https://JakartaMuayThai.com & https://BaliMMA.com – see Indonesia!

https://youtube.com/SamuraiLifeTV

Daniel S. Fletcher

https://twitter.com/Daniel_Fletcher

https://SamuraiLife.net

https://facebook.com/SamuraiLife

http://JackbootBritain.net

https://youtube.com/SamuraiLifeTV

JACKBOOT BRITAIN

https://Goodreads.com/book/show/22093713-jackboot-britain

http://amazon.com/dp/B00KG6EUKO/

http://amazon.co.uk/dp/B00KG6EUKO/

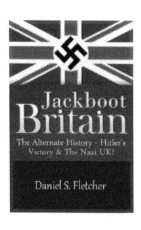

Made in the USA
Charleston, SC
15 February 2015